Arctic Sun

Arctic Sun

A Tom Fox Novel

JACK GRIMWOOD

MICHAEL JOSEPH

PENGUIN MICHAEL JOSEPH

UK | USA | Canada | Ireland | Australia
India | New Zealand | South Africa

Penguin Michael Joseph is part of the Penguin Random House group of companies
whose addresses can be found at global.penguinrandomhouse.com

First published 2023

001

Copyright © Jack Grimwood, 2023

The moral right of the author has been asserted

Set in 13.5/16pt Garamond MT Std
Typeset by Jouve (UK), Milton Keynes
Printed and bound in Great Britain by Clays Ltd, Elcograf S.p.A.

The authorized representative in the EEA is Penguin Random House Ireland,
Morrison Chambers, 32 Nassau Street, Dublin D02 YH68

A CIP catalogue record for this book is available from the British Library

HARDBACK ISBN: 978-0-241-34833-8
TRADE PAPERBACK ISBN: 978-0-241-34834-5

www.greenpenguin.co.uk

For every iteration of Charlie in my family.
And Sam, obviously.

All devils are fallen angels.
Even in hell some try to do what's right . . .

Monday 23rd November 1987 – Hampshire

It was a cold, clear day in November when eight-year-old Charlie Fox buried his mother in the graveyard across the village from his grandfather's house. The big house. The sky was blue, the clouds cirrostratus, the temperature 7 degrees Celsius. It was important to record these things. At least, Charlie thought so.

'Daddy should be here . . .'

Grandpa's hand closed on his. Part comfort, part warning that Mummy's funeral was serious so he needed to keep quiet. Across the open grave, Granny's face tightened. She thought Daddy should be here too. She didn't like him, but she still thought he should be here.

Granny and Grandpa weren't standing together, which was never a good sign. Charlie Fox was being watched. It was obvious that Grandpa and Granny were watching. They needed to be sure he'd behave; because he wasn't always sure what behaving looked like. But it was the girl under the trees at the edge of the graveyard who worried him. Becca wore black because she always did.

He'd asked his sister not to come.

'Oh God,' Grandpa muttered as a big blue Jaguar drew up at the lychgate and its suited driver hurried round to let out a passenger, who patted her hair into place, glanced at her reflection in the window, and nodded.

Graveside abandoned, Grandpa strode towards the Jaguar

XJ Series III. Not a Mark 2 or one of the classic models, Charlie noticed as he trailed after him, ignoring Granny's hissed order to stay.

'Margaret. So kind . . .'

'Of course I came.' The PM spoke carefully, sounding as if she'd borrowed her voice from someone else. All the men were looking impressed. The older ones in suits particularly so.

'We haven't started,' Grandpa said.

'Ah. And I must be elsewhere in an hour. I'm sorry.'

'Duty calls,' Grandpa said.

'Always,' the PM replied with a sigh.

Her car was really big. Even bigger than the government ones Grandpa sometimes used. Its tyres looked solid and its windows unnaturally thick.

'Bullet-proof,' Charlie said to himself.

The man helping the PM back into her car nodded.

'Must be heavy,' Charlie said.

He nodded again.

'Ah, Charles . . .'

It was the man Mummy liked before she started liking Daddy again. Charlie wasn't meant to know about that. There were lots of things Charlie wasn't meant to know about.

'It's Charlie,' Charlie said. 'But you can call me Charles if you'd like.' He was worried he might have been rude.

'Charlie.' The man tried to smile. He wanted to say something soothing, something helpful. It was just, he obviously couldn't think what.

'Mummy was dying,' Charlie said. 'It was what she wanted. It's for the best.' The last word caught in his throat and Charlie discovered he was crying. Not noisy, embarrassing-yourself-at-school crying, just crying.

2

'I should let you be.'

The man clearly didn't like it when people cried. Charlie didn't blame him. Charlie didn't like it much either.

'So you can say your goodbyes.'

The man must know Charlie had said his goodbyes already. Charlie nodded all the same, grateful to see him go. So many people who didn't know what to say. Charlie just said what he thought. He said what he thought or he said nothing. Saying things you didn't mean was confusing . . .

'Ah. There you are.'

Turning, he saw a woman with dark glasses.

'It's a terrible thing for a boy to lose his father,' she said. 'Especially before time. Although not as terrible as a father losing his boy. That's the kind of thing you don't recover from.' She was foreign, wearing too much scent, and her lipstick was purple.

'It was my mother who died,' Charlie said.

'Not Major Fox?'

'No,' Charlie said. 'Not Major Fox.'

'I see. How silly of me. He must be next.'

2

Friday 13th November – London

Ten days before the funeral of his wife – but almost two months after an attack by unidentified black boats on an East German base in Heringsdorf, about which he knew nothing as yet – Major Fox sat in a drab cubicle on the eighth floor of an office block in Lambeth, doing his best to fail a psychiatric test.

Q. A hand grenade lands at your feet. You don't know how many seconds ago it was thrown. What do you do?

Pick it up, he wrote. *Admire it.*

Q. You are trapped in a thunder-storm. Lightning has already set a tree alight. Where do you hide?

I don't. I like storms.

Q. It's night-time. You are behind enemy lines. A stray cat appears at your feet. It starts mewing. What do you do?

Adopt it.

Putting down his pencil, Tom Fox flipped open that afternoon's *Evening Standard*. Twelve people murdered by Provos at a Remembrance Day service in Enniskillen. Striking workers in Romania beaten up ahead of upcoming elections. Five members of West German CND found innocent of breaking into an airbase. Kentucky Fried Chicken to open near Tiananmen Square. What would Beijing make of southern fried chicken? Tom wondered.

Below his window, a woman. What was left of her life in a broken trolley. She made him think of Wax Angel, who'd

4

turned out to be the wife of a Muscovite commissar, a hero of Stalingrad, and an ex-ballerina. Some people came back from the streets. Some never did. Wax Angel had. Tom was glad of that.

He wondered if he would have done.

Returning to the test, he discovered he was expected to answer another twenty-five pages of questions before being allowed to skulk his way out of Century House. That insalubrious MI6 office block on Westminster Bridge Road, one of the grimmer thoroughfares in south-west London. And he said that as an army brat, born on a rotting British base in Cyprus, to a put-upon mum and a thuggish NCO who'd been court-martialled and jailed for stealing stores.

One of the better days of Tom's life.

The CIA had Langley, all black plaques, oil paintings and marble. British intelligence had rattling pipes, carpet tiles and a building that would embarrass a tax office in Croydon. Neither surprised him.

Q. What did you like most about your childhood?
Leaving it behind.
Q. What was the happiest period of your life?
I'm still waiting.
Q. Which of the following colours do you like most?
Red – Black – Blue – Green – Brown – White – Grey

Crossing them all out, Tom wrote *Turquoise*, scored through the remaining pages and scraped back his chair. The young IO who'd shown him to the cubicle looked up, surprised. Tom was only twenty-five minutes into a test she'd told him usually took ninety.

'Finished?' she asked doubtfully.

'Long since,' Tom said.

He caught the flash of relief as she realised she'd have an evening to herself after all. He'd been two hours late for the appointment, and Lambeth was already a dark and damp blur beyond their window.

'You'll get a taxi home?' he said.

Suspicion, puzzlement, mild contempt for his old-fashioned concern. He watched them chase each other across her face. 'Yes, sir,' she said. 'I'll get a taxi home.'

'Good,' Tom said. 'I'll let myself out then.'

Threading his way between cubicles, he took the stairs to minimise his risk of meeting anyone he knew at the lifts, and stopped in the foyer to sign himself out. If he never came back here, it would still be too soon.

A few minutes after he left Century House, Tom realised that he was lost. A wrong turn off Webber Street led him to one of those 1960s council estates that never lived up to its architect's drawings. These days it was all faulty street lights, heavily shuttered pizza joints that only did takeaway, and blocks of low-rise in various shades of leprous concrete. Reaching a soot-blackened church, already old when the blocks went up, his mind shied from what its graves suggested.

His memory offered a funeral in Moscow, where a Soviet officer he'd killed was buried with full honours. Tom stood by the ambassador, pretending he didn't know what had happened; while the dead man's fiancée stood stone-faced with fury. Sophia hadn't believed for one second Tom's pretence of innocence.

So many deaths. Tom had trouble keeping the past and present apart. How could his bosses expect him to talk to a service psychiatrist, when he couldn't even admit to himself half of what he'd done?

He was retracing his steps when a tail-less cat appeared.

'Meow,' Tom said.

'Meow,' the cat agreed.

It's night-time. You are behind enemy lines. A stray cat appears at your feet. It starts mewing. What do you do?

Crouching, Tom picked up the stray and felt it freeze. *Break its neck* was the right answer. When he tucked it into his leather jacket, it purred.

'Cat,' he said.

As names went, it would do.

A corner shop on the next street advertised wine, beer, spirits, cigarettes, groceries. A handwritten sign promised faxes 10p, cheap phone cards and cheques cashed. It was the old woman in a sari who caught Tom's eye. She stood stock still. As if someone had hit pause on video playback.

Facing her were two boys. Both carried knives.

Opening his government-issue briefcase, with its faded 'ERII' in flaking gold on the flap, Tom put Cat inside it. 'Wait here,' he ordered.

A bell above the door rang to tell the woman she had another customer. She looked relieved. The boys looked pissed off.

'Get out,' said the nearest.

'Now,' the other added.

'Not going to happen,' Tom told them.

Scowling, the tallest stalked towards him and jabbed his knife at Tom's face. He didn't even have time to look shocked, Tom reacted so quickly. Knocking aside the blade, he caught the boy's wrist and twisted, catching the knife as it dropped. Then he kicked out the boy's knee, yanked his head back and put the edge to his throat.

'How much does your friend like you?'

On cue, his companion dropped his own weapon.

'Kick it into the corner,' Tom told him.

It went skittering across worn lino to clang into a carousel of fading greetings cards. The first boy's name was Darren, and he lived on the next estate across. Not robbing his local store being Darren's version of not shitting on his own doorstep. The second boy didn't want to give his name. Tom was able to persuade him.

'Out,' he said.

Both boys hurried for the door.

'Wait.'

They hesitated, door half open.

'This woman is a friend of mine, understand? You come round here again, she'll tell me. I'll come looking. Believe me, I will find you. Finding people is what I do.'

Tom and the woman watched the boys close the door behind them and hurry away into the darkness. They left without looking back or seeing Tom's briefcase or the cat.

'How can I repay you?'

Tom's gaze slid to a half bottle of Famous Grouse above her shoulder. The woman was reaching for it when Tom shook his head. His wife had cancer. He still didn't know how to tell his son she had a week at most to live. If he began drinking now, he'd never stop. 'I'll take two cans of Felix,' he said.

3

Friday 13th November – Soviet Arctic

Unless they're ill, in an unwinnable battle, about to be executed or preparing to kill themselves, few people know they're about to die. The half-Leningrádka professor of nuclear physics in the Soviet Arctic certainly didn't. So she poured another coffee, without wondering whether that was a good idea, and shuffled her ageing body into heavy overalls, tied on a lead-lined apron and decided not to bother with her cap.

Electrons orbiting a Red Star decorated her left breast. Below was her name and job title: *Natalia Volkova, Senior Scientist – Midnight Sun.*

Bordering Northern Norway, and situated high in the Soviet Arctic, the Kola Peninsula was the start of the Scandinavian land mass, a precursor to the mountain ranges providing a backbone for Norway and Sweden. Salmon filled its rivers, eider ducks wintered here, and there were the reindeer, always reindeer. Although those were above ground – and she was several hundred feet below.

She imagined them, drifting like shadows through the fake village built to hide the access hatches to her complex, driven by instinct and hunger. The tail-end of a migration already delayed by Moscow's demand that the herds be tested for fallout following the disaster at Chernobyl the year before.

Nomads like her grandfather had mostly had this place to themselves. But with the Bolshevik Revolution came railroads and factories, mines, new towns and new rulers. And while many of the incoming Russians kept to the coast, the Sami were subject to relocation and collectivisation, as their grazing grounds were militarised and stripped of mineral wealth.

In summer, the temperatures on the peninsula were cool. In winter, cold. Sometimes bitterly so. Frosts fell from August onwards. Storm winds blew for a hundred days a year. Temperatures of −50 were not unknown.

'You're used to it,' she'd been told.

As if her grandparents hadn't ended up in a grim, claustrophobic 1960s Khrushchyovka block next to the Kirov railway, with lorries, arc lights and the filth of a titanium mine for neighbours. A thousand kilometres from Leningrad and even further from Murmansk, where their son still lived.

The order selecting her for Midnight Sun said she'd been chosen because her reputation was of the highest, and she was half Sami, which made it fitting. Natalia was pretty sure she'd been chosen because she was disposable. If the long nights and vodka didn't get her, radiation sickness would.

Adjusting her lead apron, she found her protective glasses and pulled on her gloves. She'd been putting off this day all week, but Moscow were becoming impatient. Plutonium was dangerous. Moscow even more so.

In the end you chose your risks.

The material she was handling wasn't even that radioactive. At least not in this state. She already knew she didn't have enough dexterity wearing gloves for what came next.

'I need more coffee.'

'Natalia,' Sergei Balov, her deputy, said.

'What?'

'Look at your hands.'

Her fingers were vibrating like the strings of a violin. She'd ingested too much already. The strip-lighting of the inner lab was giving her a headache and the dryness of the air hurt her sinuses.

'Vodka, then.'

Sergei looked at her.

'It's a sedative,' she said defensively. 'It'll help my nerves.'

'If you must.'

Stopping off at the urinals for the third time that morning, another of the joys of getting old, Sergei headed for the outer lab and one of the lead-lined cupboards marked *Danger – Nuclear Materials*. Reaching inside, he removed a bottle of Stolichnaya, and two laboratory beakers. It was an old affectation, almost a superstition, from their student days in Moscow. Back then, the alcohol had been industrial, and beakers all they had.

'To the Midnight Sun,' Natalia proposed.

Sergei raised his beaker in salute.

Behind them in an alcove, hermetically sealed behind a slab of reinforced, radiation-resistant glass, rested a crystal orb. The world's most dangerous Fabergé egg, Sergei called it. Natalia's job was to make an exact copy, only bigger.

On their lab bench lay the pieces for that job. Once assembled, the USSR would have a bomb that could kill every single living thing within a two-mile radius while leaving buildings standing. That was the theory anyway.

Made in the USSR was etched into its shell, with a flamboyance at odds with its function. Natalia Volkova had to make that true. She was terrified. Who wouldn't be? Not of handling materials she'd been handling for decades but of the responsibility her masters had put on her to deliver this project by the end of the month. America had bombs like this already. Well, perhaps they didn't. Perhaps Moscow was lying. How could Natalia know?

'You can do this,' Moscow had said.

Natalia had nodded and wished she was younger, and less aware of Moscow's reach, that her liver, bladder and nerves were in a better condition.

'You all right?' Sergei sounded worried.

'I'm fine,' Natalia said crossly. 'Let's do this . . .' She sipped the vodka to get its taste, then knocked back the beaker, inhaling alcohol vapour and feeling her lungs tighten.

'Sod the lot of them.'

Peeling off the gloves that made handling materials like this so hard, she decided not to bother with the isolation chamber either.

She'd do it her way.

Picking up machined pieces of fissile metal, she began building their precious core. She was almost done when her right hand began shaking just when she needed it to be steady. The harder she tried to control her fingers, the more they shook. The core slipped and a bright blue flame half blinded her as she tasted metal in her mouth in the split second before everything went critical.

4

Friday 13th November – Devon

'Charlie . . .'

Charlie Fox looked up from his Friday-night cocoa and Bourbon biscuit to find Peter, as Mr Todd liked to be called, smiling at him. His new form tutor was holding a letter.

'This came for you. Second post.'

At his previous school, a bigger boy would have grabbed it the moment Charlie's tutor moved on, holding it above his head to make Charlie jump for it. An even bigger boy would have asked mockingly if he was missing Mummy. Tor Point House was a different kind of school. Charlie wondered if Mummy and Daddy realised how different. It was nice not having to do lessons if you didn't want to, but it did mean you didn't really learn anything unless you felt like it. Some boys didn't even know how a combustion engine worked.

As for the girls . . .

Charlie wasn't sure how he felt about being in a school with girls. It wasn't as if he'd met many. Except his sister Becca, and she was dead.

'You should open it,' Mr Todd said.

'Later,' Charlie replied.

It was proof of Tor Point's strangeness that Mr Todd didn't immediately tell him off for rudeness, or even seem to notice that Charlie hadn't done what he was told.

*

At eight, Charlie already knew he had the blond hair, blue eyes and bashful looks to attract a certain kind of master. Luckily, his new school had fewer of those than his previous one. And the one it did have . . . Well, he's . . . *been moved on.*

That was how the other masters referred to it. Not to Charlie, of course. Those weren't the kind of conversations you had with small boys. Being moved on made him sound like a tramp who'd taken up residence in the fields. He hadn't been a tramp, just a little too keen on staring at boys during bathtime. Charlie was glad he'd gone. He felt quite self-conscious enough as it was. Particularly when having a shower. Self-conscious and being aware you were conscious were different things. Charlie knew, because he'd asked the child psychiatrist Granny had made Mummy send him to.

The lavatories at Tor Point didn't stink. That was different too. They didn't stink, they weren't scrawled all over and the floors weren't sticky. Choosing a cubicle, Charlie locked himself in, let down the wooden seat and stared at Mummy's handwriting.

Master Charlie Fox
Tor Point School
Devon

Daddy had wanted them to move to Glasgow, where his own father grew up. Since Daddy hated his father, Charlie wasn't sure that made sense. Mummy said he just wanted to get away from her parents. Daddy said he couldn't see a problem with that. It hadn't been an argument though. They didn't have arguments since the holiday in the West Indies when Mummy fell ill. They had discussions. Even the occasional disagreement. They were both much too sad for arguments these days.

Dear Charlie

Thank you for your last letter. Your handwriting is SO much better. I liked the sound of the school play where no one spoke, so no one had to learn lines. We always had to do Shakespeare.

I hope you like Tor Point. The grounds are lovely and I'm sure it's a relief not to have to do games unless you want to. You must tell me if you're homesick. Unfortunately, I won't be able to come home for exeat when Dr Miles said I could. So Daddy and I thought you might like to visit me this weekend?

Grandpa will come to collect you . . .

Mummy didn't write letters midweek. She wrote letters on Fridays to arrive at breakfast time on Saturday. That was when this letter should have arrived. Something was wrong. Charlie went back to reading it, although there wasn't much of the letter left to read.

. . . I've told Grandpa he's to go himself and not send his driver or one of his underlings! It'll be such fun to see you.

Masses of love
Mummy xxxxxxx

There were more kisses than there should be. And when had Mummy ever worried about him being homesick? Charlie took a closer look at her writing. It tailed off and grew untidy in the middle and right at the end. She'd been too tired to write it all at once and had stopped for a rest, before starting again.

So much effort to say . . . what? It wasn't what Mummy said that worried Charlie. It was all the things she didn't. He had maths for prep. He'd been looking forward to that. But now he thought he'd sit in the library and look at an atlas instead. He found atlases calming.

5

'You can't bring that in here . . .'

The tail-less cat jammed in the top of Tom's black leather jacket narrowed its eyes and stopped purring. Tom didn't blame it. The hospital receptionist's gaze took in the cans of Felix in Tom's cheap, see-through carrier bag and her eyes narrowed too.

'I said—' Her voice followed him towards the lifts '—I'm going to have to call the police.'

'I am the police,' Tom told her.

'Let me see your card.'

Stamping his way back to her counter, Tom dug out his identity card and held it up.

'That's not a police card.'

'Same job. Different branch. Feel free to call them but they won't thank you. We tell them what to do.'

This time she didn't try to stop him.

'Shouldn't have done that,' Tom told the cat.

Cat considered this.

'Keeping your own counsel? Always wise.' Tom watched buttons light floor by floor as the lift rose. Caro had a suite at the very top. Of course she did. Her father had insisted she have a good view of the Thames. Since he was paying there was little Tom could do. Maybe the view helped.

'Can I help?'

The nurse carrying a kidney tray with a cloth covering

16

stopped as the lift doors closed behind Tom. She was frowning.

'I'm here to see my wife.'

'Your . . . ?'

'Lady Caro Fox,' Tom said, falling back on what he knew would work, disliking himself for doing it and resenting that it was necessary.

'I'm afraid . . .'

'The cat comes with me,' Tom said firmly. 'He won't mess, and if he does I'll clean up. Cleaning up messes is my job. My wife will like him,' he added. For a moment, he saw pity in the nurse's eyes and that was harder to handle than her irritation.

'I'm not sure what the doctor will say.'

'You didn't see me,' Tom said. 'You certainly didn't see Cat.' He turned for Caro's room, with the tail-less street mog still tucked in his jacket and the carrier bag at his side. She let him go.

'Who's that?' Caro whispered.

'He's called Cat.'

Caro smiled. Her eyes were smudged, her cheeks hollow. Tom could see the bone beneath her skin. They both knew her death was only days away. When she tried to sit up, Tom saw her wince of pain. He was at her side before he knew it, lowering her back to her pillow. Her hand came up to cover his and she squeezed his fingers so weakly he might have imagined it. When Tom stepped back, he realised his mother-in-law was in the corner, on a blond wood chair, glaring.

At the cat? His lateness? His clothes? All three probably.

Tom nodded all the same.

'Ah. You've arrived.'

Turning, Tom saw his father-in-law behind him in the

doorway. Lord Eddington was carrying a black-lacquer tray with a plate of digestives, a proper teapot and three china cups and saucers.

'Is that animal really necessary?' he asked.

'I found him,' Tom said. 'Behind a pizza place.'

'Of course you did,' Caro said. She smiled. It was a very sad smile. '"You become responsible for ever for what you've tamed . . ." Remember that?'

'*The Little Prince*,' Tom said.

'*Le Petit Prince*,' Caro agreed. She'd bought Tom the book in Hatchards when they were first together. 'It's true too. Believe me, I should know.'

Turning to her parents, she said, 'Could you give me a few minutes with Tom?'

'You'll talk to him?'

'Yes,' Caro told her mother tiredly. 'I'll talk to him.'

'About what?' Tom demanded before the door was even closed. It shut on Lady Eddington looking tight-lipped. Lord Eddington looked deceptively benign.

'They want Charlie.'

'*What?*'

'After I die.'

'Caro . . .'

'I'm going to die,' she said crossly. 'You know that. They know that. I know that. The only person who doesn't know that is Charlie. They think he should live with them.'

'Why?' Tom demanded.

'Because you're you. You'll never change.'

'I will,' Tom promised.

'Really?'

She left a gap for him to say *Yes, I will. Of course I will.*

'He's my son,' Tom said finally.

Caro looked up.

'I love him.'

'Have you ever told him that?'

'Probably not.'

'Then do,' she said. 'Do it now.'

Caro sighed, sounding more exhausted than he'd ever heard her. 'It took until I was a week from death for my father to get around to saying that. You might not want to wait that long.'

6

Friday night was NATO pilot Major Herda's turn on the Baltic Express, as his squadron called their incursions over Soviet airspace. His US Lockheed SR-71 had broken the sound barrier before it left Norway, briefly clipped Swedish airspace and ripped out over the Kola Peninsula. Over 2,000 miles from where Lady Caro Fox lay dying in London. A city the American could have reached in forty minutes if he'd needed.

Maybe tonight was the night the Soviets would scramble multiple MiGs in an attempt to intercept him, rather than simply one or two. It wouldn't be the first time. His plane was high, though. It was fast, and with a climb-rate of 12,000 feet a minute it could outrun, outgun and outfly anything the Soviets sent after it.

The infrared camera set into its fuselage was digital. A second camera, retro-fitted directly behind it, took Kodak Aerochrome. Although Major Herda didn't know it, both would be compared with shots from a spy satellite newly placed in geosynchronous orbit miles overhead. On the one hand, satellites took days to position and a Blackbird could be run out on demand. On the other, satellites were far harder to shoot down, and the Soviets had been coming ever closer to taking out a Blackbird in the last eighteen months. So which was better?

This flight was to try to settle that argument.

Major Herda's job was to photograph a newly discovered oilfield near Naryan-Mar on the Pechora river. Today's target wasn't even that important. This was about testing new technol—

Fuck.

To the side of Major Herda the sky shimmered.

Fire rose in a pillar, cutting the sky in two. Then he was being buffeted by a shock wave, was inside the tumult and suddenly through, his instruments going haywire as his Geiger counter started screaming. Without even thinking about it, Major Herda flipped down a panel and dry-swallowed two iodine tablets for protection against radiation. Then he was into a turn, and the fact he could meant his Blackbird was at least partly functional. It was a tight turn, too tight, darkness eating the edges of his vision as G-force drained blood from his brain.

'Shit,' Major Herda whispered.

He wished he'd called his wife before take-off. Even if she did insist on referring to the plane he was so proud of as a stubby-winged black dildo.

Below him he could see little but a suggestion of snow and forests, frozen lakes and the edge of a plateau. His plane felt sluggish, slow to handle, and he wondered if it was him. The horizon kept tilting and he realised one engine was losing power. He was dropping. There was no way he could remain in stealth mode and at the right altitude on only one wing.

There were cyanide tablets behind another panel. It wasn't falling into Soviet hands that worried him. It was Moscow getting its hands on his plane and its cameras. The SR-71 surpassed anything the Warsaw Pact had. Although the MiG-25 Foxbat was fast catching up. And every digital photograph released by NATO to the Western press had been intentionally degraded to keep the world from realising how advanced the lenses now were.

Five hundred miles back to base.

He wasn't going to make it. He'd take a forced landing on Swedish soil if he could. Neutral or not, Stockholm was still cross enough about a Soviet sub sneaking into its fjords not to make a fuss. The major's speed was slowing and his height still dropping. He could see ribbon lakes clearly now. Rough roads through snowy forests. Clusters of dark houses scattered along the edge of a silvery river. Baba Yaga huts, intelligence called them. Except the stilted huts of Russia's folk-tales had chicken's legs and these had pine. Maybe 200 miles and he'd——

He saw the MiGs a moment before the pair raced past, close enough to rock his already unsteady plane. They turned in a contemptuously wide circle to bring themselves round for another run.

His plane kept slowing. Anything below 350 mph and he might as well be flying a brick. His on-board computer kept making demands his crippled craft's infrastructure couldn't meet. The skin of his face felt sunburnt. His guts hurt. Maybe the Soviet doctors would be able to help?

Probably best not.

They'd only keep him alive to let their bosses question him.

Flipping down a panel to his right, Major Herda felt for the cyanide tablets with his fingers. As he readied to swallow them, he saw the two MiGs hesitate. A Viggen fighter had appeared beside him, the three crowns of Sweden clearly visible on its fuselage. A second Swedish fighter fell into position on his other side. Major Herda waited to see if the MiGs would fire. As the MiGs began their run, the Swedish planes held their position and it was the Soviet pilots who peeled away.

The major felt like crying.

The Swedes indicated a new flight path and Major Herda forced his Blackbird into a lumbering turn. They were grinning and giving him the thumbs-up. He'd done it. He wasn't going to make it to Norway, but his plane and its cameras were back over neutral soil.

7

Friday 13th November – Soviet Arctic

'*Fuck . . .*'

Seeing a plume of heat split the sky, Dr Amelia Blackburn grabbed Per by the elbow and dragged her assistant into a frozen ditch.

'Leave it!' she snapped.

He left his Geiger counter where it was.

In the second she rolled into the ditch, Amelia saw a fleck of silver in the sky like a shooting star above her. It was forgotten a moment later.

'Under here,' she ordered.

Her Sami assistant rolled in tighter, joining her under a thick overhang cut into the gravel when last spring's torrents were in full flow. His breath was warm on the side of her face. Embarrassed, the young man began to shift away.

'Stay put,' Amelia told him.

She held him tight and pulled him closer. She was as far under the overhang as she could get, not caring that the earth bank might fall in and bury them both alive. Here, facing the risk the overhang might collapse, was safer than out there.

Per's body was whipcord thin. His shoulders stiff beneath her grip. In another situation, Amelia might have been uncomfortable, not that she really did embarrassment. But she was trying to save his life and her own. She'd seen the effects of radiation before. Watched a lover from Chernobyl die, as lesions covered her, her skin sloughed away and her liver, kidneys and lungs gave up.

Their ditch was three feet deep. The overhang wide enough to shield them from fallout. It was best not to think about shock waves and the dirt coming in. Then again, the soil was frozen. That was good. Not only did ice give dirt stability, it provided protection from radiation.

Above them, she could hear Per's Geiger counter.

She imagined he could too. Its chatter rose to a solid scream, only to begin falling far too fast, through noisy agitation, to a rapid click-track that wasn't too far above normal.

Too fast, Amelia told herself. Too fast to make sense.

'We stay here,' she announced.

'For how long?'

'Until that reaches normal. Then some.'

The Geiger counter was slowing.

'It's normal now,' Per said.

'Not quite. It's not worth the risk.'

They waited another hour, huddled together below the frozen tundra, in a crevice that grew warm from their breath and body heat. It was almost regretfully that Amelia unwrapped her arms from her assistant, announced it was time to move and felt him unwrap his arms from her. That moment was to come back to haunt her.

The reindeer in the pen behind her camp grazed on, nosing at moss and lichen beneath the snows, unconcerned and apparently unharmed by whatever had happened. A situation that wouldn't last.

Her project was ruined.

That probably shouldn't have been her first thought.

It was, though. Eighteen months before, a reactor 1,300 miles south of here had gone into uncontrollable meltdown and given the world its worst ever nuclear disaster.

Technicians, first responders and helicopter pilots overflying the disaster died, thousands became critically ill, towns and cities had to be abandoned. Swathes of agricultural land were rendered unusable. In the middle of this political, financial and ecological disaster, a plume of radiation drifted across Russia and Scandinavia, poisoning the vegetation on which reindeer fed. Amelia's job was to study the effects of that disaster on the Soviet herds.

She had only just returned from studying wolf packs at Chernobyl, and had been protesting at the peace camp at Greenham Common, when Moscow asked if she'd take this job. Her father had died in East Berlin, in exile, still wanting to come home. Her lover had died of radiation sickness. She'd quarrelled with her old professor at Edinburgh. Her friendship with Tom Fox had come to nothing. The Western press were never going to let her forget she was the daughter of a defector. And there was only so much having a camera pushed in her face she could stand. No matter how fiercely she supported picketing the US airbase.

She'd jumped at Moscow's offer.

It was to be a change of pace, she'd told herself. A chance to get some peace and the balance back in her life. And now . . . Retrieving her own Geiger counter, Amelia saw it was down to a safer level. Not safe, but definitely safer. 'I'm going to turn the reindeer loose, and leave the tent here,' she told Per. 'We'll leave at dawn.'

'Going where?'

'There might be survivors.'

'From what?'

'Whatever that was.'

'We're days from the nearest town,' he protested. 'I doubt there's a village within thirty miles. We can't walk into the middle of a weapon's test. The radiation—'

'Is falling.'

It was. Faster than made sense. And the spike hadn't lasted as long as it should have done. Running the Geiger counter over herself, then over Per, Amelia double-checked both readings. Normal.

The ditch, the thickness of the overhang, had protected them.

Tomorrow she'd find out what the hell was going on.

8

The air as Amelia climbed to the plateau was cold enough to numb her nostrils and burn her lungs. The sun reflecting obliquely off the slopes rendered her nearly blind. Usually, she liked the snow the way she liked silence, space and emptiness.

Today she simply tolerated it.

For this part of the trip, she and Per had changed into snowshoes. A far slower way to travel than relying on the skis slung across their backs, but better for the slopes they now navigated. Neither spoke. They simply put one snowshoe in front of another, steadied their breathing and thought only of reaching the top.

At this latitude, forest gave way at 350 metres to scattered trees, becoming rough grasses above. At 700 metres, it surrendered to icy desert. Since *tundra* came from the Sami *tūndâr* and meant 'treeless mountain tract' that made sense.

Not that they'd be climbing that high.

'Oh God,' Per said.

A man in a lab coat sat with his back to a stunted pine, his feet stretched in front of him. What was left of his head lolled to one side. The Tokarev he'd used to blow his brains out lay in his lap. A stain on the tree behind showed where most of them had ended up.

'Frozen,' Amelia said, removing her hand from the dead man's face. She glanced back at the sound of her assistant throwing up.

'You must have seen a corpse before.'

'Not like that.' Per gestured at the technician and then at another he'd just seen beyond. There were nine bodies in the next twenty paces. Most had killed themselves. A few had frozen to death or succumbed to radiation poisoning, their guns unfired. None of the deaths had been easy. The snow around them was coloured with vomit, shit, piss and blood. Evidence of stomachs and bowels, bladders and lungs giving way.

Having checked her Geiger counter for the tenth time, Amelia had Per give her the readout from his, without telling him what hers was registering.

Their figures matched.

'Too low,' Amelia muttered.

Snow crunching underfoot, she headed across a clearing to examine a thin woman whose face was glazed with ice. The dead woman's eyes were white. That could be radiation. Equally, it could be the cold. Both produced whiteness, although their methods of getting there were very different.

Lieutenant Anna Bobrovsky.

A military base then. Unless Bobrovsky was the KGB officer at a civilian research station, there to keep Moscow's scientists from letting data lead them to politically inconvenient conclusions.

Pulling a Praktica SLR from her satchel, Amelia photographed the woman, then went back to photograph the bodies she'd passed. In two days, she'd be on her way to Norway to present a paper on wolves to a UNESCO conference in Tromso. She'd slip the film into the post there. Friends in London would develop it, print off duplicates and make sure they reached the right places.

She'd leave them to decide what those right places were. Greenpeace would be at the top of her own list.

Telling Per to keep taking readings, she stepped back into the stunted trees to relieve herself, and stumbled over another corpse before she'd gone ten paces. Rolling the body over, Amelia raised her Praktica to record it and blinked, glad Per wasn't there to see her shock. This one hadn't shot himself.

He'd had his throat ripped out by a wolf.

Defensive wounds to his hands, wrists and forearms told her he'd tried to defend himself. His pistol still in its holster, which said he hadn't heard the wolf coming. The fingers of his right hand were chewed off. He'd lost his other hand entirely. His knee was open to the bone, his groin gone. The wolf had been hungry.

More than hungry. Starving.

She took a radiation reading from what it had left.

'Too low,' she muttered, knowing she was repeating herself. Doing it all the same.

From the start of this, every reading had been too low. No, that was wrong ... She remembered the Geiger counter screaming as she and Per huddled in the ditch under that overhang. The first reading had been terrifyingly high. It was everything after that which was wrong.

What was she dealing with? What kind of half-life were they talking about? Fallout from conventional nukes didn't degrade this fast.

Would the wolves die too? Would feeding on the dying irradiate a pack enough to weaken it genetically? Amelia didn't know. Either the physical effects of radiation on the dead should be less. Or the current readings on her Geiger counter should be higher. One or the other of those made no sense.

9

On the day Tom first met Caro she'd been wearing an Yves Saint Laurent pea coat. He hadn't known who Yves Saint Laurent was, or what a pea coat was either. She was just a girl in an increasingly febrile crowd, wide-eyed but with fear not innocence. Although she turned out later to be pretty wide-eyed with that too. Her hair had been unfashionably short, style in the late 1960s having moved on from the Mary Quant bob. She'd come to London to take part in a protest, her first and as it turned out her last, lost sight of her friends and discovered that Special Branch had every intention of turning a protest into a riot.

Everything he'd ever needed to know about her upbringing were in the first four questions she asked him. What was his surname, where did he study, where did he go to school, and who were his parents? He had only wrong answers to all those, but they'd fallen in love anyway. It was only after the birth of Becca that things started to go wrong.

The lights from Parliament reflected on the Thames.

Far below the window of Caro's hospital suite, a police boat slid downriver, its blue light revolving. Cars thronged Westminster Bridge. One of those would belong to Caro's father, who'd left his daughter's room a few minutes earlier, promising to return the next night. Tom's arrival was timed to miss him.

He wasn't sure what his father-in-law had said to upset his wife, but Caro wouldn't turn her head to look at him and her reflection in the darkened window looked furious.

'What's the worst thing you've done?' she demanded.

'Caro, what's going on?'

'It's a fair question. And if you won't tell me now . . .'

Tom stared across at the Houses of Parliament. Most of the things he'd done had been sanctioned from there. But with cut-offs and caveats. So that those above him kept their hands clean.

'Well?' she said.

'I killed a man in front of his child.'

'And what was the best?' she asked.

'I killed a man in front of his child.'

'Do I get details?'

'No one gets details.'

'Would *you* let you look after Charlie if you were me?'

Tom thought about it. 'Yes,' he said finally.

Caro smiled sadly. 'I love you,' she said. 'Strange as that sounds. And I believe you believe that.'

Affairs on both sides, a dead teenage daughter, a decade lost to Tom's undercover work in Ulster, pretending to be someone else. An earl's daughter and a boy from a children's home, where the records had been sealed and journalists from *The Times* warned off for asking questions. No one had expected them to last. Tom wasn't sure he'd expected them to last.

Until death, their vows had said.

Tom looked around the room. Machines everywhere. Tubes vanishing into Caro's wrists, and snaking under her covers. She no longer fed herself or needed a lavatory or required a bed pan. Liquids put in. Liquids taken out.

Until death it was, apparently.

This was the end of it.

They both knew that. Visiting hours were 3 p.m. to 10 p.m. Tom came at 11 p.m., at Caro's suggestion, and with her consultant's blessing. She wanted to talk to him. She needed to do it when her parents weren't around.

'It's not that I don't like them . . .' she said.

Tom snorted.

'All right,' she said. 'I love them. They're my parents. You're meant to love your parents. It's just that mine aren't always likeable.'

'And mine . . .'

'Weren't even loveable?' Caro tapped her mattress to tell Tom to sit beside her. There was something she needed to say.

'Say it,' Tom said.

'You won't win, you know. Not if this goes to court. I mean, look at you . . .'

Her gaze was almost kind.

'When did you last change your shirt? Or shave, come to that? At least you're not drunk, and you haven't brought a stray kitten this time.'

'It was a cat,' Tom said. 'And I haven't drunk in weeks.'

'Is that true?'

'If I started, I'd never stop.'

She took his hand, her grip so slight Tom could barely feel it. Her wrist was bone. Her skin yellow. Huge bruises had blossomed where the tubes went in.

'Tom . . .'

Here it comes, he thought. He steadied himself to be told that she too felt Charlie should live with her parents. Well, live with them when the poor little sod wasn't at boarding school.

'If you did have Charlie . . .'

33

He looked at her then. Properly looked at her.

Her gaze was firm. 'If you did . . .'

'He would come first.'

'Before work?'

'Before work. Before me. Before everything.'

'Swear it.'

'I swear it.'

'Swear it on your life.'

'I swear it on my life. I really do.'

Caro considered this while a wall clock ticked gently and the night darkened even further over the Thames outside. 'I'll talk to my parents,' she said finally.

When Tom looked again, she was sleeping, the rise and fall of her chest slight, almost butterfly fragile. Only the steady beep of the machines and softly rolling waves on her heart monitor told him she was still here.

It was time for him to go anyway.

Back to Cat, his memories and the Chelsea mews that wasn't his, and he couldn't have afforded to keep even if it had been. Not and pay his half of the fees for a school he hadn't wanted his son to go to in the first place.

'I'll be back tomorrow,' he promised.

She didn't hear him.

IO

November 1971 – Derry, Northern Ireland

There was the smell of beer and sweat and cigarettes you got in every pub, but the beer smell was heavier because the clientele were drinking Guinness to a man. And it was to a man if you discounted the teenager in the green velour top cut too low, and nobody was counting her because she was only there to pull pints. There was the single from a new band called Thin Lizzy on the jukebox, and the younger ones in the corner were humming along to its chorus.

This was the kind of place where putting on the wrong record might get you a beating. Safest to leave the jukebox to those who belonged. The man standing in the door looked like he should belong; but none of the regulars knew him and they watched him thread his way through the crowd.

Long hair that needed washing. Sideburns down to his chin. A cheesecloth shirt with pearl buttons. Faded jeans, denim jacket and work boots. The kind that could mete out a kicking if needs be. A hardman, in a pub given over to hardmen who wore the label because they'd earned it. And because it bought them peace from the army and the police, and from the Red Hand brigades who'd have attacked this pub at a moment's notice if they thought for one second they'd walk away alive.

'A pint,' he said.

The girl almost asked of what, then blushed. She poured him a Guinness, and his smile when she pushed it across was enough to have her blushing all over again.

'You behave,' the next man along muttered. He looked solid, sure of his right to say that, confident the newcomer wouldn't be fool enough to take offence.

'I will,' the newcomer promised.

All the same, he glanced at the girl again.

The man next to him sighed. 'She's Himself's goddaughter.'

'Ah,' the newcomer said. Apparently that was the right thing to say, because the man went back to a long conversation about dodgy odds, doped horses and a local bookies that had been burned out.

Taking his pint, the newcomer headed for a small table in the corner which had just come free. The floor he crossed was sticky with fat droplets from the kitchens, dotted with squashed cigarette butts and slippery from slopped beer.

Yeats, the famous Irish poet, was said to have frozen in the doorway of the first pub he ever visited, winced at the noise, taken one look at the clientele, turned on his heels and never gone inside a pub again. The newcomer had no idea if that was true. But if he'd reacted like that to a perfectly decent pub in Dublin ... God knows what he'd have made of an IRA watering hole on the edge of a Derry housing estate. No one came here without reason. If they were sensible, they didn't come at all.

When the newcomer finally reached the table he'd been heading for, he discovered it was taken. The man who'd claimed it indicated that the other chair was free, and the newcomer knew being beaten to the table wasn't an accident.

'Haven't seen you here before,' the man said.

He was old, sure of himself, solidly built. It was a room full of solidly built men who knew who they were and what they stood for. He wasn't the tallest of them, the best dressed or the broadest but you knew he was there.

His presence filled the room.

'I'm looking for someone,' the newcomer said.

'You found him?'

The newcomer scanned the bar, but it was crowded, the light wasn't great, and cigarette smoke smudged the faces until everyone looked much the same.

Catholics to a man.

Northern Ireland was a place where you could read a person's origins, religion, allegiances and class in a single glance. It showed in how they stood, how they dressed, how they held themselves. Most of all, in how they sounded and where you found them. There was a large Keller jar of pickled onions on the bar, a door to the gents that didn't quite shut. The place was resolutely, intentionally grim.

Rory Gallagher came on the jukebox. 'Crest of a Wave'. Five years old, maybe ten. The raw R&B guitar. That slightly broken voice. Despite himself, the newcomer grinned.

When he looked up, the other man was nodding. 'Ever see him live?'

'Never been that lucky.'

The man tipped his head slightly sideways. 'You look like him, you know. A bit.' Pleasantness done, he sat back. 'Now, why are you really here?'

'I'm looking for Pat McGrath.'

The man stilled.

'I'm his cousin.'

'Where have you been?' There was a hard edge to the question. The newcomer had gone from being a stranger to being a suspect. How or why, he wasn't sure.

'Boston,' he said.

'Pat betrayed us—'

The newcomer's seat went back so fast the table almost went over in the other direction. Rory Gallagher track or not, the pub froze. A second later, someone flicked the switch on the jukebox at the wall and silence hit.

'He didn't. He wouldn't.'

The man just sat there looking amused. After a moment, he put his hand to the newcomer's arm, almost kindly. 'It happens,' he said, pulling him back into his seat. 'It shouldn't but it does. They get their claws into you, they begin to apply pressure and then they turn the screws . . . You'd better tell me your name.'

'Jimmy McGrath.'

Around them, punters went back to their pints as they realised whatever it was was done and dusted. Someone flicked the switch on the jukebox and Rory's voice came back mid-chorus. Jimmy McGrath took his seat at the table, trying not to mind the patronising way the old man was treating him.

'How did you find out?'

'We didn't. He came to us.'

Jimmy stared at his pint and fought not to let his feelings show. Pat McGrath had gone to them? In God's name, why?

'You knew already?'

'We knew.'

Jimmy sighed. 'Christ on a bike,' he said. 'Does his mam know?'

'That he's dead?'

'That he was a traitor.'

'No. She doesn't.'

Jimmy sat back, reached for his pint and emptied the glass. 'Good,' he said. 'It would kill her. Let me get another.'

'I'll do it,' the man said.

Jimmy knew better than to disagree.

Where he'd have gone to the bar, the man simply nodded in that direction and the girl, who'd obviously been watching, hurried over. She blushed when Jimmy caught her eye.

'Behave,' the man said. 'Both of you.'

Jimmy and the girl grinned. It was conspiratorial. Intentionally so on Jimmy's part. He had nowhere to stay that night. Although, close to, he reckoned she might not be that kind of girl. Fair enough.

He'd find somewhere else.

He always did. Keeping moving had become a way of life. As had using his mam's family name. There were people who wanted him dead. He wasn't alone in that. He imagined that most of the men in that pub had people who wanted them dead. That's why they were there. That's what bound them. That, and old songs and lost comrades and enemies they wanted dead in return.

'Who turned him?' Jimmy asked.

'Why? What's it to you?'

Jimmy McGrath held the man's gaze. Watching it harden, then soften slightly as if the man was amused by Jimmy's presumption. And it was presumption because this wasn't his local, this wasn't even his home turf, and there wasn't a man in the place that wouldn't line up behind the man across the table if needs must. 'There's a debt to be paid,' Jimmy said.

'And others with a better right to pay it.'

'His brother's dead,' Jimmy said. 'Murdered by the paras. His da's gone. I'm his cousin. I'm what he's got.'

The man considered that.

Around them people traded betting tips, dirty jokes, snippets of gossip. They ordered new rounds of Guinness and fed coins into a cigarette machine that jacked out packets of Rothmans with a clang loud enough to be a cell door. The smoke grew thicker.

'Back in a minute,' Jimmy said.

He could feel the man's gaze as he pushed through the door with the gents sign above it and felt it swing shut behind him. A corridor, a pay phone bolted to a peeling green wall, the real door to the gents, and the girl in the velour top wrestling with a crate of empties.

Jimmy slapped her arse lightly as he passed, hearing her giggle. Her reaction was always going to be that, or a sharp slap to his face and a demand for an apology. She was waiting when Jimmy came out, and leant into him when he kissed her, only stepping back when he raised his hand to her breast.

'Sorry,' Jimmy said.

She shrugged.

'It won't happen again.'

'Who said you'd be getting another chance?' She headed back to her bar and Jimmy returned to his table. He hoped the man sitting there hadn't connected his reappearance with the reappearance of the girl.

He didn't have a name for her. Not yet.

He should have got a name, Jimmy thought. He couldn't just think of her as the girl. He glanced towards the bar and asked the question he'd been telling himself not to ask.

'What's her name?'

'Judy,' the man said shortly. 'She's eighteen, a good girl, and my goddaughter.'

'I'll bear that in mind.'

'Make damn sure you do.'

The two men looked at each other and Jimmy fought to keep his gaze neutral, entirely unaggressive but also unafraid. 'About Pat's handler,' he said.

The old man smiled sourly at the amount of contempt Jimmy managed to load onto that last word. 'Fox,' he said, reaching a decision. 'Tom Fox. He's intelligence. At least we think so.'

'You got a photograph?'

'You're serious about this?'

Jimmy McGrath nodded. He was serious. Look at my face, he wanted to say. Look into the anger in my eyes. How could you even doubt that I'm serious? How dare you doubt . . .

'Come back tomorrow,' the old man said.

Jimmy pushed back his stool, knowing he'd been dismissed, and knowing he'd be back at the same time tomorrow for more of the same. Smoke and beer and the stink of too many men in too small a place. The walls were lacquered with misery, the floor sticky with thoughts of revenge. These hard-faced hardmen were his future. They were what he'd become.

'Jimmy . . .'

He stopped, turned.

'He's a killer,' the man said. 'You go after him you'd better not miss.'

'I won't,' Jimmy promised.

He could feel the gaze of the girl behind the counter right the way to the door. At the very last second, he turned, and she blushed, and then the door shut behind him and he was alone on a street, with empty stores and a burned-out garage, an abandoned chopper bike, and an aquarium glow of sodium from whichever street lights weren't broken, which wasn't many.

I I

Sunday 15th November – London

Eddington was a man at odds with his appearance, which suggested someone who not only ate well, drank well and was well-dressed, but who'd aged well and took life lightly. He'd retained most of his hair, and most of his figure, and any slight defects in either were compensated for by the skill of his Jermyn St tailor and his barber at Truefitt & Hill in St James'.

In this, he was like many cabinet ministers of his political persuasion. In fact, in the eyes of the public, he and his fellow ministers were largely interchangeable. They might know his name but only those who actually followed politics could have put it to a face pulled from one of those conference photographs, where men in suits and the occasional woman did their best to look serious, heavyweight but approachable.

Charles Eddington liked it that way.

Behind the bonhomie, party bombast and carefully cultivated rumours that he'd once had an affair with Princess Margaret (untrue), had avoided death in the Brighton bombing by being in someone else's bed at the time (also untrue), and had killed his man in Malaya during the Emergency (true, but not something of which he was unduly proud), was a man who swallowed news briefs in a single skim, actually listened to his underlings, particularly the brighter ones, and bothered to read his weekly intelligence reports.

He never forgave, never forgot and he never let a debt he

owed go unpaid or a favour unreturned. People talked of how bad an enemy he'd make. Few knew, talked about or understood how fierce his loyalty was to friends.

'Sir . . .'

Lord Eddington turned, yards from his official Jaguar, to find a young man hurrying after him. The door to his car was already open. His driver from SO1 ready to take him to Caro's hospital. Eddington wasn't in the habit of working weekends but these days it was preferable to being at home. Nothing he and Elspeth could say to each other about their dying daughter made things better. In his experience, they invariably made them worse. So he was here, and she'd gone with bad grace to collect Charlie. Eddington felt guilty about that, but only slightly.

'I'm sorry, sir.' The young man gulped, to draw breath from the look of his face, which was redder than was healthy.

'We've just heard from GCHQ . . .'

Lord Eddington stopped being irritated and started paying attention. Anything the government listening post in Cheltenham thought he should know was worth hearing. 'And?' he demanded.

'They're hearing chatter that the Americans have just bombed a Soviet base in the high Arctic. Somewhere called Kola . . . Near the Norwegian border,' he added hurriedly, seeing his minister's impatience at not being given a place name he recognised.

'And did they?' Eddington demanded.

'Sir?'

'Did the Americans bomb a Soviet base near the Norwegian border?'

'I don't know, sir.'

'Then I suggest you find out.'

*

43

'Lord Eddington . . . ?'

'Dear God. What?'

Eddington saw the look on the nurse's face and shrugged apologetically. 'I'm sorry,' he said. 'It's been a hell of a day.' He nodded towards the lift leading to his daughter's ward. 'And I don't imagine it's about to get any better.'

'I'm sorry for troubling you.'

'You're not,' Eddington assured her. 'You're doing your job. That's all any of us can do. How can I help?'

'It's the prime minister.'

Eddington started.

'She's holding for you.' The nurse nodded towards a telephone on the reception counter behind them. The receptionist was casting it dark glances as if it might bite.

'Margaret . . .'

Eddington heard her take a breath. Margaret Thatcher didn't like being kept waiting. At the same time, since she'd called him here, she undoubtedly knew where he was. And being Margaret would know why, too.

'It's time?' the PM said.

'Yes,' Eddington said. 'It's time.'

'I'm so sorry.' Her voice had softened and she sounded as if she meant it.

'It's been coming for a while,' Eddington said.

'And now it's here . . . That poor girl. I remember her as a child. That terrible pony she hated. I'm sorry to call you at a time like this but have you heard from GCHQ?'

'Yes,' Eddington said.

'Do you think it's true?' she asked.

'I've told my people to find out.'

'It would complicate things,' the prime minister said.

'It would complicate them enormously,' Eddington agreed.

He took a breath. 'You could always . . .' Hell, what did he have to lose? 'You could always ask the President.'

'Assuming Ronnie knows.'

Eddington tried to hide his shock.

'Deniability,' Margaret Thatcher said. 'I'd want deniability if we'd done something like this.' She paused. 'There's no chance it's us, is there?' she asked.

'No,' Eddington said firmly.

'Good,' the PM replied. 'I'll be sure to tell Ronnie that if he asks.'

Eddington put the receiver down and realised the nurse was staring at him.

She blushed.

'I should go,' he said.

'Of course, sir. Floor ten.'

Floor ten. It had been floor ten since the beginning. The entire floor. The other patients moved out of their luxury suites. He'd insisted on it. Citing government security when the hospital administrators tried to object.

'My wife and grandson are on their way. Also, my son-in-law will . . .'

'Major Fox is already here,' the nurse said. 'He's been here a while.'

Lord Eddington's heart sank. There were a couple of things he wanted to say to Caro. Starting with sorry, and he really did love her. Always had. Things he'd never felt able to say before. He'd been hoping to get here first.

12

Sunday 15th November – London

'You're too late . . .'

Tom Fox saw his father-in-law freeze in the suite's doorway, and cursed his clumsiness. He should have found a better way to put it. But he was hollow, punched in the guts by a death he knew was coming and thought he was prepared for.

'Did she say anything at the end?'

Tom shook his head. 'She slept,' he said. 'She said, "I'm tired. I'm going to sleep now. We'll talk later."' He paused. 'So, yes. I suppose. She said we'd talk later.'

Lord Eddington walked across and gripped Tom by the shoulder. Feeling muscles rigid beneath his fingers.

'I'm sorry,' he said.

Black sky beyond the window. The bells of St Paul's ringing for Evensong. The brightness of his wife's room making the November evening look darker than it was. As dark as it felt. Tom was no stranger to death. He'd inflicted it more than most in his line of work. And although he'd lost oppos in Ulster, and both his ma and dad had died, he'd never mourned anyone before his daughter died. Now he'd lost her mother too.

'Tom . . .'

'I loved her. In my way.'

'I never doubted it. We all did. In our way.'

'That was the problem.'

46

'I know,' Caro's father said. 'Believe me, I know.' The two men stood in silence, and a world of class, education, connections and breeding stood between them. But in this they were united. Caro's loss would hit both of them hard.

Tom felt the knot in his gut tighten as he heard the lift doors open and two pairs of footsteps cross the tiled lobby outside.

'You wouldn't believe the traffic . . .'

Lady Eddington's voice was sharp. Her irritation obvious. She looked from the two men by the window to where her daughter lay dead in a hospital robe.

'Christ,' she said.

She let go of Charlie's hand.

'Why didn't you warn me?' she demanded.

'He didn't know,' Tom said. 'Charlie . . .'

The boy had slipped forward to stand beside his mother the moment his hand was released. He seemed to be considering her body.

'She's sleeping,' Tom said.

'No,' Charlie said. 'She's dead.' Reaching out, he touched Caro's face and Tom watched his son's lip tremble. He wished he wasn't watching the boy learn to swallow pain. 'It was time.'

'Charlie . . .'

'She wrote,' Charlie said. 'It took her three goes. Her writing kept going wriggly. I knew anyway. Before I arrived. I knew in the car Mummy was going to be dead.' He looked at Tom. 'Becca told me.'

'Charlie,' Tom said.

'Becca said you're to look after yourself. You're not to do anything stupid. She'll look out for you. I've got to look out for you too.'

Rebecca Innis Elspeth Fox had been Tom and Caro's

teenage daughter. Charlie's big sister. Lord and Lady Eddington's only granddaughter. On a dry day on a long clear road, when the sun hadn't been in her eyes, her car had hit a tree at speed. An accident, everyone insisted. Tom had seen the photographs. The front of Becca's Mini entirely crumpled where it slammed into an oak. She'd been seventeen and pregnant. Tom wasn't sure who the father would have been.

'Tom.' That was his mother-in-law.

Tom had seen the glance she'd given her husband at the mention of Becca's name. There was another look. A demand for back-up.

'In a dream?' Tom asked his son.

His son looked at him.

'You dozed off in the car and dreamed Becca said Mummy was dead?'

Tom held his breath.

'Yes,' Charlie said.

Daddy knew that wasn't true. He'd seen Becca too. In Russia when someone was trying to kill him.

Charlie wasn't meant to know that, but Daddy had told Mummy this summer in the drawing room, when Charlie was meant to be playing with Hot Wheels in his room but had come down to get a drink.

Grown-ups were really bad at not being overheard. They'd been talking about all the things they'd got wrong. In life, in love, in marriage. It was a very long list.

Mummy's face looked strange now there was no one inside. She looked older, thinner and definitely dead. No one could really believe she was sleeping. It was obvious she wasn't there. He could feel she wasn't in there.

Very carefully, he unbuckled the gold watch on Mummy's wrist – an Omega, she'd told him – and just as carefully buckled it onto his own. Mummy had said he should have it when she was dead.

Holding it to his ear, he heard it tick.

Like a heartbeat.

Becca had said Mummy would be dead. She'd said Granny would be furious because Grandpa was meant to be picking Charlie up and he'd gone to work instead. She also told Charlie to tell Daddy to stop agonising about her accident. Agonising was a very Becca word. Charlie liked it.

Of course, Becca didn't exist.

She'd told him that already. So had the psychiatrist Mummy sent him to. Becca didn't exist. She wasn't a ghost. She didn't come to see him. He was simply coming to terms with grief. Charlie's way wasn't everyone's way. It had to do with how his brain was wired. That was what the grown-ups said. Charlie didn't mind being odd. Not really. It wasn't as if he had much choice. Anyway, it was better than being normal.

13

Sunday 15th November – Soviet Arctic

Five hours before Caro Fox breathed her last in a private ward overlooking the Thames, Amelia's assistant stumbled over a dying Russian in a white mink coat. His breath was so slight it took Per a moment to realise he wasn't already dead. By then, he and Amelia had established that what they'd thought were a few broken huts seen through trees was set-dressing. Built to hide an underground complex.

'*Tovarisch.*'

Comrade . . .

Per Gáski dropped to his knees in the snow.

The man said something in Russian and Amelia's assistant shook his head to show he didn't understand.

'Sami?' the Russian asked. He decided Per must be because the next time he spoke Per understood him, although only just. His voice was weak, his accent atrocious. Gaps punctuated words he fought to remember.

'My coat . . .'

'What?' Per demanded.

'Undo my coat. Take it to Murmansk.'

Take his coat to Murmansk . . . Why the fuck would a dying Russian want that? All the same, Per reached for the buttons of the mink coat, and felt the last of the man's fragile body heat leach away into the sub-zero air as he undid them.

On the man's lap was a bundle.

'To Murmansk,' the man insisted. 'The police . . . no—'

He caught himself '—the army. There will be a reward. A big reward. Moscow will be pleased. It's important. It's precious. Very precious. Understand?'

He spoke as if Per was simple or a child.

'*Understand?*'

Per nodded, and the man's eyelids fluttered and then stilled. Per didn't need to put a finger to the man's throat to know his pulse was gone.

'Per?' Amelia's voice reached him.

'Give me a second.'

Inside the man's strangely metallic bag was a glass egg.

Per ran a Geiger counter over it and hurriedly rewrapped it, hearing the click-rate drop and watching the reading settle. And then, because he needed time to think about what to do next, he pushed the bundle deep into the snow beside the man, and kicked more snow over the top.

He'd deal with it later.

'Per . . . !'

'On my way.'

Her Norwegian guide emerged from the trees, still buttoning the storm front to his flies. He was looking oddly guilty. 'You all right?' Amelia demanded.

'I vomited again.'

'Check your tag,' she ordered.

Per checked the patch on his arm, which changed colour in the presence of lethal levels of radiation. It was still the right side of safe.

'Another ten minutes and we'll be gone,' Amelia promised.

'We should bury them first.'

'No time,' Amelia said. 'The ground's solid, we don't have spades or pick-axes and there are too many. I was wrong to bring you here. I shouldn't have come.'

'Amelia . . .'

'We weren't here,' she said tightly. 'Understood?'

He scowled.

'What do you think Moscow would do if they knew we'd seen this?' Amelia glared round the ersatz village, with its broken stage-set of huts on stilts. That this place wasn't marked on maps meant nothing. The whole of West Berlin didn't exist according to most Soviet maps.

'Stay here,' Amelia said. 'I'll be back.'

'I'll come with you.'

Amelia shook her head. 'Nature calls.'

She kicked a hole in a drift behind a fir, then kicked snow over the top when she was done, cleaning her fingers on the bark. Then she went to check something. The huts further into the sprawling village had been shattered, the trees uprooted. On a hunch, she began walking. Nodding when she came full circle. If all the trees faced out, then this was the edge of a blast area and in there was its epicentre.

Five minutes. Five minutes would be safe.

In the middle, where the huts had been grouped more tightly, she could trace the razed street plan of the vanished village centre. In front of a ruined longhouse, a ripped-open shaft fell away into darkness. Common sense, and the rising anxiety of her Geiger counter when pointed at the shaft, said it was time to retreat.

'Per . . . !'

Her assistant looked up from wrestling with a hatch he'd revealed by scraping away a hump of snow.

'What are you doing?' she demanded sharply.

'Seeing what's under here.'

'For God's sake.' Amelia sounded exasperated. 'It doesn't matter. Leave it.'

'We're going?' Per said.

'Damn right we are. If we leave now, we can be back at the tent in three hours. By tomorrow night we'll be in Tromso. No one must ever know we were here. Understood?'

High in the sky, in the last of the setting sun, something glittered.

They'd been photographed.

14

Sunday 15th November – Hampshire

Logs burned in the fireplace of Grandpa's house in Hampshire. Cat, now de-flead, sprawled on a tatty Persian rug in front of its flames. The red velvet curtains were drawn against the darkness of the November night. Grandpa had his back to Granny as he helped himself to a second Glenfiddich.

Mummy would have described the atmosphere as glacial.

Charlie sat on a hump-backed saddle. All that remained of the possessions of a great uncle of Granny's who'd died in 1917 as an officer in the Camel Corps. Its leather was flaky, its red and yellow embroidery was fraying, and it was so poorly cured it still stank seventy years later. Charlie loved it.

He was less impressed with his glass of slightly stale orange juice. Out of the corner of his eye, he was watching Granny take sharp, bird-like sips at her G&T, while Daddy nursed a Diet Coke, made watery by too many ice cubes. Charlie had noticed Grandpa's surprise when Daddy turned down a whisky. And the sniff from Granny that said it was too little, too late.

'I'm not sure,' Grandpa said, 'why we need to do this now.'

Granny ignored him.

'It's usual to wait until after the funeral . . .'

'The sooner the better,' Granny snapped.

The family solicitor was on his way from Winchester with Mummy's will, despite Mummy only just being dead and a long way from buried. Granny had insisted. Now she was cross because Mr Harris was late.

'All the same,' Grandpa said.

'*Charles.*'

Granny and Grandpa's arguments were polite, scrupulously so. They'd been going on, Becca said, for the best part of twenty years. That being how long Mummy and Daddy had been together. Charlie felt grateful for the sound of tyres on the gravel outside. 'Finally,' Granny said.

Mr Harris was dressed in a grey suit that Charlie suspected he'd put on especially. He was taller than Grandpa and thinner than Daddy. He was also nervous and wearing odd socks. Charlie watched him take in the room.

'My Lord . . .'

'It's Charles,' Grandpa said. 'I've told you.'

'Yes, sir.'

Charlie caught Becca's eye and they shared a smile. He was in his corner riding his imaginary camel, and she was in the window seat with her feet up on the cushions, which wasn't allowed. She was nicer dead. She hadn't been very nice to Charlie when she was alive. She hadn't been very nice to anyone.

Unhappy, Mummy said.

Apparently some people just were. Drawing his knees up and bringing the camel that wasn't there to a stop, Charlie wondered if he was one of them.

'Do you want a whisky?'

Grandpa's solicitor was caught between politeness and the truth. What he wanted, Charlie imagined, was to be allowed a weekend to himself.

'You've brought the will?'

'Yes, my lady.'

Granny didn't suggest he call her Elspeth.

She looked at him impatiently. 'Get on with it then.'

'Darling . . .' Grandpa sounded exasperated. 'At least let the man have a drink.' But Mr Harris's was already reaching into his briefcase, which was as scuffed and battered as a pair of old gardening shoes.

'Here we are,' he said.

'That's not her will.'

The solicitor turned to Granny, whose mouth tightened. His look was not nearly as polite as Granny expected. He was offended.

'My lady?'

Granny flushed slightly. 'That's white. My daughter's will is on ivory paper.'

'She remade it,' Mr Harris said shortly. 'A month ago. Since legally it couldn't be done over the telephone, she had me travel to London. Her consultant witnessed it. As did his registrar.'

'It leaves money to the hospital?'

Mr Harris shook his head.

'I think you'd better read it,' Grandpa said. He poured Mr Harris two fingers of Glenfiddich, whether the solicitor wanted it or not. Then poured another two fingers for himself.

Tom had no idea what Caro's first will said. He wasn't even sure he knew for certain she'd made one. Although, being Caro, it should have been obvious she would have done. Caro was nothing if not organised. Its replacement was short, to the point and allowed for no ambiguity whatsoever. Tom could hear his wife's voice in his mind, and imagine her dictating it to the thin man squirming in front of them. Caro's mind had stayed sharp to the very end.

It was every other part of her that failed.

Charlie was to receive the entirety of the money, land and property she'd inherited from her grandparents, to be held in trust until he was twenty-one, subject to her father, Lord Eddington, accepting the position of lead trustee.

'Of course,' Eddington said.

The reading was done. Except, it wasn't.

'"Excluded from this . . ."' Mr Harris went on.

Lady Eddington looked up.

'". . . my house in Hampshire, the mews in Chelsea, my personal jewellery, and the funds inherited from my American great-aunt, Elizabeth Warren, which are held at Coutts. All these to my husband, Major Tom Fox, with regret and sadness for the years we won't have together."'

Which might have been better than the ones we did.

Tom could almost hear the unspoken. Looking up, he saw Charlie was staring at him, and realised a second later that a single tear was rolling down his cheek.

'You're allowed to be sad,' Charlie said.

Eddington nodded.

The mews in Cheyne Walk was worth twenty times what Tom earned. The house near this one, half that. Caro's jewellery? He had no idea how to price that. Not that he'd sell. As for her American great-aunt's fortune? It was what it said on the tin. A fortune. Caro's money had been exactly that. Caro's and Caro's alone.

He'd never asked after it. Never expected it.

After probate, he'd be rich.

'The mews can't go to him.' Lady Eddington's voice was sharp. 'It had nothing to do with him. It should be part of Charlie's trust.' Even Eddington looked slightly shocked by the way things had gone.

'Did you know anything about this?' he asked, almost gently.

'I didn't even know she'd made a will,' Tom replied.

'Two of them, apparently.'

'Charlie can have the lot,' Tom told him.

'No, Major Fox . . .' Mr Harris's voice cut into their conversation. 'With respect, he can't. Your wife's will is very precise. Its conditions particularly so. If anyone attempts to overturn this will, or subvert its intentions, the entirety of your wife's estate goes to the League Against Cruel Sports.'

'She wouldn't!' Lady Eddington was out of her seat.

The local hunt met every Boxing Day outside these very windows for mince pies and port before setting off across Eddington's own fields. A local syndicate shot wood pigeon in the woods beyond and those belonged to Eddington too.

'Of course she would,' Eddington replied. 'This is Caro, for God's sake. If she can turn up at nineteen, pregnant and on the back of Tom's bloody motorbike, having met him at a protest . . .'

Tom hadn't been at the protest, he'd been passing.

It was Caro who'd been there. He'd been the one who saved her from having her skull opened with a cosh by a member of Special Branch. He'd been training for the priesthood. The baby in her belly the day they'd arrived here on his Honda Black Bomber was his. Neither one knew it was there. But he'd never forget the lay-by on the Hog's Back where they stopped on the way down.

'Tom.' Eddington was asking something.

'I'm sorry?' Tom said.

'Are you all right?'

'Thinking about Caro.'

'Mr Harris suggests you drop into his office next week.'

'Of course.' Tom nodded to Eddington's lawyer, and then decided to walk the man to the door to see him off. Charlie stood up politely and joined them. Eddington followed. Tom's mother-in-law barely acknowledged his departure.

'I'm sorry,' Tom said, watching the car drive away.

'About Mummy?' Charlie stepped between his father and grandfather and gripped Tom's hand. 'I'm sorry too.'

'Come through when you're both ready,' Eddington told them.

'Granny says I can't live with you,' Charlie said, when his grandfather had gone. 'She says it's a ridiculous idea. You'd be completely incapable of looking after me. You can barely look after yourself.'

'You shouldn't listen at doors.'

'I don't,' Charlie said stiffly. 'I can't help it if I have good hearing.'

15

Monday 16th November – London

Next day, Lord Eddington walked into his office to hear a man say, 'It's Marks & Spencer's. Three years ago. Limited run. Marble Arch, Edinburgh, Manchester . . . Washington are certain.'

Two strangers and Miss Mahon were stood by his mahogany desk, staring down at a large photograph. Miss Mahon was burning with a slow fury he recognised.

'Jenny. What's going on?'

'Sorry, sir. They were waiting when I arrived. They insisted.'

Since Eddington's PA didn't take kindly to people she didn't work for insisting anything, he looked at the two with interest. 'Boyle, sir,' one of them said. 'William Boyle. This is Edward. Sir Geoffrey Howe asked me to show the PM this. She said show you.' He pushed the photograph across.

A woman stood among dead bodies and ruined huts in a snow-covered forest staring at the sky. Firs, spruce and birch trees ringed the clearing in which she stood.

'Satellite?' Eddington asked.

'We think so, sir.'

The quality was better than anything Eddington had seen. Unquestionably better than anything the UK could achieve. That made the original source American. There was no way the Soviets could manage quality like this. Ten years in Afghanistan had nearly bankrupted Moscow and brought their military R&D to a standstill.

'What are we looking at?'

'The Kola Peninsula, sir.'

Eddington felt his heart sink.

'We're interested in the woman. The CIA say her jacket's Marks & Spencer. Winter '84. Only on sale for one season. Only sold in major stores and not available outside the UK. That's what brought Langley to us. MI5 spent the night putting a name to her.'

'And?'

'Amelia Blackburn.'

Eddington started. Picking up the photograph, he took it to the river window and stared at it in the weak light filtering across the Thames.

'Cecil Blackburn's daughter,' Boyle was saying. 'The late Sir Cecil Blackburn. The traitor and defector. It gets worse. She's a pacifist, a CND member, a Greenham Common protester . . . Also a zoologist. Specialising in wolves.'

'She told me.'

'Ah! Her file didn't say you'd met.'

'This file,' Eddington asked. 'Did it mention Tom Fox, my son-in-law? I believe they were friends.'

'More than friends, I believe.'

'Lovers, bits on the side, one-night stands? All of the above?' Eddington shrugged. 'Given my daughter's dead, I'm not sure it matters.'

'Sorry, sir. I should have begun by saying . . .'

Eddington waved the man's condolences away.

For a moment, as he watched the Thames flow below his Whitehall window, Eddington almost regretted sending Tom into East Berlin the autumn before. What the file didn't say — at least he bloody well hoped not — was that Dr Blackburn had helped Tom escape from the Stasi, avoiding what could have been a very nasty intelligence scandal.

'What's our good doctor doing on the peninsula?'

'Not sure, sir. Zoology stuff, we imagine. Given the *Guardian*'s five days' worth of woe-is-me based on her research at Chernobyl, I'd have said better there than here. At least, until now. The Security Service thought she was still picketing Greenham and writing letters to Douglas Hurd demanding assurances the Yanks weren't storing chemical weapons on British soil.'

'Christ,' Eddington said. 'They're not, are they?'

'Mr Reagan has given the PM his word.'

'Do we actually believe him?'

'Good God, sir. They're our allies.'

Eddington had his own thoughts on that.

'The thing is,' Boyle was saying, 'the CIA believe there's been a nuclear accident near Murmansk. At a previously unknown research station on the Kola Peninsula.'

'Washington didn't bomb it then?'

Boyle's face registered horror at the suggestion, and chagrin that Lord Eddington obviously knew about the explosion. 'There's no indication of that at all, sir. The Americans say it's most probably a nuclear reactor failure.'

'And all this brings you to my office, why?'

'Amelia Blackburn's on her way to Tromso to present a paper to some UNESCO bun-fight. We thought . . . that is, the prime minister feels it would be helpful for Major Fox to meet her there, regain her confidence and debrief her.'

Eddington doubted the PM thought that at all.

'And my part in this?'

'We understand he's been signed off on compassionate leave. Since he's your son-in-law, we were hoping you might persuade him to put duty first.'

*

62

Throwing out Boyle and his silent assistant might be overdoing things, but Eddington had to admit he'd enjoyed it. His office would be buzzing. His staff fielding discreet Whitehall calls enquiring if the rumour was true. With luck the news had already reached the more scurrilous of the lobby columnists. Lord Eddington was known for his politeness, his benign and patrician gaze, his sheer trustworthiness and clubability. It didn't hurt for Margaret to see the steel beneath every now and then.

Boyle had been sent away with a flea in his ear. Eddington's daughter was newly dead, not even buried, his grandson was distraught, his son-in-law grief-stricken.

How could the PM even suggest it?

News of this argument would get back to her. It was meant to get back to her. Lord Eddington wondered how long it would take her to pick up the telephone and call him herself. He'd been wanting a talk.

16

November 1971 – Derry, Northern Ireland

Judy was out back, emptying a bucket she'd just used to mop down the pub floor. Well, she wasn't. She'd stopped to adjust her knickers. 'Oi,' she said, sounding cross rather than embarrassed when Jimmy McGrath coughed loudly behind her.

'I didn't look,' he promised.

'Yes, you did.'

'Not as much as I could have done.'

Jimmy shouldn't have been there. Not least because the pub's back yard was protected by a high wall and its door to the alley was bolted on this side.

'Pub's not open.'

'I'm not here for the beer.'

Judy checked a watch, which was tiny and on a strap that was far too tight. A present from an early boyfriend or her nan, Jimmy reckoned. Someone making a big effort and getting it wrong. 'I'm busy,' she said.

'I'll help,' Jimmy offered.

'You'll hinder.' Judy looked at him. 'How did you get in anyway?'

Jimmy nodded to the door.

He'd been able to edge the bolt open with the point of a blade and shut it behind him. 'Secure it,' he said. 'Up or down, doesn't matter. Otherwise . . .'

'People like you turn up?'

He grinned.

'You been inside?'

'Not for that. Not for long.'

'But you have?'

'Aye,' he said. 'The usual.'

Building barricades as a kid, setting fire to tyres, tossing rocks at the police. She must know what he meant. This was her childhood too.

They set up in double time, changing the barrel on one of the bitters, cleaning a couple of the lines, refilling optics.

'No fruit juices,' Jimmy said.

'Who'd drink them?'

'You?'

'As if . . .'

By the time Himself arrived, the pub had been open for hours and half of the early-evening crowd were gone. They only drank here to say they did. Half from loyalty, half from belief the glamour of the hardmen might rub off.

Jimmy went over at his nod.

His journey through the fug watched by Judy, who should have been counting out change. She got the sums wrong, turning red when her customer asked if she had something on her mind.

'You don't listen,' Himself said.

'I do,' Jimmy promised. 'I have ears like a bat. I hear things three streets away.'

'What did I say about Judy?'

'She's a good girl, she's young, and she's your goddaughter. Don't mess with her . . . I'm not messing with her.'

'You were here before the pub opened.'

'I helped set up.'

'Why?'

'I like her.' Jimmy flicked hair out of his eyes, wishing he'd washed it and worn the cleaner of his two denim jackets. His 501s weren't bad, mind. Almost new.

'You had your warning.'

'And I paid attention.'

Himself considered that. His gaze flicked to Judy, who glanced away and then made herself look back. She looked worried.

'She says you've been inside.'

'Only for the usual.'

'You say you're Pat McGrath's cousin. Pat's best friend Michael doesn't know you. Says he has no idea who you are.'

'His best friend's no' Mike. It's Peter May. Pete knows me. Ask him.'

'He's dead,' Himself said.

'Fuck,' Jimmy said. 'When?'

'Yesterday . . . Bit of an accident.'

A terraced house three streets back had gone up, taking down the homes either side. Gas mains, the news said. Before they went quiet on that. Jimmy wondered if Pete May had been putting his A-level sciences to use after all.

'See that man behind you?'

Jimmy glanced at the mirror above the big man's head. Three men, all middle-aged. Drably dressed in a style that used to be called respectable. Two were engrossed in a conversation. The third was looking in Jimmy's direction.

'Brown jacket?'

'Very good,' Himself said.

Jimmy wasn't sure if he meant in spotting the man, or not doing anything crass like turn to look. Jimmy McGrath felt it best not to mention he'd seen him before. In Belfast, near the Shankill Road. Smug, rough-shaven, already pot-bellied, he'd been wearing a too-tight sweatshirt, and sprawling, knees akimbo, in a café. He'd been with a dyed blonde who could be his mother or his wife.

'What about him?'

'He says you're an English spy.'

Jimmy's guts lurched. 'What the fuck?'

Throw-away comments like that got people killed.

'Says his name's Calum Harper, born in Dun Laoghaire, moved north to help the boys. The only Calum Harper of that age born in Dun Laoghaire died of polio thirty years ago, aged five. He must think we're fools.'

'That's Fox?'

'Fox is younger. Better at blending in. Well, so I'm told.'

Himself put a folded newspaper on the table. It landed with a clunk. 'You need to prove yourself,' he said.

'And then you'll give me Fox . . . ?'

Himself didn't know whether to be irritated or amused by Jimmy's relentlessness. 'I'll introduce you to the man we have tracking him,' he said finally. 'He'll tell you more.'

'You haven't found Fox yet?'

'We will.'

Pulling the Browning from the paper, Jimmy worked the slide, let his hand drop to his side so the 9-shot semi-auto was out of sight, and pushed back his chair.

Himself grabbed Jimmy's wrist. 'What the *fuck* are you doing?'

'Dealing with it.'

'Sit.'

Jimmy sat.

'Not here,' Himself said. 'Not now.'

Slipping the pistol into his waistband, Jimmy dropped his denim jacket over its handle and reached unsteadily for his drink. He'd finished the glass before he drew breath again.

'You done this before?' Himself asked.

Jimmy shook his head.

'Leave it until tomorrow. If you can. Later tonight if you must get it over with. Not near here though, and don't let yourself be seen. Understood?'

'Understood.'

'You planning to help Judy close up?'

Jimmy glanced at the girl. He was feeling sick at what he'd got himself into, his heart was tight with adrenaline, and mostly he just wanted to be away from Himself, the pub and what he'd just agreed to do.

'Maybe tomorrow,' he said.

Himself covered Jimmy's hand with his own for a second. The gesture fatherly, almost priest-like. 'You'll be fine,' he promised.

17

The applause for Amelia's speech was polite rather than enthusiastic.

Smiling her thanks that they'd clapped at all, she half raised her hand in goodbye to those who had actually been listening to what she had to say, and took herself off-stage. Her presentation had been a success.

If by success you meant giving a couple of hundred academics news their governments didn't want to hear and would try to keep out of the papers. Wolves, Amelia's speciality, were expected to adapt to the wastelands of the Chernobyl Exclusion Zone, a circle containing everything within 30 km of the nuclear meltdown. In fact, nature had already begun to take back the derelict towns and abandoned farms. But it would be decades before even the outer edges of that circle were fit for human habitation. To put it in perspective, she'd pointed out that the zone covered nearly 3,000 square kilometres of infected land.

She'd been careful to stress the sacrifices made.

To note the extreme self-sacrifice of the soldiers, firemen and helicopter pilots who flew into the conflagration knowing they were condemning themselves to death. To acknowledge the acts of heroism on an unimaginable scale; while leaving unsaid that the response of the Soviet authorities had been far less impressive.

The Soviets regarded her as sympathetic. That bought

69

Dr Blackburn a certain amount of freedom. She had research still to do in Kola and needed Moscow onside. Those in the audience who wanted to would be able to understand her true opinions for themselves.

'Brave,' a man she didn't know said.

Amelia smiled sweetly.

In academic circles, that translated as career-ending.

She wondered which bit of her speech he had in mind and then decided she didn't care enough to find out. She had an afternoon to kill before meeting Per for early-evening drinks back at their hotel, and needed a walk.

Her assistant hadn't been in the audience. There was no need. He'd heard her practise it at least twice. Besides, Tromso was his hometown and he had family here. It would have been unfair to expect him to attend.

It was barely noon with an hour of daylight left when Amelia set off. Already the hills surrounding the city were tinged blue like a fading photograph. It was a particular quality of the light, she realised, the grey of the fjord and the steely blue of the lowering sky giving the hills their colour.

Head down against the wind, Amelia aimed for the cathedral. Officially there was only one. The other was a 1960s glass and concrete long church, which everyone called a cathedral anyway. It was the original Amelia wanted.

The only Norwegian cathedral made from wood.

Its stained-glass windows might be designed by Gustav Vigeland, the early-twentieth-century sculptor famous for his endless naked statues in Oslo's Frogner Park, but it was a small plaque near the door she'd come to see. On this site had stood an earlier church, St Mary's Near the Heathens.

Per felt sure she'd appreciate that.

His family and cousins being the heathens in question.

Amelia hadn't come to pray. She'd come for silence, solitude and to avoid the crowds at her conference hotel. While the darkening windows said daylight was fading, her stomach said lunchtime. She'd find a café on her way back. It was either that or room service. She couldn't bring herself to eat alone in the hotel restaurant. Either someone would want to join her, or she'd feel strange and antisocial surrounded by throngs of chattering academics. Not that she wasn't strange and antisocial.

In a steam-filled hut by the harbour, she ordered salt-cod stew and followed it with rice pudding, both made from scratch and cooked in a brick oven that doubled as the café's central heating. She had it because this was what the man at the next table had, and it was easier to point to his bowls than decipher Norwegian scrawled in chalk on a board behind the till. When Amelia was done, she sat with her thoughts and a mug of bitter black coffee, which the café's owner seemed happy enough to keep refilling. Amelia's bill, when it came, was ten times higher than it would have been in Murmansk. Then again, she'd been here for a couple of hours and the food was ten times better.

Amelia was about a mile from her hotel when she began to suspect she was being followed. Darkness had long since closed in. The clapboard houses lining the street had their shutters closed or curtains drawn. The only vehicles were parked up and vanishing under steadily falling snow.

Above the crunch of her boots, Amelia could hear a distant snowplough. Stopping, she stared back the way she'd come. All she could see were wooden houses stretching into the distance behind her. The road was slippery, the street lights few, and anyone with any sense was already indoors.

Since the conference centre was closer than her hotel, she

decided to head for that instead. Picking up speed, she hurried on.

Had she imagined it?

She hadn't.

Freshly fallen snow deadened the steps behind her. Amelia just had time to realise someone was there before a hand, planted between her shoulder blades, slammed her face-first into a wall. A skinning knife was at her throat before she knew it.

'Give me your camera.'

He spoke English, which meant he knew she wasn't Norwegian. Unless her clothes simply picked her out as a foreigner.

'I don't have a camera.'

Amelia yelped as the blade nicked her throat, the pain of it shocking. A trickle of hot blood ran down her neck. 'My wallet,' she said. 'It's in my pocket. It has all my cash.'

'I want your camera.'

'I don't have a camera.'

Removing his knife from her throat, the man ran it across the back of her M&S jacket, choosing his spot on her shoulder. Amelia gasped as its point pierced flesh, halted by her shoulder blade. As an afterthought, he twisted it. Amelia screamed into the hand that covered her mouth.

Laughter came from a bar along an alley behind the conference centre. The Pet Shop Boys' 'West End Girls' blasted from a jukebox. She was 200 miles north of the Arctic circle, in a city which didn't see sun from November until January. In many ways it was her idea of the perfect city. It was still one hell of a place to die.

Slowly, her attacker removed his hand.

'My watch,' she said. 'It's Longines.'

He shifted, on edge and irritated that things weren't going

his way. The nearness of the bar, the spotlight above the conference centre's rear door, unsettled him. He hadn't known to expect them. He was growing scared, and in Amelia's experience, about the only thing more dangerous in life than a scared man, was a scared man with a knife.

'I said, I want your—'

Amelia hacked her heel into his ankle, his knife pulling free in shock. Twisting, she slammed her fist into his throat and side-kicked his knee, hearing him groan as it dislocated. She stamped on his ankle with the full force of her Docs. Shattered or fractured. Either would do.

Ripping away his ski mask, she took a good look at his furious, pain-filled face, then grabbed him by the hair, yanked his head forward, slammed it backwards into the wall. Being a pacifist was like being a vegetarian.

Occasionally one lapsed.

Well, she did.

Taking his knife, she checked his pockets, feeling sick when the only thing she found was her headshot, torn from the conference programme.

'Fuck this.' Leaving the man where he was, Amelia abandoned the conference centre and headed back to her own hotel and the drink with Per. She was going to be late and she had things to tell him.

18

Tuesday 17th November – Hampshire

Daddy appeared in the drawing-room door wearing jeans and his really old black leather jacket. The one Granny hated. He had a string bag in his hand.

'I'm going to buy cat food.'

'I'll come,' Charlie said, abandoning the television.

In America, the UN General Assembly had adopted a 'Declaration on the Principle of Refraining from the Use of Force in International Relations', which sounded to Charlie like a good thing. There'd been lots of small revenge shootings and bombings in Northern Ireland after the big bombing at Enniskillen. That had been the first story on the news. Charlie didn't want to think about those.

'It's bedtime,' Aunt Agatha said.

Charlie looked at Daddy to see if he'd disagree.

Great Aunt Agatha was Granny's big sister. She'd arrived this afternoon to help Granny *in this difficult time*. Granny didn't seem that pleased to see her.

'I'll come and say goodnight,' Daddy promised. He scowled at the report about more trouble in Ulster.

'It's being dealt with,' Grandpa mouthed, as if Charlie couldn't lip-read.

'Up to bed you go,' Daddy said.

'Can I take Cat with me?'

'Yes,' Daddy said, before Aunt Agatha could disagree.

Grinning, Charlie scooped Cat from the rug in front of

74

the fire, said his goodnights to Granny, Grandpa and Aunt Agatha, and stopped so Daddy could stroke the mog.

'He shouldn't be up here.'

'Daddy said I could.'

Becca raised her eyebrows. She did it so theatrically Charlie giggled.

'Anyway,' he said, 'you shouldn't be here either.'

'I can go.'

'No,' Charlie said hastily. 'Don't.'

He liked it when Becca appeared. It made him less lonely. Granny and Grandpa's house was too big without Mummy. Everywhere was too big without Mummy. He'd rather they were at Mummy's house, even if it was only him and Daddy. He wasn't sure why they weren't.

Becca sighed. 'Because they don't want to give you back.'

Charlie was going to ask Becca what she meant, but he already knew. So he went to use the loo, and wash his face and brush his teeth in the bathroom, where he could cry without Becca seeing. Crying, then not crying, took a while.

'I'm going down to say night-night.'

'You've already said night-night.'

'I'm going to say it again.'

'I'll be gone when you get back.'

'Why?' Charlie demanded.

'Because Daddy's almost home. You shouldn't tell him you talk to me,' Becca added. 'It only makes him worried. You know it makes him worried.'

'Why can't he see you?'

'Because I'm not here, obviously.'

Charlie hesitated at the bottom of the great stairs, his hand on the carved griffin. Granny's voice was so loud she was almost shouting. Charlie wasn't sure he'd ever heard Granny shouting. Unfortunately, Grandpa's answer was so quiet Charlie missed his reply. Whatever it was, it made Granny crosser.

'He's insufferable,' she was saying. 'He's always been insufferable. Insufferable and entirely unsuitable to bring that boy up. I can't believe you'd even consider it.'

'Elspeth . . .'

'Don't you Elspeth me!'

Charlie jumped at the hand on his shoulder, and turned to find Daddy behind him. Daddy indicated the stairs and they went up together. Becca had been telling the truth. She was gone when they went in.

'I want to live with you.'

'You are going to live with me,' Daddy promised.

Charlie wondered whether to believe him.

19

She heard Per before she saw him. A high-pitched cry of, 'I don't know . . .' Followed by a long, barely human scream.

Amelia turned the corner towards the hotel at a run.

Saw a snowplough halfway along the street. Her assistant backed against a wall, his face contorted in pain. The plough had its blade to his chest and its driver was edging forward.

'*I don't know!*'

Per's protest split the night so savagely even the man driving the snowplough flinched. 'Tell me,' he demanded.

'I would,' Per whimpered. 'I would.'

'Who did you tell about the base?'

'Nobody,' Per insisted.

Keeping to the wall, Amelia reached for the knife she'd taken from the mugger and edged behind the snowplough. A siren could be heard in the distance. If it was a police car, she hoped it had proper studded tyres, not chains. The road was an ice rink.

Adjusting her grip on the knife, she hesitated.

Half a dozen paces across ice, and then she'd have to get up to his cabin, rip open its half door and . . . stab him, she supposed.

'Don't!' Per shouted.

Not at the man. He'd seen Amelia.

'Run,' he screamed. '*Run!*'

Spinning round, the man pointed his arm and Amelia saw a gun.

It was her feet sliding from under her that saved her life. Muzzle-flare lit the darkness. The bullet hissed through where she'd been, and she heard the simultaneous pop of a suppressed pistol. The bullet buried itself in a snowbank. By then Amelia was back on her feet.

She took off at a run, changing direction every few seconds. 'Weave,' Tom Fox had said in Berlin. Someone had been trying to kill her then. Someone was trying to kill her now. She jinked left, going on one knee with a jolt, and using the momentum to dig the edge of her Doc into ice and launch herself in a different direction. In the distance she could hear the siren wailing.

'Get the police!' Per shouted.

A snarl of snowplough engine cut his rising scream in two.

Amelia vomited, fish stew and rice flowing between her fingers as she fled. Pushing herself into a space between houses, she scraped between wooden walls towards back gardens and darkness. The siren was closer now. In a house nearby someone shouted a question. Across the street, a shutter slammed open.

Amelia kept backing away, only stopping when she reached a yard to scoop up a mouthful of snow and spit against the taste of vomit. Someone inside the house began hammering on a window. Ignoring their outrage, Amelia headed along a path, passing gates to darkened yards on either side.

The snow was falling fast enough to blur the houses now. So she kept walking, head down and hands in her pockets, hunched against the cold. It was half an hour before she felt steady enough to circle back to her hotel. Fifteen minutes before she could summon the courage to go inside. Even then, she used a rear door, slipping in as a sous chef headed out for a cigarette.

20

'*Tusen takk,*' Amelia remembered to say.

She passed not unnoticed but unremarked through kitchens and restaurant, threading her way between tables, surprised at how busy it was. Some of those dining she recognised from the conference. The rest were overnighting from a Fred Olsen cruise that had docked at Tromso to give its passengers time to have dinner in the city and see the northern lights. They looked bemused to find themselves among academics talking biology, zoology and university politics.

'Ah, Dr Blackburn.' The round-faced boy on reception looked momentarily puzzled as Amelia exited the restaurant. Probably because he hadn't seen her go in.

'Your friend was looking for you.'

'Per Gáski?'

'No, he left earlier. To find you – he said.' The boy looked disapproving, then abashed at letting his prejudice against Sami show. 'Your other friend.'

'Describe him.'

'Thin, dark-haired, medium height, wearing a black ski jacket.'

'He's local? Norwegian?'

'Foreign,' the boy said. 'Not staying here. Maybe not an academic.' He shrugged, half in apology that he couldn't do better than that.

'If he comes back,' Amelia said brusquely, 'let me know before allowing him up.'

Taking the lift to the fourth floor, she used service stairs back to the third, walked the length of a corridor and used the hotel's fire stairs to drop to the second, halting behind a fire door to listen. Opening it carefully, ready to run.

She stopped again at the door to her room. In her hand, the knife she'd taken from her attacker. Her plan if anyone was inside was to hit the fire alarm outside her door and sprint for reception and the safety of irritated diners streaming from the emptying restaurant. Reversing the knife, she readied to smash its glass.

Her room was in darkness. Her curtains open. Light from the street showed her duvet stripped back, her mattress half off its base. Her case on its side. The few clothes she'd brought with her were scattered across the floor.

Her bathroom was visible. No one was inside.

Locking her bedroom door behind her, Amelia put its chain in place for added – if ineffectual – security, drew the curtains and headed for her bathroom, turning on a strip light over its mirror. She couldn't afford for light to be seen from the street, so that would have to do.

Her wash bag had been emptied into the basin. Her bathroom's flip-top bin upended onto the floor. An empty travel-sized mouthwash, an empty condom packet, used cotton buds, a chocolate wrapper and a single tampon applicator were strewn across the floor.

The search had been thorough.

She debated taking off her shirt and examining the wound on her shoulder and decided she didn't have time. She'd deal with it later. It hurt. It hurt like fuck. But she could tell it had already stopped bleeding.

Taking a nail file from the basin, Amelia removed the

chrome screws securing a panel above the lavatory pan. She reached into the cavity behind, lifted free the ceramic lid to the cistern, and plunged her arm into freezing water. Her Praktica SLR was inside a plastic bag, inside a second knotted bag. She'd been intending to wind on the unused film, remove the spool and put it in the post tomorrow.

Her toothbrush, toothpaste and tampons went back into the wash bag. Her few clothes into her case. The melamine panel back on the wall. Dragging her mattress back onto the bed, she picked up papers that had been scattered across the floor, and closed the drawers to the bedside table.

She could change hotels.

Alternatively, she could take the next flight out.

She and Per were meant to be here until the weekend, but that wasn't going to happen. Changing into her spare pair of jeans, a lumberjack shirt and hiking boots, she checked how much she had in cash, and was slipping her passport and wallet into her M&S jacket when she heard someone try the door.

It was stealthy, unobtrusive.

Amelia froze.

The person hadn't knocked, they hadn't called to say 'housekeeping', and the young man on reception hadn't rung to say her 'friend' was on his way. Whoever was outside pushed at the door, and when that didn't work put a card to the latch.

Three steps took Amelia to the window.

A sloping roof one floor below, the snowy street one floor below that. Not giving herself time to think, Amelia threw up the window, tossed out her case and grabbed her camera, climbing out and pulling the window down behind her. Then she lowered herself from the sill, let herself drop and followed her case across the sloping roof below. The snowy ground came up to meet her.

21

November 1971 – Derry, Northern Ireland

If it were done when 'tis done, then 'twere well it were done quickly...

Jimmy McGrath had learned that at school, as close to a hell hole as any place he'd been. He couldn't wait. Wouldn't wait. Himself must have known that. It had been a long enough wait for Judy to ring time and the pub to begin to empty. Time enough to think about things. Even Shakespeare.

The pub door slammed open, and Himself and two others stepped into the night. Their breath rising like smoke. Others began emptying out behind them. Judy would be inside, wondering where Jimmy had gone. As she'd done every day this week, Judy would have asked if they didn't have beds to go to. An older man would have muttered something about cheeky mares. It was a routine. Regular. Safe. Also, drab. Jimmy had these thoughts occasionally. Like knowing bits of Shakespeare. He'd learned to keep them to himself.

Jimmy watched them go.

The road most of them chose looped round a council estate badly damaged in riots the summer before last. Jimmy used a footpath between ragged gardens to bring himself out ahead of the not-really Calum Harper, not really from Dun Laoghaire.

If Himself asked why he hadn't waited a day, he'd say he'd had plans for tomorrow involving Judy. Truth was, the thought of killing not-Calum frightened him. Jimmy was afraid of bottling it.

Blessing a broken street light, he hunkered down beside a phone box with smashed windows, his back to a white Transit with its doors ripped off. The mattresses behind the van were for diving practice. The mattress inside another purpose entirely. Himself's pistol was heavy in his coat.

Jimmy wanted it done.

Three of the younger men walked side by side, their conversation worn to half questions, brief answers and the occasional grunt. They were drunk but no drunker than you'd expect of men like them on a Friday night.

At a crossroads, they stopped to confer briefly, and two of them turned for the bus station. There would be no buses. Those were done for the night, and the trains were down to one an hour, but there should be taxis; and if there were not? Well, they could walk. The night was dry for once, for all the clouds were heavy and the wind chill.

It was the third man Jimmy followed.

Down a track towards the edge of town. Not that he'd be going that far. There were railway arches ahead. The kind that backed onto an earth bank and provided space for lock-ups, fly-by-night car lots, and places to hide weapons and store stolen goods. No one came here who didn't belong. Not unless they were stupid.

A silver Cortina and an early '60s Rover, the kind with the Viking badge bolted on its grill, blocked the entrance to an arch. Having glanced behind him, the man calling himself Calum Harper slipped between the cars and headed into the gloom beyond. This was a man who knew where he was going, why he was going there and whom he expected to meet. Had he been less arrogant, he might have taken more care when checking he wasn't being followed.

*

'You're late,' a voice said.

'I was working.'

'That's something, I suppose.'

The other man was English. With a voice that belonged on the radio reading out shipping reports. 'Couldn't you have found somewhere better?' he asked.

'Where do you suggest?' Calum asked. 'Your office?'

'There's no need for that.'

'What do you want?'

'A progress report.'

It was obvious the two men disliked each other. The one who'd been kept waiting was having trouble holding his temper.

'You brought my money?'

'Your report.'

'I'm in. My legend's holding up. No one suspects me . . .'

'You're sure?'

'Absolutely.'

A legend was a cover story, and the man was wrong about no one suspecting him. Himself had probably suspected him from the start. You didn't get to be a commander in the IRA, certainly not and live long, if you weren't at least as canny as those the Brits sent against you.

Shifting, Jimmy accidentally nudged a can.

'Who's there?'

'What's that?'

Calum whipped a torch from his coat, the kind watchmen carry to use as a cosh. The other man had a pistol drawn. The beam swept over the pile of scrap Jimmy was hidden behind, and settled on a rat that bared its teeth in fury.

'Fucker,' Calum Harper said.

The Englishman just laughed, then put his pistol away and pulled a wad of notes from his pocket. He'd had enough of this meeting. 'Take it,' he said. 'I'll expect a full report next time.' Tossing keys across, he added, 'There's a present for you in the Cortina.' He couldn't quite make himself shake his contact's hand, so he slid between the cars blocking the entrance to the arch instead and hurried away.

Jimmy let him go.

'Stuck up little shit.' Calum's accent grew harder, more obviously Protestant now he was away from the pub and his handler had gone. He counted the notes by the light filtering in from outside. From his scowl, he'd been expecting more.

Very slowly, Jimmy stood.

He was hidden in shadow beside the wall.

Equally slowly, he pulled the Browning from his coat. It felt large, clumsy and unfamiliar.

One shot, he told himself. All it needed was one shot. He could kill the man outright; or wound him so he'd bleed to death, but not before Jimmy had asked a few questions.

Himself would like answers. Unfortunately, Jimmy had forgotten to ask to which questions.

'Who—?' The man said, realising someone was there.

'Me,' Jimmy said. Then fired.

22

Wednesday 18th November – London

'You should read this, sir.'

Eddington took the report and skimmed the first paragraph, going back to read it again more thoroughly. The report was a page and a half long and comprised all of six double-spaced paragraphs. He read the remaining five paragraphs carefully, only noticing its date at the end.

'This is two months old.'

'Yes, sir.'

'Why bring it up now?'

'A week after this, an East German weapons dump exploded.'

'And now a Soviet research facility on the Kola Peninsula has exploded?' Eddington thought about that. Weapons dumps exploded. The soldiers manning them died. It was a hazard of the job. Research facilities? That depended on what was being researched or who objected.

'Odds on it being true?' he asked.

'That a week before a GDR arsenal exploded, it was attacked by Soviet commandos, who found it guarded by *spetsnaz*, who died to the last man? It makes no sense whatsoever, sir. Why would Moscow attack their closest allies?'

'Why indeed?' Eddington asked.

He had his own thoughts on the increasingly frosty relationship between East Berlin and Moscow, but they were his thoughts. He wasn't ready to share them yet.

'Where is Heringsdorf anyway?'

'Pomerania, sir. On the Baltic, as far east as you can go without being in Poland. Used to be called Kaiserbad.'

Now there was a name Eddington recognised. His grandmother used to take the waters at the spa in Kaiserbad before the Great War, back when the world was a bit more civilised. 'Ask our friends in Bonn what they know of this. Let me know the moment you hear back,' said Eddington, and promptly put the report out of his mind. His assistant hadn't quite finished though.

'Forgive me, sir. The other matter . . . ?'

'I'm dealing with it,' Eddington said crossly.

Meals were provided, sheets washed. No one had to think about shopping. There was a housekeeper, a gardener, and a cleaner. All so invisible they might have been ghosts. Eddington's house still felt like prison to Tom.

He didn't exactly dislike Caro's childhood home; and he knew she loved it, with a fierceness he found impossible to understand. Her childhood had been easier than her adolescence, but not even her fiercest teenage arguments had been enough to tarnish Caro's love for the place.

Tom wished he liked it more.

He also wished it, and he, were somewhere else.

Within easy drive of London via the M3, secluded but not isolated, set in its own grounds, complete with barn, stable and a picturesquely derelict tennis court, it had paddocks, a couple of huge fields hired out to a local farmer, and its own woods, which came with the advantage of added tax breaks. It was what living in the country looked like if you were rich and didn't like the country very much.

It was also not far from Fort Monckton in Gosport, where intelligence agents did six months' basic training, and SIS ran more intensive courses for those in the field. Monckton wasn't one of Tom's favourite places either.

Tonight's chat with his father-in-law in the blue drawing room, the two men together drinking whisky and remembering Caro, was never going to be just that. Having refused a whisky, Tom watched Eddington pour himself a Laphroaig, add a dash of warm water and drink it down. There was probably a doctorate in what Eddington's various choices of whisky said about that day's thought processes. Should anyone be able to extract the information.

'Sure you won't have one?'

'What do you want?' Tom demanded.

His father-in-law didn't even pretend to be offended. 'To talk, away from my wife, her dreadful sister, and your boy, obviously. Something's come up. Something serious. I'm going to need your help.'

'Why mine?'

'You have the experience.'

'A dozen men have that.'

'No,' Eddington said flatly. 'They don't. Your stuff in Moscow. Dealing with that issue in East Berlin. You've become a name, Tom. Even the Blessed Margaret asks how you are.'

That issue in Berlin. One way to describe a murdered defector, not to mention Tom's closest brush with death since a multi-storey in Derry.

'I don't want to be a name,' Tom said. 'I don't want the PM asking after me. I'm not an agent. I'm an asset . . . *was* an asset.'

'Hoping we'll throw you out?' Eddington asked.

'Yes,' Tom said. He'd been wondering when Eddington would mention the questionnaire.

'You should have come to me, you know. Said you wanted out. You didn't need to go through all that tomfoolery.'

'I did come to you. Remember?'

88

Eddington had the grace to look embarrassed.

Tom let the silence between them grow. Losing himself in the crackle of kindling and the hiss of flames. A log as thick as an elephant's foot burned in the great fireplace. Velvet curtains kept out draughts from sash windows, and flames threw swirling orange shadows on the oak panelling around them. A mahogany standard lamp provided the room's only real light.

He couldn't imagine what it would have been like to grow up here, cosseted and constrained at the same time. Everything allowed, except for the things that weren't. All the rules so firmly fixed they never needed mentioning. Everything of real importance said in the silences between words. He didn't want this for his son.

'You're serious about not drinking?'

'If I start . . .' Tom replied.

'That's a surprisingly honest answer. Let me get you something ghastly.'

In the seconds Eddington was gone, Tom checked the notebook left on the Regency card table by his father-in-law's chair. Little arrows led from one bullet point to the next. It had been left out for him to read. Eddington's idea of subtlety.

Kola Peninsula
↓
Amelia Blackburn
↓
Tromso
↓
Tom
↓
Debrief

'Here we go,' his father-in-law said.

Opening the Coke, Tom took a mouthful and almost smiled at Eddington's horror. He poured the rest of the can into the Bohemian tumbler provided.

'About Charlie,' Tom said.

'I wanted to talk to you about work first.'

'All the same,' Tom said firmly, 'he's my son. I'm not parting with him.'

'You're not parting with him because he's your son?'

'I'm not parting with him because his mother's dead, he needs looking after, and I can do the job as well as anyone else.'

And I promised Caro.

'Let's come back to that,' Eddington said.

In his gaze, Tom saw the man who'd manoeuvred himself into a prime position on the Joint Intelligence Committee, while manoeuvring two of his rivals off. 'Now. What do you know about the Soviet–Norwegian border?'

'Little enough.'

'It's in the high Arctic, less than two hundred miles long and unusually porous. We guard our side, they guard theirs. Everyone behaves.'

'How novel,' Tom said.

'Five days ago there was an explosion too close to the Norwegian border for comfort. A nuclear explosion.'

'An accident?'

'We think so. At least we hope so. If it was a test, it went wrong. Which I guess would make it an accident anyway. There were fatalities. Numerous fatalities.'

'The Soviets have admitted this?'

'Of course not.'

They'd only admitted Chernobyl when the fallout became

too extreme to hide. Even then, they'd lied about practically everything that came after, from when it happened to the levels of radiation released and the numbers dead. They'd lied to themselves, to each other, to their bosses and the West.

Eddington pushed a photograph across.

Tom's eyes widened. 'That's . . .'

'Aye,' Eddington said. 'It is. A friend of yours. The traitor's daughter.'

'Sir Cecil tried to come back—'

'Vanity,' Eddington said, cutting him off. 'Vanity, ill-health and the hope of a publishing deal.'

Taking the photograph to the lamp, Tom examined it. Amelia stood in deep snow surrounded by bodies. A lot of bodies. Someone in Whitehall had probably been given the job of counting them.

'She's in Tromso,' Eddington said. 'At a conference. God knows, I know it's a lot to ask you with Caro dead but . . . well, she was a friend of yours.'

'Find someone else.'

Eddington watched Tom leave the room and sighed. It was the answer he'd expected, which wasn't at all the same as him accepting it. Caro was dead. His son-in-law was feeling guilty. So maybe mentioning Amelia in those terms had been unwise. Although, God knows, it wasn't as if Caro had been a saint either.

'What were you talking about?' Eddington heard his grandson ask from beyond the door.

'Stuff,' Tom said.

'What kind of stuff?'

'*Stuff* stuff,' Tom replied. 'What are you doing out of bed?'

'Mrs Ross has gone home.' Charlie might have considered

that answer enough, but his father obviously didn't. Charlie sighed. 'I was making cocoa.'

'Of course you were,' Tom said. You could almost hear his smile.

Give me a lever, Eddington thought, and I can move the earth. He'd have another word with Tom tomorrow.

23

Wednesday 19th November – Hampshire

'You let the milk bubble over,' Becca said.

She was standing in the bay of Charlie's bedroom. The one with the stained-glass windows and oak shutters that creaked. It wasn't really Charlie's, it was simply where he slept. Although 'Charlie's room' was what Granny called it. Charlie liked it, though. Its window was twice his height, with sandstone pillars, and he enjoyed making the shutters creak and pretending it was a ghost.

Becca was right. He'd left the pan on the Aga while he went to the hall.

'I was—'

'Listening at doors. And then you burned your fingers trying to clean up. I don't know what we're going to do with you.'

'You can't do anything with me,' Charlie said crossly. 'You're dead.'

'That's mean.' Becca sounded hurt.

'I'm sorry,' Charlie said. 'I didn't mean it.'

'Yes, you did. It's all right though.'

'Does it hurt being dead?'

'Not at all. It didn't hurt dying either.'

'It must have done.' Charlie had seen the photograph of her Mini after the crash. He wasn't meant to have done but he did. There wasn't very much of anything left. Car included.

'It was so quick I didn't feel a thing.'

93

Charlie didn't believe her.

'Look at the snow,' Becca said.

'There isn't any snow.'

'Of course there is.'

Scrambling from his bed, Charlie ran to the window, yanked open its shutters and was staring at tundra below. The lawn, the paddock and the cherry tree were gone. There was snow as far as he could see. The woods beyond didn't look like Grandpa's. They were firs, birches and spruce, with sharp, slate-coloured mountains rising behind them.

The sky was on fire . . .

'It's called the aurora borealis,' Becca said, sounding grown-up. 'It looks impressive but doesn't give as much light as you'd think. You won't do it until geography O-level.'

'How does it work?' Charlie asked.

'Solar wind hits the magnetosphere and everything glows like Christmas lights.'

Charlie liked the sound of that.

'When did it snow?' he asked.

'When you were asleep.'

'I haven't been to sleep.'

'You're asleep now,' Becca told him.

'No, I'm not.' Charlie touched his cocoa to make sure. It was still warm in its mug.

Becca grinned. 'If you say so.' She stood so close that Charlie could almost feel her. It felt like wind slipping between the sashes of a tall window.

'Grandpa's right,' she said.

'He's not,' Charlie said hotly. 'I'm not living here.'

'Of course you're not,' Becca said dismissively. 'That's a really stupid idea. I mean about the other thing. Daddy has to go away for a few days. It's important. Anyway, it's the Wolf

Lady. You like the Wolf Lady. Also . . .' She hesitated. 'You shouldn't listen at doors.'

'You did.'

'That was different.'

'Wasn't different at all.'

'You never hear anything good,' she said. 'Well, I never did.'

'Will Daddy be back for Mummy's funeral?'

'Of course he will.'

Charlie thought about it. He didn't want to be here alone, but Becca might be right, she usually was. Not an endearing quality, as Mummy used to say.

While he thought about it, Charlie considered the snow, which was deeper than could fall in one evening. And the stars were all in the wrong places. Even if only by a little bit. That had to mean something.

'I'll talk to Daddy tomorrow,' he promised.

24

Thursday 19th November – London

'That supposed Soviet attack on the GDR arms dump on the Baltic, sir . . .'

'*Supposed?*'

The lift Lord Eddington had been waiting for opened and he waved at those inside to let it shut without him. He was on his way back to Hampshire to have another go at pressing Tom to track down Cecil Blackburn's daughter. A fact that wouldn't make his son-in-law happy, and would undoubtedly make Elspeth even more furious than she currently was.

His car could wait.

'What have you heard?'

'The West Germans say it's fantasy. According to an NVA asset of theirs, a fire went out of control at an arms dump. I don't doubt the GDR are lying about the death toll. We'd probably lie ourselves. But speedboats full of Soviet commandos machine-gunning *spetsnaz*? I'll be telling our own man we don't appreciate being taken for mugs.'

'Ask him where these boats that didn't exist came from.'

'Sir?'

'Ask him,' Eddington ordered.

'Yes, sir. There's something else . . .'

'Isn't there always.'

'One of ours in Washington was talking to one of Langley's a few months ago. Rumours of an Arctic research station came up. Soviet. Purely zoological. No military application.

It's just . . .' Eddington's assistant paused. 'Rumour said the station was designed in two parts. The laboratories walled off from the living quarters. For safety reasons.'

'For zoological research?'

'Quite, sir.'

'Tell the CIA we'd like everything they have, and we'll share anything we discover as a quid pro quo.'

'We did, sir. They deny the conversation took place.'

Lunch had started when Eddington got home, which was his own fault for dropping by the Carlton for a discreet word with the Foreign Editor of *The Times* in case he'd heard rumours of trouble in Kaiserbad.

He hadn't. Nor would he print the rumours. Eddington had his word on that. He would, however, be first in line if putting the story in print made sense. And it might yet. Eddington felt West Germany's rejection of the idea was a little too over-egged and emphatic for comfort.

'*What* did you say to Charlie?'

Eddington didn't even have time to sit before Tom rounded on him. His wife froze, a fork of pheasant and lardon pie halfway to her mouth. Charlie wasn't there, which wasn't that surprising. He liked eating in the kitchen with Mrs Ross, who gave him less grief about sitting up straight and finishing his plate.

'Well?' Tom demanded. His voice was hard, his fists clenched at his sides. The expression on his face didn't belong in polite company.

'Tom, what's this about?'

'Did you talk to my son about Tromso? Did you mention Amelia? Did you tell him I had to go?'

'Good God. Of course not.'

'Are you lying?'

'Tom . . .' Elspeth Eddington was outraged.

Her husband held up his hand. 'No,' he said. 'I'm not. I give you my word. I've said nothing about any of this to Charlie.'

'About what?' Lady Eddington demanded.

'I'll tell you later . . .'

Tom ran his hand across his face.

'What's going on?' Eddington asked.

'Charlie says I should go. He says that the Wolf Lady needs my help. Mummy would insist.'

'He used those words?'

Tom nodded.

'We'll skip pudding,' Eddington said. 'My driver's outside. Ride with me and we'll talk on the way. I'll have Marcus turn round and run you back when we're done.'

Tom was pretty sure that wasn't acceptable use of a ministerial Jaguar, but Eddington was a law unto himself. Advisers, confidants and allies came and went. Eddington remained.

'I don't give a damn about Caro's money,' Tom told his father-in-law the moment the car's doors were shut and Eddington's SO1 driver had turned off the intercom and raised the glass. 'I don't care about Chelsea or her house here. You can have those too. Charlie's different. He told me about your argument.'

'With Elspeth?'

Tom nodded. 'He can go to that damn boarding school if you insist. But he's mine, and my responsibility, and in the holidays he lives with me.'

'That's your price?'

'I shouldn't need to buy him back.'

'You're buying peace. Peace, and my support.'

'You'd take my side in a custody battle?'

'You'll get on a plane?'

'Now. If you swear it.'

'Your plane better be first thing tomorrow. I'll have the chaps fix you an Amex and a passport. And they'll need to knit you a legend.'

'Swear you'll take my side in any custody battle and I'll get on your plane.'

'Now?'

'Now.'

'On my hope of heaven,' Eddington promised.

Tom wondered if the old fraud really expected heaven to take him in.

25

Stamping along the line of traitors, recidivists and saboteurs, Colonel Sergei Rostov grabbed the director of the Kola Institute by the hair and dragged him into the middle of the clearing. It didn't matter that Comrade Sholokhov was a Hero of the Soviet Union. If he'd been a real hero, he'd have died when his scientists and technicians did, a week earlier.

Throwing Sholokhov to his knees, Rostov yanked free his Tokarev 7.62, told the man to bow his head and put the muzzle to the back of his skull. The director knew what was going to happen. He'd known the moment Rostov arrived.

Blood, bone and brains splattered the snow in front of the man, who fell sideways as the noise of the shot set wolves howling somewhere in the forests beyond.

'Hold the rest here,' Rostov ordered.

These were the few he'd found. The ones who'd been in the living quarters rather than the labs, the ones not lucky enough to die in the explosion. A couple of them were already so eaten up with radiation they looked like walking corpses. The rest . . . ? He could smell them from where he stood.

Shit, piss and fear.

Their stink destroying the purity of the Arctic air.

'You,' he said to his lieutenant. 'Come with me.' The boy wanted to protest. Of course he did. Zhidkov's father was a Politburo member. As his grandfather had been. A posting to this border was meant to be close to not serving at all.

'Could be worse,' Rostov told him. 'You could be in Afghanistan fighting American-armed fanatics.' He watched the boy's face close down and smiled to himself.

'You've found me a way into the labs?' he asked his sergeant.

'Yes, colonel. If you'll follow me . . .'

Little enough was left of the fake village built to hide the air ducts, entrance hatches and pipes down which water could be delivered. A few of the more distant huts still stood, either cracked open or listing on broken stilts. It was obvious the explosion had been contained within the labs, then exploded up a shaft and risen like a geyser into the air. It must have been some sight. It still didn't explain why those people were still alive though. Unless the reinforcements between labs and living quarters had been at near nuclear bunker levels.

'Here, sir.'

Rungs descended into darkness.

Rostov held out his hand and the sergeant handed him a torch.

'Stay here. And you—' Rostov nodded at Zhidkov '—follow me, and try not to fall off the bloody ladder.'

The colonel went first, descending rapidly and stopping every twentieth rung to angle his torch down the shaft and check his way was clear. At the bottom was a hatch with a handle and Rostov swung on it, shouldering open a heavy blast door.

A bulkhead light showed sullen orange, its paint burned back to scorched steel beneath, its shattered glass held in place by wire mesh within. Most of the support system for this place had been lifted from a nuclear submarine. Somewhere the central generator was still working.

'Sir . . .'

'What?'

Zhidkov pointed at his radiation patch, then at its equivalent on his boss's uniform. Both had begun to darken.

Rostov shrugged.

'Sir, we're . . .'

Flicking open a lock-knife, Rostov hacked the badge from Zhidkov's uniform.

'Feel better?' he asked.

The corridor into the laboratories was a darkened tunnel of melted walls, missing ceiling and twisted metal. A sprinkler system had come on – unless its nozzles had simply disintegrated. Drips fell from twice their height to splash into the ankle-deep water they waded through. From its slow and steady dripping the system hadn't been turned off. Its tanks were simply empty.

Rostov matched the mess to his memory of a map.

'This way,' he said, clambering over fallen rock. He was talking to himself. Zhidkov was too junior, too effete and too obviously one of the new breed to merit more than open scorn and direct orders. In the area beyond the rock fall, the walls had melted entirely, revealing yards of fire-blackened granite.

'Now where?' Rostov asked himself.

He found it eventually.

A ripped-open chute leading to open sky.

High above, he could see the faintest shimmer of the northern lights as darkness approached and the aurora prepared to fill the sky. He wasn't given to sentimentality, but standing in the centre, where the explosion had escaped, he admired the approaching light show for a second or so and knew he was unlikely to see it again.

'Open that,' Rostov ordered.

'It's jammed, Comrade Colonel.'

'Try harder,' he told Zhidkov.

Beyond the first steel door was a second, beyond that a third.

The air scrubbers, the water purifiers, the bomb-proof bulkhead lighting, even the thick metal hatches. Pretty much everything lifted from a submarine had proved up to the job. He had no doubt the reactor, buried deep below this level, would keep running long after the base was abandoned. Consulting the map in his head, he turned into a corridor that looked less damaged than those before it.

'Now that,' he ordered.

Zhidkov wrestled with the handle of another steel door.

Beyond was a tiny room, almost undamaged. Between it and the hellscape they'd passed through was a window a metre or more thick, its reinforced glass made from layers of polymer, woven glass fibres and radiation-resistant lead glass. From inside the room, its millions of cracks looked like patterns in ice.

'Fuck,' Rostov said.

'Sir?'

'It's not here.'

'What isn't, sir?'

'None of your damn business.'

The colonel spun on his heel, ready to head back the way he'd come, then changed his mind. Turning, he pulled his pistol from its holster and shot Zhidkov through the head. 'Call that a kindness,' he said.

The little fool had seen too much anyway.

'Who took it?' he demanded of the woman kneeling in front of him.

'Took what, Comrade Colonel?'

Bone and brains sprayed from the back of her skull. The

roots of a fir tree acquired an ugly scar and a varnish of blood and jelly.

'Well?' Rostov said to the next in line.

This one had wet himself. Since he already looked like a swaying corpse that might have been radiation sickness. 'How the fuck would I know?' he replied.

Another bullet. Another man.

'At least that one had guts,' he told his sergeant. The NCO nodded, looking at the five men remaining. None would know where it was. Whatever the fuck *it* was. The Comrade Colonel hadn't bothered to share that information.

If they did know, one of them would have broken by now.

'Round,' Rostov snarled, stalking down the now shorter line. 'The size of a child's ball. Filled with metal and made of glass. Ring any bells?'

The men looked at each other.

They'd have lied and pretended to know where it was if they thought they could get away with it. None of them bothered. Sickness, or a bullet. They were dying anyway.

'Shoot the lot,' Rostov said tiredly. 'And call in a clean-up crew.'

The Mil Mi-26 helicopter came in low over the trees.

Winter-white and lacking markings, the low thud of its rotor could be heard across the plateau, as could the blades of the helicopter behind it, and the one behind that.

Birds rose in the forest. Wolves howled. Bears shuddered in their early sleep. Arctic foxes froze invisible against snow. It hovered low, its blades kicking up a blizzard that obscured the white-uniformed soldiers racing down its ramp. The nearest hatches were quickly lifted, bodies tossed into the shafts, hatches bolted again.

It was swift, efficient, practised.

'Now scrub it,' Rostov said.

Fire, bright as burning phosphorous, lit the dark, blazing from the nozzle of a flame-thrower as the first soldier took up his position and began to burn the trees around the splintered longhouse, the longhouse itself, and the ruined fake buildings back to nothing. Others joined him, moving in a line as snow melted before them, turning back on themselves to lay waste to the ground again.

26

Fourteen-thirty hours.

Welcome to pitch darkness.

Tom re-checked the time on his Rolex Day-Date, as his Scandinavian Airways DC-9-21 touched down on the runway at Langnes, just outside Tromso.

All my love, always.

It was fifteen years since he'd last worn it and its bracelet felt strange. Caro hadn't added her name to the back. There was no need. Who else would give him a watch costing half a year's wages? Although by then he'd learned to call it a salary.

At least when her family were around.

The last half hour of Tom's flight had gone through dusk into darkness, the airport lights as they were landing unnaturally sharp and bright. Nothing showed beyond the runway's perimeter. Not even mountains, sea or sky. Those clambering to their feet around him were oil men. Neat haircuts, gold Rolexes, suave suits, which they were now covering with elegantly cut overcoats.

Tom's own was M&S. His suit Burton. He'd been outfitted by his father-in-law's office with items they defined as *academic, smart*. He wanted his black leather jacket and jeans back. At the very least, he wanted his flying jacket from the days when he'd first met Caro, which had basically been a

sheep turned inside out and fitted with a zip. It was the warm-
est thing he'd ever owned.

Tom shivered.

'We'll have you inside soon, sir.' The stewardess smiled.
'We're just waiting for permission to disembark . . .'

A snatch of Norwegian came from the speakers.

'Ah,' she smiled again. 'Here we go.'

A gale buffeted Tom the moment he reached the steps,
and he hugged his greatcoat tighter, wishing he'd worn
gloves. There was snow. A lot of it. And wind.

The 1960s arrivals hall was concrete and functional.
Being Norwegian, it was also clean, in good repair and
everything worked. No one was there to meet him. Not
that Tom was expecting anyone. No one at baggage
reclaim seemed interested in his arrival either. Or, if they
were, they hid it well. He took the eight-seater airport bus
into town, along a three-mile road being scraped by
snowploughs.

'You're checking in, sir?'

Brushing snow from his coat, Tom nodded and put his
newly printed passport and Amex on the counter without
being asked. A-ha's 'Take On Me' drifted from the lounge
next door. Becca's boyfriend had bought her the single. She'd
played it once to keep him happy, then gone back to Soft
Cell. All the same, they'd stayed together until the day she
died. Even if the baby in her belly wasn't his.

Information Tom extracted from the boy with his fists.

Not his finest hour.

'Professor Conway?'

Tom looked up.

The receptionist's smile was slightly strained.

'Sorry,' Tom said. 'Long flight and an early start.' He reached for his hotel key and wondered if he'd get used to answering to Professor, which was the rank Eddington's office had selected for him with the agreement of an acquiescent Oxford college.

'The conference is almost over, sir.'

'I know,' Tom said. 'This is a last-minute trip to catch up with an old friend . . . An academic colleague,' he added. 'Amelia Blackburn. The zoologist.'

The receptionist's face froze.

'What?' Tom demanded.

'I'm afraid . . .'

'She's hurt?' he said. 'An accident?' An accident that was anything but . . . ? Tom waited while the receptionist visibly composed herself.

'Dr Blackburn is missing.'

'How do you mean, missing?'

'She went up to her room two days ago and hasn't been seen since.'

'Show me.'

'I can't,' she said. 'I shouldn't even be discussing it. I can't let one guest into the room of another. Regulations.'

'Her things are still there?'

'I believe so.'

'Then get me the manager.'

The Norwegian girl looked even more unhappy. 'Mr Hauge is away,' she said. 'He'll be back tonight.' She peered through the lobby window at fast-falling snow. 'Unless the weather gets worse. In which case it will be tomorrow.'

'Do you have a map of Tromso?'

The receptionist looked surprised. 'Of course, sir.'

Unfolding the map, Tom told the receptionist to circle the

police station and have his case taken up to his room. He stamped off into the snow, leaving her looking worried.

'I'm afraid not, sir.'

Inspector Dahl's English was perfect, for all her accent was obviously Scandinavian. Replacing the receiver on its cradle, she shrugged apologetically.

She'd called Tromso hospital on Tom's behalf, then Nordkjosbotn, a smaller hospital forty miles away. Tom had insisted she try, while agreeing it was unlikely his friend would have strayed that far.

'She's an adult,' Inspector Dahl said. 'You said her things are in her room. As you know, there's a conference on. She might simply have not returned yet.'

Yeah, Tom had heard that kind of thing about conferences too. All the same . . . 'How long before you can put out a missing person?'

'Is there something you need to tell me?'

Tom shook his head. 'I'm sorry,' he said. 'I'm just worried for my friend. I don't suppose you could try the morgue?'

'We have only one body,' Inspector Dahl said, her voice studiedly patient. 'A young Sami crushed by a snowplough. He was drunk and probably went to sleep in the snow. We're still looking for the driver responsible . . . Believe me,' she added, 'if we had a dead academic, I'd know about it.'

27

Friday 20th November – Moscow

A tragic fire on the Kola Peninsula has resulted in the complete destruction of a zoological research station. Despite heroic efforts from the Red Army, who flew the latest Mil Mi-26 helicopters into notoriously difficult Arctic terrain in the middle of winter to help with the evacuation of the wounded, there were no survivors and the buildings could not be saved.

Pravda

The USSR Academy of Sciences is sad to announce the death of Professor Natalia Volkova, one of our finest academics, in the recent fire at the Kola Zoological Complex in the Arctic. As a young woman, Natalia Volkova worked alongside Professor Yulii Borisovich Khariton at Arzamas-16 as part of the All-Russian Scientific Research Institute of Experimental Physics.

A good Party member, and a Hero of the Soviet Union, she will be remembered best as an outstanding theoretical physicist, for her contributions to the greater good, and her unquestioning devotion to the Motherland.

University of Moscow Gazette

Radioactive Wolves?
Glow-in-the-dark reindeer?
Mutating magic mushrooms?

Given Dr Volkova's part in establishing the USSR's nuclear weapons programme, her university's insistence that she died at a 'zoological research station' is interesting. What was she doing there? We shall probably never know.

Krokodil

28

'Is the manager back?'

'It's two-thirty in the morning, sir.'

'I didn't ask you the time,' Tom said flatly. 'I asked if the manager was back . . .'

The reception staff had changed and night shift at the hotel was taken by 'Erik', if his name badge could be believed. It was the young man's wristwatch, Tom realised. Large, black, sterile dial, cloth strap. It screamed special forces when the soft-faced, floppy-haired Norwegian boy was anything but.

'Is he back?' Tom demanded.

The young man nodded reluctantly.

'Get him.'

Erik looked at Tom's expression and decided not to argue. The man he brought back was older, busy trying to force a smile onto his face and struggling into a jacket. Mr Hauge had the look of a man who'd only just got to sleep, having spent several hours driving through a blizzard.

'Can I help you?' he asked.

Tom looked at Erik. 'You can go.'

Receiving a nod from the manager, Erik scowled and took himself into the back. A moment later the background music turned up a notch, and then changed to something angrier. The manager sighed.

'What's the problem?' he asked Tom.

'I'm a friend of Dr Blackburn's. I'm told she's missing.

That she didn't check out, that she wasn't seen coming down. She simply disappeared. I'm told her stuff is still in her room.'

'I can't discuss other guests.'

'Your Inspector Dahl says it's too early to issue a missing persons. The inspector's also checked Tromso hospital for me, and the hospital in Nordkjosbotn. There's only one body in Tromso morgue and it's not hers. I'd like to check her room.'

'You think she's in danger?'

'She's either hiding, has left Tromso or is already dead.'

Extracting his wallet, Tom reached into a slot behind his credit cards and pulled out an ID. A younger version of himself stared from a card that gave his rank, his thumbprint, and announced his employer as SIS London. A note on the back asked authorities in all Allied countries to render him any help necessary.

'This isn't the name you're registered under.'

'No,' Tom agreed. 'It isn't. And I didn't show you this, and you don't tell anyone what you didn't see.'

The manager re-read the card.

'I can have someone from E-tjenesten call you if that helps?' Tom said, using the shorthand for Norwegian intelligence.

'No need, sir.'

They took the lift in silence and the manager put his finger to his lips, then smiled apologetically as he led Tom past occupied rooms. People talking. A couple making love. Someone watching a late-night film. Someone flushing a lavatory, then cursing as they walked into furniture in the dark.

The noises anyone would expect.

Sliding his key into Amelia's door, the manager stepped back to let Tom in first.

Her bed had been remade. A jacket hung in her wardrobe. A tatty sweatshirt had been left neatly over the back of a chair.

Chinua Achebe's *Anthills of the Savannah* rested on her bedside locker. 'Shortlisted for the Booker Prize', announced its sticker. A price tag in Norwegian kroner suggested Amelia had bought it at Fornebu Airport in Oslo when changing planes. The lock on the door into her room was undamaged.

'Her room's been tidied?'

Mr Hauge glanced round. 'I imagine so.'

On the desk was a copy of the paper she was here to present. It was short, dry, notable for what it didn't say. Very Amelia. Tom read the title aloud, flicked through the first two pages and shrugged. He understood one paragraph in three.

Under the hardback was a page torn from *Die Bild*, the West German newspaper. It reported a break-in at an airbase near Bonn by armed activists from Greenpeace. Armed had been circled in red. 'We have NO armed activists,' Amelia had scrawled across the page. She'd been angry enough for her biro to go through the paper. A final thought was written below: *If not us. Who?!*

No passport, no wallet, no black leather satchel she habitually carried. What she'd taken said more than what she'd left. Almost as an afterthought, Tom flicked through the novel. She'd read halfway, tucking in the flap to keep her place. Tom was shutting *Anthills* when a photograph slipped to the floor.

A young Sami stood beside her, grinning.

Per was scribbled on the back. The name of the boy killed by the snowplough. She'd dated the photograph three weeks earlier. A string of numbers underlined his name. It looked like code or an overlong telephone number. It wasn't, though. In very Amelia-like fashion she'd geolocated the hills, birch trees and lake in the background.

29

Saturday 21st November – Tromso, Northern Norway

Amelia's toothpaste was in the bathroom, her toothbrush and wash bag gone. The soap was dry. The hotel shampoo and conditioner untouched. Tom stared round the little room, all too aware that Mr Hauge was watching from the door.

'Is she really a friend of yours?' Mr Hauge asked.

'We met in East Berlin the year before last. Her father had died. I was there on assignment. Circumstances threw us together.'

She saved my life.

'Almost done,' Tom promised.

He lifted the lid of the lavatory and the cardboard tube from a tampon floated below. The room hadn't been that well cleaned then. Absent-mindedly he flushed it.

The cistern sounded loud as a waterfall.

Domed screw-covers held a panel in place, cross-threaded screws behind them. Not even done up tight. Tom undid them under the uneasy gaze of Mr Hauge. Behind the melamine panel was a cistern, uncovered. Its ceramic lid leant against an inner wall. A plastic bag on top of that.

A plastic bag, inside a plastic bag, inside a plastic bag. A couple of thick rubber bands lay below. Anyone else, and Tom would think they'd been hiding money, drugs or a pistol.

Amelia, though?

Inside the inner bag Tom found a lens cap, a lens brush and a cleaning cloth. Eddington was right. She'd seen enough to know it was important, and from the look of things she'd photographed it too. He wondered where the reel of 35mm was and who else was after it.

Per dead. Amelia gone. Her room . . .

Tom tried to reconstruct events. She'd come back to her hotel, frightened or soon to be frightened. She'd changed quickly. Cared enough about what she had on film to burn seconds removing the panel. Grabbed her passport and wallet, and abandoned everything else.

How had she exited the hotel?

'She wasn't seen leaving?'

'Definitely not.' Mr Hauge shook his head. 'She wasn't even seen coming down. The front door, the lifts and the stairs are clearly visible from reception. It's manned at all times. She went up. She never came down.'

No blood, no one seen taking her corpse out in a rolled-up carpet. She wasn't someone who'd go quietly if kidnapped. Tom had once watched her feed an enemy of his to the wolves.

'Was her window open?'

'Not that I've been told.'

Which meant nothing. Tom checked the drop to the street. Two floors below, but only one if you were aiming for the sloping roof and its drop to the road. Better than death if you were desperate.

'Pass me that torch.'

Pulling the torch to be used in a blackout from its clip by the door, the manager did as Tom asked. There was a dip in the snow, as if someone had slid down the roof. It was vanishing under endless fresh snow, but it was definitely there.

*

'How do I get an outside line?' Tom asked.

'Dial 9,' the hotel manager told him.

Picking up the receiver, Tom dialled the international code and then Lord Eddington's number. He waited for the international dialling tone to change to a local one. It took twenty rings before the phone was answered.

'Charles . . . ?'

'Do you know what the time is?' Lady Eddington demanded.

'Is your husband there?'

There was an icy silence. 'It's three-thirty in the morning, Tom. Are you drunk?'

'I'm in Norway. Is he there?'

'No,' Lady Eddington said, 'he is not. He decided to spend the night in London. He mentioned booking a hotel.'

'Did he mention which hotel?'

'Not that I remember.'

Tom sighed. 'I'll call his office first thing then.'

'He won't be there. He's needed in Lympstone. Something to do with funding for the commandos. I've no idea what.'

'Via the house?' Eddington's home was roughly halfway between London and the Royal Marine base in Devon.

'He did mutter something about changing clothes.'

'Then could you give him a message? The person he sent me to meet is missing. I'm going to try to find her. I might need a day or two.'

'Your wife's funeral is on Monday.'

'I know when my wife's funeral . . .' Tom took a breath. 'I'm sorry, Elspeth. That was uncalled for. I know when Caro's funeral is. I know I should be with my son. I'll be there. I promise.'

30

Saturday 21st November – Kola Peninsula

Today's mission was unprecedented.

Three Lockheed SR-71 Blackbirds ripped over the Soviet border, already at supersonic speed and increasing velocity with every second. Inside their cockpits, G-force pushed three US pilots into their seats and reduced the world to a tight circle of vision as blood left their brains.

Three flights on the Baltic Run was unheard of. Almost intentionally provocative. At $50 million-plus per plane and $85,000 an hour to run, it was irresponsible to risk even one unless needs must. And every flight on this run was a risk; even if no planes had been lost yet, at least not that the Pentagon would admit.

On Soviet soil, MiGs scrambled. Three North-West Sector airfields flinging whole squadrons into the air in response to shocked reports from their local flight controllers, and anxious requests for instructions flooding in from VV watch-towers along the border.

Calls were already being made to the Kremlin, threat levels raised, leave cancelled, the Minister of Defence, the Chief of General Staff and the First Deputy Minister of General Affairs locked in an argument about what three SR-71 Black-birds at once meant.

The MiGs began their climb and the Blackbirds climbed higher, pushing into the stratosphere at speeds the MiGs couldn't yet match. With a climb-rate of 12,000 feet a minute and a ceiling height of 85,000 feet, the NATO pilots were out-running their Warsaw Pact counterparts, and the Soviet pilots knew it.

And far below all this, barely above tree height, a newly built US drone began a great looping flight that would take it over the Kola Peninsula and back to Kirkenes, the northernmost Norwegian town near the border. A place where Norwegian intelligence had kept a small outpost for decades.

Constructed from fibreglass over balsa wood, carbon composites and Kevlar, the drone's 9-foot wingspan and stumpy body was powered by a heavily silenced 2-stroke burning 100-octane aviation fuel. Its profile, lack of mass and limited use of metal parts, unless entirely necessary, gave it a minimal radar signature.

This was the drone's first flight. Its launch timed to use the 167 minutes of daylight available this late into November. Although the test had originally been scheduled for the Black Forest, the drone – minus its designer and most of its engineers – had been commandeered by AFNORTH and shipped out in the middle of winter; its support crew reduced to one engineer and a programmer, people who might actually be useful. In its nose was a camera and a Geiger counter, both set to activate when the drone flew over the site of last week's explosion.

The drone almost failed to cross into Russia at all.

Flying low over snow-covered wastes, it drew the attention of a white-tailed eagle, which folded its wings and dived, only veering off in the last second. On the drone flew, over phosphate pits and fur farms, over a lakeside village abandoned fifty years before, and a Tsarist mine that never produced an ounce of silver, despite a frenzy of speculation.

The drone knew none of these things. Had those who programmed it known, they probably wouldn't have been interested. The drone had one purpose only. Overfly the ruined research station, photograph it and record its radiation levels.

This it did, the Geiger counter taking multiple readings, and the camera with its shielding and lead-glass lens working perfectly. Job done, it continued its looping trajectory towards the Norwegian border. All was going well until a Soviet hunter looked up from stalking a rogue wolf, saw what he thought was a huge bird flying low over the trees in front of him, and shot it from the sky.

31

Saturday 21st November – Soviet Arctic

'Where's your pet Sami?'

'My assistant, you mean?' Amelia Blackburn stared at the pudgy young *militsiya* officer who hadn't bothered to climb off his police-issue snowmobile.

'Well?' he demanded.

'You are?' Amelia asked.

The young man glared at her.

Some faceless would-be apparatchik then. Who fancied himself a power in the Murmansk Oblast and resented having to ride out here to question a foreign academic, even if she held favoured status and was here at Moscow's request.

Behind the young officer, two *militsya* men in winter whites sat on Buran snowcats. Both machines were police issue, which meant bonnet-mounted spotlights, a slot for a two-way radio, whether one was fitted or not, and a lieutenant back at the Rybinsk Motor Factory whose sole job was to ensure that those building *militsya* and border-force machines didn't turn up drunk, used the correct screws and remembered to tighten *all* the bolts before signing new machines off.

Civilian vehicles were built on a different production line, and if their owners found themselves stranded on broken machines because pistons had seized, or parts fallen off, or someone had forgotten to fix the fuel tank into place properly, that wasn't a problem. Well, it wasn't the lieutenant's problem.

The young man from Murmansk scanned Amelia's camp.

'Just you?' he said.

Amelia didn't like the way he asked that.

'Just me,' she said. 'Just me, my Geiger counter, my tent, my working notes.'

'Remind me again why you're here?'

'The Politburo asked for me.'

She watched him digest that.

His Buran had a single ski at the front and lightweight caterpillar tracks behind. It was powered by a screaming two-stroke, which would have disgraced a Japanese lawnmower. Its seat was probably vinyl over shaped cardboard. She didn't doubt his journey out had been smelly, bumpy and cold. His journey back would probably be worse.

'Would you like some coffee?' she asked.

He blinked. Wondering what the catch was.

Amelia's glance included the other two in her offer.

'You have American coffee?' the nearest asked.

'South American,' Amelia said. 'Columbian. Bought in Norway. And I'm Scottish, not American. You don't mind drinking it black?'

He didn't. His comrade didn't either.

Get them onside, Amelia told herself.

They looked to their officer, who nodded grudgingly.

Let them return to Murmansk and say the foreign professor was happy, relaxed, busy examining moss growth and wolf droppings. Let there be no suggestion anything was wrong. And absolutely no suggestion that someone had tried to kill her four days earlier and a thousand miles away. Or that she'd been anywhere near a disaster at a research station.

Lighting her hurricane lamp, Amelia hung it from a birch. Then lit her primus and filled her saucepan with snow, taking her time. Throwing dead twigs on the fire, she followed those with a couple of small branches and watched the fire she'd lit the night before to keep predators at bay grow brighter.

She'd been expecting a visit. The Soviet authorities liked their numbers to tally. Two people in her party had flown out. Only one had flown back in. That would need accounting for. She'd half expected to be stopped when flying in to Leningrad.

That the young man chose to arrive in what counted as almost light rather than pitch darkness was good. If he'd really wanted to scare the shit out of her, he'd have declared himself KGB and turned up at night. Night being most of any given day that wasn't now and an hour either side.

'Your Sami . . .'

'He stayed behind.'

'We know that. We want to know why.'

Her Sami? Outright prejudice, or unthinking urban arrogance?

The young officer made Per sound like a pet. Per's people didn't have that great a time of it the Norwegian side of the border, but they had a far worse time here. Biting down on her anger, Amelia pulled a large bar of Freia's Melkesjokolade from her pocket. It might not be Swiss but Norwegian chocolate was at least as good as anything they could buy in Murmansk.

The two conscripts' eyes widened as she broke the bar into pieces still in its wrapper, tore the wrapper open and put it on the ground in the middle so everyone could reach. The officer wasn't finished, though.

'You haven't told me why he stayed behind.'

'Family stuff. I imagine.'

'You were sharing a hotel?'

'No,' Amelia said. 'I was in the Lux on Fiskergata. My assistant was staying with an uncle outside Tromso.'

Not entirely true. Per had a room. He just never used it.

They'd shared a bed in the Lux the night before he died though; but it was her bed, and her room, her choice, and his. This man didn't need to know that.

'He didn't show up at the airport?'

'No,' Amelia said. 'He didn't show up.'

The officer sucked his teeth in a way that suggested he expected no better, and reached for a square of chocolate. 'We'll send you another assistant. Maybe two. Just in case you lose another one . . . Now, you left here what, four or five days ago?' Although he said this as an afterthought, Amelia wasn't fooled. She nodded, and he dropped his real question.

'Where were you before that?'

Amelia named a lake miles from where she'd really been. Far enough from the ruined research station for him not to worry.

Tipping a tablespoon of ground Columbian into the now-boiling snow, Amelia wished the officer and conscripts to hell. She'd left Per where he was, run for her life and kept running. Cutting short her Norway trip and trading her return flight for an earlier one. Her smile, the coffee, the chocolate were lies. Lies that soured her stomach. All that mattered was that they believed nothing had happened in Norway.

Nothing untoward happened there. Nothing untoward happened here either. She'd presented her paper in Tromso, picked up an award and enjoyed herself. Everything went as planned. These were the lies she needed them to believe.

Amelia had decided this was her safest move.

She was right.

32

Saturday 21st November – Tromso, Northern Norway

A wall of cigarette smoke hit Tom as he opened the door to the bar and felt the tiny room's heat flood out into the night around him. Every eye in the place turned to watch him. No one's gaze was welcoming.

He made himself go in anyway.

The man behind the counter had a greying moustache that looked half grown for all he had ten years on Tom. His hair was tied back with a black ribbon. A grey felt tunic was fixed at his waist with a broad belt. His eyes never left Tom's face.

'Coffee,' Tom ordered.

The man snorted and pointed to a row of bottles. Mostly akvavit, a couple of different types of vodka, a clear bottle of something with no label at all.

'I'm not drinking,' Tom said.

The man considered this.

'You're here to work the rigs?'

He meant the oil platforms offshore that were making Norway rich. Although perhaps by now that should be 'richer still'. How much of that money trickled down to the people in this bar Tom didn't know. A little. Maybe.

'I'm visiting.'

'Just as well. You wouldn't last a winter on the rigs without alcohol. No one would.'

Reaching for a shot glass, he filled it and banged it down

in front of Tom. It was water, but looked like the spirits being drunk around them.

'No charge,' he said. 'Now, what brings someone who doesn't drink into a bar like this? Even the Norwegians stay away.'

'Here,' Tom said.

He watched the barman examine the picture of Amelia Blackburn and her assistant. Saw him note the tent, the birch trees, the lake and snow. Caught the exact moment he glanced beyond Tom to a group in the corner.

'This isn't the first Sami bar you've visited. Is it?'

'No, it's not.'

He'd started with the ones in the centre and worked his way out in a circle, drinking the occasional coffee, endless glasses of water and, in one place, a fruit juice with a cartoon of the Pink Panther on the label.

'I'm looking for the boy.'

'He's dead.'

'Killed by a snowplough?'

'Why ask if you already know?'

'I didn't. I knew there was a young Sami in the morgue. The police told me.'

'Why would they tell you?'

'I'm also looking for her.'

'Your wife?'

'My wife's dead.'

'And you're still not drinking?'

'His name was Per,' Tom said. 'That's all I know. He was in Russia with this woman.'

'Working.' There was something off about the way the barman said it. The man shrugged. 'None of my business. It doesn't matter now.'

'He had a girl back here?'

'In Geilo. They were due to be married. He went to university in Oslo. Before this. He was clever. Maybe too clever.'

'Too clever?'

'He's dead, isn't he?'

The barman must have signalled to the men in the corner, because one of them drifted over to stand at Tom's shoulder. He was stocky, of indeterminate age but fit. With the skin of someone who lived outdoors and cheekbones to make Nureyev look moon-faced. Taking the photograph from Tom's hand, he stared at it.

'Where did you get this?'

'Amelia's hotel,' Tom said. Sometimes the truth was simplest. 'It was marking a place inside a book she'd left by her bed.'

'Amelia?'

'The woman in the photograph.'

'Dr Blackburn,' the Sami said. 'My nephew called her Dr Blackburn. Always. I'd never seen Per impressed by a woman before. I used to wonder what it was about her.'

'I once watched her feed a man to a wolf. I left. She stayed to watch it eat him.'

'That would do it.'

'What can I buy you?' Tom asked.

'Akvavit,' Per's uncle said, pointing to an unopened bottle of Aalborg behind the bar. 'I'll take the bottle.'

Tom paid, over the odds, he imagined. Took his change and went to have a look at the jukebox, leaving the barman and Per's uncle space to have a short and impassioned conversation. Choosing the records took longer than he expected. 'Harry's Game' from Clannad, just because. Bon Jovi's 'Living on a Prayer', because that was what he was doing. 'This

Corrosion', if only because Becca played Sisters of Mercy loudly enough to annoy Caro. Something by the Raga Rockers. He'd never heard of them before but he liked the name. And finally 'Whiskey in the Jar' for old times' sake. He'd have chosen Marianne Faithfull's version of 'As Tears Go By' if the jukebox had had it. Caro's song.

'Hope you chose well,' Per's uncle said.

Tom looked at the man.

'They'll throw you out if you didn't.'

Moya Brennan's voice rose from the speaker, her words carried on Clannad's haunting tune. Per's uncle listened to the first few lines, realised they weren't in English and asked, 'What's she say?'

Tom laughed.

'What?' the man demanded.

'A Russian friend asked exactly the same.'

'And the answer?'

'Everything that is and was will cease to be . . .'

Per's uncle thought about that and then nodded grimly.

He chose a dark corner of the bar, and had his friends withdraw to a distance where they could pretend not to be listening. The bottle of akvavit was opened, and Per's uncle introduced himself as Hárri, Per's father's brother. He shook Tom's hand with a firm but not aggressive grip, and readied himself to fill Tom's glass.

Tom put his hand over the top.

'You don't drink?'

'I did,' Tom said.

'And you stopped? Per stopped too.'

'The police said he was drunk.'

'So much easier,' Hárri said, 'to dismiss a drunk Sami and say it was an accident than discover who murdered a sober one and why.'

'You think he was murdered?'

'I know he was murdered,' Hárri said flatly. 'Per didn't drink. A bottle was found beside him. Someone planted it.'

'I'm told he stank of drink.'

'The murderer poured it over him.'

'Alcoholics relapse. I should know. Still, the autopsy will show whether he was drinking.'

'What autopsy?'

Tom and the man sat in silence for a while.

33

November 1971 – Derry, Northern Ireland

'Import and Export,' the operator said carefully.

The caller snorted.

'Can I help you?'

'Yes. I'd like to speak to Mr Mackenzie-White.'

Flipping open a folder, Miss Browne ran her finger down a list of suitably anonymous names, and her eyes widened.

'I'm sorry . . . Could you repeat the name?'

Her caller did.

Inside her head, Miss Browne swore. Her boss was in a foul mood. The PM had decided to impose direct rule on Northern Ireland. There were, according to her boss, a dozen good reasons why that was a terrible idea. He'd been overruled.

'Who should I say is calling?'

'Mr White-Mackenzie.'

Her caller had reversed the code. That was the point Miss Browne decided the sooner she made this call somebody else's problem the better.

'I'll connect you now, sir.'

'It's me,' the caller said.

Eddington almost asked, 'Who?'

But he knew, at least he did the moment he wrenched his thoughts away from Edward bloody Heath's latest stupidity.

'What do you want?'

'I've gone rogue, sir. You're worried I'm out of control. It's just a feeling. But all the same . . .'

'Rogue?'

'Feral, in fact. Tell someone in army intelligence you trust. Then someone you don't.'

'How close are you?' Eddington asked.

'Closer by the day. Someone's after me. I may need to let them catch me. Make sure the men you talk to know someone's after me. Say you think that's what's got me rattled.'

There were plenty of questions Eddington could ask. All questions for which it would be best he could swear on oath he'd never had answers. 'Will do,' Eddington said.

Both men put the receiver down at the same time. Neither bothered to say goodbye.

34

Saturday 21st November – Tromso, Northern Norway

The air in the bar grew so heavy with alcohol fumes that Tom eventually stopped wanting a drink. He'd inhaled enough to relax.

No one thought to open a window. Then again, it was −10 outside.

Hárri's friends had long since stopped listening and gone back to playing *Idioten*, banging their cards down on the table in turn. Sharp bursts of laughter punctuating a conversation about something else entirely.

It was a good hour before any of them even glanced over. Hárri's bottle of Aalborg was three-quarters gone. The old man downing akvavit with such heroic determination Tom knew he was working himself up to something.

'You won't find her,' Hárri said suddenly.

Tom froze.

'She's gone,' Hárri added.

'Dead?' Tom asked.

The man shook his head. 'She left the night Per died. We didn't know he was dead or we wouldn't have let her go. My cousin drives taxis. There aren't many who'd take a fare in the middle of a blizzard, with the darkness in and wind howling off the fjord. It was a bad drive out. Snow so thick he almost lost the road.'

'The planes were flying?'

The Sami snorted. 'Not then, obviously. But come morning,

after they'd scraped the runway. Up here if we stopped for a bit of snow no one would ever get anywhere.'

The alcohol was making him talkative.

'Where was she going?' Tom asked.

'Home,' Hárri said. 'Tromso to Oslo, Oslo to Leningrad, Leningrad to Murmansk. That's what she said. She'd had enough of conferences. She wouldn't be coming back . . .' He paused, thoughtful. 'She left a knife on the back seat.'

Tom blinked at that. 'What kind?'

'A skinning knife. Good quality.'

'Your cousin still has it?'

'Maybe,' Hárri said. 'Maybe not.'

'Did he say how she seemed?'

'Why?' Hárri demanded.

'I'm interested.'

'She kept looking back.'

Don't we all? Tom thought.

Amelia had obviously been worried about being followed. That suggested whoever killed Per knew who she was. Also, he doubted she'd have abandoned Per if he'd simply been injured. So, she'd known he was dead. Most probably before she went back to the hotel. Which explained the speed with which she'd vacated her room, and the route she'd taken on leaving. Perhaps the knife had been Per's and she'd taken it for protection?

Tom fitted the pieces together in his head.

Either Amelia had seen it happen, found Per's body or been told he was dead. Whichever, she was scared enough to abandon most of her possessions, and get herself, her camera and whatever she knew the hell out of Tromso. If she had any sense, she'd tell the Soviets her conference was a success, find an excuse for Per not returning, and hope the lie didn't come back to bite her.

Chances were she'd get her wish. A dead Sami might make the local news, but Tom doubted it would spread much further. She couldn't guarantee that whoever murdered Per wouldn't come after her. Although obviously that depended on who they were. If they were Soviet, she'd delivered herself into the lions' den. If they were from the West, few places would be safer than the far side of the Iron Curtain.

Tom would need to clear his next move with London. 'If needed,' he said, 'could your taxi cousin get someone over the Soviet border?'

Hárri gaped at him.

'He would be well paid for his help.'

'They'll shoot you. You know that, don't you?'

'It won't be me. I'm needed at home.'

'How would this man find her?' Hárri asked.

Picking up the photograph of Per and Amelia, Tom turned it over and pointed to the numbers: 68° 09' 10.3" N 34° 47' 19.7" E.

'Those are the co-ordinates for the lake. I'll suggest he starts there.'

'I'll ask my cousin,' Hárri said.

'And I'll make a call.'

Fighting his way to the door through a crowd of young men entering, Tom stepped into the darkness of pre-dawn and realised it was now the next day.

The heavy snow had stopped and the clouds thinned. The northern lights were an iridescent curtain above the horizon. He wondered how it was possible to be somewhere so incredible and feel so bleak.

35

Sunday 22nd November – Tromso, Northern Norway

'*Wait . . .*' Tom was nearly back at his hotel when he heard Hárri behind him. Turning, he saw the man trudging through the snow, head down and puffing like a dragon as he tried to cut Tom off. Reception was in sight. A couple of bedroom windows were already lit. After twenty-four hours awake he wanted his bed and sleep, but what he'd do was make a couple of phone calls, pack his stuff and get himself to the airport. Eddington, or his department, could pick things up from here.

He needed to be home for Caro's funeral.

I'm not sure you deserve her.

His Muscovite friend Ivan Petrovich Dennisov had said that. In Russia, in the middle of a blizzard. The night he saved Tom's life. *Your wife came to my bar*, Dennisov had said, glaring at him. *She told me about the deal you made. A woman like that. I'm not sure you deserve her.*

And now he didn't have her either.

A woman he'd never loved as much as he should.

'Per told me,' Hárri said.

'Told you what?'

'About the glass ball. That's what you're after, isn't it? That's why you really want to find Dr Blackburn. No point. She doesn't have it. She doesn't even know it exists.'

Tom's mind fought to catch up.

Hárri carried on as if Tom had already asked the obvious

questions. 'Per hid it. It's valuable. Very valuable. He said we were all going to be rich. He hid it under the snow, and then under a manhole cover. He said Moscow will pay to get it back. People will pay for Moscow not to get it back.'

'This thing. Where did he find it?'

'At the base,' Hárri said, as if that should be obvious. 'The base with the dead people. Dr Blackburn said he must never tell anyone he'd been there.'

'But he told you . . .'

'I'm family. We have family there too. We can help you. They can help me. It will work.'

'You're in contact?'

'People come and go,' Hárri said vaguely.

'Did Per say how big this thing was?'

Hárri sketched something the size of a grapefruit. 'A man was holding it,' he added. 'A dead man in a fur coat. Clutching it to his chest like a baby.'

Tom considered that. 'We should talk.'

A Fred Olsen liner, several cargo boats, a couple of container ships, half a dozen trawlers, a pair of lighters with 'Statoil' stencilled on the side. A huge rig, like a giant spider, some distance offshore. The docks were bigger than Tom expected.

Cranes clanked, and trucks growled. There were already lights in the windows of the harbour offices and warehouses. Dockworkers and seamen coming and going. The aurora was still just visible, despite the lights and dawn's approach.

'The fire fox,' Hárri said.

Tom looked at him.

'My grandmother was Finnish. She believed the *revontulet*, the fire fox, ran so swiftly over snow it kicked sparks into the northern skies. The nights we see the lights are the nights it goes hunting.'

Tom smiled. Knowing Charlie would like that.

The young woman running a café by the docks looked at them askance. As if saying, *And who are you?* She took their order though, between calling greetings to those she knew. Rye bread, Gudbrandsdalen brown cheese, pastries and coffee.

It was the coffee Tom needed.

He and Hárri chose the quietest corner, and watched fishermen, truck drivers and crane operators buy coffee, wolf down flatbread and cheese, and leave just as swiftly.

'You. Me. We'll split the money,' Hárri said.

'What money?'

'Per said people would pay millions.'

'Did he say which people?'

'The man he took it from . . .'

'You said he was dead.'

'Dead. Dying.' Hárri shrugged. 'They're close enough. He told Per it was precious. Per had to get it to Moscow. There would be a reward. A big reward. The Kremlin would want it back. Per thought the Americans would pay more.'

Too clever for his own good. Seemed the old Sami was right.

36

Sunday 22nd November – Tromso, Northern Norway

Aunt Agatha's voice was as clipped as ever. She sounded less than pleased to have been called to the phone before breakfast.

'Do you know what time it is, Tom?'

'Nine in the morning here. So eight a.m. with you.'

'Precisely eight a.m. On a Sunday morning.'

'Could I speak to your brother-in-law?'

'Eddington has a name, Tom.'

'Is he there?'

'No,' she said. 'He's not.'

'He got my last message?'

'I've no idea. What do you want?'

Apart from my wife back, and to be with my son? 'Ask Eddington if he's heard anything about a glass ball. Say it's urgent. Say it was found . . .'

Tom hesitated.

'Found where?'

'Where Amelia was.'

'I suppose, given your habits, it might be best not to ask who Amelia is.' Tom winced at the bitterness in Charlie's great-aunt's voice. 'Anything else?' Lady Eddington's sister asked, and put the phone down before Tom could answer.

She hadn't asked if he wanted to talk to Charlie. She hadn't mentioned Caro's funeral, which was tomorrow. When Tom thought about it, the reason for her silence was obvious. The less contact he had with his son the easier it would be to paint him as entirely unsuitable if this came to court. And Tom had a nasty feeling that Charlie's grandmother and great-aunt wanted it to go to court. Whatever Elspeth Eddington said in public, and she'd probably been saying a lot, when it came down to it her outrage if he missed Caro's funeral would be a lie.

She didn't want Tom there at all.

Eddington wasn't at his office or club. His office claimed he'd gone home and couldn't be disturbed. The Carlton said they hadn't seen him in days. He wasn't at the Savoy or the Ritz either. Tom left the number of his hotel in Tromso with all four, stressing that it was urgent and they should tell his father-in-law so.

He spent the rest of the day not being telephoned back. Darkness fell, the afternoon and evening passed in a slow crawl of waiting for a reply that never came. His follow-up calls were no more successful. The first of them went through to Aunt Agatha. The second to Elspeth Eddington. Both promised to pass his message on.

He believed neither.

The next call reached a telephone that had been disconnected. Later calls did the same. By the time he went to bed Tom was wondering if it was Eddington who'd cut him adrift.

37

Becca was in the trees.

'Like the baron,' she muttered.

Charlie spread his hands to show he didn't understand, and she gave him that look she used to when she was being grown-up. The one that said, *You're six, how could you possibly understand.* He was eight now though.

He still didn't understand.

She was up in the trees on a slope, where she used to go to smoke Gitanes and meet the man from the village who wasn't her boyfriend. No one was meant to know about that. Not even Charlie.

'What's wrong?'

That was Great-aunt Agatha, Granny's sister.

It was obvious from her expression that *Nothing* was the only acceptable answer . . . Charlie wanted Becca down here. She deserved to be down here. Mummy was being buried and he had to be very brave. He'd feel braver if Becca stopped hiding on the slope and came down here to stand beside him.

'Agatha . . .'

Grandpa's voice was tight. There'd been an argument about whether Charlie should be here at all. Grandpa thought not. Granny and Aunt Agatha said eight was quite old enough to bury your mother. For once Charlie agreed with them.

He wished Daddy was here though. He really wished Daddy was here.

Not just because Great-aunt Agatha was being horrid about Daddy to everyone when she thought Charlie couldn't hear. *What could anyone expect from a man like that?* she'd said to the new padre. Then looked at Charlie with a saccharine expression that didn't reach her eyes. Charlie liked the word saccharine. It meant artificial.

Becca used it.

Daddy would be here if he could.

Charlie knew that. He'd told them that, and Grandpa had nodded in a way that said he wasn't really listening, while Great-aunt Agatha and Granny hadn't even bothered to do that.

The inside bit of the service was done.

There'd been prayers, poems and a reading from John 14: 1–3. The bit that says 'My father's house has many rooms'. Cousin Arthur, who was a bishop, spoke about an illness bravely borne and a life lived to the full, and a little girl who grew up loving ponies and country walks. None of it really sounded like Mummy.

Dust to dust. Ashes to ashes.

'Now,' Granny said.

Now what? Charlie wondered.

Then he remembered he was meant to toss dirt on Mummy's coffin. Only he'd forgotten to pick any up. Scrabbling for a handful, he felt tears run down his face. Everybody noticed. That's why he'd been trying not to cry; because everybody would notice. He felt a hand on his shoulder, brief as anything and soft like wind, and knew it was Becca. That made him cry all the more.

'I'm sorry,' he said. 'I'm sorry.'

Grandpa took his hand, and the priest delayed the blessing he'd been about to start. And into the silence, which was slightly embarrassed, intruded a loud and insistent electric buzz.

Everyone looked at Grandpa. While Grandpa glared furiously at the briefcase on the grass behind him. 'If you'd excuse me . . .'

Charlie liked that he didn't wait for a reply.

'Eddington,' he barked into a grey plastic telephone the size of a brick, with a curly black cord that vanished inside the case. Let it be Daddy, Charlie whispered. Let it be Daddy saying he was on his way.

38

Monday 23rd November – Kirkenes, Norway

Twelve hours before they buried Caro, a Volvo taxi set out from Tromso on the longest trip Anders Hassi would ever take. He'd been told by his cousin that his fare was American.

Tom Fox was happy to leave that lie uncorrected.

749 km to Kirkenes.

The sign loomed in the snowy dark and was gone. Kirkenes was the last town in Norway's high Arctic before the border. He'd cross there into Russia. Unable to reach Eddington, and uncertain what he should do, he'd been forced to make a decision. So he had. He had to believe it was the right one.

'Broken,' Anders said when Tom asked him to turn the heater up. 'Look behind your seat.'

Tom stared at the pelt in disbelief.

The old man laughed. 'My cousin in Spitsbergen won it at cards.'

Wrapping himself in the polar bear skin, Tom huddled down. Tromso was behind them, the road ahead pure ice, and they'd travelled barely fifty kilometres in the last hour. The noise of snow studs on ice limited the chance of conversation; although Anders didn't look the talkative type, and Tom's thoughts at missing Caro's funeral were too dark to share.

He hated himself for not simply flying home.

He'd told himself he'd done it to ensure he got Charlie. That after this, Eddington had to back him. A bit of him knew, though, that he'd been institutionalised before he even reached adolescence. The school for problem children in which he'd found himself had seen to that.

'Here,' Anders said, passing an empty bottle.

If Tom needed to piss, he could use that. If he needed to do more, tough. They'd risk stopping to refill from petrol cans in the boot but that was it. Anders wasn't going to stop more than that in case his engine stalled and his battery failed. It could be a week before another vehicle passed, and by then starvation would have killed them both if hypothermia hadn't got there first.

'And this,' Anders said. 'This will warm you up.'

Tom swigged from the thermos and swore.

'Spirits,' the old man said. 'Made it myself.'

Half the houses in Norway had stills for producing alcohol, according to Hárri. Owning one wasn't illegal, drinking what it produced was. So you signed a form saying you intended to use the alcohol for industrial or agricultural use, and then drank it anyway. It was so rough Tom could imagine it knocking the average pub-goer unconscious.

'I get a third,' Anders said.

'Of what?'

'The cash. When you sell the icon.'

'Sell it?'

'Hárri told me. It's okay. You can trust me.'

Anders gulped at his thermos, swerved slightly and rammed the open flask between his thighs as he settled his old Volvo 142 for the approach to a bend. His headlights barely penetrated the falling snow. He seemed to be driving this bit of the road from memory.

'You know where this icon is?'

'My other cousin . . . He will have it.'

Will have it? Or will know where to find it? Tom wondered. Hárri had assured Tom it was the first. But then he'd told his cousin the orb was an icon.

'I get a third,' Anders repeated. 'Okay?'

'Okay,' Tom said.

'It's valuable. Very valuable.'

'Believe me,' Tom said, 'I wouldn't be making this trip if it wasn't.' Wrapping himself tighter in the polar bear skin, he pushed back in his seat to escape the draught, and settled in for the next stretch.

'You asleep?' Tom asked the man a few hours later.

Anders jerked awake, steadying his taxi which had been drifting towards the edge of the road. 'Sleepy,' he admitted.

'We could pull over. Leave the engine running?'

'Too cold, and we're almost there.'

He took a swig from his flask, choked slightly and peered through his filthy windscreen at a sign looming ahead. Kirkenes 460 km. 'All right,' he said. 'Not exactly there. You were with Per when he found the icon?'

'A friend of mine was.'

'Ah. The woman.'

Whatever Hárri had told Anders, it obviously wasn't that Per found an almost-dead Russian clutching a strange glass orb. An object so valuable Per was murdered and Amelia had fled. If he had, Tom doubted he'd be on his way to the Soviet border with the promise that a cousin of Hárri's wife would meet him on the far side in return for 200 Western cigarettes, a copy of *Hustler* and a bottle of Aalborg.

Kirkenes 68 km.

'Half your family live in Russia?'

'We live all over.'

Hárri had said something like that too.

'But you're Norwegian?'

'First Sami, second Norwegian, third Finnish.'

'How does that work?' Keep him talking, Tom had decided.

With steadily falling snow the only thing visible through the car's windows, Tom could imagine them both falling asleep, and Anders' taxi sliding off the road and into a ditch or over a ravine. If the crash didn't finish them, waiting for rescue would.

'Norwegian mother. Finnish dad. They met when he moved here after the Winter War.'

'The what?'

'Finns against Russians, 1939 to 1940. Again in 1941 to '44. We didn't win and they didn't win. We fought the bastards to a standstill twice – and signed a treaty that gave them thirty per cent of our economy and ten per cent of our land. And people wonder why we sided with Berlin in '41.'

'Your father fought with the Germans?'

'No, he was here by then. When they invaded Norway in 1940, he pretended to be Norwegian and the Germans never knew. His brother fought with them though. He died at Stalingrad. His cousin came back. Addicted to the amphetamines he'd been issued to keep out the cold.'

Kirkenes 19 km

'It was a hard war? This Winter War?'

'You know what *sisu* is?'

'No,' Tom said.

'They all had it. Determination in the face of adversity. My dad was fifteen when it began and sixteen when it ended. His unit were the White Guard, named for their uniforms which blended against snow. White uniforms, white-wrapped sniper rifles, white groundsheets to hide beneath. It was their

146

land. Their forest. Their trees. They had a saying, "The forest will answer you in the way you call to it." And it never let them down. His CO used to send Dad out to string wire across the road at head height between trees to decapitate dispatch riders.'

Anders laughed sourly. 'Best days of his life, he called it.'

Clambering from the taxi, Tom checked his Rolex.

Charlie would be at the graveside now. Other mourners watching him. Or else, he and Caro's parents would be at the house, preparing to walk down through the lych-gate. Eddington would insist they walk.

Tom wasn't sure what Charlie saw when he looked at the world, but it wasn't what others saw. Sometimes he saw deeper, sometimes he didn't seem to see what other people saw at all. Tom's eyes stung with tears. He blamed the wind. How could he forgive himself for missing Caro's funeral?

How could he not miss it?

What choice had he had?

'Good trip,' Anders said happily.

'I need to call England,' Tom told him.

Anders looked doubtful. 'Well. We can try.'

39

Grandpa shot Great-aunt Agatha a glance so cross that even the new padre looked shocked. 'Did I get the message you left with my sister-in-law? No,' Grandpa said. 'I didn't.'

He listened some more.

'You also left one with Elspeth?'

The person on the other end said something strange, because Grandpa looked puzzled, then scowled because he hadn't understood. 'A glass what?' Obviously remembering the other mourners, he swallowed whatever he'd been going to say next. For another minute he listened intently. He said 'yes' once, 'no' once, and 'quite' three times.

Charlie tugged at Grandpa's hand. 'It's Daddy, isn't it?'

Grandpa hesitated. Then shook his head.

'I don't care if I was at Chequers,' he was saying. 'Geoffrey should have used his initiative. He left an urgent message? I haven't been near my office in two days. You called again last night? You couldn't get an answer? Of course you couldn't. We've been up to our necks in bloody reptiles wanting quotes.'

Eddington ran his hand across his face.

'Tell me again about . . .'

The conversation became stranger. More than once Grandpa glared at Granny and Great-aunt Agatha, and once he glanced round at the mourners, obviously wishing them all elsewhere. The priest was looking worried. Everyone else looked embarrassed. Mummy's coffin was in the ground, the tears on Charlie's face were drying but his fingernails were still dirty from the earth he'd scooped up.

'Are you sure it's not Daddy?'

'Charlie . . .'

That was Granny. He ignored her.

'*Over here.*'

The whisper was in his head.

Becca was standing on the far side of Mummy's grave. She looked sad and alone, and Charlie wanted to go to her but knew he'd be in trouble if he swapped sides. And in even worse trouble if he let anyone know why. 'Look.' He nodded to the telephone that Grandpa gripped so tightly his knuckles had turned white.

Becca rolled her eyes.

Grandpa had no more questions. He was listening intently now. Occasionally he'd grunt. Mostly he scowled. Half the grown-ups were pretending not to watch Charlie grip his fistful of earth. The other half were pretending not to listen to Grandpa's strange conversation. Charlie had seen some of these people on television. One had been on the front of yesterday's *Times*.

Charlie hated being watched, and he hated being lied to. It was Daddy. He knew it was Daddy. Grandpa knew he knew it was Daddy.

Plastic, Charlie decided. Plastic pretending to be metal. Grandpa's telephone wasn't even real.

Charlie hadn't known telephones could be carried, though. The curly black cord disappeared inside the leather case, and Charlie realised the case was just big enough to hold a big metal box. It was metal too, not plastic pretending. There was a tiny red diode on top, beside a switch. Its light was on. There were no words to tell you what the switch did.

'Don't,' Becca said.

Charlie did anyway.

40

November 1971 – Belfast, Northern Ireland

'Religion?'

The muzzle touched the back of Jimmy's head a second ahead of the question. The questioner's voice was deceptively soft, his accent imprecise. Welcome to Belfast, where the wrong answers got you killed. Two hours hitching late-night lorries, ten minutes in the city with the stink of cordite still on his fingers from shooting the man who wasn't Calum Harper, and now this . . .

Unless he was imagining the cordite.

'Well?' the voice asked.

Catholic or Protestant?

One of those was right, the other might get him killed. And religion wasn't the question anyway. Republican or Unionist. That was the real question. At least it was in Ulster in the winter of '71 if you wanted to stay alive and were unwise enough to stray outside your box. Here on the front line, where the cities within the city overlapped, everyone was out of their box.

'I said . . . ?'

Jimmy flinched despite himself. 'I'm a fucking atheist,' he snarled. 'Pull the trigger or don't pull the fucking trigger. Just don't put your shitty questions on me.'

There was a moment of stunned silence.

'What are you doing round here?' the man asked.

'Trying to find somewhere to buy a pint of fucking Guinness.'

You could almost feel the questioner relax. Guinness was a Republican drink. Well, it was a fuck of a lot more of a Republican drink than it was a Loyalist one.

'You're an atheist?'

'Look around you,' Jimmy said. He turned his head to look himself, feeling the barrel scrape against his skull. 'Do you see anything that suggests God?'

'Where are you from?'

'Nowhere,' Jimmy said.

'Where did you grow up?'

'An orphanage. Full of fucking nuns.'

'Best get that Guinness,' the man said.

Jimmy did. In a pub on the corner three roads in. A grand Victorian hostelry gone to seed like those inside. There was a sleaziness to its tarnished gilts and worn velvets that made Jimmy feel at home. Having washed his hands twice in the slimy green soap that dribbled from an upturned chrome dispenser, he ordered a pint, then another. He was still there next lunchtime, one overnight lock-in and more Guinness than he could bear to remember later.

It was Himself who found him in the pub in the backstreets of Belfast. The older man was wearing a tweed jacket, fawn slacks and a Tattersall shirt. He didn't look happy to be put to the trouble of travelling. Judy was at his side in her usual jeans and sweatshirt, looking somewhere between worried and cross enough to want to slap Jimmy herself.

'She insisted,' Himself said.

Jimmy looked up from his pint. Empty glasses crowded the table. He had no idea how many of them were his. All of them, possibly.

'Didn't want me doing you damage, I imagine.' Himself's face said that's exactly what he'd be doing if Judy wasn't there. 'Go order some food,' he told his niece.

Judy opened her mouth to say Jimmy was in no state to eat, took one look at her uncle and went to order food anyway.

'Keep these seats for me.'

The big man was talking to the next table. No please, no if you could. The men nodded. They might not know who Himself was but they recognised what.

'You,' Himself said to Jimmy, 'with me.'

Lifting Jimmy by his collar, he pushed him towards the gents, silencing someone who tried to intervene. His punch took Jimmy in the guts the moment they were through the door, pint after pint of Guinness spewing out across the tiles as Jimmy doubled over and fell to his knees. There was a pasty he'd eaten for breakfast and a lunchtime Mars Bar in there somewhere too.

'All done?' Himself asked.

Jimmy nodded.

'Quite certain?'

Jimmy nodded harder.

'Right then.' Himself pointed to a bucket and mop. 'You'd best clean this up. No reason her behind the bar should do it.'

Judy and Himself were sat at the table with a half of Guinness and a pineapple juice. Their neighbours and the empty glasses on their table were gone. Both tables were still damp from being wiped clean.

'Faggots and mash,' Himself said. 'Three times. Judy paid. Make sure you pay her back.'

'I will,' Jimmy promised.

No one said anything else until the food arrived, and they

didn't say much then either, just muttered that it was good and wolfed it down. It helped, the food. It helped enough for Jimmy to stop wanting to vomit.

The hours he'd spent in a drunken haze, wondering what he was doing and why, were fading. By the time his plate was clean he felt better all round. He hadn't even known he was hungry.

'Right,' Himself said to Judy. 'It's your birthday next week. Go buy yourself something nice.' He extracted one of those long leather wallets from inside his tweed coat, removed three £10 notes and pushed them across.

Judy's eyes widened.

'Something nice now.'

She glanced at her uncle, then at Jimmy.

'Don't worry. We'll still be here when you get back. Your pretty boy will be fine.'

Judy blushed.

Both men watched her thread her way between tables, glance back once at the door and vanish through it into the winter drizzle of Belfast outside.

'Right,' Himself said. 'You want to tell me what the fuck's going on?'

'His real name was Eddie Haig,' Jimmy said after a second. 'Ex-RUC. He was working for Billy McLean, who's tied to a UVF splinter group. McLean also doubles as British black ops . . . I've currently got a Cortina boot full of Armalites under those arches, and a thousand in twenties in my jacket. Just don't look in the boot of the Rover opposite. It was a nasty death.'

Himself stared.

'The piece?' he asked a minute later.

'In the river, in bits, wiped down and scattered. Don't worry. There's another five exactly like it in the Cortina's boot.'

'Shit,' Himself said, half in admiration.

'Yeah,' Jimmy replied.

'Any papers?'

'Only fakes. An Irish driving licence made out to Calum Harper. A union card for the GMB. A letter from the dole office . . .'

'How do you know they're fakes?'

'He said so.' Leaning forward, Jimmy glanced either side to check he wasn't being overheard. 'It seems Billy McLean delivers bigwigs to Kincora. Stands guard while they enjoy themselves . . .'

Kincora was a Belfast boy's home with a bad reputation. Reputedly visited by local and visiting VIPs. Rumour said the Brits had it bugged for blackmail purposes.

'He told you this?'

Jimmy paused. 'Eventually.'

41

Monday 23rd November – Norwegian–Soviet Border

The wind was bitter both sides of the border, the birches restless and looking no different here on Soviet soil. What light there was came from a half-moon refracted and reflected between sky and snow. The shimmering violets and greens of the aurora lit the horizon as solar wind hit the earth's magnetic field seventy miles overhead.

The trees stood like sentries. The real guards, Moscow's Vnutrenniye Voiska, patrolled five miles behind Tom, drifting ghost-like between birches and firs. Their NATO counterparts doing the same on the border's far side.

The taste of calling Eddington was still sour half a day later. Caro's father had broken the link without saying how Charlie was holding up, or how her funeral had gone. A rudeness so unlikely Tom wondered if he'd been right; if Eddington was on the edge of disowning him.

Plausible deniability.

It wouldn't be the first time his father-in-law had stood up in front of a select committee at the House of Commons and told them to their faces he had no idea what they were talking about.

Stopping by a granite slab that jutted through the snow, Tom checked the way ahead. Trees and the shadows of trees created a dark arena in which anyone could be waiting. He had a packet of Eventyr in his pocket. A parting present from Hárri's cousin Anders. Sheltering in the lee of the slab, and hiding the flame with his hand, Tom risked a cigarette.

The match flare was shockingly bright.

He looked round and saw the same trees, the same shadows.

Nothing but rustling branches and snow. Anders had also provided a pair of plastic snowshoes. He'd wanted 100 krone for those. They were broad enough to stop Tom sinking into the crust, though they left a more obvious trail than he liked and were impossible to use at speed. That was why he was late. An hour late, maybe more. A cousin of Harri's wife was waiting for him beyond a local war memorial. It would be fine, Anders had assured him. No one went there any more and only old people even remembered it existed.

An idealised statue of Soviet youth clutched a rifle and looked lost, unloved, forgotten. Tom stopped fifteen paces from the memorial to three teenagers who ambushed a German patrol in this forest and died for their pains; as did their entire village, which was burned to the ground.

A man waited at the far edge of the clearing.

So far as Tom could tell, and he'd made a complete circle of the woods to check, the man had come alone. Something felt wrong though, unnatural. Tom was still trying to work out what. So he watched and waited some more.

The figure stood between two trees, his head tipped back and his arms outstretched in welcome. If it hadn't been so unlikely, he might be praying to the darkness above him. Five minutes later, he still hadn't moved. By then Tom had checked again for others; letting his eyes adjust to the shadows and searching for movement.

Anything to suggest an ambush.

All was stillness and silence. Too still?

A snowy owl hooted, and a squirrel scuttled overhead, spooked by the owl's call. He was being over-cautious, Tom decided. Except there was no such thing as over-cautious. Not out here, five miles the wrong side of the Soviet border. Didn't matter if it was the most porous border in the Eastern Bloc, he was still the wrong side of it.

Tom advanced slowly, still watchful.

The man heard him coming and tried to look. His face falling forward with the effort of twisting his head.

A handful of steps closed the gap, and Tom gasped to see savage twists of barbed wire circling the old man's skull. It was only the nails through his hands that kept him upright, his arms outstretched between firs. The felt of his tunic had a rent in its side and blood oozed from a stab wound beneath. Sub-zero temperatures had reduced the flow to a dribble.

'The ball?' Tom said in Russian. 'Where is it?'

The man looked terrified.

Tom had no idea if the man was Lutheran, Russian Orthodox, Communist, or held to old Sami shamanistic traditions. He believed the crucifixion of this man was aimed at him, though. Tom had trained in a Catholic seminary, been ordained into the Protestant tradition. This was a message.

Someone knew he was coming.

Tom yanked at one of the nails and the man swore.

There was no easy way to extract them. They'd been hammered too deep, and their heads were too broad to be pulled through the wounds in the dying man's palms.

'Finish me,' the man begged.

'They took the glass ball?' Tom demanded.

'I never had it.' His voice was a whisper. His face hollow with pain. Questioning him was cruelty. Tom did it all the same.

'Then who has it?'

'Per's professor.'

'Dr Blackburn. She has it?'

'Per hid it. She will know where.'

'You told the Russians that?'

'I told them nothing. I told them I had nothing to tell. They'll be back, though. They said they'd be back. For you, and to question me.'

'About Per's professor?'

The man raised his head long enough to look Tom in the eyes. 'Not yet,' he said.

It was a challenge. It was meant to be a challenge.

Flipping open his lock-knife, Tom put his hand over the old man's mouth and stilled his heart with a single stab, just as a white-uniformed figure on skis materialised on the clearing's far edge. Shouting an order not to move, the Vnutrenniye Voiska man reached for the rifle slung across his back.

Tom ripped his knife from the old man's chest and threw . . .

42

Monday 23rd November – Hampshire

'You should be asleep.'

'So should you,' Charlie said.

Becca snorted. 'Dad's in trouble,' she said.

Charlie stopped trying to remember Grandpa's conversation, which is what he'd been doing instead of sleeping. He was sure Grandpa had been talking to Daddy. He just didn't know why Grandpa would lie.

'Where are you?' Charlie said crossly.

His bedroom curtains fluttered, and there was a brush of wind as his dead sister put her hand on his shoulder. She was beside him, in his bedroom on the third floor of Grandpa's house, and only he knew she was there.

It was unlike her to pretend to be invisible.

Climbing from his bed, Charlie headed for the window, feeling a breeze as Becca followed. He listened for her footsteps but heard only his own. From this window you could see the churchyard where Mummy was buried. On the slope above was Becca's grave.

Rebecca Caroline Everard Eddington Fox

1969–1985

Say not in grief that she is no more

But say in thankfulness that she was

'How do you know he's in trouble?'

'I just do. There's snow,' she added, before Charlie could

interrupt. 'And it's cold. Very cold. And it's dark and there are bears.'

'Polar bears?'

Becca thought about that.

'Brown bears,' she said finally. 'Brown bears and white wolves.'

'I met—'

'That's where he's gone, isn't it? To meet her. That's why he's in trouble.'

'What should we do?' Charlie asked.

'You have to help him,' Becca said. 'I can't. You know I can't.'

'How should I help him?'

Becca shrugged. 'I don't know. You're the clever one. You work it out.'

Charlie didn't think Becca had ever called him clever. Not for real. Not when she was . . .

'You're talking to yourself.' Grandpa stood in the doorway in his dressing gown. This was red and quilted, and Mummy had said it was very old. He looked sad and tired. Grandpa never looked sad or tired. His voice was kind, though.

A little worried, maybe.

'I was dreaming,' Charlie said.

Grandpa helped him back into bed.

43

Monday 23rd November – Norwegian–Soviet Border

Tom's blade rotated once and buried itself in a fir tree next to the Vnutrenniye Voiska man's head.

'*Gavno!*' the Russian shouted. Shit!

He stared in shock at the quivering knife.

And Tom used the moment to step back into the trees, almost falling as his cheap snowshoes slid on icy granite stripped clean by the wind. Regaining his balance, he turned for the border, relying on a run of rock to hide the tracks that would betray him if he returned to the snow.

'Halt!'

He increased his speed.

A rifle bullet splintered a pine trunk beside him. Another buried itself in a tree beyond. As Tom wove his way between firs and birch, heading for a frozen river, he found his way blocked by a fallen trunk. Clambering over it would disturb the snow coating it and prove he'd come this way. Although the guard must know . . .

'Halt!' This time the shout came from close behind.

Levering himself over the tree, Tom half skated a dozen paces along the frozen river, then doubled back to scramble under the trunk. The direction of the half-moon threw his side into shade. In the last second, he stuffed snow into his mouth so the condensation from his ragged breathing wouldn't give him away. He hoped it would be enough.

He could hear a guard approaching.

The soldier grunted as he removed his full-length skis, before cursing his way over the fallen tree and halting at the river's edge. He tested the ice with his foot, grunted to himself when it held. He stood not far from Tom's head, facing the river.

Keep going, Tom thought.

The man didn't. He simply stayed there.

Tom was surprised the guard couldn't hear his stifled breathing. Christ, he was surprised the man couldn't hear the thud of his heart. It felt so loud. Tom was reaching for the man's boot, ready to take him down, when snow crust fell on his hand and he realised a second soldier was clambering over. This one still wore his skis. As did the next, and the one after. All four stood with their backs to Tom, staring along the dark thread of frozen stream.

'Get me Murmansk,' Tom heard one say.

There was a hiss as a military radio tuned in, and a crackling exchange about a crucified Lapp and the fact the Lapp's attacker was heading towards the border. The sergeant intended to leave one man here and go after the criminal with the other two. 'No need for paramedics,' the sergeant said. 'Better send a snowcat to collect his body though. The brass will want it as evidence.'

Three of the guards skied away upstream: and a second after they'd vanished into the darkness, still gathering speed on ice that somehow held, Tom acted. Punching the back of the remaining man's knee, he crushed his larynx and broke his neck a second later.

A teenager. Barely older than Becca.

Tom thought of Caro. The graveyard, his daughter's grave. Now it held his wife's grave too. It was years since he'd believed in the resurrection, and he was no longer convinced by the life eternal.

Which was worse, Tolstoy had asked, the wolf who cries before eating the lamb or the wolf who does not? Coldly, methodically, Tom stripped the boy's corpse of its skis, boots and snow-white uniform.

He was checking the boy's Simonov for rounds when the low thud of an approaching helicopter woke sleeping birds and sent them skywards. Rolling his victim under the fallen tree trunk, Tom kicked snow over him and stood to wave the rifle as the Mil Mi-1 caught him in its spotlight. Just another Vnutrenniye Voiska going about his business. When the first Mil Mi-1 was joined by another, and they both began sweeping the forest between the river and the border, Tom accepted the inevitable and slipped away in the opposite direction.

An hour later, having relied on his stolen skis for speed and his new snow camouflage to keep him safe, he was fifteen miles the wrong side of the Norwegian border, and five Mil Mi-1s could be seen lighting up the darkness. He was grateful when the clouds came in, the half-moon vanished and a blizzard began.

44

November 1971 – Derry, Northern Ireland

'Police,' one of the drinkers said.

It was the night after Himself brought Jimmy back from Belfast. He was sat in the corner, showered, shaved and feeling sorry for himself. A Diet Coke was on the table in front of him. He'd barely touched it all night.

'Army,' another said.

'Which is it?' Himself said crossly.

'Both,' a man by the windows said.

'Anyone carrying, get out of here.'

'Too late,' Judy said. She was in the door to the yard, a crate of empties in her hands. Beyond her, Jimmy could see the silhouette of two soldiers blocking the yard door, which they'd taken off its hinges with a squat hydraulic ram.

Stepping into the yard, Judy put down her crate and calmly returned to the bar, shutting the door on them, exactly as if they weren't there.

'Bolt it,' Himself ordered.

A couple of drinkers with their backs to the wall were wiping down pistols, which they dropped to the floor and kicked under their seats. Another man simply dropped out the clip on his Browning, counted the rounds, put the clip back and jacked a round into the breech. If Jimmy had been out front, that's the one he'd be worried about.

The pub door slammed open.

In it stood a crop-haired RUC officer in a flak jacket. Behind him hovered two Green Jacket soldiers in flak jackets and helmets, rifles ported and fingers alongside the triggers.

'We don't want trouble,' the RUC officer said.

Himself stared at the man.

'This is an arrest for murder. Not a raid. Not a search.'

'Go on,' Himself said.

'We take our man. We leave.'

The drinkers waited to see what Himself would decide.

Soldiers at the front. More out back. Jimmy didn't doubt the road through the estate was locked off by Saracen APCs. There'd be snipers. Night-sights. Men in reserve. The half dozen Green Jackets were simply those you could see.

'Who?' Himself demanded.

The RUC man pointed at Jimmy.

'What's the charge?' Jimmy demanded.

'You know the charge,' the man told him.

'Fucking Prod,' Jimmy said.

The blow knocked him from his stool, and Green Jackets stepped into the pub and had their rifles raised before anybody could scrape back their seats.

Himself shook his head.

'Not me,' Jimmy said, picking himself up. He could taste blood in his mouth. One of his teeth felt loose when he tested it with his tongue. 'You've got the wrong man.'

'Your fingerprints are all over it.'

Jimmy stared at him.

'You think we wouldn't find you?'

'Who?' Jimmy demanded. 'What? When?'

'You tortured Eddie Haig to death. Stuffed his body in the boot of a Rover. In that junkyard under the arches down there. You might have moved his body. But his blood and your fingerprints are all over it. Ring any bells?'

'That junkyard's mine,' said a thickset man Jimmy had never met. 'The boy kills the rats for me, stops people dumping their shite, keeps an eye out for scrotes. His fingerprints are bound to be on things.'

'Council say he's on the dole.'

'It's unofficial, like.'

'Maybe we should take you in as an accessory.'

'Just back from Majorca. I haven't been down there in weeks. You can ask anyone.'

The RUC man sighed.

'You're under arrest,' he told Jimmy.

Having read Jimmy his rights, to jeers from those watching, the officer spun Jimmy round, yanked his hands behind his back and snapped on a pair of handcuffs. The two Green Jackets covered the room while the RUC man dragged Jimmy from the pub and threw him into an unmarked van. The first kick came before the back of the van had even closed. Jimmy didn't doubt those crowding the pub door saw it. He didn't doubt they were meant to.

The van went in one direction. The soldiers in another.

'Name,' a desk clerk demanded.

Jimmy gave his name.

'Your real name.'

'That is my real name.'

A punch to the kidneys dropped him to the tiles. A guard yanked him to his feet by his hair and shoved him along a corridor. Prisoners were howling from cells on either side. Walls being hit, doors being kicked. Mixed into the fury of the incarcerated were shrieks from those being tortured, questioned or simply softened up.

This wasn't a normal police station. If those even existed

these days. It didn't seem like part of an army base either. In both of those, there might have been a pretence of keeping to the law. From what Jimmy could tell, here anything went.

When they dragged him into the showers and Jimmy found it already occupied by a naked man tied to a stool wearing a bucket on his head, he wasn't even surprised. The metal bucket was being hit with a spanner. The noise in the shower room was painful. Inside the bucket, it must have been insanity-inducing.

'Take it elsewhere,' Jimmy's escort said.

The man putting dents in the bucket looked as if he might object, then shrugged. 'Feel free. Got fucking arm ache anyway.'

'In you go,' Jimmy was told.

A kick drove him under the shower, and a second later frozen water powered from the nozzles, soaking his clothes and chilling him to the bone. Every time Jimmy tried to crawl out, a guard kicked him back in. Minutes became hours and Jimmy couldn't stop shivering. The cold bit so deep he couldn't breathe.

'Right,' a guard said.

He reached into the shower, gripped Jimmy's long hair and forced his face upwards. Water filled his mouth and ran into his nose. He swallowed desperately.

'Why did you shoot Eddie Haig?'

'I didn't shoot him.'

'How do you know how he died?'

'You just said.'

'I said, *Why did you kill Eddie Haig?*'

'You didn't,' Jimmy said desperately. 'You said why did I shoot him.'

Water poured into his face and filled his sinuses. His body

was fighting not to die. You're not dying, he told himself. You're not dying. They're not really going to kill you. His body didn't believe it. It could feel itself drowning. Jimmy wasn't sure he believed it either.

'Your fingerprints are on the gun.'

'There isn't a gun. I've never owned a gun. I didn't kill him.'

'There are witnesses.'

'There can't be. Ask them why they're lying.'

The man let Jimmy's head drop.

Jimmy slept on the concrete floor of a cell and was woken at dawn by a kick in the guts from the guard in civvies who'd questioned him the night before. Jimmy wondered where the man had been in the meantime. Nowhere that made him any happier. His breath was rank, and he stank of a slow-burning anger that filled Jimmy's cell like rancid sweat.

'Come with me,' he ordered.

On his way out, Jimmy caught sight of himself in a window. Split lip, black eye, swollen cheek, bruised jaw. His shirt, jeans and jacket were somewhere between damp and still sodden. He'd lost his wallet on the way in, and wherever he was being taken no one looked like they were going to give it back.

'I want a lawyer,' Jimmy said.

'I want a lawyer,' the man mimicked. 'Where you're going a fucking lawyer won't do you any good.' He dumped Jimmy on a chair in reception and told him he'd break both his arms if he even thought of fucking moving.

Half an hour later, a conversation took place between the man who'd questioned Jimmy, and a young man who looked like a clerk but merited *sir*.

'No fingerprints?'

'Not inside the car boot.'

'But outside, sir?'

'They prove nothing.'

'So we're letting the little shit go?'

'Not a chance. We're going to move him somewhere discreet. Sit on him for a few days. See what he'll tell us. You can trust me for that.'

The man looked happier.

45

Tuesday 24th November – Norwegian–Soviet Border

Moving got you killed. Staying still got you killed too.

Tom's plan, formed on the fly, was to trek inland and keep his head down for long enough for the Soviet helicopters to decide he must have escaped. He wanted to go to ground. Gut instinct said hide. His training said keep moving.

He kept moving.

He used the snowstorm and darkness to hide his move deeper into Soviet Russia; and the first two hours of daylight to run parallel to the border, up the frozen length of a ribbon lake whose ice he trusted, being hard as concrete and feeling as solid. Twice he had to throw himself flat to avoid being seen by trucks carrying supplies on a road above its shore.

In a pocket in the uniform was a bar of Alyonka, which his body heat had softened enough not to break his teeth. He ate the bar of chocolate in one go, and almost crumpled its wrapper but folded it instead. So as not to crease the moon-faced wee boy smiling out at him. In the afternoon he worked his way back towards Kirkenes. It was too dark by then to see what kind of trail he was leaving, but he knew he had to be leaving one. Taken short, he buried his spoor and smoothed the snow.

Wherever possible, he kept to ice or ice-glazed rock rather than fresh snow, for all it was more dangerous to ski. He chose the middle of frozen rivers and avoided the banks.

Anything to hide the tracks left by his skis. All went as planned until early evening, and then Tom felt the helicopter as a low thud in his chest before he heard it, and an Mi-1 skimmed overhead. He heard the dogs a second later. The exultant cry of hounds picking up scent.

He ran. Well, he dug in the stolen skis and kicked off, taking the fastest route away from the dogs, even when it took him to the very edge of a drop. With snow thinning to ice crust, and then frozen grit grinding under his skis, he ran an incline so suicidal he was certain he would fall. His heart was pounding. His mouth dry.

He was so cold it was in his bones.

He could hear the dogs, but further back, and the Mi-1 was away to one side. He had a mile at most to the border. The sudden whine as someone kickstarted a snowcat to life was a brutal surprise. It had been waiting in the trees.

With no time to think, Tom sidestepped as the soldier tried to run him down, whipping his ski stick across his attacker's throat. The Vnutrenniye Voiska corporal went backwards off his bike, which came to a halt fifty paces on.

'No you don't,' Tom said.

He snapped the man's neck with a twist.

Take the snowcat or keep going on skis? Skis were quieter, the snowcat would be faster. Tom went to examine the thing. A heavy-duty battery behind the snowcat's seat was wired to a two-way radio below the windscreen.

Tom flicked a switch and the speaker crackled as voices faded in and out. The aurora overhead interfering with radio waves. If he'd had a compass, its needle would have been quivering from the magnetic disturbance. They were hunting him, and the radio was tuned into the hunt. Use this, Tom told himself.

He needed to throw them off the scent.

He needed to channel his friend Ivan Petrovich Dennisov.

A veteran of Afghanistan who'd fashioned a leg for himself from the landing spring of a Soviet helicopter downed by a US missile supplied to the mujahideen. The man was nails. Steadying himself, Tom summoned up his friend's best Moscow drawl. 'He's doubled back. Repeat. Doubled back. Heading away from the border. Repeat. Away. Get on it. Stop him before he goes to ground.'

Tom killed the link before anyone could question what authority he had to give that order. A second later, the Mi-1 peeled away from its path. Behind him, the hounds began protesting as they were stopped in their tracks and turned with orders to find a new trail.

46

Tuesday 24th November – Hampshire

Cat wasn't sure about horses.

Charlie didn't blame him. He wasn't sure about them either. Granny had bought Misty as an early Christmas present. Charlie hadn't asked for a horse, but Granny had decided Charlie should learn to ride. And Misty wasn't a horse, so she kept telling him. Charlie hadn't helped by saying as far as he was concerned a pony was simply a horse subset.

'Honestly,' he heard her say after he'd finished his cornflakes and asked to be excused. 'Where does he get his vocabulary?'

'He reads dictionaries,' Grandpa said.

'Really?'

'Yes,' Grandpa said. 'Really.'

Grandpa was waiting for his official car. He was meant to be taking a week away from the Ministry, compassionate leave, which was like time off for sadness. He'd managed three days, and one of those had been burying Mummy.

Charlie didn't recognise the man in the black hat who climbed the stile at the end of Grandpa's paddock and began picking his way through brambles towards what had been a tennis court, before the netting rotted, frost ate the asphalt and the chain-link fencing began to fall down. That was when Mummy was little, before he was born.

'Charlie,' the man said.

Charlie wondered if he was meant to know who this was.

'Are you a journalist?' Charlie asked.

'Why?'

'Because I'm not meant to talk to journalists.'

The man considered that. 'Very wise,' he said.

Had this man been at Mummy's funeral? Lots of people were. The picture in the *Sun*, taken by someone hidden in a bush beyond the churchyard wall, made it look like a party. Serious, properly dressed, but very busy and a bit crowded.

'How are you, Charlie?'

'Very well, thank you. How are you?'

'I'm well too.' The man seemed amused by Charlie's answer, which seemed odd because it was the right answer. The one Mummy said to use.

'Have we met?' Charlie asked.

'I know your father.'

'My father?'

'Your grandfather, too.'

The man's accent wasn't English, Scottish or Irish. It might be American, Charlie decided. Daddy had friends there. He'd sent Charlie a postcard from Annapolis, which was a naval base. And from Langley, which wasn't. All the sailors Charlie knew had beards and this man didn't. When Charlie asked if he was from Langley, the man's face froze. 'Your pony?' he asked, changing the subject.

Charlie nodded glumly.

'You don't like ponies?'

'It bumps up when I bump down.'

'You'll get better.'

Charlie doubted it.

'But you like cats?'

Fur damp from that morning's dew, and picking his way

with distaste between sodden clumps of winter grass, Cat had come to see if the stranger brought food.

The newcomer held out his hand.

Cat stopped to sniff.

'You like cats?' The newcomer repeated.

Charlie nodded, wondering why it mattered.

Cat didn't seem thrilled to be picked up and flicked the stump where his tail should be. 'Have you seen your dad recently?' the man asked.

Charlie didn't call him Dad. Becca did – well, had. Probably because it annoyed Mummy. Although, as Daddy pointed out, he didn't mind and Becca would probably go back to calling him Daddy if Mummy didn't make it so obvious she minded.

'Charlie . . .'

'Yes?' Charlie said, remembering the man was there.

'Your dad. Is he here?'

'No,' Charlie said. 'He went . . .'

'Went where?'

'I don't know,' Charlie said.

That was the truth, mostly.

Daddy went where the Wolf Lady was. That could be anywhere with wolves, which ranged from Norway to almost Japan. America and Canada had wolves too. Those were of a different kind. Becca had said there was snow. Snow, and trees. Or maybe just snow and he'd made the trees up. Perhaps it had been Grandpa who mentioned snow in that strange telephone call of his. You found snow almost everywhere you found wolves so that didn't help.

'He hasn't phoned you?'

Charlie shook his head sadly.

'Not even on the day your mother was buried?'

'No,' Charlie said crossly. He wasn't sure who he was

crossest with. Daddy, this man for asking or Grandpa for lying. Probably all three. Cat was swishing his stump. The man didn't appear to notice.

'What about Eddington? I mean, your grandfather. Has your dad called him?'

When Charlie hesitated, the man tightened his grip on Cat, who suddenly went very still.

'You're hurting him,' Charlie protested.

'No. He likes it.'

Charlie could tell Cat didn't like it. Charlie was getting worried. He knew this because he'd started feeling sick. That's what worry felt like. The child psychologist said so.

'Your grandfather,' the man said. 'Has he heard?'

'He says not,' Charlie said.

Cat yowled. It was a horrible yowl.

'Granny did,' Charlie said frantically. 'And Aunt Agatha. Daddy left messages.'

'For your grandfather?'

Cat was scrabbling now. His eyes wider than Charlie would have thought possible.

'He wanted to know if Grandpa knew about a glass ball . . .'

The man let Cat go.

The animal streaked away into the hedge by the footpath and Charlie knew it was going to be hours before he came back. If he ever did. That thought made Charlie even sicker.

'Well,' the man said, 'I'd better be going.'

He made it sound as if they'd just had a nice talk. As if he really was a friend of Daddy's and Grandpa's. Charlie didn't believe he'd been at Mummy's funeral at all. The man began to head for the stile and the field that fat Farmer Wilson rented beyond. A footpath would take him to the village. After a moment's thought, Charlie followed.

47

The man's car was big and black. It had a strange number plate on the back and one of those oval stickers that usually said things like EU, or GB for Great Britain, or IRL for Ireland. This one said CD.

Charlie wasn't sure what that stood for but he'd find out when he wasn't busy. The man himself was in the village phone box, having first gone into the Post Office to buy a paper to get change for the telephone. Charlie knew this because he'd watched through the window. The man bought the *Telegraph*. Charlie wondered if that was significant.

It was the first paper in the row, the first the man came across, so possibly not.

There was a small steel mirror above the coin box in the red telephone booth that let people see if anyone was behind them. The man wasn't looking in it, and Charlie wasn't tall enough to be seen in a mirror that high anyway.

Bending as if to tie his shoes, Charlie watched the man punch in a number. Charlie was too far away to see the buttons, but he memorised their positions and promised to check when the horrid man was gone.

He had something to do first. He'd need to run, though.

'My bike's broken.'

Mr Turner looked up from the rear of a Hillman Minx that

had seen better days. He squinted into the light. Smiled as he recognised Charlie in his workshop doorway.

'Bring it in then.'

'I'd rather do it myself.'

'That's the spirit. Where is it?'

Charlie hated lying. He wasn't very good at it either. Except when it really mattered. Then he was good at it because for a few seconds, inside his head, the lie became real. 'I left it by the telephone box.'

'Flat tyre?'

'Chain,' Charlie said. 'It's slipped off. And the bit the pedals are fixed to . . .'

'Chain-ring,' Mr Turner said.

'That's loose.'

'Help yourself,' Mr Turner said, pointing to a box of tools. 'Remember to bring them back when you're done.'

Charlie grabbed a screwdriver and a spanner. Then, checking Mr Turner wasn't looking, he added a handful of nails and a hammer. 'Thank you,' he said.

His shirt was sticky with sweat by the time he reached the big black car. The man was still in his telephone box though. Still talking. Only now he seemed cross.

'Stay there,' Charlie told him.

Dropping to his knees by the big car, Charlie gave thanks for the bread lorry alongside that gave him cover, and considered his options. What he'd really like to do was remove all the nuts from the wheels, but he didn't have the right tools and wasn't strong enough anyway. Letting the air out was too obvious, both to do and because the man might work out that it had been him.

Then he might come back. Charlie didn't want the man coming back. He felt sick just thinking about Cat being hurt some more. He wanted the man to go away. Go away and never come back.

Charlie was about to hammer a nail into the side of the tyre when he had a better idea. Among the nails he'd grabbed he found a screw, a broad-headed tack, and a flat nail of the kind the Victorians used to secure floorboards. He fixed the screw between treads on the driver's side front wheel, leaving most of it sticking out, then carefully hammered the tack, which was long, jagged and black, into the back wheel on that side, but not far enough to puncture the tyre. At least, not yet.

The Victorian nail he pushed between the rubber of the tyre and the shiny metal of the rim. He wasn't sure it would do anything much but he liked its shape too much to waste it.

Charlie was in the village store buying a bag of flying saucers when the man abandoned the telephone box, stamped to his big black car and shut its door with a slam. The engine roared, sounding far too noisy for a car that square and ugly, and it pulled away in a squeal of wheels.

Charlie wondered how far he'd get.

With luck, the motorway.

48

Tuesday 24th November – Kirkenes, Northern Norway

'You!'

The Norwegian in the doorway of Tom's hotel room carried a baseball bat and looked as if he'd been working himself up for this confrontation.

'Me,' Tom agreed.

'I'd heard . . .'

What? Tom wondered. That he was dead, under arrest, had absconded?

There was only one tourist hotel in Kirkenes. A long, low wooden building painted rust-red and set back from a memorial to the resistance. Further east than Leningrad, or even Istanbul, Kirkenes was one of the most bombed towns in Europe. What the Soviet Air Forces didn't destroy, the Red Army did, driving out the Wehrmacht. Only nine houses survived, according to a sign half obscured by snow.

Tom's room was at the back.

He'd kept it on because he'd only expected to be gone for a day collecting whatever the hell it was Per believed to be so valuable. And he'd arrived back to find it ransacked, his case upturned. Luckily, by the time the hotel manager had plucked up the courage to check who was in there, Tom had changed back to jeans and a sweatshirt and his stolen Soviet uniform was bundled under the bed.

'I didn't see you come in,' the hotel manager said. The

light from the corridor was behind him and he was peering into the darkness of Tom's unlit room.

'I used the window.'

'Why?'

'Reasons,' Tom said. A man would need reasons to climb the outside of a building in a snowstorm and force a window sash rather than use the front door.

'There was a burglary,' the manager said.

'The whole hotel or just my room?'

His clothes were scattered across the floor, the passport he was travelling on and his wallet gone from where he'd taped them to the back of a drawer. That had been the first thing he checked. Luckily, his SIS ID was still where he'd left it. Under the insole of an M&S brogue he'd tossed, along with its companion, into a cupboard before leaving.

'Well?' Tom said.

'You're the only guest.'

'Just my room, then?'

'Nothing else worth taking, I guess.'

'Did you call the police?'

'Of course. They wanted to know where you were and when I expected you back. I said I hadn't known you were going anywhere. That was yesterday.'

'What can I get on room service?'

The man looked at him.

'I need food,' Tom said. 'Food, a bath and sleep.'

'What happened?'

'I got lost in a forest.'

The man nodded, looking thoughtful. 'That happens,' he said.

49

Wednesday 25th November – Hampshire

Charlie had a letter to write.

It was important he wrote it carefully.

Actually, he had two letters to write. One to Granny and one not. Granny liked things neatly written, so Charlie took extra care to make sure his lines were parallel, his paragraphs had proper margins and his letters didn't slope. He would leave it on his pillow in an hour or two, before he walked into town.

Dear Granny,

Please feed Cat for me. I am going to London to the Natural History Museum to study wolves. I will be very careful when crossing the road and make sure not to talk to strange men.

Much love
Charlie

The letter looked a little too short to be polite, so Charlie added: *PS I will be back in time for supper.* And then, because that still wasn't quite long enough: *PPS I have already checked the timetable for return trains.*

He'd managed to fill a page. Mummy always said letters to anybody should be at least a page. Anything less was rude. Folding the sheet of slightly blue Basildon Bond, Charlie slid it into an envelope and wrote *Granny* on the front, remembering to add *By Hand* at the top right. He underlined it once, because *By Hand* needed underlining, but only once. Two lines was too emphatic. Charlie wasn't sure why. He'd looked up 'emphatic' in a dictionary and didn't see how it applied to lines. Filing that as a problem to come back to later, he returned to bed.

Very early next morning, long before it was light and well before the first robin was awake, Charlie changed his mind about leaving the envelope on his pillow. Instead, he left it on the little inlaid card table in the hall. The one that looked Georgian but was only Edwardian.

There was a map of the Underground on the back of Grandpa's *A–Z* of London and Charlie had memorised the tube lines and the stations where he'd need to change. If he forgot, he could check a map on a wall. There had been maps on the walls the time Mummy took him to Madame Tussauds. And if the map didn't help, he'd ask somebody. But not anybody who could be considered Strange.

'Bye, Cat,' he said.

Cat had come to see who was in Grandpa's study. He wanted breakfast. He didn't seem amused when Charlie scowled at his Seiko and headed for the door. 'I'm going to be late,' Charlie explained. 'Mrs Ross will feed you.'

'Do you have anything on wolves?'

The woman behind the counter of the gift shop at the Natural History Museum in South Kensington had watched the small boy come in by himself and wondered where his parents were. Children, especially boys, could be a problem, particularly if they arrived in a school party. This one looked harmless enough.

'Where are your parents?'

'Mummy's dead. Daddy's talking to a friend.'

'Ah . . .' The woman seemed disconcerted by that.

'About wolves,' Charlie reminded her.

'Oh yes. We have this.'

It was heavy and hardback and very expensive.

'Perhaps for my birthday.' Picking up a guide to the museum, Charlie said, 'I'd better have this instead.'

Holding his guide tightly – proof that he'd visited the Natural History Museum and hadn't lied – Charlie headed for the huge doors he'd used to enter and let himself out again.

Now for the second part of his plan.

'I'd like to see the ambassador.'

The sergeant inside the gates of the Soviet embassy in Kensington Palace Gardens looked down at the small boy standing just beyond. The boy was holding a guide to the Natural History Museum, which was a brisk fifteen minutes' walk from here.

'Please,' Charlie added.

The soldier shook his head.

'I wouldn't ask if it wasn't important.'

The place with the most wolves in Europe was Russia, which formed most of the western part of the USSR. And Becca had said there was snow. Russia had lots of snow. The Wolf Lady had been in Russia before East Berlin. It would make sense for her to return there. And if Daddy had gone to see the Wolf Lady . . .

Charlie had worked it all out.

'Please,' he said again.

'Can I help you?'

Charlie examined the smiling man who'd just appeared

on the far side of the gate. He looked very young to be an ambassador.

'I work for him,' the man said when Charlie asked. 'We all work for him. Do your parents know you're here?'

'Mummy's dead,' Charlie said, forgetting to say 'my mother' as he'd meant to. 'I think my father's in Russia.' Not only did the man look surprised, he looked suspicious, which Charlie thought was unfair. 'Perhaps I should talk to the ambassador instead,' he said.

'He's not here.'

Charlie stepped back. That possibility hadn't occurred to him.

'When will he be back?' Charlie knew he sounded worried. He couldn't help if he sounded worried. He was.

'What's this about?' the young man asked.

His accent was very Russian but entirely understandable. He also wore a rather nice tweed jacket, which surprised Charlie. The sergeant who'd gone to get this man wore uniform, obviously. He was standing to one side, looking interested. Probably not very much happened when you guarded a gate.

Kensington wasn't that exciting.

The man with the tweed coat was waiting for an answer, and Charlie felt he should give him one. 'Do you know Wax Angel?' he asked.

The Russian looked puzzled.

'She was at Stalingrad,' Charlie explained. 'A sniper, and then a ballerina. Joseph Vissarionovich put her in a camp, and when she came out she was a beggar in Moscow. She used to steal candles from churches and carve angels to sell to tourists. Then the Commissar found her again and she made him comb his hair and start being nicer to people. I need this to get to her. Please.'

Reaching into his jacket, Charlie pulled out the other letter he'd written. He'd taken care with the address. It was in his neatest writing.

'Wax Angel?'

'She lives in the Lion House,' Charlie said.

'In the House of Lions?' The man's eyes had widened.

'That's the one.' Charlie nodded happily. 'She lives with the Commissar. He's very old now. Could you forward this to his wife and say it's urgent.'

'*Marshal Milov?*'

'Yes,' Charlie said. 'The Commissar.'

'How do you know about Madame Milova?'

'She's a friend.'

'And your mother is dead? And your father . . .' He left that bit unfinished.

'Yes,' Charlie said to both.

He'd taken great care with the letter. Even more than with his note to Granny. He'd kept it simple too. Only including the bits that mattered. Those bits being the Wolf Lady, his father, the glass ball, Grandpa being very cross, the strange woman at Mummy's funeral who thought they were burying Daddy, and the appearance of the man Cat didn't like.

50

November 1971 – Derry, Northern Ireland

'Tom Fox? Never heard of him.'

Jimmy watched the inmate walk away. They were in the yard under the watchful eye of soldiers up on the walls. This place must have been an ordinary prison at some point. There was a Victorian grimness to its red brick that spoke more of punishment than rehabilitation. The only modern touch was razor wire wrapping its courtyard. That, and the strangely squat rifles carried by its guards. No regimental badges. No name tags. No badges of rank. Jimmy suspected this place didn't exist. Not officially, anyway.

'You were asking about Fox?'

Jimmy turned to find a wiry man behind him. His hair was sandy, his skin freckled. His eyes watchful, almost anxious. You'd have overlooked him in a pub, and probably regretted it if things turned nasty. The scars to his hands said he'd been in more knife fights than most. 'You know where he is?' Jimmy asked.

'What's your interest?'

'He killed a pal of mine. I intend to settle the debt.'

The man thought about that, then thrust out his hand. 'I'm Vince,' he said. 'There's a queue for Fox and I'm at the head of it. But the Big Man wants a word with Fox first. If you're out in time, come find me. You can help settle the debt.'

Jimmy stared at him.

The man smiled. 'I'm out tomorrow. They say.'

*

There's the smell of beer and sweat and cigarettes you get in every pub, but the beer smell is heavier because the clientele are drinking Guinness to a man; and that's intentional, and it is to a man if you don't count Judy, who's glowering so fiercely she's practically her own exclusion zone.

When she sees Jimmy in the doorway her face is unreadable.

At least it is for the first second, then she blushes and scowls, and even the drunk she's been serving with such bad grace, who's on his fifth pint of the evening, realises something is wrong and turns to see what's going on.

It's been five days and Jimmy's blackened eye is nearly open, his bottom lip is less swollen than it was, and his jawline has begun to turn yellow. He stopped off at the wee flat where he's dossing to change his clothes and take a shower.

He watches her stalk towards him.

'Idiot,' she says.

Her slap knocks his head sideways, and then she's hugging him and he's trying not to gasp from the pain in his un-mended ribs. 'It's grand,' he tells her when she steps back looking concerned.

'Jimmy . . .'

Himself's up from his table. He grips Jimmy's hand and it's a fierce handshake and Jimmy has to try not to wince at that too.

'They let you go.'

'Didn't do anything. They had no choice.'

Himself smiles at Jimmy's bravado. They both know that's a lie on so many levels. 'Sit down. Judy can bring you a drink.'

'Food. If you have it. I'm starving.'

'They didn't feed you?' Judy asks.

'Not without spitting or pissing in it first.'

*

189

Jimmy drank sparingly, shook his head at an offer of a lift home, and helped Judy clear away the glasses, empty the slop trays and wipe down the old mahogany counter. After that, he helped her empty the ashtrays, sweep the floor and put out the empties.

'The back gate's been mended?'

'Aye,' she said. 'Thicker door. Better locks.'

Judy flicked off the overhead lights when they were done and turned for the stairs. Leading him up them without a word being said. Her living space was tiny. A small kitchen that needed new units, a toilet squeezed between a yellowing bath and a chipped basin, a bedroom with barely space for a bed, for all it was a single. Clean bras, knickers and shirts folded neatly in piles along the wall. Everything else hung from hooks fixed above.

'I don't bring boys here,' she said, seeing him look.

'Thank you,' Jimmy said, meaning it.

'For what?'

'Making an exception.'

'More fool me.'

She ran Jimmy a bath without asking if he wanted one, and told him to get in, waving away his protest that he'd already had a shower. 'They worked you over well.'

'Aye. They did.'

'Why you?'

'Not just me,' he said. 'Everyone there. They wanted confessions.'

'But you wouldn't?'

'I didn't do it.' Jimmy shifted slightly under her gaze. 'Well, they certainly didn't have any evidence of that.'

'Your fingerprints . . .'

'Were on the outside of the car. And the other car. And on everything else. Just not inside the boot where they said the body was originally.'

'They said?'

Jimmy nodded.

'Shift up,' she said.

The bath was too wee for both of them and Judy didn't object when Jimmy climbed out, wrapped himself in her off-white towel, and sat on the floor to watch as she stretched out as far as the bath would allow. She had a soft body with small-ish breasts and pale nipples.

Looking up, he found her watching him.

'Sorry,' he said.

'If I'd wanted you not to look, I'd have said don't look.'

So he watched her some more, and after a while she closed her eyes and settled so low that everything except her knees and face was below the surface of the slowly cooling water.

'Throw me the towel,' Judy said.

Blinking, Jimmy looked up and realised he'd been close to falling asleep.

'Where were you?' she asked.

'In the home.'

'It was bad?'

This wasn't a conversation he wanted to have. Not here, not with her, not now.

'Bad enough,' he said, and she let the subject drop.

Just before they climbed into the single bed, Judy put on a fresh pair of knickers, having tossed the ones she'd been wearing, along with that day's bra and shirt, into a wicker bas-ket in the bathroom. She looked at Jimmy to make sure he understood the point she was making. He did.

They slept in each other's arms, and Jimmy dreamed of his time in the children's home. He woke wondering where he was, and then wondered why, and how he found himself in the places he did. He didn't ask Judy about her own dreams.

51

Wednesday 25th November – Kirkenes, Northern Norway

'Professor Conway?'

Tom looked up from the map of Kirkenes he'd borrowed from the manager. A police officer stood in his hotel doorway. The manager stood behind him, looking anxious.

The policeman's gaze went to the Tokarev 7.62 pistol held loosely in Tom's hand, then to the Soviet rifle on the bed beside him, still wrapped in its white camouflage rags.

'Precautions,' Tom said.

The policeman's eyes widened.

'You didn't knock,' Tom explained. 'And I'd locked that door and you obviously have a key.' That was where the hotel manager came in, Tom imagined. 'How can I help?'

To give him his due, the policeman didn't falter. 'Professor Conway, I'm arresting you on suspicion of murder.'

Tom had a choice.

It took him less than a second to make it.

With a sigh, he jacked open the slide and ejected the round in the Tokarev's breech, catching it in mid-air. Dropping out the clip, he thumbed the unused round back into the magazine, locked the slide in the open position, and put the sidearm on his bed. 'Whose murder?' he asked.

'A Sami. In Tromso.'

'In Tromso?'

'Is there another I should know about?'

192

Tom thought of the old man crucified between trees and shook his head.

'I'll need your passport,' the policeman said.

'It's been stolen.'

'When?'

'Ask him.' Tom pointed to the hotel manager, who'd stepped right back at the sight of the Tokarev, and showed no sign of stepping forward again. The policeman ignored Tom's suggestion.

'You don't know when you were burgled?'

Tom had been careful not to take anything that could identify him into the USSR. Right down to cutting the labels from his clothes. Although those were so obviously Western, it would have made little difference if he'd been captured.

'I was out,' he said.

The afternoon smelled of drifting wood smoke. The yellowing light over the hotel's front door barely reached the steps. A lone snowplough was clearing a single strip down the middle of the road. It was not yet mid-afternoon, and already felt like midnight. Tom had no idea how they stood it.

'We'll walk,' the policeman said.

Tom slipped twice before he'd gone fifty paces. The second time it happened, the policeman uncuffed him. 'It's either that or freeze to death while you find your balance,' he said sourly.

His station was a rust-red hut lined with filing cabinets. A black heater pumped out warmth and paraffin fumes in equal measure. On a pinboard, along with yellowing posters about drink-driving, fishing licences and the value of vaccinations, was a brand new one of Tom. It was him, right enough. The name below was his current alias. His date of birth a lie.

Tom grinned.

There was no way Per's death merited that, poor bastard. But how better to focus the attention of local forces than an APB for murder? Someone in authority somewhere had been hoping for a sighting. 'My better side,' Tom said.

'Do I need to handcuff you again?'

Tom nodded to the poster of the fugitive Professor Conway. The number to be called if he was sighted. The promise of a reward. 'You'd need a crowbar to get me out of here.'

'Then I'd better tell Oslo you're here.'

Reaching into a steel box with 'TBK' stencilled on its side, he removed a heavy-looking telephone, hit the cradle a couple of times and listened for a connection, then spoke in rapid Norwegian. Whatever the reply, he didn't like it. He looked royally pissed off.

'He wants to speak to you.'

'Who does?'

'No idea.'

'Fox?' The man's voice had a Nordic lilt, but otherwise he spoke perfect English. A printer was running in the background and someone nearby was typing. This stopped the moment the person typing realised the other was on the phone.

'Yes,' Tom replied. 'Major Tom Fox.'

'Can I ask where you've been?'

'I went to see a friend. Unfortunately he was indisposed.'

'Seriously so?'

'Very seriously . . .'

'Your zoologist friend is still in Russia.'

'That's certain?'

'We watched her go. We know she has not come back. Phone home. Do it now.'

The line went dead and Tom was left with whispering static.

'You're not Professor Conway?' the Kirkenes policeman asked.

'Not any longer,' Tom said.

'His lordship's not here.'

The young woman on the London end of the connection sounded flustered, and not at all happy to hear who was calling. Not what Tom expected from one of his father-in-law's highly intelligent, highly educated, highly ambitious assistants.

'When's my father-in-law due back?'

'I'm not sure, sir.'

'Did he say where he was going?'

'He said . . . he said he was needed at home.'

Tom didn't like the sound of that at all.

'Is your husband there?'

All Tom got was icy silence.

'Elspeth . . . Lady Eddington. Can I speak to your husband?'

'Your own wife's funeral,' Elspeth Eddington said furiously. 'You couldn't even be bothered to turn up to your own wife's funeral. Where were you . . . ? Drunk in a gutter? In some whore's bed?'

'Elspeth. Please. My son might hear.'

'He's run away. A dead mother and a useless father. God, how can you possibly believe you're fit to look after that boy?'

'Run where?'

'The Natural History Museum.'

'Good God. Why?'

'Charles is bringing him back. Bloody useless man.'

It took Tom a moment to realise Elspeth Eddington meant him and not her husband.

'Marrying you was the worst thing my daughter did. She could have had anybody.'

'She chose me.'

'To spite us.' The telephone receiver went down with a bang, and when Tom turned he found the Norwegian policeman staring at him. It made him wonder how much the man had heard and understood.

52

The nasty man was here.

He was following Charlie. Charlie knew he was.

What he wasn't sure about was how the man knew he was in London. Perhaps he'd seen Charlie at Waterloo. Perhaps he'd been waiting at the station when Charlie joined the train. Perhaps he'd followed him from Grandpa's house. That thought made him shiver. Not as much as it should, though.

He wasn't good at recognising danger. Well, he could *recognise* it. He just wasn't very good at expressing it. Charlie sucked his teeth. He wasn't sure learning to feel what other people felt was going to be possible. He'd been trying really hard and it hadn't happened yet. 'Concentrate,' he told himself.

Charlie had caught sight of the man in a bakery window when he'd stopped to look at buns. It was his eyes. They were flat. Cruel. The kind that belonged to someone wicked enough to hurt cats. Charlie didn't dare look round and didn't know whether to go back to the Natural History Museum, which is what he'd been intending to do, or try to lose the man in a side street.

Becca would know.

He'd hoped Becca might appear but she didn't like crowds. She never had. Now he was alone on a busy pavement and getting frightened. Charlie knew he was getting frightened because his chest had tightened and he was finding it harder to breathe.

Fuck this, Dancer thought.

All these posh people, and not one of the muppets stopped to drop even 10p into his tin. It was shit living on the streets. This was meant to be a good site too. All these tourists. All these rich parents taking their kids to the museums. You had to be rich to take your kids to museums. Well, Dancer imagined so. His ma had never taken him anywhere near one. His da? His da died early. Killed in front of him.

Looking up, Dancer saw the kid.

He checked for the kid's parents and didn't see them.

There was a man behind the boy though, ten paces back and weaving through the crowd at speed, with the look of someone who thinks the city belongs to him. No awareness of pavement artists. No checks to see if he was being watched. The wee kid's jaw was tight, his face pale, and if he walked any faster he'd be running. Dancer knew exactly what fear looked like. He'd felt it, and he'd inflicted it.

Too much of it.

He was scrambling to his feet, wondering how best to handle this and knowing he'd probably just punch the pervert in the throat and be done with it: when he spotted a smart young woman cutting her way through the crowd towards the man. She'd seen what Dancer had seen. But she didn't stop when she reached the man, she kept going until she reached the boy, and put her hand on his shoulder, smiling kindly when he swung round, eyes wide with panic.

'Charlie Fox?' she asked.

The boy stared at her.

And Dancer took a longer look at the kid, matched him to a photograph of a funeral he'd torn from the previous week's

Evening Standard, and blinked. Charlie Fox, son of Tom Fox, grandson of Lord bloody Eddington. God indeed worked in mysterious ways.

'I'm from the embassy,' the woman whispered.

'Wax Angel's embassy?'

She nodded.

Charlie breathed a sigh of relief.

She moved Charlie aside so the nasty man could pass; and because he couldn't very well stop, he did. That was when the beggar with the straggly beard and tin cup in front of him sat back down again. He was staring at Charlie, and Charlie wondered if he knew the man from somewhere.

'We'd better hurry,' the woman said.

'Why?' Charlie asked.

'We don't want the café at the Natural History Museum to run out of cake.'

Well, Dancer would be fucked.

It really was the kid he'd seen in the *Standard*. In the photograph that showed Lord bloody Eddington standing by a grave. The wee boy beside him. Hampshire, the paper had said. It hadn't said where, though. Not that it mattered, Dancer could find out. An easy job for someone of his somewhat specialised experience.

Eddington was involved in the nastier end of British intelligence. Rumoured overlord of the bits Westminster denied, and would go on denying until the end of time. The bits that had seen cross and double-cross, bribery, blackmail, and morality-free handlers in Northern Ireland feeding Catholics to the Protestant paramilitaries, and occasionally the other way round.

Dancer hadn't always lived on the streets. No one on the

streets had always lived on the streets. People ended up there via bad luck, bad decisions, and occasionally because the anonymity it offered was the only thing keeping them alive.

Dancer had a family once.

A wife, a child, a house, a job.

His day job had been working the docks. His night job . . . His night job had brought him into conflict with bad men. There'd been a firefight and by the end of it, Dancer didn't have a wife and he didn't have a child and there was nothing in his house worth going back to. Now here was Eddington's grandson delivered on a plate. Until it arrived, Dancer hadn't even known this was the moment he'd been waiting for.

Charlie was sitting at a Formica table with half a bun, a mostly drunk glass of orange juice and what looked like a very expensive picture book about wolves in front of him. He was talking animatedly to a smart young woman in a black jacket, who pushed back her chair the moment Charlie Fox's grandfather appeared.

She clearly recognised him.

'Valentina knows Wax Angel,' Charlie said excitedly.

'I heard Madame Milova talk once about her experiences as a sniper in Stalingrad,' Charlie's companion said. 'I was very young.'

Eddington didn't bother to say the woman still looked young to him. He simply waited for her to finish extracting a slightly bent business card from her handbag.

Valentina Kosterova, it read.

'An aide at the Soviet embassy?'

Charlie opened his mouth to explain but the young woman beat him to it. 'I come here in my lunch hour,' she said, 'because I find natural history restful. I saw your grandson by himself and we got talking. About wolves. And snow. We have lots of wolves in Russia. Lots of wolves. Lots of forests. Lots of snow.'

Charlie grinned. Valentina was going to keep his secret. He wasn't sure she would, even though she'd promised not to get him into trouble. He liked her even more now he didn't have to tell Grandpa about writing to Wax Angel.

53

Wednesday 25th November – Lubyanka Square, Moscow

Sophia Petrovna's uniform was sea-foam green, her shoulder boards cornflower blue. Her cap had the red band of a general, as specified by the Presidium under its decree of June 1945. No one watching her step off the Moscow metro doubted for a second where she was headed.

None dared meet her eyes.

She had a 1985 ZIL saloon at her disposal, the latest model, but chose to travel by underground. That was her right. Her duty. The Moscow metro was a glory of the Motherland. An architectural triumph. Besides, she liked the effect her KGB uniform had on those around her.

It was fifty years since gutters had been installed in the prison floor on Lubyanka Square. They'd been needed to cope with the blood of traitors, recidivists and intellectuals executed to keep the Soviet Union safe. Then Stalin had died, and that had seen an end to traitors being shot on a regular basis. Five years ago the entire prison floor of the KGB HQ had been turned into a cafeteria. A decision that newly made general Sophia Petrovna considered disgusting. No wonder things were going to the dogs if those now in authority had so little respect for tradition.

Saluting the statue of Iron Felix, Sophia Petrovna turned back for an admiring look. Felix Dzerzhinsky had founded the Cheka, predecessor to both the KGB and the Vnutren-niye Voiska. Sophia owed her job to her father, whose father had known Felix himself. Her fiancé, may he rest peacefully in his grave, had been a Vnutrenniye Voiska rising star, whose father had known Iron Felix also.

It was Felix Dzerzhinsky who suggested turning Alexander Ivanov's ornate offices for the Tsarist All-Russia Insurance Company into the headquarters for a very different kind of insurance business. One dedicated to guaranteeing the safety of the new Soviet state. A job they still did. A job they would always do.

Striding towards the Lubyanka's great door, Sophia glanced at the huge banner of Lenin above, and her heart soared. This was her world. She would protect it.

'Rostov. Which floor?'

The lieutenant on the reception desk looked up and was saluting Sophia Petrovna before he even realised he'd jumped to attention.

Behind him, his chair clattered to the floor.

'Fourth, Comrade General.'

Sophia turned to go.

'He's . . .'

'What?' Sophia demanded.

'Sorry, Comrade General. Nothing, Comrade General.'

Sophia strode towards the lifts. There were three places in Moscow where the lifts could be relied on to work: the Kremlin, the House of Lions, which housed retired grand marshals of the Soviet Union, and here. Three officers stepped aside to let her enter. Sensibly they didn't try to follow.

There would be another lift. Let them take that.

'Rostov,' Sophia demanded again, stepping out of the lift.

The major, grizzled enough to pass for a bear and with a chestful of medal ribbons, took one look at Sophia's face and stopped what he was doing.

'This way, Comrade General.'

He led her through corridors Sophia half remembered. The All-Russia Insurance Building had always been maze-like, and while the redevelopments of 1947 and 1983 might have doubled its size, they did little to simplify its floorplan. The Lubyanka was a city inside a city. It always had been.

'Here, Madame.'

The major didn't try to follow.

'Rostov!'

A gaunt officer looked up from a desk so tidy Sophia wondered if he'd done anything in his first hour at work beyond arrange his fountain pens in a neat line.

'Look at you,' she said. 'You're dying.'

The man's face said he knew.

'And you're a fool. That explosion wasn't an accident. It was sabotage.'

'I was told—'

'You were told it was believed to be an accident. It was your duty to investigate. To discover the truth for the sake of the Motherland. You should have stayed. Examined the evidence. Meticulously. Not just tidied up and left.'

'Comrade General . . .'

'Sabotage,' Sophia said vehemently. 'By the West when we're at the very point of outdoing them. Minimal structural damage. High initial death-rate. Short half-life . . .'

She glared at him.

'We could clear Kabul in a day, send in clean-up squads and move the Red Army in a week or two later. This changes everything.'

'General . . .'

'The prototype still exists. We have reports that it has been offered for sale. It is my duty to stop it falling into American hands. Also, my duty to kill those who sabotaged the base and any who offer it for sale now.' She glared at him, and Rostov got the feeling she was seeing him properly for the first time.

For a second, her expression was almost sympathetic. Maybe she saw the man he'd been before the sickness set in. Maybe she saw her father. A great man torn apart by disappointment and pain. 'Go home,' she said. 'See your family. Say your goodbyes. Make peace with anybody you need to make peace with. And prepare to die.'

54

Thursday 26th November — Moscow

The marble foyer of Moscow's House of Lions near Patriarch Ponds was not somewhere Valentina Kosterova had
expected to find herself when she was sent after a worried
small boy in Kensington. But here she was, with instructions
to hand deliver the boy's letter. In an impossibly imposing
retirement home built by Wehrmacht prisoners, on Stalin's
orders, for marshals of the Soviet Union.

Well, the ones he hadn't killed.

Valentina glanced round. Suddenly worried that someone
might have overheard her thoughts. Her only companion
was a huge bust of Lenin on a green marble plinth, and he
looked as if he agreed with her. Ahead was a row of lifts.
Valentina had never been in a lift that had mahogany panelling, tiled floors, and an oil painting on its wall.

'Miss Kosterova?'

Valentina stepped out to find herself facing a bird-like
woman wearing a long black dress that looked far too well
made to be Soviet. 'Schiaparelli,' the woman said, seeing her
gaze.

She blushed.

'I'd have been cross if you hadn't noticed.'

Valentina hadn't met a living legend before.

'Don't look so impressed,' Maya Milova said. 'It doesn't
suit you. Now, I believe you have a letter for me . . . ?'

'Wax Angel?' Valentina asked apologetically.

Madame Milova smiled. 'So it's true then. You've met Charlie? He told you my nickname?'

Valentina nodded. Smiled in turn.

'Good. You've read his letter?'

'No, madame.'

'But someone has or you wouldn't be here.' Taking the envelope, Maya Milova looked impressed. 'Still sealed,' she said. 'No signs of having been opened. Very neatly done. Very neatly done indeed.'

Slitting it open, she read and reread its contents.

Valentina hadn't been there when the letter was steamed open, and a decision taken at ambassadorial level that passing it on as swiftly as possible might be best for all concerned, so she had no idea what it said. It had, however, been serious enough for Ambassador Zamyatin to tell her to get the next flight to Moscow and hand deliver it. Next flight, not next Aeroflot flight. It was clearly important. Ambassador Zamyatin was not fond of spending hard currency if he didn't have to.

A door twice as high and half as wide again as a normal door opened onto a decaying apartment full of oil paintings of battles, snow scenes and rolling plains. Every inch of the floor was covered with tatty rugs and heavy leather furniture that hadn't been in fashion for decades. An old man with an embroidered skull-cap was scowling at a huge samovar.

'It's empty.'

'Fill it then,' Wax Angel told him.

Valentina hesitated in the doorway.

'Come in then,' Maya Milova said tartly. 'He wants to meet you.'

'Sveta or Dennisov?' her husband asked, once the nervous girl was gone.

Wax Angel looked at him.

She adored the Commissar, which was how she still thought of him, even after all these years. Now he was cleanly dressed and his hair trimmed, he looked nothing like the lion-maned scarecrow he'd been back in the days when she was living on the street, and he'd only abandon his dacha to come into town grudgingly. To meet Sveta, his granddaughter, or to have his enemies shot. Wax Angel adored him. But he was so busy plotting that he didn't always pay attention to life.

'Sveta's pregnant,' she said shortly.

'No she's not,' he replied. 'She's had it.'

'Again.'

'How did that happen?'

Wax Angel snorted.

'Dennisov then,' Marshal Milov said.

Ivan Petrovich Dennisov was his granddaughter's would-be husband and the father of her first child. Apparently, soon to be father of her next one too.

'Don't get him killed,' Wax Angel warned.

Milov looked puzzled.

'Sveta would never forgive you.'

55

November 1971 – Derry, Northern Ireland

Major Tom Fox could remember when army surplus stores were popular. In the late sixties everyone had wanted those big greatcoats with the turned-up collars so they could look like the Beatles. Now that look was out of fashion and the Beatles had broken up, which was fine with Fox – he'd always been more of a Stones man.

The one he wanted was in a staunchly Protestant area, within walking distance of the Foyle, and almost in sight of St Columb's Park. An Indian restaurant, a funeral director and a sauna offering heavenly massages were its nearest neighbours. The massage parlour had a handwritten sign saying it was closed.

There was a rack of coats inside the window, and the usual motley collection of rotting gas masks, German helmets and worn boots. A Hitler Youth dagger, its handle inlaid with an enamel swastika, was visible under the counter's glass display. It looked too new, too shiny and too decorative to be real.

'Help you with anything?' a thickset man asked.

Fox nodded towards a vivid Red Hand of Ulster pennant hanging on the wall behind the man. 'Nice,' he said.

The man relaxed.

Credentials established, Fox drifted off to look at the displays. He was confident of his anonymity in a blue nylon windcheater, a benny hat, cheap aviators. He looked down-at-heel, a bit seedy, a bit unwashed. Like half the people in Derry really. The owner wouldn't remember him if anyone asked, not that anyone would.

Half a dozen bayonets rested on tatty velvet inside a battered display case.

'Okay to look?'

The man thought about coming to supervise, then shrugged. 'Help yourself,' he said. 'The top's not locked.'

The long bayonets were World War 1, the short ones World War 2. All MOD, except one with a paler olive scabbard.

American, Fox imagined.

'I've got these,' the man said. 'If you're interested.' He held up a couple of Iron Crosses.

Fox muttered appreciatively.

'What about this?' Fox picked up the biggest kukri he'd seen.

'World War 1,' the man told him. 'Battlefield issue. Take a man's head right off.'

Fox wrapped his fingers round its buffalo-horn handle and drew the blade. It was thick, and surprisingly heavy. He didn't doubt it could do what the man said.

'1917,' he said, reading the date.

'And the broad arrow.'

Fox nodded. It had the arrow mark indicating it was official government issue. Its sheath was wood, bound in pale leather, and looked newer.

'I'll take it,' he said.

'Let me wrap it,' the man said. 'You don't want trouble with the police.'

Fox agreed, he didn't. He paid the asking price without haggling, said his goodbyes, and bought a sharpening stone and a padlock elsewhere. His final purchase was a small bottle of Kensington Gore, from a theatrical shop halfway across the city. A mixture of syrup, water and food dye. It was indistinguishable from real blood, unless you decided to taste it.

Now to bait the trap.

56

Thursday 26th November – Kirkenes, Northern Norway

A knock at the door woke Tom.

If not for the digital clock by his bed reading 08:27, he wouldn't have known what time it was. His room was black, the sky beyond his blinds the darkest of greys. The only source of light was the green glow of the digits telling him he'd fallen asleep without realising it. Rolling off the bed, he headed for the door.

The worst thing about being trapped in Kirkenes was not drinking. Alcohol might just about have made this limbo life bearable. Then again, this was Norway, there was a distinct absence of a minibar in his bedroom, alcohol was prohibitively expensive, and some provinces were apparently still dry.

'You?' Tom was bemused.

He'd been expecting the hotel manager. He'd got the local policeman instead.

'There was a telephone call,' the man said tiredly. 'For you. It came into my station. They're calling back in five minutes.'

'Who is it?' Tom demanded.

The policeman shrugged.

Without handcuffs this time, Tom made it down the hotel's icy steps without falling. A couple of school kids on plastic skis glanced at the policeman and him, obviously wondering what was going on. That was it. Everyone else was safe inside their rust-red houses. Coffee and a hot breakfast in front of them, and shutters locked against the dark and cold if they had any sense.

'Eddington,' Tom's father-in-law announced, when Tom reached the phone.

'About bloody time. Did you find Charlie?'

There was silence.

'Is Charlie safe?'

'Yes,' Eddington promised. 'Safe. Unharmed. Entirely unconcerned. Probably buried deep in his bloody wolf book. How do you know about—?'

'I called your office. They said you'd gone home. I called the house. Elspeth wasn't happy to hear from me . . . She didn't tell you, did she?'

Eddington didn't answer.

'Sort it out,' Tom said furiously. 'Or bring me in from the cold.'

'Pretty glacial, I imagine.'

'For fuck's sake . . .'

'Christ, Tom. That was meant to be a joke. Do you know where he was? In the Natural History Museum having tea with a cultural aide from the Soviet embassy. Apparently she asked him where his parents were and he said his mother was dead, you were abroad, and his sister was dead too. Only Becca didn't like being dead very much. Although she liked it slightly more than being alive.'

'Oh God.'

'Quite. The Russian decided to babysit Charlie until a responsible adult arrived.'

'Do you believe that?'

'Not for a minute. Her name's Valentina Kosterova. I fed her through the machine. One of their rising stars. Shortly after leaving me, she caught a plane to Moscow.'

'What else?'

'She left a message saying she had Charlie with my office.'

'*She did what?*'

'She called her embassy from a telephone box at the museum, and they called my office. You can imagine how that went down.'

Eddington was talking too much, offering too much detail, and doing his best to appear relaxed. As if they were having a chat over a Glenfiddich in the Carlton, rather than talking down a bad line in different countries a thousand miles apart.

'What do you want?' Tom demanded.

'Tom. Please.'

'I know you,' Tom said. 'What do you want?'

'We have a situation,' Eddington said vaguely.

Now we get to it, Tom thought.

57

Thursday 26th November – Kirkenes, Northern Norway

Snow rose in a flurry. The air so thick with flakes that the descending helicopter made it look as if someone had picked up Kirkenes and shaken it like a snow globe. Half the town had turned out. In summer, maybe this pitch was used for football. For now it was an impromptu landing pad.

The first man off was MI6, someone Tom hadn't seen since Frankfurt the year before. He almost didn't recognise him.

'What are you?' Tom asked. 'The old bastard's bag carrier?'

'Something like that.' Peter glanced around. 'I see they're still sending you to all the best places. Must be pretty important if you rate your own helicopter.'

'Sod off.'

'Ditto.'

'Let's go inside,' Tom said.

'No time. Can't stay.'

'Okay. Better give me the bundle.' Tom was expecting a new passport, a new wallet, currency in two or three denominations, briefing papers to be burned after reading, possibly a pistol. The usual.

'I have to brief you first,' Peter said. 'And, before that, I need a rundown on what you've been doing for the last week. His lordship wants details.' He stepped back, indicating the helicopter. 'We'd best get airborne.'

'My things are at the hotel. All of them.'

'Anything you can't afford to lose?'

Tom shook his head.

'Didn't think so. Come on. We're cutting it fine as it is.'

He waved Tom into the helicopter and climbed up behind him. The local policeman didn't look sad to see them go.

'Take us up,' Peter told the pilot.

'Christ, you're lucky,' Peter said when Tom had finished filling him in on Tromso, Kirkenes and the cross-border jaunt. 'His lordship would have had to disown you if you'd been caught by the Ivans. London would have insisted.'

Tom shrugged. It hadn't occurred to him that Eddington wouldn't.

Leaning forward, Peter tapped the pilot on his shoulder. Tom heard *Mayday Mayday Mayday* a moment later. The international call for help.

'We're in trouble?' Tom asked.

Peter grinned. 'Engine failure. We're going down. Probably going to be a nasty landing. With luck, not *too* nasty.'

The helicopter felt fine to Tom.

'Not yet,' Peter said. 'Ten minutes from now. Fifty miles from here. Place called Ivalo.'

'Norway?'

Peter shook his head. 'Finland. All a bit embarrassing given this is a NATO helicopter and we'll have strayed into their neutral airspace.' Passing Tom a weird-looking viewer, with a full reel of Super 8 one side and an empty spool the other, he nodded to a pair of headphones. 'You'll need these too.'

Tom plugged them in.

'Ten minutes to bump-down and the tape lasts eight. You get one viewing. So concentrate . . . Don't look at me like that. Blame his lordship.'

Peter flicked a switch.

'What am I looking at?' Tom demanded.

'Foyer. British embassy. Helsinki. Yesterday. A walk-in. The cine-camera's in the wall beside the receptionist's shoulder. The microphone's in the bell push. That metallic strip on the opposite side to the film's perforations carries a soundtrack.'

58

Thursday 26th November – Finnish Airspace

Walk-ins were randoms claiming to offer intelligence. They were more common than the public thought, and rarely worth the effort spent investigating them. Invariably they wanted something in return.

Balancing the Super 8 viewer on his lap, Tom concentrated on the events unfolding on its little screen. A young woman on the reception desk of the British embassy in Helsinki was looking up from her typewriter and scowling. A civilian was pushing his way through revolving doors. A civilian being anyone not associated with the embassy.

'Can I help you?'

The man swayed slightly and Tom wondered if he was drunk. His greatcoat was tatty and he obviously hadn't shaved. He gripped the counter to steady himself.

For a second, he hesitated.

Then he drew himself up and made his decision. Tom could see in his ruined face traces of the man he must have been before hunger or illness hollowed him out. 'I am Sergei Rostov,' he said. 'Sergei Mikhailovich Rostov, Colonel, KGB. I am dying. Radiation sickness. I have information of great value. You would be wise to listen.'

To her credit, the receptionist barely blinked.

'If you'd wait here, sir.'

The man watched her leave.

He glanced slightly nervously at the revolving door, as if

wondering whether he was visible to passers-by on the street, but didn't move out of its line of sight. Tom noticed how tightly his fingers gripped the counter.

Anxiety, or the effort of holding himself up?

'If you'd come with me, sir?'

The next camera was also hidden. Colonel Rostov, if that was his real name, showed no awareness of being filmed. Although he glanced once round the small room as if looking for microphones, and dipped his head to look for them under the table too. He'd just straightened up when someone knocked at the door.

Tom liked the knocking. That was a nice touch.

'Ah, Colonel ... Rostov.' The young man who'd just entered hesitated slightly at the name. As if he too wasn't certain it was real. 'I'm told you wished to speak to me.'

'You are ... ?'

'Jamie Giles. I'm—'

'The cultural attaché? Isn't that what London usually calls its local spy-masters?'

'Actually,' Giles said, 'these days we're as likely to be billed as trade. Sadly, money opens more doors than art in these benighted times.'

Rostov smiled. 'Here,' he said, placing a KGB identity card, Party membership card, driving licence and Soviet passport on the table.

'All of these can be faked,' Giles said.

'Of course. I've issued fakes of all these in my time.'

'You don't mind if I ... ?'

Rostov sat back and watched in sour amusement as Jamie Giles photographed the military ID, the driving licence, the Party card, and every page of the passport.

'You'll find them real.'

'I already know they're real,' Giles replied. 'HQ has a file on you as fat as a paperback from your time in London. They faxed me a photograph while you were waiting.'

He put the fax in front of Rostov, who peered at it closely.

'You're younger, obviously.'

'Also, not dying.' Rostov pushed the fax back and scooped up his documents. Jamie Giles made no attempt to stop him. 'I have radiation poisoning from an explosion at a research station in the Arctic. Take too long to make up your mind about trusting me and you'll be too late.'

'There was an accident?'

'Sabotage,' Rostov said. 'Apparently.'

'What are you offering up and what do you want in return?'

They'd got to the nub of it and Rostov's relieved expression said he was glad the fencing had stopped. He sat back, his shoulders relaxing slightly.

'Can I get you water?' Giles suddenly asked.

Rostov shook his head. 'It hurts to swallow. It hurts to do pretty much anything. Let's get this done while there's still time.'

'Let's.' Lifting a Sony cassette recorder from his briefcase, Giles put in a brand-new cassette, and pressed record and play. 'You're on,' he said.

'This is to do with Midnight Sun . . .'

Giles opened his mouth to ask a question and Rostov held up his hand.

'I'm offering you my notes of what happened on the Kola Peninsula. The recordings from a US drone downed over the site. And the plans themselves.'

'Midnight Sun is a weapon?'

'Beyond anything the West has developed. Close to full non-residual radiation. Or so the scientists at the Institute of Experimental Physics promise us.'

Jamie Giles' eyes widened. 'A neutron bomb?'

'In return,' Rostov said, 'I want ten million dollars in used notes and safe passage to London for my teenage daughter.' He pulled out his wallet and extracted a tatty photograph of a girl whose fair hair fell in plaits either side of her slightly round face.

'She was twelve then. She's older now,' Rostov said. 'Fifteen.' He sighed. 'No more smocks. And she's cut her hair.'

'Tell me more about Midnight Sun.'

Rostov shook his head, his mouth setting in a stubborn line. 'I want to meet the man who will collect my daughter and take her to safety in London. No more answers until he and I meet.'

'Why not take this to the Americans?'

'I don't trust them.'

'But you trust London?'

'Over Washington? Every time.'

The film cut off and Tom put the viewer down. His head ached from watching the shuddering little screen. Something worried him about that conversation. He couldn't put his finger on what. He would, though. Given time.

'One extra thing . . .'

Wasn't there always?

'You're going to need this,' Peter said. He pushed a bulky envelope into Tom's hand, and Tom recognised his father-in-law's handwriting.

'This is from Eddington, obviously. If you get your hands on the plans you're not to let go. They mustn't fall back into the hands of the Soviets.'

'You *know* about the plans?'

'Plans for what? Of course I bloody don't. I'm just delivering a message . . . It could be for a chocolate-making machine for all I know. Now, buckle up and hold tight. We're

221

putting in a final distress call. And then we're going down. We don't want you breaking anything too early.'

The engine shut off, the overhead rotor lost lift and the tail rotor stilled. In the sudden silence that followed, the helicopter fell the last twenty feet and thudded to the ice of a little lake. An echoing boom said its surface had cracked beneath them.

Added realism.

59

November 1971 – Derry, Northern Ireland

Patched jeans, long hair, Jesus sandals and patchouli. A pair of unlikely Derry hippies were making out between the bins of a tenement on Strand Road, just down from the round-about. The bins stank and vile liquid from beneath was threatening to reach their feet. They both noticed Tom, but only for as long as it took to check he wasn't police.

Suppressing a smile, Tom limped on.

He was pleased with his limp. Mostly because it looked like something he was trying to hide, rather than something he was putting on. As he headed down Strand Road towards the burger bar and wine lodge, he thought about what he'd seen. How desperate did you have to be for privacy for a slot between bins to be your best option? No better than his child-hood. No worse either. Just different.

The bars that caged those kids weren't his.

His had been literal, black-painted bars set into the stone sills of a boarding school for children of problem parents, which was where he'd ended up. Before that he'd been a squaddie's brat, dragged from pillar to post. His dad had come south, got a local girl pregnant and married her. The man would have been happier, and his mum safer, if he'd simply done a runner. Instead, Tom was born dead at a mili-tary hospital in Cyprus, and kickstarted back to life with a slap from a corporal in the Nursing Corps who decided she had nothing left to lose by trying.

Glancing behind him, Tom saw the kids by their bins, still doing the things kids that age did. They wouldn't remember him.

It was best for everyone they didn't.

The multi-storey car park Tom was heading for had a ground level, four floors above that, and a half-sized basement level reserved for the high heid yins of the city council. Its ramp, which took vehicles in both directions, had been cast as a single twist of concrete. In the year it was built, it won three major architectural awards. That was before cracks appeared, pillars started rotting and chunks began falling off. Two expensive attempts at repairs later, the multi-storey was closed, barely ten years after it opened.

Now it lay abandoned, destined for demolition and re-development by a council that seemed in no hurry to do either. Part pillared maze, part rat-trap, it had taken Tom weeks to find, and as much time again to formulate a plan and bait his trap for the rats he was after.

Pulling a quart of motor oil from his coat, Tom splashed it along the runner of the entrance grill at the open mouth of the ramp. That done, he took a beer crate from outside a seedy-looking discotheque opposite and used it to reach the upper runner, splashing oil along it too.

He needed the grill to open and shut silently.

Nobody passed while he was doing this; and if they had? Well, he was wearing a blue donkey jacket of the kind worn by council workmen. He was returning the beer crate when he saw a packing case. It was wooden and half rotten. One side kicked in and rusty nails showing. Tom smiled. It wasn't a kind or easy smile.

Having checked the coast was still clear, he ripped the

crate apart, chose the pieces with the longest nails and deposited them inside the entrance to the multi-storey.

He'd be needing them later.

Taking the four flights of stairs at a steady trot, Tom stepped out onto the multi-storey's roof to be greeted by fading parking lines, a rusting ticket machine and a lowering Derry sky that was readying to rain. Its default setting these days.

Having prised open the lift doors, he cut the thin, high tensile wire designed to keep the doors closed, ducking when it pinged like a snapped guitar string. It was a long drop to where a broken cage waited at the bottom. Now for the door down there too.

He cut its identical wire, checked the doors now opened and shut easily, and removed the lift's ceiling hatch. Seeing daylight show through open doors four floors above.

The rest was housekeeping.

The planks from the broken crate he hid on top of the lift cage, nail-side down for now. He slid the kukri from the army surplus store into a gap above a concrete beam dotted with bulkhead lights and running the length of the ceiling. The bottle of Kensington Gore he tucked into the flatbed of an abandoned truck on the ground floor. The padlock he hooked through the grill without locking it. When Tom left, it was in a different direction, donkey jacket now discarded.

He no longer walked with a limp.

60

Thursday 26th November – Kemijärvi, Finland

The man shuffling into Kemijärvi Station three hours after a NATO helicopter crashed 200 miles north had his collar up and his head down against wind that threatened to go right through him. If doing both of those also hid his face from view that was fine.

Major Tom Fox was blending in.

The station at Kemijärvi was a low pink building, boring enough to be a Home Counties bungalow if not for snow two feet thick on its pantiled roof. Half a dozen Finns waited impatiently on its poorly lit platform, deep in their own thoughts. The weather this November was brutal even for Finland.

No one even glanced at Tom.

We've booked you onto the sleeper to Helsinki.

Eddington's letter made it sound civilised. As if the Helsinki sleeper was the Scandinavian equivalent of the Orient Express. To judge by the pinched faces and drab clothes of those around him, Tom doubted it.

Getting here had taken three hours in a taxi, a conversation in broken Russian and most of Tom's Finnish cash. The only good thing about the hard landing was the burst helicopter door, which let him use the snow it threw up to roll out of sight of the shore. By the time the Finnish police decided the ice was safe for their car and the ambulance they'd sent for just in case, Tom was long gone. Air traffic control had been told two men were in that helicopter and two men was what they found.

An announcement burbled over the station tannoy. As tinny and incomprehensible as station address systems anywhere in the world. A minute later the sleeper appeared and Tom headed down the platform to find his carriage. Five men and one woman got on. None showed any interest in him.

A bunk with a duvet and two pillows, and a wash basin. Tom opened what he thought was a cupboard and found a lavatory inside. Presumably, booking him into first class meant Eddington felt guilty. Tom hoped so. The bloody man deserved to be racked with guilt.

Having shaved, washed, and bound the knee he'd twisted on landing, Tom headed for the restaurant car. He was the only passenger eating.

Since Tom understood no Finnish, the elderly waitress removed the menu card she'd brought for him and made her own choices. A hot pastry to start, topped with a mixture of butter and chopped egg, followed by a bowl of carrots, onions, potatoes and what might have been steaming chunks of beef. She gave him a little round sponge cake topped with icing and pulped berries to finish. Tom wolfed it all down with such enthusiasm she forgave his ignorance of her language.

Back in his berth, he bolted the door, stripped to his briefs and fell back on his mattress; grateful to be the still point in a swiftly moving train.

How much more of his life did he have to live before he would face the fact he kept moving because he didn't know how to stay still? That he'd built his life around a job he professed to hate because it gave him a reason for existing? When Caro, Becca and Charlie should have been reason enough, and would have been if he'd been brave enough to let what happened to him in that school go.

Dozing in the darkness, listening to the wind rattle the door of his compartment, Tom asked himself what he'd need to do to turn his life around. Like firm answers, sleep eluded him. All he had was the whine of the wheels, and the growl of a diesel dragging his night express south through the snows of central Finland.

Maybe they were running old rolling stock that week.

Maybe the Night Express still had to be updated. But his compartment walls were wood, and his ill-fitting window let in a draught so fierce that what passed for the heater stood no chance. Pulling his duvet tighter, Tom finally began to drift off to sleep. And hesitated on the precipice edge.

His door had stopped rattling . . .

61

Friday 27th November – Central Finland

Snapping awake, Tom opened his eyes in time to see a shadow slide through his closing door. Two steps brought it closer, a knife stabbed down and Tom flung up his arm just in time to block the blade. Gripping his attacker's wrist, he twisted and heard a grunt of pain. Tom forced himself upright and struck for his attacker's throat, losing his grip on the man's wrist as he jerked away.

A shadow, if barely. No light reflecting off the blade.

No light to reflect, come to that. Tom's attacker was still in the compartment. Having lost his element of surprise, he planned to wait Tom out. He needed Tom to make the next move. Make the next move and make a mistake.

Tom steadied his breathing.

He let his heart settle. Excitement and fear are inextricable, and both are as addictive as amphetamine in their way, but he needed stillness. He tried to listen for movement, for the sound of his attacker's breath, but all he could hear was the creak of wooden walls and the hammering of steel wheels on the track below. And then, as the Night Express raced through a small town and light suddenly showed from behind the blinds, he spotted the assassin by the window.

Launching himself from the bed, Tom grabbed at his knife hand. The answering head butt might have broken Tom's nose but caught his cheek instead. It hurt like fuck all the same. Keeping his attacker's knife trapped, Tom swung his elbow into the man's jaw, feeling him stumble and pull free.

Tom flicked on a light, blinked.

The woman he faced was young, crop-haired and whip-cord thin. A scar across her right eye twisted her face slightly. The sourness of her smile said she knew exactly why he was surprised. As swiftly as he flicked the light on, she smashed the bulb with her hand and threw their fight back into darkness.

Tom twisted, and her blade slipped by.

He blocked, jabbed for her throat and backed away. He was being herded into the corner, and if he let that happen, his actions would become defensive and this would all be over. She was younger, faster, fitter. The odds weren't in his favour. It was a hell of a time to regret not going back to his hotel in Kirkenes for the pistol.

Reaching behind him, Tom felt for something to use as a weapon. All he found was the built-in basin, and that was screwed tightly to the wall; then his other hand found the windowsill, and he swung on his hands, his double-footed kick catching her gut and driving her into the door, which burst open with a bang.

Barrelling her into the dimly lit corridor beyond, he blocked a slash to his throat, took the blade on his forearm and gasped as it bit bone. Grabbing her knife wrist, he pivoted to grip the same wrist with his other hand and twisted, his movement fluid and brutal.

He caught her knife as it fell, and drove it hard into her guts.

The woman grunted in shock, winded.

The blade had been blocked by body armour. The next time Tom stabbed, she was ready. A straight-fingered blow froze his arm. Her knife clattered to the floor and Tom kicked it away before she could grab for it. For a split second, her eyes flicked away from him. Something was coming.

Had her Muay Thai jump-kick connected he'd have been down; unquestionably unconscious, quite possibly dead. But the slight telegraphing was warning enough. Instead of blocking, he dropped under the kick, driving his fist up hard. He got in a second strike before she went down, her head hitting the floor.

Dragging her back to his compartment, he smothered his would-be murderer with a Finnish Railways goosedown pillow and began going through her inside pockets. A KGB card. A wallet stuffed with roubles, US dollars and Finnish markka. A photograph of a soft-faced, sensitive-looking young man. Tom looked at the dead woman and had trouble imagining them together.

Her oversized leather jacket was interesting. Reversible, black or white, lined with what looked – from the cut Tom had put in it – like chainmail but felt ceramic. The jacket wasn't light, but good leather is always heavy and the mesh added protection for surprisingly little extra weight.

Tom brought an ex-biker's eye to things.

He tried it on for size and liked it. There were zipped pockets either side. One was empty, the other held photographs, and Tom felt his chest tighten. The first was him in Regent Street. The second Amelia at Patriarch Ponds in Moscow. The third had Amelia in a ruined village, staring at the sky.

Having returned wallet, KGB card and photographs to their pockets, Tom retrieved the knife from the corridor floor, checked the coast was clear, and opened the train's door. Ignoring the snow that swirled in, he threw the body through it.

62

Friday 27th November – Hampshire

Charlie was in trouble.

He knew that before Mrs Ross even told him he was wanted in the big drawing room. Usually she was smiling when she came to find him. This time she looked serious.

Granny and Aunt Agatha sat side by side.

Grandpa's big red chair was empty because he was in London. Something was happening and Charlie wasn't allowed to know what. Nobody was.

He wished Grandpa was here.

'This isn't a smiling matter,' Aunt Agatha snapped.

'What isn't?' Charlie asked.

Granny said, 'Grandpa's rabbit rifle is missing.'

'Perhaps he took it with him.'

'Don't be ridiculous.'

'I'm not.' Charlie couldn't see what was ridiculous about that at all. The .22 rifle that Grandpa kept in the corner of his study wasn't here and neither was Grandpa. It seemed obvious to Charlie that one might be connected to the other.

'Have you asked him?' Charlie asked politely.

'Oh good God,' Aunt Agatha said. 'Are you entirely sure the boy is normal?'

Granny shot her a look. That was unusual.

Aunt Agatha was Granny's older sister and had a title. She also had the house Granny grew up in. Grandpa had once said Granny and Aunt Agatha didn't really like each other.

232

Charlie thought that strange because they spent lots of time together. Mind you, Grandpa and Granny didn't like each other either and they were married.

'Are you listening?' Granny's voice was sharp.

Charlie looked up guiltily.

He had orders not to touch the rabbit rifle and he didn't. At least not very often and only when grown-ups weren't around. He'd taken it apart once to see how it worked and whether he could put it back together. He could. It was hard, but no harder than a thousand-piece jigsaw. The rifle had a five-round magazine holding very small bullets. Their brass bits were shiny, which meant they were new. The rocket-shaped bits he could scratch with his fingernail . . .

'I said . . . *Did you take it?*'

'No,' Charlie said. 'Of course not.'

'She's going to call the police,' Aunt Agatha warned him.

'It should have been in his gun cupboard,' Granny said crossly. 'That's what the police will say. They'll be right too. Oh God, what if the bloody papers find out?'

She was talking to Aunt Agatha obviously.

'I didn't take it,' Charlie promised.

'Don't lie,' Aunt Agatha said.

'I don't lie,' Charlie said. 'I never lie. Mummy said my life would be easier if I did.'

Being sent to his room was new.

Mummy didn't do it. Charlie couldn't remember Daddy doing it either; but then Daddy was mostly away working until Mummy got ill, so that didn't count. He had to stay there until he decided to tell the truth, Granny said. Since he was telling the truth already, he imagined he'd be there for ever.

Trousers, two shirts, three pairs of socks, his toothbrush.

Running away was like packing for school, except the clothes list was shorter, he didn't need his trunk and he didn't have to pack games stuff. That was good. He hated games. On his way out, Charlie stopped on the darkened half-landing to touch the huge kukri for luck. It was dated 1917, hung on the wall and had a broad arrow stamped on it to say it belonged to the King. Granny told people they inherited it from Grandpa's father, who'd brought it back from the Western Front.

Charlie knew that wasn't true.

Daddy put it there. Mummy hadn't been pleased.

Charlie was in the kitchen making cheese sandwiches for later, in case he got hungry, when Cat wandered in demanding his share. Charlie decided he'd better pack Cat too.

63

November 1971 – Derry, Northern Ireland

'I don't kill him,' Vince said. 'You don't kill him either.' He sounded regretful. 'Not before Himself's had a word.'

'You sure Fox will be here?' Jimmy asked.

'I'm telling you so.'

'Himself said?'

Vince sucked his teeth. Told Jimmy to fasten his denim jacket, lace his boots tighter and pull his hat low. This was the first time Jimmy had seen Vince since that day in prison. He'd picked Jimmy up at the pub where he was living with Judy these days. Jimmy wished he felt a bit less guilty about that. She must know he'd be moving on.

Vince was older than Jimmy remembered. Late forties? Old, anyway.

'You can tell me,' Jimmy protested.

'Jesus, Mary and Joseph,' Vince said. 'Why am I doing this again?'

'Himself's orders.'

'And why's Himself bothering with the likes of you?'

It was a real question. One that Jimmy knew required an answer. Himself was one of the big beasts, and it was the nature of things he'd have disciples, acolytes and hangers-on. It was also the nature of things that he barely bothered to acknowledge them. What made this particular long-haired, skinny kid in a denim jacket different?

'I did a job.'

'Plenty of us done jobs.'

'It was messy. The Specials grabbed me.'

'You didn't talk?'

'You saw me. Remember?'

'Dozens been messed up worse.'

'Six days they had me,' Jimmy said. 'I wore gloves though, didn't I? Ditched the pistol and collected the brass. They couldn't make anything stick. Fuck knows they tried.'

'That's it?'

'I'm friends with Judy.'

'And you still have your balls? Your legs are still unbroken? Christ, he must really like you. Come on then . . .'

'This UFF prick. Does he have a name?'

Vince shook his bull-like head. 'Leave it,' he said crossly.

'But he's a nasty piece of work?'

'He is that.'

'So we kill him too?'

'Not our job. Not today.'

Jimmy opened his mouth and Vince held up his hand. 'We let them talk. We kidnap Fox. We let the other cunt leave. That's how this works. You don't have the balls for it? Fine. Fuck off.'

They'd reached a multi-storey, deserted from the look of it. Lights were on in the street behind, cars splashing past. Just another winter day in Derry, where it rains as often as not. Half the kids huddled in doorways in denim, making out or smoking, the other half, barely older, dressed in fatigues, carrying rifles and failing to hide their jumpiness. If nothing else, the drizzle should keep tonight's trouble to a minimum. Jimmy was glad for that. The last thing he and Vince needed was the RUC or soldiers setting up roadblocks.

'Your rules,' Jimmy said.

Vince nodded. 'My rules.'

64

Friday 27th November – Helsinki, Finland

Helsinki's Café Aalto had clean lines, chrome rails and enamel lights that hung low over surgically white Formica tables. Situated on the mezzanine of the Akateeminen Kirjakauppa bookstore on Keskuskatu, it looked down on the shelf-filled, hangar-like well of Helsinki's biggest bookshop and felt to Tom like the set of an avant-garde 1960s film. The kind with no plot, but plenty of foreign awards.

A Caro kind of film.

When he thought of cafés, he thought of the ones she'd introduced him to. All gilt and velvet, offering hot chocolate, expensive coffee, and cakes with cream. The grand, haut bourgeois meeting places beloved of Paris, Vienna, Venice and Berlin. Haut bourgeois was what Caro called them.

She didn't even mean it as an insult.

This was something else entirely. A bright Scandinavian temple to sharp-edged modernism and minimalist design. If he hadn't been meeting his local handler, he'd have found somewhere he felt more at home.

'Ah. Max. There you are . . .'

A smart young woman waved from a table by the balcony, standing slightly when he reached her. Tom did a double-take as she pulled a fat file from a briefcase. 'Last week's political press,' she muttered. 'We subscribe to Durrants, the cuttings service. Not entirely sure why. The ambassador never reads them. Still, they'll make us look convincingly business-like.'

She pushed her card across the table.

It gave her name as Emma McCoy and her Glaswegian accent suggested that might even be real.

'Trade?' Tom asked.

'Of course.' Emma raised her voice. 'You're here to buy Finnish vodka, after all. Well, your company wants to import it. My job is to help that happen.' She smiled breezily at the man taking a seat at the next table. He flushed and shifted himself, his coffee and that day's edition of *Helsingin Sanomat* to the one beyond.

'Someone you know?' Tom muttered.

'Supo like to keep an eye on us. Luckily, they really do think I'm trade. And their government is desperate to export vodka. So we'll probably be left in peace. Poor bastards, I wouldn't want the Soviets as my neighbours either.'

Straightening her leg, she nudged a holdall towards Tom.

'There you go,' she muttered. 'Ten million in US notes. One use for the diplomatic bag, I suppose. In return, London gets the plans, the Geiger counter from the downed drone, and Rostov's daughter. Exchange takes place twelve noon tomorrow. Across the Sound.'

'Across the what?'

'In Tallinn. Across the water. From the moment you board the ferry, you're Finnish, off to take in the sights . . . No worry,' she added, 'thousands of Finns make the trip every year. Your ticket's for a three-hour, two-way booze cruise, with time for lunch and an hour's sightseeing either side.'

'I'll need to buy Rostov's daughter a ticket.'

'You won't.' She pushed the folder across. 'It's in here.

Also, a passport. A Finnish paperback. A girl's purse for her to carry. A faked photograph of you together . . .'

'You have a picture of her?'

Emma looked at him. 'It's a random wee child. London took your face from the files. Pretty good for a rush job.'

She leant closer.

'You watched the tape?'

Tom nodded. He was finding it hard to forget the bloody thing. Colonel Rostov's eyes were those of a man staring death and disgrace in the face. Whatever had happened on the Kola Peninsula, the grim reaper was closing in on Rostov, and Tom wasn't surprised the man was in a hurry to get his daughter to safety.

'About that,' Emma said.

Here it came.

'Your priority is the plans. The Nuclear Weapons Authority at Aldermaston are desperate to get their hands on them. Next, the Geiger counter from the drone. We want the readouts. Getting the girl out comes . . .'

'What are you saying?' Tom asked.

Emma's gaze was unflinching. 'If there's any trouble, Rostov's daughter is the first thing you sacrifice. Right. Any problems on your way down?'

'Someone tried to kill me.'

The young woman's eyes widened.

Tom watched her think this through. Decide she didn't like it.

'No one was meant to know you were on that train.'

'Quite,' Tom said.

'What happened?'

'I threw her off.'

'Any idea who *she* was?'

Emma didn't like that the would-be assassin had been female any more than Tom did, he could hear it in her voice. He thought of the KGB card. The photograph of Amelia, and the street-shot of him in central London. He wasn't sure how much he trusted anyone these days.

'Not a clue,' he replied.

65

Saturday 28th November – Hampshire

The sun was almost up, the boy from the village shop had been to deliver the papers, and the cows in the big field had been taken in for milking.

Charlie smelled the man before he saw him. He thought it was a fox at first. Foxes smell like sour pee. This was not that though. This was more sweat and dog dirt and the urinals from his previous school.

The man was on his hands and knees behind the old barn beyond the paddock. The one that was falling down and Charlie wasn't allowed to go inside. There was a thin trickle of saliva the consistency of glue running from the man's mouth to a puddle between his hands. He was staring at the yellowy puddle as if surprised it was there.

'You,' the man said, looking up.

'Me what?' Charlie asked.

He tried not to sound offended in case that was rude. The man had long straggly hair parted in the middle, and a face that hadn't quite made up its mind whether to have a beard or not. Close to, he wasn't as old as Charlie thought, and Charlie had a feeling he'd seen him before. The rifle next to him Charlie definitely recognised.

'That's Grandpa's!' he said, outraged.

'It's mine.'

'No,' Charlie said. 'It's not.'

When the man doubled over, Charlie decided the rifle could wait.

'Are you ill?' he asked.

The man grunted and Charlie wasn't sure if that was a yes or a no. The vomit obviously wasn't a good sign, and he was very thin and there was sweat on his face, which suggested he had a temperature. Also, his face was filthy.

'You need a bath,' Charlie told him.

The man glared.

'It's not your fault,' Charlie said hastily. 'You probably haven't been anywhere that has baths.' He tipped his head sideways, thinking.

'You look like Jesus.'

'I am Jesus.'

'No you're not,' Charlie said. 'And that was a stupid film.'

The man's mouth twisted. '*Whistle Down the Wind*,' he said. 'Alan Bates and Hayley Mills. Watched it once with my nan.'

Nan meant gran, Charlie knew that.

Charlie bit his lip and considered what to do next. He couldn't take the man back to the house because, one, he was running away, and two, Granny wouldn't let the man in anyway.

'You're running away?' the man said, when Charlie explained this. 'Why? What are you running away from?'

'I'll tell you another time,' Charlie said. That was what Mummy always said when he asked a question she didn't want to answer.

'You haven't run very far.'

'I know,' Charlie said miserably. 'But I have to wait for Cat.'

'The cat?'

'No *the*. Just Cat. He's running away too.'

'He's probably back at the house.'

Charlie shook his head. 'I locked his window and I have all his food. I promised Daddy I'd take care of him.'

'Daddy's not home?'

'No,' Charlie said. 'He's in Russia.'

'And you're here . . .' the man said thoughtfully.

He had two old coins on a string round his neck. When he saw Charlie notice, he tapped them. 'They're my conscience,' he said. Which made no sense at all.

Charlie decided he couldn't keep thinking of the man as 'the man'. So he gave his own name, and put out his hand.

The man took it. 'I'm Dancer,' he replied.

66

Saturday 28th November – Gulf of Finland

Tom didn't doubt that getting out of Tallinn would be harder than getting in, but he still felt his guts tighten as he dropped his key into a slot on the empty reception desk of his hotel behind Helsinki's Orthodox cathedral, and headed downhill towards the quayside and the day's booze cruise.

The MS *Georg Ots*, which sailed daily between Helsinki and Tallinn, had all the charm of the Dover–Calais Channel ferry, for all it was named after a famous Estonian baritone and featured daily ballroom dancing to a live orchestra.

The sea was slate-grey and sullen. The wind had those waiting to board hunching their shoulders and turning their backs. And yet, for a dark, bitterly cold weekend in November the *Georg Ots* was surprisingly popular. At least fifty cars and a dozen trucks waited to board, and the queue for foot passengers filled the gangway ahead of Tom, and soon stretched for a hundred paces behind him.

Clutching his cheap nylon holdall, he waited impatiently for his turn. Inside his holdall, $10 million in high-denomination notes hid below a black suit jacket, yesterday's edition of *Hufvudstadsbladet*, Finland's Swedish-language paper, that month's Swedish edition of *Playboy*, random dirty washing, and a litre bottle of vodka.

Presenting his ticket to a harassed woman, Tom stood

silently while she checked his face against a fake Finnish ID and matched his name to the ticket.

'Move along,' she ordered.

The engines rumbled, the steel deck shook and the 12,666-ton vessel backed from its concrete berth and began a lumbering turn towards the fifty miles of grey sea separating neutral Finland from Moscow-ruled Estonia. Seagulls screamed overhead as the gangway was dragged free by a tractor and left beside a redbrick warehouse. He was on his way. Shaking the tension from his shoulders, Tom lit a Klubi cigarette so raw it made him cough, watched gulls fight for scraps and did his best to look like no one very much.

An announcement in Estonian, followed by one in Finnish, sent passengers scurrying to the stern, and Tom followed the crowd as it flooded down steel stairs into a huge lounge below. The table holding that day's buffet stretched across a far wall. Those who'd made the trip before were down there already, plates in hands as they helped themselves to slices of sausage and cheese, smoked herring and rye bread, and cucumber and tomato. A woman brought out a huge metal tray of hot pastries filled with rice and carrot and they vanished within seconds.

Tom managed to grab two.

It was forty-eight hours since he'd eaten properly, and his brief stop at Café Aalto had taken in a single espresso and a cardamom bun. Having finished one plateful of food, he went back for more. By the time he reached the table the second time round, most of the passengers had long since finished and headed for the dance floor. Stopping off first for vodka or *shampanskoye*, Soviet champagne.

Three hours later, with Estonia in sight, the number of

Finns able to walk in a straight line had halved; and Tom was wondering how most were going to get down the gangplank safely, never mind round Tallinn and back to the ferry for their trip home.

'Stolichnaya,' Tom demanded.

The barman looked at Tom and decided he was drunk enough to overcharge, giving him back a handful of Soviet kopeks for the Finnish markka he'd pushed across.

Carrying his Stoli back to the table, Tom upended the vodka into his mouth without swallowing, and banged his glass down. In the gents, which stank of piss, alcohol and vomit, Tom stepped in sick, dripped half his vodka down his chin, gargled the rest and spat it into a basin. Not drinking it was one of the hardest things he'd ever done. Getting out of East Berlin included.

The green-uniformed Soviet customs officer looked at Tom's Finnish ID and then jerked her chin at his tatty hold-all. Tom swayed slightly. Only slightly, because he didn't know how drunk was too drunk to be let in. The woman's nose had already wrinkled as he stepped up to her counter, and she'd stepped back when he breathed vodka at her.

She barked something in Finnish.

Hoping it was 'Open your case,' Tom lifted it noisily onto the counter.

Dragging the bag towards her, she removed its bottle of Finlandia and the newspaper under that, then peered at the *Playboy* beneath. She stared at him.

Tom stood, shame-faced.

Pulling out the magazine, she flipped it open and examined a centrefold, her mouth wasp-like with disgust. She pushed aside the black jacket below, found Tom's cheap white shirt, and pushed that aside to find a vest beneath. Dirty this time.

Tom could feel sweat bead under his arms. Now was when

246

things could go wrong. Badly wrong. No excuse or cover story would get him out of this if she dug further. The penalty for currency smuggling was death. No exceptions.

But the woman had had enough.

Putting the vodka under her counter, she tossed his *Playboy* into the bin and jerked her head towards the exit. Tom went, not even bothering to close the holdall.

He was through.

67

Saturday 28th November – Tallinn, Soviet Estonia

Tallinn's best restaurant was not for everyone. If you hadn't booked, your chances of getting a table on the twenty-second floor of the Hotel Viru were non-existent. It was as well the lift worked. Tom hadn't fancied arriving out of breath, having dragged $10 million up twenty-two floors. He'd stopped off first at a public lavatory to wash the ship's vomit from his shoes, rinse the vodka from his mouth and swap his leather jacket for the black one he hoped would be smart enough to gain entry.

Politicians from the local soviet, Party members, rich tourists, Western businessmen on buying trips . . . The restaurant smelled of fried meat, human warmth and faint despair. Unless that was just Tom. The maître d' was all ready to block his entry when Tom held up his hand. A gesture both peremptory and entitled.

'I'm meeting someone.'

Into his voice, he put the drawl of a KGB general he'd helped in Berlin the year before. Grigori Rafikov was monstrous, a murderer. His main advantage in Tom's eyes was that he was less monstrous and less murderous than the English agent who'd been hunting Tom. One of life's ironies.

'Sir . . . ?' The maître d' was suddenly more attentive.

'Rostov,' Tom said. 'Colonel Rostov.'

'If you'd follow me, sir?'

The man from the reel Tom had watched on the helicopter

248

rose unsteadily from a chair. He was in uniform, although the last of his hair had gone.

'Colonel Rostov,' Tom said.

'You're late.'

Tom glanced at his watch. A good replica by Poljot of a Soviet tank commander's watch from the last war. He'd found it in Emma's holdall. Tom liked that touch. He'd been careful not to put it on until he was safe on the Tallinn side of the Sound.

'Ten minutes,' Tom said.

Rostov jerked his head at a spare chair. 'Ten minutes matters when you're dying.'

The maître d' wisely took himself elsewhere.

'You have the money?'

Tom put the holdall down.

Rostov's eyes went to the bag and then back to Tom.

Tom held his gaze and shivered. He'd never seen anyone quite so focused by his own impending death.

'Show me,' Rostov demanded.

'Here?'

'You might be lying.'

Easing back the zip, Tom dug for a single block of currency. Fifty $10,000 bills secured by a paper wrapper.

'They look old.'

'Withdrawn from general circulation in 1969. Still entirely legal. The preferred denomination for all Swiss banks.'

Taking the bundle, Rostov stuffed it into his pocket.

'You have the blueprint?' Tom asked.

'The what?' Rostov's voice was a croak.

'And the Geiger counter.'

'That's with—'

A waiter interrupted and Rostov ordered for them both. Verivorst with mulgipuder, blood sausage with mashed barley, potato, bacon and sautéed onions, plus black bread. He told the waiter to make sure his food was heavily seasoned. If it wasn't, he'd be sending it back. 'I'll barely taste it as it is,' Rostov muttered, watching the man hurry away.

'You were saying,' Tom said. 'The Geiger counter is with?'

'My daughter.' Rostov sounded cross that Tom could be stupid enough not to understand that.

'We meet her after this?' Tom asked.

'Of course not,' Rostov said, sounding exasperated. 'There was never any question of that. I can't possibly let my daughter see me like this. I'll be dead before you have time to collect her.' He looked at Tom, hesitated. 'Do you have a daughter?'

'She died,' Tom replied.

'I'm sorry.' For a second Rostov sounded almost human. Reaching into his uniform, he pulled out a photograph. It showed a teenage girl with cropped blonde hair and a slightly wide face. She was smiling reluctantly for the camera.

'Rivka,' he said.

Tom felt his heart clench. 'How old?'

'Fifteen,' Rostov said proudly.

Two years younger than Becca had been. Tom pushed that thought away. He'd taught himself not to pick at Becca's death like a scab. He'd promised his wife he'd let it go.

'She is my life,' Rostov said.

He produced a second photograph. This time of a small girl on a tricycle. In the background was an old wooden dacha surrounded by birch trees. 'Fourth birthday,' he said. The child was grinning from ear to ear.

Tom looked at Rostov.

'She takes after her mother,' Rostov said wryly. In talking about the girl he seemed to almost forget about dying. He hadn't, though. Leaning forward, he gripped Tom's wrist.

Any lack of strength in his fingers was made up for by the fierceness in his voice. 'Promise me,' he said. 'Promise me you'll get her to safety. Whatever happens, you won't abandon her . . .'

'I promise,' Tom said.

'How do I know I can trust you?'

'I just gave you my word. Besides, you have no choice.'

Colonel Rostov sat back, exhausted. 'That at least is true.' He smiled sourly. 'You meet her at the complex. Five days from now.'

'*What?*'

'I said this. You don't need to worry about interlopers. I had the whole area declared a hazard zone.'

'Is it?' Tom demanded.

'Yes and no,' Rostov said. 'Also, less so by the day. You can leave the money with me. Rivka will bring what you want.'

Tom hooked the holdall closer.

'About time,' Rostov said when the waiter returned. 'A man could die waiting to get fed round here.' He peered at the blood sausage, then shrugged and cut himself a chunk.

'Tasteless,' he said.

Tom could see the thick layer of pepper from where he sat.

'Where were we?' Rostov said. 'Oh yes, you were being difficult about the money. Keep it then. Give it to the boy who delivers Rivka. He's family. You can trust him.' The man put another chunk of sausage into his mouth and had obvious trouble swallowing.

'Eat up,' he insisted.

Tom cut into his own sausage. When he looked up, the man was watching him. 'You get used to it,' Rostov said. 'A man can get used to anything if he has no choice.'

Tom didn't think they were talking about sausage.

Around them, rich Finns and Estonian bigwigs dug into their meals, swilled wine and knocked back vodka. Like the grander hotels in Moscow, this place was reserved for those with hard currency or harder connections.

'About the blueprints,' Tom said.

Rostov sat back. 'Blueprints, plans, call them what you like. They don't exist.' He paused for a moment, obviously enjoying Tom's shock.

'You said—'

'I lied,' Rostov said. 'For simplicity's sake. What you get is better. Rivka has the prototype.' He jerked his chin at Tom's holdall. 'Once you've handed over the money, that will be plenty big enough to carry it home. It's no bigger than a grapefruit. It's not even that heavy. A Fabergé egg among bombs, some fool called it.'

Tom chewed thoughtfully.

So that was where Per's glass ball had gone.

68

There were twenty-two buttons in the elevators at Hotel Viru and twenty-three floors. Access to the twenty-third was via an express elevator reachable only from the outside. Its door was marked *Electricity. Dangerous. No Entry.*

KGB officers and support staff manned the floor day and night.

Just as the rooms grew grander the higher you went, so did the level of attention paid to those occupying them. The lowest floors had simple bugs, which were tended by junior stenographers with three or four rooms to oversee. Drunken conversations, barely adequate sex, complaints about hangovers, shop prices and workmates. Not much of value was extracted here.

Each middle room had a middle-ranking stenographer. These rooms catered for visiting trade unionists, local politicians, their mistresses, and British and European buyers tying up wholesale deals for kitchen units made by slave labour. Something both sides knew but nobody was indiscreet enough to mention.

The floors above housed foreign politicians, visiting journalists, rich tourists and anyone else the KGB regarded as persons of interest. These had two-way mirrors, cameras built into their light fittings, and a plentiful supply of hidden microphones to ensure adequate stereo recording.

Only the suites had actual cine-cameras. These were built

to the highest specification in East Germany by Zeiss. Each one costing more than a luxury car, had luxury cars been available.

The KGB colonel eavesdropping on Tom Fox's conversation with the disgraced Sergei Rostov cared nothing for any of this. He'd flown from Moscow that morning, having been told a British agent had boarded the Helsinki–Tallinn ferry. A full ashtray and an almost empty bottle of Stolichnaya stood in front of him. In fairness, the bottle had only been two-thirds full when he started.

A KGB sergeant had offered to fetch him an open sandwich, but the colonel had turned it down. Food would disturb his concentration, he said. And this conversation was fascinating. More so than either of the men having it realised.

'Almost done,' the KGB colonel said.

The microphone allowing him to listen to Tom Fox's goodbyes was in a marble and ormolu ashtray on the restaurant table one floor below. Every table had an ashtray. Every ashtray was bugged.

'What do we do now, sir?'

He looked at the sergeant, who was in her early twenties, probably ten years younger than him, and wide-eyed at finding herself shadowing a staff officer sent by the Kremlin itself. 'Nothing,' he said firmly.

Major Fox's meal with Colonel Rostov was ending. On the floor below, the British agent was scraping back his chair. The goodbyes had been perfunctory but respectful, at least on Major Fox's part. It was obvious that neither man expected to see the other again. Pulling off his headphones, the colonel indicated that his companion should do the same.

'I'll take that,' he told her.

The sergeant looked at her carefully transcribed notes.

Every word that could be heard, with the few words that couldn't marked as inaudible.

'Sir, I have to—'

'File it. Yes,' the man said. 'I know how this works. All the same.'

She handed him her notes.

'Was the conversation also recorded?'

'Of course, sir.'

'Fetch me the reel.'

She hurried away looking worried, returning half a minute later with a spool taken from a VM-70 military-issue tape recorder, which she handed across, looking more worried than ever when he produced a gold lighter from his pocket.

The unravelled tape burned more fiercely than she expected.

A couple of local officers glanced over and had the sense to look away.

The colonel found it hard to believe this was the first time they'd seen that happen. Dropping what was left of the tape into a bin, he headed for the exit. As he reached the door he turned back.

'Best not mention today to anyone. Understood?'

69

November 1971 – Derry, Northern Ireland

'Why here?' Jimmy McGrath asked.

He meant why this particular multi-storey. With its peeling signboard out front announcing a supposed date for demolition eighteen months in the past.

'Why the fuck not?' Vince said.

'You're certain this is it?'

'Jesus,' Vince said. 'Will you just shut the fuck up?' Reaching inside his jacket, he let a pistol hang by his side. No one would see it unless they were looking and they wouldn't be. Himself's orders were *Don't be seen. Don't use the pistol unless he had no option.* This was the big one. *Don't fuck it up.* Sometimes the Big Man liked to advertise what he was doing. Other times . . .

'Let's go,' Vince said.

A shaven-headed bull of a loyalist, his brown suit jacket strained across his shoulders, waited at ground level, half hidden between a shiny Volvo 144 and a Datsun truck encrusted with pigeon shit. Its rotting tyres said it had been there since the multi-storey closed.

The man looked furious.

'Where's Fox?' Jimmy whispered.

Vince glared him into silence.

Dull bulkhead lights bolted to a run of central pillars lit an oil- and water-stained concrete floor. Street lights bled through gaps in concrete slats lining the building's sides, and gave up long before they reached the middle. A sign by the lift gave the number to call if the ticket machines weren't working. The nearest one was beyond not working. A bit like Ulster itself, Jimmy decided.

He would remember this place.

He would remember its smell, the coldness of the wind through the walls, the sudden hammering of the rain as the skies decided to open again. Mostly, he'd remember this aquarium gloom in which the world beyond no longer felt real.

He and Vince watched. And waited.

Then waited some more.

'Fuck,' Vince whispered finally, watching the loyalist simmering in his own fury. 'Fox isn't showing.' He glanced behind him, face tight. 'I wouldn't trust the bastard not to have set us up.'

'Want me to go look for him?'

'No,' Vince said. 'Stay here. I'll do it. Don't show yourself. Even if he does show. Don't try to take him on your own. Don't even fucking move a muscle. Understood?'

'Understood,' Jimmy said.

Rolling silently from the flatbed of the Datsun, Major Tom Fox scuffed his shoe on concrete and watched the loyalist realise someone was standing right behind him.

'Don't turn round,' Fox ordered.

'How the fuck—'

'I don't want to know your face. I sure as fuck don't want you to know mine. Even the slightest flicker of recognition on the street could get us both killed.'

'You're late,' Billy McLean said. 'Have you any idea how fucking late?'

'You're being watched.'

257

McLean froze.

'If you weren't so useless,' Fox said, 'you'd know that. There's a kid behind that pillar over there. The other's gone up a level.'

'Why?'

'He's looking for me.'

'We need to leave.' The man turned for his Volvo, which still ticked and clicked slightly as its engine cooled. He'd had a long drive in.

'Wait,' Fox hissed.

McLean hesitated.

'There are three Provos out front, one with night-sights on a converted No. 4 sniper rifle. There's a door through to the council buildings on the floor below. It's locked. We'll get out that way.'

'How?' McLean demanded.

'I have the key. But first . . .'

'What are you going to do?'

'Kill that boy and the man he came with.'

'Give me the key first.'

'Later,' Fox said. 'Now go.'

McLean swore, glanced towards his Volvo and headed reluctantly for the ramp to the council's private parking area below. He turned back to say something but Fox was gone.

70

Saturday 28th November – Hampshire

The boy was missing.

That in itself was trouble.

Dancer had come round from fever dreams to discover the day was half gone and the boy had stolen away. Back to the warmth of Lord bloody Eddington's mansion probably. What kind of fool gave his nickname to a boy he was half minded to kidnap, if not worse?

Dancer's kind, obviously.

At the very least he'd need to change camps.

Maybe even write off his plan and get out of here. Head back to the smoke and anonymity. Back to hiding in plain sight. All that brat had to do was mention his nickname to his grandfather and armed police would be here. Dancer had better things to do with his life than die in a shoot-out in some toy forest in Hampshire. Although just now he couldn't think what they were.

Revenge could wait. Then again, revenge never waited.

Except, it had already waited this long.

He needed skag and food. Most of all he needed to be someone else. The pain behind his eyes was fierce. The sweats setting in. His body was gearing up for the shakes to try to take it apart. Staggering to his feet, he managed to make it out of the ruined barn before voiding his bowels in the nearest ditch.

From habit, he kicked dirt over his spoor. Half to

extinguish its rancid smell, half to hide its presence from him, and his presence from the world. Dancer was cross with himself. He should have acted the moment Charlie Fox appeared. *If it were done . . . then 'twere well it were done quickly.* They'd given him an education, if little else. He could have had the brat's body buried deep enough in his own grandda's woods for no one to ever find it. Let Major fucking Fox deal with not knowing what happened. Not knowing if his son was alive. Half hoping he was. Always suspecting he wasn't.

A sob caught in Dancer's throat and turned to vomit as his stomach emptied onto the leaf mould in front of him. Fuck, his mouth tasted vile.

He needed water. No, what he really needed was another fix. Although he'd settle for a bottle of Thunderbird or anything resembling brandy. Either of those would keep you sedated and keep you warm; and in late November, in woods this dank, and in a world like this, you needed all the warmth you could get.

He should have planned properly, put supplies in place rather than going with his gut and deciding to busk it. Everyone bigged up instinct as if it was magic. Experience beat it every time. Tossing earth and leaves over his vomit, Dancer went to wash his hands in the ditch.

'You're not very well, are you?'

Dancer spun. Knife already in his hand. The boy looked so shocked, and so unexpectedly frightened, Dancer found himself apologising.

'You made me jump.'

'I've brought food,' Charlie said.

He put a carton of orange juice, a packet of Mr Kipling Fancies, a white sliced loaf of bread, one of those round packets of Dairylea and a block of bright yellow cheese on the ground in front of him and reached into his pocket for a bone-handled butter knife. 'It's all right,' he said. 'No one saw me. It's Mrs Ross's afternoon off. And Granny, Grandpa and Aunt Agatha are in the big drawing room arguing.'

'What about?'

'Me,' Charlie said, sounding resigned. He took a packet labelled Chocolate Hob Nobs from his jacket. 'These are new. Just invented. Granny doesn't approve of them. She thinks I should eat proper food like everyone else. But Mrs Ross buys them without telling her. Mrs Ross is the housekeeper.'

'Of course she is.'

'I'm sorry the cheddar is processed.'

'Processed?' Dancer said.

'Mrs Ross uses it for cooking.'

Dancer pointed at the orange juice. 'Bring me that.'

As the boy stepped into reach, Dancer adjusted his grip on the knife. It would have to be done sometime. Might as well be now.

'Are you feeling all right?' Charlie asked.

Dancer sighed.

71

Saturday 28th November – Tallinn, Soviet Estonia

Tom knew he was being followed the moment he left the Hotel Viru. Stopping in Tammsaare Park to tie his shoelace, he glanced back and saw a group of Estonian punks leaning on a bronze frieze of heroic workers. The workers carried pickaxes and wore singlets showing off bulging muscles. To a man, their chiselled profiles stared into the hopeful future. The punks, in contrast, had long coats, lace-up boots and messy hair. One wore a leather tank cap, its flaps loose around his ears. All sported mirror shades, despite daylight being mostly gone. They were sneering at a group of Finnish tourists picking their fastidious way between puddles.

It was the contempt of kids half as old and a tenth as rich for those whose lives were not theirs and probably never would be. Neither punks nor sightseers showed any interest in Tom.

Next time he stopped it was to read a sign bolted to a medieval wall in the Old Town. Once part of the Hanseatic League – along with fifty or so cities, including Hamburg and Bergen – Tallinn had traded widely with Greater Europe. In a state of ruin at the end of the Great Patriotic War, the building behind the wall had been restored by order of the Presidium of the Estonian SSR.

The sign didn't mention that those bits of Tallinn not destroyed by the Luftwaffe in 1941 had been reduced to near rubble by the Soviet Air Forces in the months that followed.

An attrition that culminated in the March bombings of 1943, when fires swept through the entire city and thousands became homeless.

Tourists were Tom's best cover.

At least until he identified who was shadowing him.

Turning back, he spotted the Finns not far from where he'd left them. He ignored the glare of the Intourist guide, who obviously regarded him as a free-loader, and smiled at a Finnish woman who moved slightly to make room.

As Tom didn't speak Finnish, he had no idea what was being said, but he stared on cue at arrow slits in a tower, the lopsided façade of a merchant's house, which was either truly ancient or a good post-war reconstruction. Finally, he stopped with the others to look at a half-naked verdigris dryad who might have been a personification of the city or just the sculptor's mistress, or both. In every case, his real focus was on those beyond the group's edge . . .

All he saw were young couples, mothers and children, men in clusters. Hopes, dreams, squabbles. The life of a city anywhere. No different for being inside the Soviet Union. Maybe he'd been wrong?

If so, it was time to head back to the ferry.

Falling back as the Finns rounded a corner, Tom checked no one was watching and cut across cobbles between two high stone houses and found himself facing a waterlogged expanse of wasteground. Ahead of him, out of sight behind a chain-link fence and the long line of a rotting warehouse, he could hear the whirr of cranes and a foghorn. He was heading in the right direction.

Tom was searching for a way through the fence when he heard wet gravel shift, started to turn, and felt himself grabbed from behind. Breaking his assailant's grip, he lashed his elbow back, simultaneously stamping on his attacker's instep.

Pain lanced up Tom's own leg. Stamping on metal does that. Spinning, his fingers rigid for a throat strike, Tom saw his attacker stumble back, clutching his ribs. A KGB officer's cap tumbled into a puddle.

'For fuck's sake,' Dennisov croaked.

'What are you doing here?'

'Your son wrote.'

'*My son what?*'

'To Wax Angel. About you, the Wolf Lady, and the glass ball.'

'Fuck,' Tom said.

'Good to see you too.'

72

Saturday 28th November – Tallinn, Soviet Estonia

'How's Yelena?' Tom asked.

Dennisov smiled at the thought of his sister. 'Banging around with her pots and pans, creating recipes that taste like everything else she cooks.'

Hot, filling and highly spiced. Tom could remember.

'And your other sister?'

'What other sister?'

Tom looked at him.

'We don't talk. We never did. Now it's worse. I'm sleeping with the enemy, and Sophia . . .' Dennisov shrugged. 'She's not going to forgive that.'

'She doesn't approve of Sveta?'

'It's Sveta's grandfather who's the problem. He's one of Gorbachev's. Or Gorbachev is one of his. Sophia takes after my father. No weakening. No negotiation. No compromise with the West.'

'I'm sorry.'

'About what? It wasn't like we ever liked each other. Now, we need to get you off the streets.' Dennisov put his arm round Tom's shoulders, and scowled when Tom pulled away to unzip the leather jacket he'd put back on after leaving Viru.

'Ever seen something like this before?'

'Makes you look like a ballet dancer.'

'Took it off a KGB agent yesterday,' Tom said, his gaze on

Dennisov. 'She was trying to kill me. I killed her instead. Know anything about that?'

Leaning closer, Dennisov examined the mesh beneath the slash. Ran his thumb over it. 'You think Moscow made this?'

'Are you saying you didn't?'

Dennisov smiled sadly. 'You know what the Finns say? What doesn't whirr and doesn't fit in your ass? A Russian ass-whirrer – a vibrator,' he explained, seeing Tom's confusion. 'A saying as old as those punks you thought might be watching you. If we'd made something like this, it would be three times thicker, five times the weight, and only available in the wrong size. Also, it really does make you look like a ballet dancer. That's not a compliment,' he added. In case Tom thought it was.

'So not you wanting me killed then?'

Dennisov looked hurt. 'We're friends,' he said. 'I'm here to keep you alive.'

'But there *are* people who want me dead?'

'You . . . me . . . There will always be those who want people like us dead. You know this. Now, let's get you off the street. I could do with a drink.'

You smell like a distillery.

'I have a ferry to catch,' Tom said.

'No,' Dennisov said. 'You don't. I have a message from the Commissar. And I meant it about needing that drink.'

'How's it doing?' Tom meant Dennisov's leg. The one he'd had hacked off, eight inches below his balls, in a field hospital in Afghanistan. The last time Tom had asked that question, the stump had been rubbed raw while saving Tom's life and was refusing to heal.

'How do you think it's doing? It hurts. I drink.'

'Tell me on the way to the harbour.'

'You *want* to die?' Dennisov demanded.

Tom stopped, shocked.

'Shit,' Dennisov said. 'When did you get so stupid? The Americans have an assassin on that boat. He's going to shoot you and toss your body over the side.'

'Not going to happen.'

'Churning engines,' Dennisov said. 'Howling winds. Seventy kilometres of darkened water. Hungover Finns hiding in the lounge. A sudden rush of lead to the brain. You don't even hear it coming. No one sees you go into the sea.'

'You mean this?'

'Of course I fucking mean it.'

'Why would Washington want me dead?'

'Good question. Let me know if you come up with an answer. Apart from the usual, obviously. Killing people being the American way.'

The bar was in a basement. A neon beaver holding a bottle flickered in its window. The glass of the window had already steamed up from inside. Customers looked up, eyed the obviously drunk KGB colonel clutching a cap that still dripped from where it had fallen into a puddle, and went back to their beers. Shortly afterwards they decided they'd rather be somewhere else.

'Two Stolies,' Dennisov demanded.

The barman looked at a litre bottle with a tattered and faded label, quailed under Dennisov's gaze and reached under his counter for the real thing. Given the speed Dennisov drank his first shot down, Tom doubted its authenticity mattered.

'Drink up,' Dennisov ordered.

Tom pushed his drink across. 'I promised Caro . . .'

'Shit, shit, shit.' Dennisov's face changed. 'I'm sorry. I should have remembered. I only met her the once. That time she came to my bar to tell me the deal you'd made to save Masterton's daughter. Your life for hers. A woman like that . . .'

He downed Tom's glass. 'To Caro.'

'To Caro,' Tom agreed. 'Now. This letter of Charlie's?'

'Hand-delivered to our embassy. *Daddy's in trouble . . .*'

'Daddy's in trouble?'

'That was when Wax Angel decided you needed help. Well, the old man decided, but only after Madame Milova told him to. I don't know what else she said, but the Commissar spent the rest of that day on the telephone. Shouting at people.'

'You have a child,' Tom said, remembering.

'A girl,' Dennisov said happily. 'It's strange.'

Tom waited.

'You and me,' Dennisov said. 'Our childhoods.' Turning, he pretended to spit. 'And then. You have one and . . .'

'You move heaven and earth to stop history repeating?'

'See,' Dennisov said. 'That's why I like you. You understand.'

73

The doors opened onto absolute silence, and Tom and Dennisov entered a swimming pool with emerald-green wall tiles, and brass-inlaid doors leading through to a steam bath beyond. Marble pillars soared to support a wrought-iron and glass roof of the kind found on the Grand Palais in Paris, built in the same year. Heat rising from the water melted snowflakes before they could settle on the glass above.

On the walls, mosaics of naked water sprites smiled coyly, their bodies, expressions and backgrounds picked out in semi-precious tesserae. A simpering marble nymph did her pre-Revolutionary best to look simultaneously virginal and inviting. Tom could imagine what Caro would have to say about that. The city might be Leningrad now, but these baths personified St Petersburg.

'This used to be a gentlemen's club.'

'And now?' Tom asked.

'It's still a gentlemen's club.'

'Where is everyone?'

'It shut unexpectedly. Essential maintenance.'

'The Commissar?'

'Of course.'

'I don't imagine that will make its patrons happy.'

'I don't imagine he cares.' Stripping off his shoes, Dennisov kicked them under a marble bench with legs that ended in lion's claws. He draped his KGB jacket over the nymph's arm, wrapped his trousers round her shoulders, tossed his shirt and pants at her feet, and put his officer's cap on her head.

'Suits her better,' he said.

Dennisov's body was whipcord thin. Since Tom had last seen the man, he'd acquired blue stars either side of his chest, new and obvious among old bullet wounds and fading knife scars. The only time Tom had seen tattoos like those he'd been in a sauna in Moscow and they'd been on the chest of a Georgian mafia don called Erekle Gabashville, now dead. Tom had liked the man.

'Does the Commissar know about those?'

'I wear them on his orders.'

Tom couldn't hide his surprise.

'Life is strange. And getting stranger.'

'In the Soviet Union?'

Walking naked to the steps, Dennisov unbuckled his leg and dived into the pool, leaving his prosthetic looking like an amputated limb on the side. 'Yes,' he said, surfacing. 'Especially in the Soviet Union.'

They swam ten lengths and, not bothering with towels, headed for the steam baths. After five minutes, Tom could feel the sweat dripping off him and was ready to leave. Dennisov, on the other hand, had his eyes shut and his head lolling back against the tiled wall. He looked more relaxed than Tom could remember.

'I'll see you outside,' Tom said.

'Lightweight.'

'My turn,' Dennisov said, lowering himself into the freezing plunge pool. He swore, grinned, grinned some more and ducked under the icy water, puffing like a grampus when he surfaced. 'I used to cut holes in the ice.'

'After a sauna?'

'A steam bath,' Dennisov corrected. Clambering clumsily from the pool, he added, 'Of course, I had two legs then.'

In a white-tiled changing room filled with rows of mahogany lockers, two small cardboard boxes sat in string bags on a stripped oak bench. Beside each bag was a pile of clothes. Very ordinary clothes.

'Here you go.' Dennisov tossed Tom a thick woollen shirt, a kapok-filled jacket, some heavy jeans, a crude leather belt and a pair of tan hiking boots. 'Keep the leather jacket,' he said. 'I want to look at it later.'

Tom had been intending to keep it anyway.

Removing a new leg from a locker, Dennisov strapped it on. 'Carbon fibre,' he said. 'Ratchet joint. Very light. Very modern.'

'And your other?'

'It'll be collected,' Dennisov said. 'My stuff, your stuff. We'll get it back later. Assuming there is a later.' He scowled, then shrugged. 'And if there isn't we won't be around to worry.'

Russian shirt, Russian jeans, Russian boots. Copies of Western items but still obviously copies. He'd pass, Tom decided. At least he'd pass in the street. And this far west, his Russian accent would probably pass for Muscovite too. They looked like the Russian equivalent of the Bridge and Tunnel crowd. In from the country or suburbs. Here to see the sights of the big city.

'Where now?' Tom demanded.

'Finlyandsky station,' Dennisov told him. 'Via a vodka shop.'

74

Sunday 29th November – Leningrad, Soviet Russia

'You want us to travel in that?'

A dozen tatty wooden boxcars were ranged behind an old-fashioned TE3 diesel that would have been consigned to a scrap heap anywhere but Soviet Russia. Weather-bleached pine showed through peeling paint. A row of rusting padlocks secured rickety sliding doors. A train guard, in soiled uniform, watched them dead-eyed as he swigged Zhigulevskoye straight from its bottle.

The thought of doing a twenty-four-hour trip to Murmansk in a boxcar was grim. Dennisov, however, was whistling happily to himself – 'Stuck in the Middle with You', a song that had been on a compilation tape Tom sent Dennisov's sister Yelena.

When Tom looked across, he smiled innocently.

'What are you looking so happy about?' Tom demanded.

The train guard, who obviously disliked having his beer disturbed, shouted at them to move away. Dennisov's smile grew wider.

'Let me,' he said.

It was amazing the change in attitude a KGB card could produce. Halfway along the line of boxcars was a secondary engine, a black-painted slave unit, and Dennisov stopped to examine it with an engineer's eye. Tom had been wondering how the TE3 was meant to drag this many boxcars.

'You look dreadful,' Dennisov said.

Tom scowled.

'Badly dressed, limping, unshaven, sullen. No, keep it up. That's good. You could be Russian.'

The string bag probably helped.

Idly, Tom tapped his knuckle to the boxcar they were passing, and its peeling, supposedly wooden side rang with the unmistakable note of solid steel.

'What . . . ?'

'Welcome to my world,' Dennisov said. 'Where nothing is what it seems.'

Knocking three times on the next boxcar's door, he stepped back as it slid open. A Soviet commando blocked their way. The man's Kalashnikov had its slide back and his finger was alongside the trigger. From where he stood, Tom could see the door was an inch thick and armoured.

Dennisov presented a written order.

The soldier looked at it, glanced at Tom and came to attention.

'We've been expecting you, sir.'

Shaking away the man's offer of help, Dennisov levered himself onto the train. Tom followed, and found himself in a command car with a huge map of Western Europe on one wall, and bank after bank of radio equipment bolted to the others.

'Follow me,' Dennisov said.

'Oh shit,' Tom said, as he saw what the next boxcar hid.

The boxcar's roof was on rails, which looked recently oiled. A hand-winched system for winding back the roof had been replaced with something electric and more modern. An intercontinental missile on a hydraulic launcher filled the floor.

Every other boxcar they passed through contained a missile, launching gear, and a mechanised winch to open its armoured roof.

'This is recent?'

'No. We've had them for years. Your satellites simply see goods trains. How many of those are there in the Soviet Union? Thousands. Tens of thousands. How could you possibly keep track? How could anyone?'

'You know I'll report this?'

'Of course you will,' Dennisov said. 'There are games when it helps to keep your cards secret. Others where you need your opponent to know exactly what hand you're holding. The Commissar's counting on it.'

'What's the game?'

'No idea,' Dennisov said. 'I don't do politics.'

At the very end of the run of boxcars was a caboose, one of those wooden carriages invented in the nineteenth century for crews of goods trains to live and cook and sleep in on long journeys across countries like Canada, China and Russia. It was old, wooden and draughty.

Dennisov seemed delighted.

'That's your bunk,' he said. 'That's mine. Everybody else has been told to leave us alone. Now show me this evidence of KGB involvement you say you found.'

Tom handed him the wallet taken from his attacker on the Kemijärvi–Helsinki train and watched in silence as Dennisov went through it. He stopped at the photograph of Amelia at Patriarch Ponds.

'Your Wolf Lady?'

Tom nodded.

'Did your wife know about her?'

'Caro knew about most things, and there wasn't much to know.'

'You must tell me about her sometime.'

'Sometime,' Tom agreed.

'Unfortunately,' Dennisov said, 'I can guess where this

one was taken.' He was looking at the photograph of Amelia in the clearing. Putting it aside, he opened the KGB card and examined it for several minutes, turning it over and taking it to the light.

'East German,' he said finally.

'You're sure?'

Dennisov seemed so certain that Tom wondered what he'd missed.

'The jacket was hers?'

'Yes. It was.'

'Could your people make it?'

'I doubt it,' Tom replied.

'Then American,' Dennisov said. 'As I said.'

'You said East German.'

'No. You misheard. Now, look carefully at the crest, remembering this card was supposedly renewed three months ago.'

Tom did, not understanding.

Pulling out his own KGB card, Dennisov began pointing out differences. 'See? The red is slightly wrong. The embossing too deep. And though this card is new its crest is not. We haven't used this version since 1984.'

'Inbuilt deniability,' Tom said. He watched his friend consider the possibility that the KGB had issued a slightly faulty card so it would be discounted.

'I'm not sure we're that clever,' Dennisov said sadly.

75

Sunday 29th November – Leningrad, Soviet Russia

'At the swimming pool, you said . . .'

Dennisov scowled, shook his head and took a swig of vodka, pushing the bottle across to Tom, who shook his head in turn. 'Suit yourself,' Dennisov said.

He drank in silence, the train shuddering into life around them.

The next time Tom opened his mouth to say something, Dennisov pulled out his cigarette papers, a tobacco pouch and a tiny propelling pencil.

Pozdyeye, Dennisov wrote. *Later.*

Our carriage is bugged?

Of course it is.

But you're a KGB colonel and this is a military train, Tom wanted to say as he watched Dennisov fill the paper they'd written on with black Moldavian tobacco, roll it, glue it and seal the end with a twist.

He lit it with a gold lighter.

'Long story,' Dennisov muttered, seeing Tom's glance.

They lapsed back into silence as Dennisov worked hard to empty his latest vodka bottle, and smoked his roll-up down to a tiny stub. Mikhail Sergeyevich Gorbachev might be in power, and Perestroika, that famed appeal to openness, the order of the day, but Tom wasn't naive. The Soviet Union obviously hadn't changed as much as the Kremlin would like the West to believe.

All the same . . .

They were still bugging their own officers?

Cigarette and bottle finished, Dennisov put his finger to his lips and shook free from their string bag the two cardboard boxes. Inside the first box was another, paperback sized.

Tom lifted the lid on his.

It contained the smallest pistol he'd seen.

Dropping out its clip, he realised it took Winchester ACP, which was both impressive and a surprise. ACP being the most potent .32 cartridge developed. A Seecamp LWS. Steel chassis and slide. Delayed blowback. Minimal working parts. Six-round magazine, plus one. Why American? Tom almost asked. Then worked it out. If they had to kill anybody, the Soviets would blame the Americans first.

'Let's get some air,' Dennisov suggested.

They held themselves in place on the observation platform by clinging to its safety rail as the wind howled around them, while using their free hands to ward off swirling snow. They were leaving a city gripped by winter for Arctic wastes where daylight wouldn't be back for months.

Around them, the marshes on which St Petersburg had been built were hidden under a bleak run of sixties housing that even the heaviest snow couldn't make picturesque. The classical heart of the city was behind them; still haunted by its ghosts from the war, from the revolution before that, and by the ghosts of the thousands of carpenters, stone-cutters and labourers who died to ensure an improbably beautiful city could rise in such an unlikely place.

'Let's see them bug this,' Dennisov shouted.

Tom laughed. 'What did you need to say?'

'Marshal Milov wants London to have Midnight Sun. Lord

Eddington wants London to have Midnight Sun. Marshal Milov and your father-in-law have this in common.'

'That's treason,' Tom said.

Dennisov shrugged. 'He knows.'

76

Fox had been lying when he said three Provos guarded the multi-storey's exit. His business with Billy McLean wasn't finished and he didn't want the crop-haired loyalist doing a runner. It wasn't a big lie though. There were two of them now heading for the multi-storey, one after the other. Their hands were in pockets that undoubtedly held pistols.

It seemed Himself was taking no chances.

Fox had a pistol of his own. A Browning, with an extra clip of 9mm. He'd left it at his digs, taped to the underside of a drawer. Taped beside it was a Russian-made silencer and a pack of Libyan cigarettes. He'd left the silencer where it was and brought the cigarettes. Dead Provos, Libyan cigarettes. Let the police have fun with that one.

Kill these two men or let them in?

Fox let the first head up the spiral, then slid from behind the entrance pillar and cut the other's throat. The work of a moment. A hand over his mouth, his head yanked back, the femoral artery severed. The man shat himself. They usually did. That was the only thought Fox allowed himself before he lowered the man's twitching corpse to the ground.

'Steve?' a voice called from the spiral.

Fox grunted a reply.

'Keep up. Keep the noise down.'

Fox looked at the already cooling body and was grateful

279

for the award-winning curve of concrete that kept him hidden from the man's companion ahead.

'Martin?' Vince whispered into the dark.

'Aye. It's me.'

Vince was beside a pillar. His silhouette barely visible in the yellowing light that seeped between the concrete palisades of the outside wall. Fox let his breath settle before creeping closer.

It was a few seconds before Martin realised his companion hadn't followed.

'I'll get Steve,' he said.

'No,' Vince replied.

'He's probably just—'

'He'll be dead,' Vince said flatly. 'Jimmy was. His throat cut, blood everywhere. Dumped face down in the flatbed of that ruined truck.'

Fox went back the way he'd come.

The kukri was where he'd hidden it. In the gap above the concrete beam. Hanging it from his belt, Fox headed through the entrance and pulled its grill shut behind him, securing it with the padlock. Now for part two. And for that, all he needed was to make sure the men inside couldn't get out. Walking to the rear of the multi-storey, he looked up at the walls rising above and without giving himself time to think he began to climb.

77

Sunday 29th November – Leningrad–
Murmansk Train, Soviet Russia

Darkness in the shop doorway, rain beyond. Those hunting him through the city would kill him eventually, but not before they'd tortured him first. Tom knew this. In the butcher's window were the bodies of those they'd killed already. Hung like meat on hooks for display.

An arm here, a leg there. Guts piled in sausage-like heaps.

His chest was tight. He couldn't breathe.

Wake up, he screamed at himself.

Wake up . . .

Horrific things don't have to make you horrific.

Although they might, they don't have to mean you can't meet people you admire, and have good and happy days, whatever horrors visit at night. *Surface*, Tom ordered himself. Sweat prickled his scalp, his face felt greasy. He was hot and cold in the same moment. So cold he might as well have been . . .

'Dreams?' Dennisov asked.

Until his friend lit a kerosene lamp Tom hadn't realised Dennisov was at the fold-down table, with the caboose's rear door open to the blizzard beyond. He wore his prosthetic and nothing else. He seemed to be taking a shower in the snow.

'How did you know?'

Dennisov snorted. 'We're brothers,' he said. 'You said that in Moscow when you gave me what had been Gabashville's . . . People like us. We have the same dreams.'

Tom doubted it. For most of the night he'd been in the school for children from difficult families. An institution somewhere between boarding school and a borstal, where he'd done much of his growing up. Most of it far too soon.

Only at the end had the nightmare pivoted, putting him back in bloody Derry, knowing it was the night he'd probably die.

'I still have vodka,' Dennisov said.

'And I'm still on the wagon.'

'These then.' Dennisov hooked a pillbox from his pocket. 'It's not like we're getting off anytime soon. With these you can sleep through a mortar attack. Believe me, I've done it.'

Dennisov was playing patience with grimy American cards featuring pneumatic, Stetson-wearing cowgirls in various stages of dishabille, when he looked from the tattooed, six-gun-toting ace he held to his friend, who was curled into a ball, dead to everything. 'Brothers!' he said, raising his glass.

He was three shots from finishing the bottle. Drink them, or save them? Save them, he decided, at least for now. Besides, he'd had an idea.

Staggering to the door, Dennisov realised he needed to be wearing more than his prosthetic leg and returned to the table. 'This won't take long,' he told the girl on the playing card. Although that proved optimistic, because first he had to dress while drunk, and then it took him the best part of an hour to identify a sergeant who could help and hunt the man down. He'd just gone on duty but proved willing enough to be pulled off it and go fetch his needles on the orders of a senior officer.

'These,' said Dennisov, opening his shirt.

The NCO blinked and then caught himself.

The officer was KGB. The officer was an officer. It was the officer's business if he had *Voryvzakone* stars on his chest. And if this was what the officer wanted.

'If I may, Comrade Colonel?'

Undoing Tom's shirt, the sergeant splashed the last of Dennisov's vodka across Tom's chest, wiped it down and set to work with his needles. In total, the stars took three hours to ink and Tom slept through the entire thing.

78

Sunday 29th November – Hampshire

The tatty square of newspaper was folded in eight and tucked under the wipers of Lady Eddington's Volvo estate. Eddington spotted it through his bathroom window as he brushed his teeth before bed and hurried down to intercept whatever it was before Elspeth saw it.

The bit he could see included an ad from a Toyota garage in Belfast for models that were ten years out of date, at prices which would now be impossible. Eddington took the square of paper inside, stopping in the hall. He'd been hoping it was from Charlie. To be honest, he'd been hoping Charlie would simply come home. It wasn't as if he hadn't run away himself a couple of times. Once for one night, once for two. He'd been beaten on his return both times, obviously.

Unfolding it revealed a story about Earl Mountbatten holidaying in Sligo. Since Lord Louis, better known to Eddington as Dickie, had gone to meet his maker six years back, that made the cutting old. If Mrs Ross had been here, he'd have asked if she'd noticed anyone, but she'd left for the day. His wife was in bed. Well, Eddington assumed she was. He wouldn't know. He couldn't remember the last time he'd gone to her room. As for Agatha, Elspeth's wretched sister had finally gone home. Thank God.

Realising he could put it off no longer, Eddington unfolded the last square of newspaper, turned it over and felt sick. It led with a massacre in a Londonderry multi-storey. The details were vague, and Eddington's department had worked hard to keep it that way. The death toll was accurate, though.

Eddington remembered the case.

Stalking into the house, he dialled the night desk at his office and gave orders that two armed officers from SO1 be despatched to his house immediately. He knew now who had taken Charlie. This clipping told him why.

It wasn't information he could share.

He felt glad, God help him, that his daughter was dead. She'd never have been able to bear it if anything happened to Charlie. Now she'd never need to know. He only hoped the bastard had given Charlie a clean death.

It took several whiskies and an hour of despising himself before Eddington realised the truth. All but one of those connected to that night had died in the massacre or been killed in the years that followed. Only Tom was still alive. But then Tom was the last person in the world likely to hurt Charlie.

Besides, it would be far crueller, if you were going to kill the boy, to leave Eddington unknowing. Let him wonder for years if his grandson had run away or been abducted, how he died, whether or not he was even dead. This note was a kindness, almost.

So, who *had* taken Charlie? How could Eddington keep any mention of Ulster out of the conversations now necessary? And what exactly should he do next? In his head, he began picking his path carefully through assorted half-truths, prevarications and lies. That done, he reached for the telephone and began making late-night calls, the first of these to his local chief constable.

'John, I'm sorry to trouble you. My grandson has run away . . .'

79

Monday 30th November – Hampshire

Monday morning brought fog and a long line of Hampshire police and volunteers from the village sweeping the fields surrounding Lord Eddington's woods. Charlie had come back from stealing food last night and Dancer had been strange, very strange. Now he was missing, and—

'Charlie!'

The voice came from a man at the front wearing a huge khaki trench coat with its collar turned up. It wasn't quite a shout. More a pronouncement. He sounded like a very serious actor being serious in an old film.

'I know you can hear me.'

No you don't, Charlie thought. You don't know anything of the sort.

He could have been anywhere. The problem was, he wasn't. He was here, and the woods were running out behind him. He'd be in the fields soon, and those were huge and open, and even bigger now the hedges had been grubbed up.

He was trapped in a little strip of trees.

The man didn't know Charlie was trapped.

Except that Charlie was worried that perhaps he did. Perhaps he was right and he did know that Charlie could hear him. Charlie's mistake had been staying too close to Grandpa's. He should have run away properly.

The line of police and volunteers was advancing through

286

Grandpa's woods towards him. What if there were more police and volunteers behind?

And Cat . . .

What about Cat?

He'd gone off to do cat things and how would he know where to come back to? Charlie bit his lip and tried very hard not to cry. He had to work out his next move, but couldn't come up with an answer.

'No one's angry with you . . .'

That was a lie. Grown-ups were always angry.

'We just need to know you're all right.'

He had been, until a long line of policemen turned up. If he hadn't heard them coming, he'd never have known to run. Charlie shuffled backwards, a dozen raindrops from a bramble tumbling onto his head. His clothes were already sodden. His hands were covered in mud.

He was crying. Charlie hated himself when he cried. It was always at the wrong moment, when he needed to remain calm. Behind him was a stream. That was all right. It wasn't as if he could get any wetter, was it? Charlie shuffled backwards, and felt himself being grabbed by the shoulder, as a hand covered his mouth.

'Shut it!' Dancer said.

The man smelled. This close, he smelled really bad.

He'd been drinking too. Charlie knew what alcohol smelled like.

'I'm going to take my hand away, and you're going to stay schtum, right?'

He was meant to nod, Charlie realised.

'Good boy.'

Dancer dragged Charlie to his feet. Lifted him up and pushed him towards the branches of a Douglas fir that

Grandpa's grandpa had planted. It was huge, really huge, and its needles stung where they scraped his face.

'Climb,' Dancer hissed.

Charlie looked at him, and realised that Dancer meant it. From the scowl on his face, he was going to be very cross if Charlie didn't.

So Charlie climbed.

'Faster,' Dancer whispered.

He did that too.

'What are you doing here?'

Dancer stared up from trying to light a fire with damp twigs and a Bic lighter that was almost out of fuel. He stared owlishly at the man in the raincoat.

'What does it look like?' he asked.

Every last inflection of Irish was gone from his voice. He could have been born within the sound of Bow Bells and lived his entire adult life on the London streets. Lord Eddington – and Dancer knew it was Eddington, from that picture in the *Standard* – pushed himself forward.

'That camp back there. You?'

'Yeah. Me.'

'You're trespassing.'

Dancer shrugged.

A policeman dragged him to his feet, and took a step back when Dancer turned to complain. The policeman looked a bit sick. Up in his tree, Charlie sympathised.

'He's drunk,' the policeman said.

'And he stinks,' Eddington said. 'I know. I can smell him from here.' He planted himself in front of Dancer. 'We're looking for a boy,' he said. 'He's missing from the village. A small boy. Have you seen a small boy?'

'Neither hide, nor hair,' Dancer said.

'Search him,' the plainclothes officer ordered.

The two local police found nothing but an old military ID Dancer had robbed from a Brummie outside a medical centre for street people in Soho. The clean-cut teenager in the photo didn't look much like Dancer, but then it hadn't looked much like its original owner either. Living on the streets changed you.

'Ex-Para,' one of the local policemen said.

'Ulster?' Eddington asked.

'Falklands,' Dancer said. 'Wounded, wasn't I?'

Pulling off his tatty combat jacket, he began undoing the filthy shirt beneath. Only stopping when Eddington held up his hand, his shirt already half off one bony shoulder.

Reaching for his wallet, Eddington pulled out a £50 note.

Dancer gave a sloppy salute and let one of the local policemen lead him, staggering, towards the road, only turning back at the last minute. 'Good luck finding that boy.'

80

Tuesday 1st December – Kola Peninsula, Soviet Russia

Amelia Blackburn had gone to ground.

Not literally digging in like a hunted animal. In her head, though, she was holed-up for the long haul. From her camp high on the granite of the Kola Peninsula's central plateau she could have seen for miles in high summer, but the midnight sun was many months away and the long night ruled.

Still, out here in the cold, with her wolves, Arctic foxes and snowy owls, she was safer than back in the human world. Harder to reach, harder to find. Very much out of sight, and she hoped very much out of mind.

Dragging on a foul-tasting *papirossa*, Amelia tossed a branch on the fire, tossed the cardboard stub of the cigarette after it, and listened for anything that wasn't the snap of burning wood, the hoot of an owl or wind through the birches.

She liked fires. There was a time . . . Amelia tried not to think about that.

Trying to burn down your home got you sent to boarding school. Well, it got her sent to boarding school. If she'd been less privileged, she'd have been taken into care. What would the punishment be for burning down Roedean? She'd never had the courage to find out.

Out here, life thinned to a razor's edge. You died or you survived, and many of the animals she shared the plateau with had little hope of the latter.

If she was one of them . . . ?

'If there is no God, everything is permitted.' So said Dostoevsky. And Amelia lived in a world where everything seemed to be permitted, and God presented zero evidence of existing. She'd been nine when she stopped believing. Thirteen when she announced marriage was an abomination. Fifteen when she decided manners were a weapon in the arsenal of cultural oppression. Her contempt for middle-aged men was fixed by seventeen. It had taken turning nineteen to decide humanity was a cancer the earth would one day shake free. Although that might simply have been a reaction to her boyfriend of the time. The only laws she believed in were laid down by physics, biology and chemistry. Everything else was sociology.

Lighting another *papirossa* from habit, she took a drag and wondered why she'd bothered. Its rough tobacco tasted as foul as ever. She tossed it into the flames, her attention suddenly on a nearby run of trees.

She'd heard something.

Amelia was sure she'd heard something.

A lone wolf would have made more noise, and she'd have heard howling before it reached her. There were stray reindeer, but not many and they'd be heading in the wrong direction. Eight foot tall and weighing in at over 200kg, *Ursus arctos* seemed her obvious answer. Except brown bears were meant to be hibernating by now; no need to urinate, their arses stuffed with faecal plugs, their guts with berries, their heartbeats slowed to eight beats a minute like a winding-down clock. She wished the two new 'helpers' Murmansk had insisted on providing hadn't taken the camp's only rifle with them when they vanished to replenish the larder.

The one time they might actually have been useful and they weren't here.

A woken bear would be bad. Wolves even worse. A life's

study had given Amelia a healthy respect for *Canis lupus*, their perseverance, hunting skills and ingenuity. If cats were fascists, wolves were Cossacks. Utterly unforgiving to anything weaker.

It wasn't that she feared them. Respected them, yes. Feared them, no. But a hungry wolf in winter was a hungry wolf in winter, and this winter was as brutal as any she remembered. Pulling a flaming branch from her fire, Amelia held it aloft as she scanned the trees. If there was a pack, she'd see them as shadows first.

Something was out there. Amelia was certain of it.

The creature loomed, broad and bipedal.

A lone bear then, shaken from a hibernation that had barely begun. It would be foul-tempered, furious at being awake, but still replete with fat stored in the autumn. That was good. The less starving it was, the less she'd look like a meal.

Edging forward, Amelia lifted her branch high. Look big, look dangerous, don't run. She knew the routine.

The northern lights flailed and snapped in a celestial wind.

They were the snow fox. They were a bridge between worlds. Tom's nan had called them the Dancers, although she never said why. Tonight they were only just visible. Some nights, he'd heard said, they were as bright as moonlight on ice. There would be a reason for the difference. Tom didn't know it.

He knew his mind was wandering, though. His arms and legs losing strength as the reptilian bit of his brain worked out what it could afford to shut down. He hadn't known what cold to the bone meant until the wind on his way here ripped every last shred of the heat from his body, then tried to take more. Heading for the fire, he stumbled, dropping his rucksack as Amelia swung a flaming branch at him.

'Stop!' he said. 'It's me.'

The branch stopped moving.

'*Tom Fox?*' Amelia said in disgust. Her face was thin in the firelight, almost skeletal. Her hair in knots, her padded jacket filthy. She looked furious and nearly feral. 'What the fuck are you doing here?'

Crouching in front of her fire, Tom pushed his gloves at the flames.

'I need to show you a photograph.'

'Of *what?*'

'You.' Tom fumbled at the toggles of his kapok-filled jacket.

Turning for her tent, Amelia said, 'A bear would have been better.'

She returned with a Gaz lamp that she pushed into a snowbank, before lifting away its opaque glass shade and lighting the ring with a twig taken from the fire. Having let the mantle settle, she adjusted the brightness until there was enough light for Tom to see both her tent and a hut built from branches and covered with skins.

'You have company?'

'I have helpers.'

'Where are they now?'

'Hunting. You're lucky they didn't decide you were prey. Now, show me this photograph. Then get the fuck out of here and leave me alone.'

'Amelia . . .'

'The photograph.'

She stared at the aerial shot of herself at the base. Her eyes flicking from one dead soldier to another. Her face bleaker than ever. She stared at it for a long time.

'They're going to kill us all,' she said.

81

Amelia's helpers trudged into the camp carrying five dead
rabbits between them. They were wrapped tight against the
snow, with wolf-fur caps pulled low over high cheeks and
watchful eyes. Only their polyurethane skis slung across their
shoulders stopped them looking like they'd stepped straight
out of history.

'You told the Soviets about Tromso?' Tom asked.

She looked shocked, then resigned that he knew about
Tromso.

'Of course I didn't.'

'But they sent new helpers?'

'Per wasn't a helper,' she said tightly. 'He was my assistant. A brilliant young doctoral student who happened to be
Sami. A *militsiya* officer came out from Murmansk and
insisted on inspecting my letter of authorisation from Alexander Yanshin at the USSR Academy of Sciences. He sent
these two.'

A short while later, two of the rabbits were gutted, skinned
and impaled on sticks over the fire, while the other three –
also gutted and skinned – hung by their heels from the door
of the hut. Apparently the two men were going back out the
moment they'd eaten.

'Do you trust them?'

'Of course I don't. Their grandparents were kulaks,' she
added, grudgingly passing Tom a sliver of rabbit that would

294

have burned his fingers if he'd had any feeling in them. 'Exiled here after their farms in the Crimea were broken up. They adapted well enough. But I was hoping for Sami.'

Having stripped the carcase of the rabbit they were sharing back to bone, the two men put on their skis, picked up the rifle and disappeared. But not before one of them had turned back to glare at Tom.

'They don't like me here.'

'I don't like you here,' Amelia said.

She was taking his arrival badly. Partly it was the photograph, which she refused to give back and had put firmly in her pocket. There was more to it than that, though.

'Why?' she demanded suddenly.

'Why what?'

'Why now? Why you?'

'Would you have trusted anyone else?'

'What makes you think I trust you? After . . .'

After Berlin, where they'd shared a bed. Although they'd done nothing much. At least, not that he could remember. Berlin. Where she'd saved his life and he'd saved hers, and they'd promised to stay in touch and he hadn't even acknowledged her first letter, never mind her second.

'I'm sorry,' Tom said eventually.

'A whole year,' Amelia said. 'I thought . . .'

She hesitated.

'What?' he demanded.

'I don't make friends easily. I thought we were friends. Oh, don't worry. I get that you still love . . .'

Tom watched her search for the right name. They'd talked about Caro only once. The lies, the evasions that filled that marriage. Mostly on Tom's side.

'Her name was Caro.'

Amelia stared at him.

'She died two weeks ago,' Tom said. 'Cancer. I missed her funeral. I was in Tromso looking for you. You were gone. The police showed me Per's body. That was his name, wasn't it? Your assistant. You might want this.' Reaching into his jacket, Tom pushed across the photograph he'd found beside her hotel bed. Per and Amelia smiling beside a frozen stream.

Guilt hit Tom when tears filled her eyes.

'He was brilliant. Probably the best postgrad I've had.'

'What happened?'

'I left him there,' Amelia said. Her face was wretched, her eyes haunted. 'I left him where he was, crushed to death by a snowplough, and ran.' She sounded as if she couldn't believe she'd done that.

'Better than getting yourself killed.'

She nodded doubtfully.

82

November 1971 – Derry, Northern Ireland

'He's not here,' Martin said.

'Of course he fucking is.' Vince's voice was tight.

They'd rattled the grill. Martin was certain that Fox had locked them in and gone on his way. He was having a hard time accepting Vince's assurance that this wasn't how Tom Fox worked. They died, or he did.

Fox would be satisfied with nothing less.

'The basement then,' Martin said.

Vince sucked his teeth. 'Use your fucking brain.'

Stalking to the body Fox had left at the foot of the ramp, Vince glanced at it. His face unreadable in the squares of light filtering through the grill beyond. He considered laying Steve to rest beside Jimmy in the flatbed of the abandoned truck, but they didn't have time.

'We should check the basement.'

As if on cue, a bang came from high overhead.

Fox was on the roof. Except by now he was heading down a level or three. He imagined Vince would take his time heading up. They'd been hunting each other long enough for getting it right to come first. Vince made Fox wait an impressively long time. And then, having made him wait, he made him wait some more . . .

Shit.

Fox felt a jolt of adrenaline as he snapped awake, his head against the pillar he'd been kneeling behind when he nodded off. How long had he been out? A second? Ten seconds? Longer?

He stared round the cavernous floor, trying to work out if anything had changed. The same shadows, the same silences, the same reluctant glow from bulkheads along the central run. Everything looked the same.

He couldn't be confident it was though.

Fox stopped, stilled his breathing, and listened.

The wind through concrete slats, the rattle of wires hung along an outside wall, rain starting up again, and teenagers shouting as they left the discotheque. Not much traffic though. Not at this time of night. Quietly, discreetly, Fox flipped the cover hiding the dots on his watch dial. Ten minutes to black-out.

To cut costs, Belfast council had night savings. Their central switch, already adjusted for sunrise and sunset, now turned the city lights off an hour after midnight and back on two hours before dawn. The bulkheads of the multi-storey were included in this, although they shouldn't have been connected at all.

Any second now . . .

One moment the car park felt dark, the next it was. Pitch dark. In that moment, Fox heard movement and knew Vince had been waiting for darkness too. The merest scuff of a heel on concrete between wind and rain. Someone was on the ramp leading up from below.

If Fox was lucky, it would be Vince.

He fell back into darkness, reaching for a coin in his pocket. Shadow, darkness. Shadow, darkness. Fox tracked the man's approach against fractal differences in the sky just visible through gaps in the multi-storey's slats. The darkness was at its deepest where Fox waited, hardly daring to breathe.

He slowed his heart.

Weighing the kukri in his hand, Fox adjusted his grip.

His victim had stopped to look back, scared that Fox had got behind him. Not Vince then. The other one. Martin . . . Satisfied that he hadn't been blindsided, the man started forward, spinning as Fox tossed the coin away to the side.

Martin was peering into the darkness when Fox stepped up behind him. The man in the army surplus shop hadn't lied. The kukri could take a head from a man's shoulders with a single blow. It bounced once and Fox kicked it down the ramp to where Vince would be waiting. It happened so fast, Fox doubted Martin had time to know he was dead.

83

Tuesday 1st December – Kola Peninsula, Soviet Russia

'Turn off the lamp,' Tom ordered.

When Amelia hesitated, he did it himself; searing his fingers on the lamp's glass in his hurry. Plunging his fingers into snow, he hoped that would be enough to stop them blistering. It was dark now and Amelia's assistants were still out there somewhere. This wasn't them, though.

'I'll put out the fire,' Amelia said.

'Too late,' Tom told her. 'They're close.'

Above the crackle of the fire they could both hear the whine of a snowmobile grinding its way towards them. 'How did you get here?' Amelia demanded.

'Train, truck, skis.'

'You were followed.'

He wasn't. Tom was certain of that.

He'd checked. At least, as much as was possible in a landscape that alternated between absolute darkness and near-absolute, with brief forays into moonlight and the pyrotechnics of the aurora's spectral glow. Mind you, anyone with a torch would have been able to track his skis.

'You're from the Academy of Sciences,' Amelia told him. 'Sent out from Moscow. Speak only Russian. Better still, don't speak at all . . .' Pushing herself to her feet, she glanced back to check Tom had stayed put, and went to meet the headlight crawling up the slope towards her.

The figure who climbed from the saddle swept his gaze

round the fire-lit camp, missed Tom in the shadows of a tree, and demanded: 'Where's Major Fox?'

'*Dennisov?*' Tom was on his feet. He still hadn't forgiven the bastard for the tattoos, which itched to fuck.

Dennisov was dressed in snow fatigues. An SVT-40 rifle slung across his back.

'We need to leave.'

'Why?'

'Ask her.' He jerked his head towards Amelia.

'I have a name,' Amelia told him. 'And I'm here at Moscow's invitation.'

'You're here because Moscow allows it, which isn't remotely the same. If you don't come with me, you'll find yourself on your way there to answer questions.'

'About what?' Amelia demanded.

'I imagine the people following me will start with why you didn't report the murder of your assistant. And move quickly on to what you might have seen, said or found that got him killed.'

'I didn't—'

'Get him killed, or find anything? Doesn't matter. I don't believe you and they certainly won't.'

'*Dennisov . . .*'

'We're wasting time,' Dennisov said crossly. 'I'll tell you on the way. She's to take me to the site of the explosion. Now get her moving.'

'You can't just—' Amelia began.

'Of course I can,' Dennisov said. 'I can arrest you. I can have you deported. I can have you detained indefinitely. I can shut down your investigation into the effects of fallout on Arctic reindeer. If necessary, I can make you disappear.'

'There are wolves out there,' Amelia told him.

'There are wolves everywhere,' Dennisov replied. 'Some worse than others.'

84

Charlie's life hung on the toss of three coins.

The first was an old penny with George V's head, the second a Victorian sixpence Dancer had taken from a dead priest. If it was meant to be lucky it hadn't worked that time. The third coin existed only in Dancer's head.

Dancer wasn't sure Charlie knew how close he was to death. Just how irritating was his blind faith that Dancer was a friend. The wee boy had a galling, unswerving belief that Dancer needed his help. Without for one second understanding his father and grandfather were the reason Dancer was here. He'd practically greeted Dancer's return with open arms.

A life for a life.

An equation so simple even God couldn't disagree.

Then again, company was company. And who was going to creep back into that big house and steal Dancer bread, cheese and bottles of brandy if not this boy?

Dancer sucked his teeth.

Those were yellow. Just as his hair was matted, his fingers nicotine-stained. His bloodshot eyes given to weeping in the wind. Dancer had no illusions about how soiled he looked. Let the outside match the in. There was a famous quotation about that but Dancer couldn't be bothered to recall it.

This filth was his disguise.

The disgust of others his armour.

Who'd look for a famously dapper, fanatically fastidious Belfast hitman in the shambling husk of a vagrant squatting beside a fire in the middle of a wood? Dancer was trying to work out what came next. What should come next . . .

Taking the slate-dark penny, Dancer flicked it into the air. Heads, the boy died. Tails, Dancer faded into the trees and Charlie never saw him again.

Heads.

One down. Two coins to go.

Dancer tossed again. His silver sixpence spinning up, hanging suspended for a second and tumbling back to the leaves.

Tails.

One die. One live.

It all depended on the final coin.

The one in his head, whose design kept changing. Dancer tossed it up, seeing it clearly, and watched it hang motionless. Heads or tails? Live, or die? Tails, he decided before it even hit the ground. Maybe it should have been heads, though. Only he couldn't change it. Not now.

And he couldn't throw again for a week because those were the rules. A man had to live by rules. Especially a man like Dancer. He'd shift camp instead. Shift camp without telling the boy and see how the coins fell next time.

85

Wednesday 2nd December – Kola Peninsula, Soviet Russia

In between taking part in the coup that overthrew Tsar Peter, stealing Crimea from the Ottomans, and acting as Guardian of Exotic Peoples at the All-Russia Legislative Commission, Prince Grigori Alexandrovich Potemkin created fake villages to prettify the routes taken by his lover Catherine the Great, empress of all the Russias.

The village Moscow had built above their underground complex on the Kola Peninsula was undoubtedly less pretty but just as fake as anything Potemkin ever ordered. Although, they'd skipped the bother of filling it with freshly washed peasants in unrealistically clean smocks.

It existed solely to convince NATO overflights that any comings or goings were village-related. While its ramshackle stave church was to convince anyone examining photographs that it had always been here.

A village had, just not this one.

Rewsk was so old it predated both the Soviet Union and the Romanovs before it. It stood on stilts because stilts protected it from predators and vermin, keeping inhabitants and their food supplies safe. Stilt villages were found in Northern Norway, Finland and here. There might be a few in the USSR still inhabited. But not this one. Not now.

It had been small, poor and thinly populated by the time engineers turned up to relocate its original and increasingly elderly inhabitants, dig out their mountain and hide a complex under a bigger village next door.

Now, of course, the fake church, village hall and stilted huts were ruins or ash. What the explosion hadn't destroyed had been burned by the clean-up team sent in to rewrite history, and make sure another nuclear catastrophe wasn't added to the Kremlin's sheet so soon after Chernobyl. Only on the western edge of the fake village, where it became the original hamlet, did half a dozen huts still stand. Although set on fire, their wood was so hard, old and cold that the flames burned themselves out.

'Take a reading from the longhouse,' Dennisov ordered.

Amelia bristled. She'd been about to do that anyway. She didn't need telling to do her job. Especially not by some oaf who didn't even bother to hide the half of vodka jutting from his pocket.

'It's too low,' he muttered when Amelia gave him the reading. She looked like she wanted to argue. Instead she nodded.

'How much too low?' Tom asked.

'Impossibly so,' Dennisov replied.

'It does seem unlikely,' Amelia admitted grudgingly.

'And yet here we are,' Dennisov said, shining his torch round the burned and broken ruins. 'Right on the edge of hell, which looks altogether less hellish than it should.' The snow helped, of course. It blanketed the dirt that had been sterilised by flame-throwers. And the bodies were husks. Incinerated half-corpses that looked . . .

'Like Giacomettis,' Tom said, voicing his thought aloud.

Amelia snorted. 'You have a sick mind.'

'That's why we love him,' said Dennisov. 'Who's Giacometti?'

'Italian sculptor,' Tom said.

Dennisov's torch lit shattered trees, snow-covered husks and burned huts. 'We're probably safe to move closer to the centre,' he said. When Amelia realised he was looking for confirmation, she nodded.

Amelia went first, Geiger counter in hand, then Dennisov on his snowmobile, Tom hitching a lift on his skis by grasping its side.

'Strange,' Amelia muttered.

'It's not going up?' Dennisov asked.

'Not as fast as I'd expect.'

'Try that.' Dennisov indicated a half-ruined hut and the thrown-back hatch it had been built to hide. Edging his snowmobile closer, Dennisov stumbled climbing from its saddle.

'What's wrong with his leg?' Amelia whispered.

'It's missing,' Tom told her.

'You may want to give me a moment,' Dennisov added as he reached the hatch. One frozen corpse, then another, and finally a third were dragged from the hut. He tossed the first two down the slope.

'Wait,' Amelia ordered when Dennisov readied to do the same with the third. Dropping to a crouch beside the body, she ran her Geiger counter along its length. The machine's clicks were slow, almost lazy. Steadying herself, Amelia unzipped the dead woman's overalls and tore open the vest beneath.

Pale flesh, frozen hard.

Her eyes were white, which could have been radiation, but since sub-zero also turned eyes white, it probably wasn't. The clue was that her chest didn't look mottled, there were no lesions, her skin hadn't started to slough away. Amelia knew the symptoms for radiation sickness. The report she could recite from memory was dictated by a lover at Chernobyl who'd died the next day.

This woman had rushed from a warm underground room into the cold, found an outbuilding to hide in and discovered it hadn't been enough to save her.

'What killed her?' Tom asked.

Amelia looked at the woman's stark ribs, her shrunken stomach. 'Starvation probably. Possibly starvation, hypothermia and low-level radiation poisoning. But only low-level. Ask a pathologist.'

'No pathologists,' Dennisov said.

He tipped the body into the shaft without bothering to zip its overalls first and kicked the hatch shut.

Two ruined huts were chosen, Tom and Dennisov in one, Amelia in the other. The broken walls provided no heat and little defence against the wind. Amelia's Tartar helpers were probably back at her original camp, wondering where their boss had gone. As Dennisov said, if they had any sense they'd just go home.

'Do you trust her?' he asked Tom suddenly.

'She saved my life in East Berlin. She didn't have to.'

Dennisov nodded to Tom's rucksack. 'Does she know about the ten million?'

Tom shook his head.

'Does she know you're here to make an exchange?'

'No,' Tom said. 'She doesn't.'

'Have you told her about Midnight Sun?'

'Not yet.'

'Then you don't trust her that much, do you?' He pushed across his half bottle of vodka. 'Here,' he said. 'It will help with the cold.'

'If I start . . .' Tom said.

The mantra that had kept him sober.

Dennisov laughed. 'Look around you,' he said. 'Where do you think I'm going to find another of these?' He waved the bottle in Tom's face. 'This is my last. When this is gone, it's gone.'

'My wife's dead,' Tom said. 'Her father thinks I'm a useful idiot. Her mother hates me.'

'All the more reason to drink. Besides, you need to finish it before I do. Otherwise I'm going to forget what we're meant to be doing tomorrow.'

Tom hadn't known they were meant to be doing anything.

'We have a meeting before dawn.' Dennisov laughed, slightly bitterly. 'Or when dawn would be if it came to this benighted place. Just you and me.'

'The exchange isn't for two days.'

'I know.'

'This isn't a meeting about that?'

'Why would we need a meeting about a meeting? What kind of fool would do that? We're meeting a Sami. An expert hunter.'

'Of what?' Tom demanded.

Dennisov grinned. 'Aeroplanes.'

He held out the bottle and Tom drank.

86

Wednesday 2nd December – Hampshire

It had been a water tower, built by the Meon Valley Water Board in 1910 and designed at the demand of the original owner of Lord Eddington's estate to look like a castle turret, then abandoned and left to rot.

When Dancer first saw its red brick hidden under ivy and set back from an A-road that had fallen into disuse after the building of a dual carriageway, he'd thought it a folly. One of those weird ruins rich Englishmen build to make their over-designed gardens look wild and picturesque. He wouldn't put that past Eddington.

God, Dancer despised him. He quite liked his water tower, though. Its lines were business-like. Its location discreet. He particularly liked the big red sign on its front door reading *No Entry – Dangerous Structure.*

The internal staircase had been ripped out, making it impassable. Half the ceiling above had fallen in, giving the interior a deserted and dangerous look. It stank of mould, mildew and foxes. The ground around the tower was slick with rotted leaves and criss-crossed with brambles. No one passing would suspect it was occupied.

An excellent quality in a look-out post.

Iron staples in the rear wall led to a copper tank at the very top. And best of all, the tightness of an oak tree to the wall hid Dancer's climb. The view from the top was magnificent. A man had a clear shot in three directions.

He could see Golf GTIs and Peugeot 205s on the road, their striped-shirt boy-racers believing they were speeding unobserved. He could see village kids sneaking into Eddington's woods: the ones too classy to make out behind bus shelters. He could see their mothers jostle for parking outside the village shop.

Dancer's name was on a kill list. The man who'd put him on it lived down there. You'd have to make allowances, of course.

Adjust the shot.

The bullet from a .22 rifle rises roughly 2 inches in 50 yards, then drops 10 inches by 100. The waves created as the bullet slows from super- to subsonic causes further inaccuracy. That said, .22 Long Rifle was still the most popular round in the world. Good to 100 yards, pretty good up to 150, able to kill at 400, and capable of travelling over a mile.

Its stopping power wasn't great. But its killing power, particularly for humans, particularly in the hands of a professional . . . People underestimated that.

Dancer grinned.

A rifle, a ruin, a stake-out.

He was enjoying himself. It felt almost like the old days.

87

Wednesday 2nd December – Kola Peninsula, Soviet Russia

'Fuck,' Dennisov said. 'Will you fucking look at that . . .'

Tom squinted along the beam from the snowcat's head-light and wished he hadn't. Fat flakes were falling in a flurry and he was having trouble focusing. He saw it though. And wished he could unsee it.

The body of the hunter they'd come to meet had been mutilated. Before death, if the quantity of blood soaked into the snow crust around him was an accurate indication. His tongue had been cut out, his eyes removed. A hatchet indicated how his hands had been taken off. These were between his knees. A nail hammered into the back of his skull between his third and fourth vertebra had finished him off.

'How very traditional,' Dennisov said.

Dropping to a crouch, Tom put his hand to the snow. The blood was cold, as sticky as a milkshake but not yet frozen. 'Why?' he demanded.

The *who* could wait.

'It's a message,' Dennisov said.

'Obviously. For us?'

'Who the fuck else would it be for?'

'Who was he?'

'Called himself Beaska-Sáve. Sáve Who Wears Reindeer Skin. It's not his real name. There's no one on Murmansk's Sami register called that. We . . .'

Tom waited for Dennisov to put his thoughts in order.

This took a good few minutes while Dennisov tried to get the snowcat going again, and finally conceded that it was out of petrol and therefore so much junk. In between this and looking for a fuel tap that might have a reserve setting, and realising there wasn't one, Dennisov stared at the body, stared at the blood on the snow, and then at the sky, which had brightened slightly on the horizon, where an unseen sun had edged high enough for its rays to almost reach them.

'I don't know how they stand the darkness,' he said finally.

Tom had to agree.

'A week ago, a Sami hunter shot down a plane. We asked what happened to the pilot. He said it had no pilot. The Israelis have pilotless planes. If the Israelis have them, then the Americans have them. Perhaps we have them too.' Dennisov scowled. 'I'm sure we do,' he said. 'I'm sure ours are better. I just haven't seen any.'

'Why didn't you tell me this on the train?'

'Why didn't you tell that woman about the ten million?'

'When did you stop trusting me?' Tom demanded.

'Who said I ever trusted you?'

'I thought we were friends?'

'Not necessarily the same thing.' Dennisov hesitated. 'The Commissar has heard a rumour,' he said carefully. 'That you changed sides in Berlin. That you came over to the KGB. That Grigori Rafikov turned you.'

'This would be a problem?'

'Of course it would. The only reason I've ever trusted you is because you're one of them. We knew where we stood. Either side of a fucking line, with more in common with each other than our bosses.' Dennisov sounded as if he took the possibility of Tom's defection to the Soviet side personally.

Tom remembered the stars on Dennisov's chest. The stars

he'd had tattooed onto Tom's chest in turn. Was it possible to be a KGB officer and a high-ranking member of the Russian mafia simultaneously?

Apparently so . . .

Tom doubted his own side would take kindly to a Russian mafia boss considering one of London's own a brother-in-crime, should they find out.

'That rumour's untrue.'

'Who started it then?'

'I did,' Tom said. 'Well, Grigori did. It kept me safe. Not from my side or yours. From *spetsnaz* and the Stasi.'

'Nasty to tangle with,' Dennisov said. 'Brave, though . . .' He looked as if he was about to add something and then nodded to Tom's rucksack. Not even bothering to pretend he wasn't changing the subject. 'The money's still in there?'

'I'm keeping it safe.'

'Stopping that woman from finding it, you mean.'

'She has a name,' Tom said.

'Don't we all,' Dennisov said. 'Give me a bundle of it. Think of it as leaving a calling card.'

Tom gave him a single $1,000 note.

'Cheapskate.' Prising the nail from the dead man's skull, Dennisov picked up the discarded hatchet, reversed it and used its flat end to nail the $1,000 note to the tree against which the dead man slumped. 'That should get their attention.'

'Who's they?' Tom asked.

'Does it matter?'

This was the version of Dennisov Tom recognised.

88

November 1971 – Derry, Northern Ireland

Halfway through basic training, an NCO had told Tom that he'd make a good sniper. Snipers being antisocial, up themselves, happy to be left alone, not given to conversation and willing to stay put for long periods of time. It hadn't been intended as a compliment.

Tom had thanked him all the same.

The darkness of the lift shaft in the multi-storey was deeper than the dark clouds and night above him. Tom had no idea where exactly Vince was. It didn't matter.

Jumping for the cable, he slid faster than expected. He should have allowed for it still being greased. Steel cable slipped through his fingers, his boots failed to get a grip, and the roof of the cage four floors below was there before he had time to brace. Breath rushed from him as an ankle twisted, his knees punched his chest, and he gasped in agony as a lower rib snapped. Hooking his fingers under his diaphragm, he yanked it back into position.

Nearly blacking out from shock.

Vince would know where he'd gone from the thud of his landing. And Vince would follow him down. Tom was counting on it.

Still swaying with pain, he fumbled for the bits of broken crate he'd hidden. The ones with the rusting nails. As quickly as he could, he arranged them in a ring around the cable that rose away into the darkness. Then he tumbled through the ceiling hatch into the lift, replaced the hatch, yanked back its doors and staggered out onto ground level.

There was no way anyone could get through the locked grill, but he scanned the level just the same. Long stretches of darkness, broken by faint light through gaps in the concrete palisades. It felt vast, empty and claustrophobic at the same time.

How the fuck did he end up here?

How far back would he have to go to find an answer to that? There wasn't much point in asking the question anyway. He was where he was. Maybe there hadn't been a branching point anyway. Maybe here in the darkness of a derelict multi-storey, with all his sins come back to haunt him, was where he was meant to be.

Vince landed on top of the lift.

Tom heard it happen.

The man's scream was loud, blasphemous.

'I'm going to fucking kill you!' Vince howled.

Nails through both feet with any luck. He'd have slid down the greased cable as hard and fast as Tom had, hitting the lift's roof with equal force. The nails in the booby trap Tom had left for him were long enough to hold a crate together. Strong enough to punch straight through the soles of whatever boots Vince was wearing.

'You bastard.'

They were into the endgame. It was time to head down a level.

The grill might still be locked but Billy McLean's Volvo was missing. Tom had time to wonder when and why the loyalist thug had moved it, before staggering down the ramp into the absolute darkness of the private parking floor below.

'Fox!' the shout came from behind him. 'You're dead . . .'

And you're alone, Tom thought.

His heart was pounding, his ribs burned, his jaw felt as if it had also been fractured in the fall. The hardest part was not dragging huge mouthfuls of air into his aching chest.

Silence. Silence was what he needed.

Footsteps approaching.

Ten paces away, fifteen . . . ?

Taking another step back, Tom clipped a pillar with his kukri's blade. Ducking down as Vince fired. Muzzle and cylinder flare lit the basement level, the noise of the shot rebounding in brutal waves from windowless walls. The bullet passed so close Tom felt it. A jagged sliver of concrete exploded from the pillar behind. Blood ran down his fingers from the hand he'd thrown up to block the glare.

Ricochet damage.

'I thought you had orders to take me alive?'

Tom was expecting a second shot in answer. By the time it came, he was ducked behind Billy McLean's car. The Volvo that shouldn't have been there. He felt for the door handle and edged it open, feeling it yanked back from inside.

A second later he heard it lock.

89

Wednesday 2nd December – Kola Peninsula, Soviet Russia

'Your friend's passed out.'

Tom glanced over to where Dennisov slumped in a corner of the hut they'd agreed to share. It being on the outer edge of the old village, and the only one with unbroken walls, for all it leant at a sickening angle. Dennisov had a reindeer hide pulled over his head. The skin was only mildly radioactive. That was, sleeping under it for one night was equivalent to living in Cornwall for five years, where granite raised background radiation. Amelia's reference points weren't everybody's.

'He's being tactful.'

'KGB colonels aren't noted for their tact.'

'He thinks we need time to talk . . .'

'About what?' Amelia's voice was tight.

'I returned from Berlin to find my wife dying,' Tom said flatly. 'My father-in-law not expecting it to affect my work, my son withdrawing inside himself . . . Further inside. He's never been good around people at the best of times.'

'Like his father,' Amelia said.

Tom grunted.

'You told me you had reasons for being the way you are,' she said, her voice studiedly neutral. 'Does your son?'

'Christ. I hope not. At least, not the same ones.'

'Perhaps it wasn't what happened, whatever it was, that made you like this. Perhaps this is who you are. Who you were meant to be. After all, I'm just me. Nothing makes me this way.'

'Your father defected. Your mother had a very public breakdown. She lost her family home. You were exiled to boarding school.'

'Life happens,' Amelia said. 'In Berlin, you said Caro was having an affair. But intended to end it. Did she?'

'I believe so.'

'And you? Were you faithful?'

'In the year we had left? Yes,' Tom said. 'I was.'

Amelia considered that. 'I liked Charlie.'

'And he liked you.'

They'd met only once, Amelia and Charlie. Outside the terminal at Heathrow, after Tom and Amelia returned from East Berlin on the same plane. If Caro had minded her son talking about Daddy's friend the Wolf Lady, she never let it show.

Then again, Caro always kept her emotions siloed.

Had kept, Tom reminded himself.

'I think of her,' he said.

'You say that as if it's strange.'

'I doubt I thought of her more than a couple of times a year for most of our marriage. Except in the early days and at the end.'

'What *were* you thinking about?'

'Staying alive,' Tom said. 'Staying in character.'

'You were undercover?'

'In Belfast,' Tom said. 'Occasionally Derry.'

'Aren't people like you meant to call it Londonderry?'

'Borders blur,' Tom said. 'After a while you realise people like you aren't like you at all. The only ones like you are the ones you're hunting or being hunted by. We were tools. Expendable. At least they get to boast about their kills. Our bosses denied we even existed.'

'Your wife didn't know any of this?'

'Not then. Not for years. I was in training to become a priest when we met. I ended up as an Anglican one in a regiment in Ulster. Only to lose my faith altogether and get sucked into intelligence. From there . . .'

'You graduated to killing?'

'Something like that,' Tom agreed.

90

Wednesday 2nd December – Hampshire

Dancer was gone when Charlie got back from stealing cans of tuna. He'd had to turn back for a tin opener, which meant he took twice as long as he intended. When he got back, Cat was being sick by the light of the moon and the man was gone. Charlie was so taken up with worrying about Cat he didn't notice Dancer's rucksack was also missing. At least, not for a while.

'Bones are bad for you,' Charlie said.

Cat glanced back from slinking into the wet undergrowth. It was a Paddington sort of stare. He'd be back soon enough, with another fluttering bird. Then there'd be more bones, more feathers and another pile of vomit. He had a delicate stomach for a cat found behind a pizza joint.

Charlie wondered whether to bury what was left of the thrush and decided that would be too odd. He did, however, throw dirt over the vomit, and apologise to the bird's ghost. 'He's not really my cat,' he added, in case that made it better. Perhaps it did. Daddy would know. He'd ask him.

It was only then that Charlie realised Dancer's fire was out and his rucksack missing. The tramp kept the flames fed night and day, using only dry wood so smoke didn't give them away. It was meant to be a good luck thing. But the fire was out, buried under handfuls of earth. Kicking it away, Charlie found blackened twigs and embers hot enough to blow back into flames when he fed them with slivers of wood.

No kettle, no sleeping bag, no canvas windbreak camouflaged by twigs and broken branches. No food either; Dancer had taken everything they'd had left.

'No!' Charlie said aloud. It was almost a wail.

He'd just remembered the rifle. And the rifle was very definitely gone.

He needed to get it back. It was Grandpa's and Grandpa would be cross. Besides, the rifle was Charlie's proof he hadn't stolen it. Really, he needed the rifle *and* Dancer. Then Dancer could say he was the one who stole it. Granny would have to believe him. So Charlie needed to find Dancer.

To do that he'd have to track him.

Charlie ran through what he knew about tracking. It wasn't much. But before he started looking for footprints or broken branches, bent grass or tufts of cotton on barbed wire, he needed Cat to come back. He'd use the time between now and then to get the fire going again. For luck.

91

Thursday 3rd December – Kola Peninsula, Soviet Russia

'Darkness, snow, silence,' Amelia said. 'No one within a hundred miles. It begs the question, what are you running from?'

'What have you got?'

Amelia sighed. 'Brando. 1953, *The Wild Ones*.'

'Very good,' Tom said.

'I'd have thought *Apocalypse Now* was more your style.'

'Never seen it.'

'Probably just as well.'

All Tom could see of Amelia was her nose and chin in silhouette, barely lit by the hearth they'd let burn down to flickering embers. Her question came out of nowhere. At least, it seemed so to him.

'Yourself?' she said. 'Your past? Charlie?'

'Christ . . .'

'You're here,' Amelia said. 'Your son's there. There must be a reason you're not at home with him.'

'Eddington . . .'

'Fuck Eddington,' Amelia said. 'You can say no to Eddington. You've always been able to say no. You never do. Why?'

Tom stared into the darkness of that question for longer than he liked, and hoped Dennisov really was asleep, not just being kind or tactful. Dennisov was his friend but this was going places Tom didn't want to go.

'Well?' Amelia demanded.

She was waiting for an answer. If he didn't give her one,

322

she'd never trust him again. Tom wasn't sure why that should matter. It did, though.

'What do you know about a glass orb?'

Amelia turned. When she spoke her voice was flat, as if she believed his question was asked to shut down hers. It wasn't.

'Nothing,' she said. 'Absolutely nothing.'

Shifting, Tom fed the fire with slivers of kindling he'd cut from a door frame. When the flames caught, he added a length of broken board and considered the stone hearth, set on the tilting floor.

'Displacement,' Amelia said. 'You should look it up.'

'I'm thinking . . .'

'About what?' she asked.

'Your question. Eddington's demands. Per's orb.'

'*Per's?*' Amelia sounded shocked.

'He found and hid a glass orb. Priceless, he told his cousin.'

'That's what got Per killed?'

'Most probably. You're lucky they didn't kill you too.'

In the light of the re-built fire, Tom watched her think that through, and realise something. Something she didn't like.

'Per found it here?'

'So he said.'

'He found it and didn't tell me?'

Tom wondered if she realised how much the hurt in her voice revealed her feelings for the young Sami researcher, and how she thought he'd felt for her.

Perhaps he had.

'It's valuable,' Tom said. 'Incredibly valuable. The man Per took it from told him Moscow would pay a fortune for its return. I imagine Per realised that was a lie. Moscow's most likely response would be to kill you both to ensure your silence . . . Per, because he knew about it. You, because they couldn't be certain you didn't. He obviously decided it was

323

safer for you, and more profitable for him, to sell it to the Americans.'

'Fuck,' Amelia said.

'Aye,' Tom agreed.

'You know where this thing is now?'

'No,' Tom said. 'I don't.'

'You know *what* it is?'

Tom hesitated, then shook his head.

'He does,' Amelia said, nodding to Dennisov curled under his rotting reindeer hide. 'So do I . . .' Her face was still in the firelight as she vanished inside herself.

When she finally spoke, her voice was entirely flat and she could have been reading figures from a spreadsheet. 'The bomb dropped on Hiroshima incinerated 80,000 people and destroyed four square miles of city. Another 60,000 civilians died of burns and radiation poisoning inside a month. The final death toll, including cancers, was over a quarter of a million. Three days after Hiroshima, the Americans dropped another. St Mary's Cathedral in Nagasaki was incinerated, along with its congregation, and another 70,000 in the streets around them. The altar went up in flames, the bells in the tower melted, the wooden head of the Virgin survived.'

'Christ,' Tom said.

'I doubt he had anything to do with it.'

Tom waited for Amelia to say more. He had the feeling she was still working out whether to trust him. Whether she should say more.

'We're at ground zero,' she said finally. 'Not in the traditional sense, or we'd be dying. And in this case, ground zero was underground, which undoubtedly helped. All the evidence suggests a relatively low-level explosion generating high levels of fast-decaying radiation. Theoretically, there's a bomb that can do this. It's a tenth of the size of a conventional nuclear weapon, produces a fifth of its blast, kills over twice the area, and degrades fast. There's also an international agreement not to build it. Neutron bombs aren't meant to exist.'

'How do you know this?'

Amelia looked at him. 'CND,' she said. 'Greenpeace. The picket at Greenham Common. You think we act on emotion? That we don't gather intelligence? Co-opt academics to our cause? Undertake research?'

Tom held up his hand in apology.

'You asked what I was running from,' he said. 'The answer's obvious. Myself. My childhood. What I think it made me.'

'It was bad?'

'It wasn't fun.'

'You don't want that for Charlie?'

She saw or maybe sensed his shock. Of course he didn't . . .

A moment later he realised her question worked on two levels. The one he'd reacted to, and the one asking how much of what he did for a living was driven by what had been done to him. He didn't have an answer to that. The trouble with having your childhood taken from you, is you tend to romanticise the normality of everyone else's. And Charlie was Charlie; he looked at the world in ways most other children didn't. His childhood was never going to be that normal anyway.

'I need Eddington's help to get Charlie. That's the deal. I go to Tromso. I talk to you. I find out what the fuck is happening. In return, he backs me in court if necessary.'

'That's blackmail.'

'It's not like that,' Tom insisted.

'It's exactly like that. Now, I heard you talking to him.' She jerked her thumb towards Dennisov. 'You said it depends on tomorrow . . . What does?'

'Everything,' Tom said.

92

Thursday 3rd December – Kola Peninsula, Soviet Russia

In the far corner of the Baba Yaga hut, Dennisov rolled over and climbed unsteadily to his feet. He blinked a handful of times in the firelight and seemed to be having trouble recognising where he was. His Tokarev pistol was at his side, and Tom realised he'd been holding it in his sleep.

'I'm going to stand guard.'

'You're drunk,' Tom told him.

'Worse,' Dennisov said. 'I'm sober.'

Tom laughed.

'Don't laugh,' Dennisov said, sounding offended. 'It's almost dawn. There are people who want us dead. Someone should be out there trying to stop them.'

'We're too late in the year for dawn.'

'Whatever you want to call this then,' Dennisov said crossly.

'I'll do it,' Tom offered.

'Stay here. Have another chat. Besides—' Dennisov tapped his artificial leg '—there's less of me to get cold.' He nodded to the sleeping Amelia. 'Also, you need to tell her the truth. The whole truth. Nothing but the . . .'

'About what?'

'Being heartbroken. About Caro being the best part of you. About how losing Becca destroyed you. How much you love Charlie. You, me, we don't do emotion. But women like it. What have you got to lose?'

Grabbing skis, Dennisov tossed them into the cold.

'See you,' he said.

'He saved my life,' Tom said later, as if that explained everything. 'He appeared out of nowhere in a bloody helicopter with Yelena at his side.'

'A girlfriend of yours?'

'His half-sister. I'd killed the son of a Politburo general. The Politburo general wanted revenge. Almost got it, too.'

Tom was remembering the burning huts in what had once been a prison camp. How close he'd been to becoming another name on the list of those whose fates were unknown. Caro wouldn't have missed him, back then. Charlie barely knew him anyway. And Becca . . . ? She was already dead. Tom was where he was because he was trying to save the life of a girl. As if saving Alex Masterton could have made up for letting Becca slip through his fingers.

'You really trust him, don't you?'

'Dennisov? He's a lunatic.' Tom thought of the tattoos, which began to itch on cue. 'More than a lunatic. But he put his life on the line for me. So, yes, I trust him.'

'It's never occurred to you that his friendship is a front? That this commissar of his dispatched him for one reason only – to stop you recovering this orb? To take the monstrous thing back to Moscow?'

'We're brothers,' Tom protested.

'In arms? Bullshit.'

'*Voryvzakone.*'

'You said he was KGB.'

Tom found himself telling Amelia about Rostov, a man so ill from radiation poisoning he could barely sip water, never mind taste food. About the crucified Sami, and the long hours of darkness it had taken to retrace his steps to the

Norwegian border. The hotel in Kirkenes, the arrival of the NATO helicopter. The faked crash-landing.

'All this to get Charlie?'

'Yes,' Tom said.

Until her hand came up, Tom hadn't realised he was crying. And for all his face was cold, her fingers were colder.

'It's not just that though, is it?' Amelia said. 'You're doing it because you believe you must.' She sighed, half frustration, half regret. 'Give me the child until seven, and I'll give you the man.'

St Ignatius Loyola. Tom recognised the quote.

'They got to you early, didn't they?'

Tom nodded.

93

Thursday 3rd December – Hampshire

Someone was inside the tower.

Dancer froze on the iron ladder on the rear wall, thinking back to the wet oak leaf resting on a rusting lower rung where he'd left it. It had looked untouched, undisturbed. Seems he was wrong. It had been replaced.

From the other side of the hatch came a click, as whoever it was put something down. Drawing his knife, Dancer held it in his right hand and pushed the hatch open with his left, leaving himself room to strike.

'It's me,' Charlie said.

'Fuck! What are you doing here?'

'You should have left a note to say where you were going.'

The boy sat cross-legged in the empty water tank with the rabbit rifle on his lap. He was field-stripping it, with his bloody cat at his feet, tail stump twitching and one eye open to check for danger. As Dancer watched, Charlie removed the bolt and put it to one side, removed the barrel, and unscrewed and lifted away the breech block. The magazine he'd removed already.

The rounds were lined up like tiny chess pieces.

'Who taught you to do that?' Dancer asked.

'I taught myself,' Charlie said. 'Taking things apart is how you find out how they're made. Then you put them back together.'

'And they work?'

'Not always,' Charlie admitted. 'Mostly, though. Grandpa's Bang & Olufsen record player didn't. His radio did though. I haven't tried the television yet.'

'How did you find me?'

'I tracked you,' Charlie said proudly. 'I knew you couldn't have gone far if you needed to watch the house, and there aren't many places round here to keep dry. Also the ground's still wet because it rained yesterday.'

'Footprints?'

Charlie nodded. 'You took all the food,' he added. 'And the kettle, and my matches and the gun.'

'I thought you'd go home.'

'I can't.'

'You mean you won't.'

'Can't,' Charlie said. 'Not without this.' He tapped the bits of rabbit rifle.

People like Charlie didn't say 'can't'. They said 'cannot', or found another way to word it. But Charlie liked can't. He liked nice too, and you weren't meant to use that either. It was a nothing word, Mummy said. Charlie hadn't had much need for it. Not much had been nice since Mummy died. Not that much had been nice before that either.

'Are you going to rob Grandpa's?' Charlie asked.

'What makes you ask?'

'It's just . . . There are guards now. So it might be best not. Unless you really have to. It's all pretty old and most of the antiques aren't that good.'

'You really think I'm a burglar?'

'You look like a burglar,' Charlie said. 'And you spend all your time watching the house. You watch who comes and goes. You watch very carefully. I've noticed it.'

'Have you?'

Charlie nodded. 'There's an alarm box above the front

door and a panel in the hall to make it work. There are bells everywhere.'

'Sounds tricky,' Dancer said.

'It is.' Charlie seemed relieved that Dancer understood.

Sitting himself down, Dancer reached for the bits of the rifle and began putting it back together. 'Tricky is fine,' he said.

94

Thursday 3rd December – Kola Peninsula, Soviet Russia

There were easier ways to hide work tools but few more discreet. Putting his back to a fir tree, Dennisov unbuckled his prosthetic leg and reached inside, pulling free a ratchet wrapped in rags to stop it rattling.

He glanced to the hut where Amelia and Tom dozed, and was glad to see it looked deserted, uninhabited. A drab, broken silhouette. Not even a flicker of hearth fire showing. Above it hung a wavering wall of northern lights, too ethereal tonight to do more than look pretty and light nothing. He'd been worried a glow from Tom's fire might show through the hut walls. It didn't, which was something at least.

He wished his fiancée was here.

She'd like it. Sveta had the soul of a peasant and her grandmother's ability to see meaning in natural things. He wasn't sure he had a soul at all. Then again, in another way, he was glad Sveta wasn't here. Dennisov wasn't sure that any of this was going to end well.

The tight cluster of the original village gave way to the remains of the sprawling fake. The hiss of his skis across snow crust sounded loud to him, but that was only because the wind had dropped, the trees stopped rustling and for a second the village and the forest around it were silent.

An ersatz square with the burned-out ruins of a meeting house told Dennisov he was where he needed to be. Air

Hatch 15, the Commissar had said. Dennisov had not enquired how that information was extracted or who from.

Fifteen. Counting from where, damn it?

Scraping the crust off a snow-heavy hump, Dennisov revealed a manhole, but domed and weighty. Nothing suggested it was vented. Air hatches should have holes in the top or at the sides, surely? Nothing on it to indicate a number either. Angrily, Dennisov kicked snow crust from another three hatches. Finally finding one that looked like an oversized, upturned sieve. No number, obviously. That would have been too simple.

Perhaps the numbering was unofficial? Maybe Milov's information hadn't been accurate in the first place? Dennisov had better things to do than freeze his balls off in the Arctic while Sveta's grandfather stamped round his warm apartment in the House of Lions, complaining about how long this was taking. Because he would be complaining. Complaining, fretting and plotting.

Particularly, plotting. That was how he'd stayed alive when so many of his enemies perished in the purges. There weren't that many who'd worked closely with Stalin who survived.

Start with the main entrance, Dennisov decided.

It was beneath what had been the meeting house. Dennisov could see the logic in that. Enemy overflights might see people going in and out; but since it was so obviously a village hall that would be unexceptional.

Call the entrance zero. The nearest air hatch should be one.

Walking in a growing circle, Dennisov began kicking snow from hatches, finding another perforated hatch four mounds later. They were the biggest. He kept that in mind. Number 15 was in the trees. A corpse lay across it. Long dead, deep frozen and wearing a full-length white mink coat. A rifle at his side.

Dennisov tried on the coat and liked it.

He put his ratchet to the first bolt. His fingers were cold and the bolt rusty, but he had desperation, the Commissar's orders and a hangover from hell on his side.

It shifted eventually.

One bolt down, he tried the next.

His ski gloves were ripped, he was frozen to the bone and his hands were torn by the time he got the last bolt free. It was too cold for the cuts to bleed, and too cold for him to care.

Wrestling the hatch upright, he reached down. Resting on a tray-sized filter, where Per had hidden it, was a glass egg wrapped in a metallic blanket. Dennisov had expected his prize to be bigger. Football-sized at least. This was barely larger than an orange. Men had been shot for it, their careers ruined, their establishments closed down. It seemed a very small object to have caused so much trouble.

95

Dennisov was gone when Tom awoke.

He was gone and Amelia's assistants were back, having tracked her through freshly falling snow to her new camp. Something Amelia considered unexceptional and Tom found miraculous, given the twenty hours of darkness and four hours of twilight that currently passed for a day.

It gave him a new respect for the exiles.

Tom's skis and half of what remained of their chocolate were also missing. Dennisov had taken his rifle and pistol too, but left the money. That puzzled Tom.

'Some friend,' Amelia said.

The tracks leading away from the camp passed under an old Norway spruce that towered above the other trees. It would do as a marker. Something for Tom to look for when he made his return.

'*Picea abies*,' Amelia said. 'Clonal *abies* can be thousands of years old . . . Sprouted from root systems,' she explained when Tom looked blank.

'That's meant to make me like them?'

'Respect them,' Amelia said. 'Liking comes later. Love later still.'

Tom wondered if they were still talking about trees. Picking up his rucksack with the money, he went back to staring at Dennisov's ski tracks. He felt sick, but that might be the second day of his hangover. It was certainly responsible for the return of his shakes.

'Where are you going?'

'To do the job I was sent to do.'

If Dennisov hadn't got there and done it first.

'You're being set up,' Amelia said. 'It's a trap. I mean, who the hell sets up a meeting in a place like this if it's not?'

'Someone who needs to stay under the radar.'

'You want me to come with you?'

'Why would you do that?'

'Go then,' Amelia said crossly. 'Be an idiot. Why the fuck would I care?' She seemed surprised when Tom leant in to kiss the corner of her lip.

'What was that for?' she demanded.

'Luck,' Tom told her.

Hoisting his rucksack with its $10 million, he slung it loosely over his shoulder and took a deep breath. Rostov's daughter, the bloody glass ball and the plans would be waiting. He knew which of those he was meant to save if it came to it.

And which one he would.

In the early 1920s a Muscovite geologist discovered a large deposit of apatite in the Kola, a mineral used in the production of phosphorus mineral fertilisers. And it was this discovery that sped up the collectivisation of the reindeer herds, which in turn curtailed the migrations of the Soviet Arctic's nomads.

A stone plinth, half buried in snow, marked the place on a hillside where the geologist froze to death returning from a later trip. The hide Tom built twenty paces from it was simple. A half circle of snow strong enough to support a lattice of fir. Within a minute, falling flakes had begun to smooth off the roof. Within five minutes, the hide was indistinguish-able from any other wind-blown mound of snow. You could just about see the narrow eye-slit he'd left himself, but only if you knew where to look.

Three reindeer being driven by a Sami boy trudged a route that would take them to slopes where richer moss and lichen might be enough to see them through the winter to better months ahead. Tom could smell them. A sourish, musk-like odour rank enough to carry on the freezing wind.

Their breath rose in clouds, and the boy swore when one of his animals stopped dead to grub in the snow for lichen. As it did, the others halted behind it, and Tom watched the boy grow furious as he tried to get them moving. As Tom suspected they would, they moved on when they were ready.

After that, nothing.

For at least an hour, he lay in his hide, grateful for the warmth it trapped and glad of the camouflage it offered. There'd been days like this in Ulster. Never with snows this thick or temperatures this cold, but days where you waited and waited and wondered if what you were waiting for would arrive.

He remembered those, well enough.

Twilight was almost done and a pale green and purple-tinged aurora showing at the edges of the sky when they finally walked out of the trees. A man and a girl, walking side by side. The man in the uniform of a KGB captain, the girl with her cap pulled low, wrapped in a greatcoat so large it made her look tiny. A canvas bag was slung across her shoulder.

They came to the plinth marking the death of the pro-spector and looked around them, to the slopes above and back to the trees and the way they'd come. Snow had been falling all day, disguising ditches and crevasses, and Tom's hide was long since entirely hidden. The man said something and the girl shook her head. Tom would have said they were arguing.

Standing slowly, he brushed snow from his front and went to meet them.

'Rivka Rostova?'

The girl looked up then. Blonde hair and a face in shadow below the cap she'd pulled down to her eyes. She seemed older than Tom expected.

'Major Fox?' she asked.

Tom nodded.

'This is for you.' Reaching into her coat, she produced a small revolver and fired. Flame blasted from its barrel. Tom felt the round hit in his hip and stumbled sideways. Falling as the roar of the shot echoed from low cliffs on the slope above.

He could see snow in front of him. Feel the world go dark at its edges. He tried to stand and couldn't. Looking up, he saw the girl stalk towards him, revolver in hand. As he watched, she raised her weapon once more and aimed it straight at his head. He watched her finger tighten on the trigger.

96

November 1971 – Derry, Northern Ireland

The stupidity was that Tom had more in common with Vince than with his own wife, the teenager he was sleeping with, the smug bastard he worked for, or anyone in his family. Maybe that was why they were trying to kill each other. Two sides of the same hellish coin. It was darker than hell, though.

A darkness not even lit by the glowing coals hell offered. Tom backed away, gripping his ricochet-damaged wrist. Blood still seeped between his fingers. He needed time to tie it off. He didn't have time. His kukri was down in the dirt somewhere. He needed that too. The bulkhead lights in the multi-storey would come back any minute now and he'd be exposed. A sitting target in the car park's lower-ground floor.

'Should have brought a gun,' Vince shouted.

Dropping to his knees, Tom edged towards where he thought he'd lost the kukri. The concrete was cold and slick with old oil from cars long since gone to the breakers. No outside lights to filter into this lowest level, nothing to give him a sense of direction. He had no idea whether Vince was nearby, or hidden behind a pillar twenty paces distant.

Tom stopped to listen.

The dull thud of an early-morning rubbish lorry. The clatter as crates of last night's bottles were collected from outside the discotheque opposite. Beyond that, nothing. Tom edged forward, fingers searching filthy concrete for a weapon.

'Give up!' Vince shouted.

He was away to the left, Tom decided.

The kukri had to be here. Tom swept his hand across the cold floor, finding nothing. Shifting, his heel caught the fallen blade and Vince fired again.

Flame lit the space.

Noise hit the walls and rebounded.

And a round passed like a wasp over Tom's head and pierced a 500-gallon tank of heating oil, which should have been emptied eighteen months before. By then Tom had rolled behind a pillar. He had the kukri now. Instinct, visceral terror and training combining to make him grab it as he rolled.

Vince had nails through his feet, Tom reminded himself. His own blood must be leaching away. Every step would be agony. At least Tom hoped it was.

Heads or tails. What did it matter?

Reaching into his pocket, he found one of the new 50p pieces – queen's head one side, Britannia the other – and hurled it towards the oil tanks, hearing it hit one with a satisfying clang.

Vince's response was immediate. The sound of a round piercing an oil tank mixed with the echoing roar of Vince's shot.

Four rounds down.

The Provos had taken a cargo of Smith & Wesson Model 20s that summer. Redundant stock from a Boston PD armoury, put on the open market and bought through a front company. There were rumours that Colonel Gaddafi intended to arm the Provos too. Tom had no idea if that was true but he wouldn't put it past the bastard.

Oil, Tom thought, nearly slipping.

He could feel it underfoot, spilling out from the holes punched in the council-owned tanks at the back. How long now before the bulkheads came back? Minutes? Seconds?

'You die here,' Vince called.

'How many have you lost tonight?' Tom asked him. 'How many dead little simpletons? What lies will you tell their mams before you pull on a balaclava and go fire rounds over their graves?'

Vince fired and missed, the lights came back, and in the second that Vince went wide-eyed with shock at how badly he'd been fooled, Tom threw his kukri. The blade spun once to bury itself in the other man's chest.

His last bullet going wide.

'Christ . . .' Vince said.

'. . . has enough sins of his own.'

Vince looked into the face of the man he knew as Jimmy McGrath, boyfriend to Judy and newly promoted acolyte to Himself himself. Fake blood dripped from Tom's neck where he'd splashed himself with Kensington Gore. Playing dead on the flatbed of that abandoned truck, knowing Vince might come closer, had been the most dangerous part of this.

'Fuck me,' Vince said.

Ripping the kukri from his chest, Tom nodded.

The Provo dropped, shuddered once and died with his eyes wide. The last thing he saw was Tom turn away, Vince's death already dismissed as the headlights of Billy McLean's Volvo caught Tom in their beam.

The vehicle accelerated, intending to pulp Tom into a wall. McLean was behind its wheel. Behind him, wide-eyed with shock, was a wee boy.

97

November 1971 – Derry, Northern Ireland

Not having time to think, Tom threw the kukri he'd ripped from Vince's chest as hard as he could at the Volvo's windscreen, and jumped out of the way as Billy McLean braked instinctively, putting his vehicle into a skid.

The rear just missed Tom as the Volvo twisted sideways on spilt oil and thudded into one of the ruptured tanks, coming to a halt with a crumpled side door.

'Stay in there!' McLean shouted.

The wee boy didn't look as if he was going anywhere.

Slamming open his own door, McLean grabbed a sawn-off from under his seat and turned towards Tom. He skidded on oil, found his balance and lost it again as Tom closed on him and ripped the shotgun from his hands. Slipped himself, and just had time to send the shotgun skittering into a corner before hitting the concrete with a grunt.

Tom and McLean stared at each other.

Both men rolled away and came to their feet.

'Da . . . !' The boy tossed a baseball bat towards McLean, then slammed the driver's door shut and ducked out of sight at a glare from his father. McLean bent for the bat.

Tom had his back to a corner. Windowless concrete forming an amphitheatre around him. Unable to retreat, his ankle still on fire, he reached into his pocket for his lock-knife and did the only thing he could. He went to meet the man.

He went fast, knowing his boots wouldn't hold on the

lethally slippery floor. That in any fight against an uninjured man with a baseball bat he'd be the first to go down. He wanted speed. He needed to hit McLean full on.

McLean raised his bat.

He could outreach Tom, his bat could smash Tom's skull, break his arm, or batter the knife from his fingers. This was a bad place to die.

Anywhere was a bad place to die.

But here, on the lowest level of a multi-storey car park in the arse end of a city he'd be happy never to visit again, at the end of a life he wasn't sure why he'd bothered living . . .

Fuck it.

Dropping to his knees, Tom ducked the slash of the bat. Reading in that single split second McLean's shock that his blow hadn't landed. And then Tom crashed between the man's legs, carried by speed and oil slicker than ice, his knife flicking up to half castrate McLean and open his femoral artery.

McLean's scream was higher than a gelded colt's. It echo-ed off cast concrete as loud as any shot. Pure fury and fear. McLean looked in shock at the blood pumping from his groin and fell to his knees. 'Fenian bastard,' he said.

'Not me,' Tom said.

'You're—'

'No,' Tom said, 'I'm not. Believe me, I'm not. Jimmy, the good little Provo, doesn't exist.' He smiled bitterly. 'Why the fuck did you think I didn't want you to see me earlier. You really bought that "not recognising each other on the streets" bullshit? I'm Fox.'

Billy McLean was closer to death than he realised.

'Why me?' he demanded.

'Kincora.'

'You were there?'

'I'm the start of the clean-up team.'

Shock filled the man's face and then he was beyond shock and life itself. As Tom watched, he pitched forward to land on his face. And behind him, baseball bat in hand, stood the small boy. One of his eyes had been shut by a punch some days before. The other was wide. He was too terrified to go to his dead da. Too terrified to attack. Too terrified to run. Too terrified to do anything but stand there not knowing what else to do.

'My da,' he said.

Tom still had a lock-knife in his hand. The boy was a witness. A danger. Common sense said he needed to die. Tom touched his hand to his own eye.

'Your da did that?'

'Aye.'

Tom looked from the boy to the man. He knew what he should do. He knew he wasn't going to do it. No matter how heavy the knife was in his hand.

'Go,' Tom said. 'Go find . . .' He was about to say a policeman but stopped himself. What would happen to the boy then?

'Where's your mam?' he asked.

'She left.'

As mine should have done, Tom thought.

'You have a nan?'

Tom could remember his.

Your grandmother, Caro called her.

Such a formal word for someone who shuffled through life in the two tatty dresses, one for summer and one for winter . . .

'Aye,' the boy said. 'I have a nan.'

'What's her name?' Tom demanded.

The boy gave it. This man had something on him now. The boy knew that.

'What does she call you?'

Tom expected a diminutive of the boy's name. But the boy just smiled tremulously. 'Dancer,' he said. 'She calls me Ya Dancer.'

'You know where she lives?'

The boy's look said, of course he did.

'Go find her,' Tom said. 'Tell her she has to look after you. I'll come looking if she doesn't.'

'You'll kill her?'

'I will if she doesn't look after you.'

'You're no' going to kill me?'

'Not this time,' Tom said.

By nightfall, Tom was in Liverpool. Newly showered, his ankle strapped, his bleeding wrist bound up, his beard cut back to stubble and his hair in a ponytail.

His Belfast accent thick enough to render him almost incomprehensible to the customs officer who waved him through. Just another young Irishman wanting work. The kind to attract a warning from the police to keep his nose clean. And free drinks in two or three dockyard pubs, and a warning from like-minded comrades to stay away from the Special Patrol Group.

Not that Tom went anywhere near a pub that evening.

The afternoon after that he was in London.

His hair newly cut, his stubble gone, his tattered denim jacket, Levi's and black t-shirt stuffed into a bin on the Intercity 125. In their place he wore a white shirt, a silvery tie and a grey suit from M&S, anonymous enough to make him look like a publisher's rep. He travelled in a smoking carriage, second class, read that morning's edition of the *Mail*, and ate a British Rail cheese sandwich with every appearance of enjoyment.

*

'Well,' Eddington said, pushing himself through the door of the seedy office behind Piccadilly Circus that his department kept to handle people like Tom, 'I don't know whether to promote you or fire you . . .'

'Does Caro know I'm back?'

'Of course not,' his father-in-law said. 'And let's keep it that way. Use a hotel tonight. No point unsettling things by going home. You can send her a postcard from Boston.'

'Why Boston?'

'That's where you're heading next.'

98

The man's fingers danced over the parts of the .22 rifle as he put it together without even glancing down at the pieces in front of him. Charlie liked that. He liked the way Dancer could fit the bits together without looking. Almost as if he could see with his fingers. Unless he knew his way round rifles so well the pieces put themselves together for him.

He seemed lost in thought.

Wherever he was, Charlie didn't think it was here in the ruined water tower. Dancer's face was too blank. His thoughts too hidden to reach his eyes or even twitch his mouth.

He might as well have been wax.

Except for the movement of his fingers, obviously.

Becca had looked like that at the end. In the days before she died. In the accident. She was lost, he knew that now. Charlie had thought about it a lot in the last few days. Mostly he wondered why she'd abandoned him.

He felt abandoned.

It was a kind of empty feeling.

Before the thinking he'd simply done a lot of listening at doors. Grown-ups said a lot when they thought he wasn't around. Mummy, Daddy, Granny, Grandpa. Everyone talked about Becca in the weeks that followed the crash. Unless he was there. Then they didn't. Could they have seen it coming . . . ? Could they have stopped it . . . ?

Now they talked about him. In the same hushed tones. In

the same concerned voices. Where he should live. Who he should live with. All the reasons he couldn't live with Daddy.

Looking up, Charlie found Dancer staring at him.

The man's eyes were dark and flat. His face unmoving. Having carefully loaded .22 rounds into the rabbit rifle's magazine, Dancer slotted the magazine into place and worked the bolt to put a bullet into the breech. Never point a gun unless you intend to use it, Daddy said.

Charlie wondered if he should be afraid yet.

99

Thursday 3rd December – Kola Peninsula, Soviet Russia

The firing pin fell, primer ignited and propellant exploded, driving the bullet from the barrel at 2,750 feet per second. It spun three times in the split second it took to close the gap, and the girl with the revolver stumbled backwards, drilled through her forehead. A second later the KGB captain joined her in the snow, his own pistol half drawn.

Blood splattered white like an abstract expressionist painting. Long streaks of it, dotted with bone. *Death*, by Jackson Pollock. Tom's own blood loss made him light-headed. It certainly played havoc with his thoughts. He watched winter birds circle against the aurora in the stunned silence that followed the shots.

His body had entered what laymen called shock.

It wasn't shock, though, not in the strictest medical sense. Tom had had enough bullets in him to know that. Adrenaline and endorphins were flooding his body. Keeping pain at bay, while he decided on fight or flight as his best choice to stay alive.

Dennisov walked down from the trees wearing a full-length white mink like some Mosfilm movie star. His face unreadable as he gazed at the bodies. Rolling the first over with his foot, then doing the same for the second. He looked puzzled.

'Recognise them?' Tom demanded.

'No,' Dennisov replied.

A burst of irritated Russian came from the girl's kitbag, and Dennisov knelt to undo its drawstring, shaking out a military radio and a battery pack the size of a brick. A man's voice was demanding to know what had happened. It was clipped, impatient to the point of anger.

Dennisov turned it off.

'Where did you go?' Tom asked.

'I just saved your life,' Dennisov said. 'And that's your response?'

'I owe you,' Tom told him. He held Dennisov's gaze. 'Now, where did you go this morning? Why weren't you there when we woke?'

'You don't trust me?'

'I don't trust anyone,' Tom said.

Dennisov grinned. 'Good. We'll make a Russian of you yet. Now. Are you quite sure you didn't become our double-agent in Berlin?'

'Positive,' Tom said.

'That's also good,' Dennisov replied. 'I would hate to have to kill you.' Dropping to a crouch, he went through the girl's pockets. Two bars of Alyonka chocolate. An unopened packet of Cosmos 20s and a cheap lighter, which clicked up to reveal wick, flint and flame when he pulled its trigger. In the man's pockets, Dennisov found a knife, more chocolate and a flask.

'Vodka,' he said happily.

'*Dennisov*,' Tom said.

'I came out here, all right?'

'Before me?'

'Yes. Long before you.'

'And that ridiculous coat?'

'Provides the perfect camouflage. I found it back in the trees. Its owner had passed beyond needing it.'

Tom didn't know if he believed him.

Without giving Tom time to object, Dennisov took a gulp from the hip flask, flicked open the knife he'd found, sliced open Tom's trousers at the hip, and spat vodka into the wound.

'*Christ!*'

'Fifty per cent alcohol,' Dennisov said proudly. 'Maybe fifty-five. That's good. Too little alcohol it's not going to kill the germs. Too much, weirdly, it helps them.' Cutting a square from the girl's coat, he wadded it into a pressure pad and tied it into place with the cord cut from her kitbag.

'In and out,' Dennisov said. 'Didn't even hit bone. Nice.'

He reached for the dropped revolver.

'Röhm RG-14. Six-shot. The weapon used in the attempt on President Reagan's life.' Dennisov shrugged. 'It's hard to know these days what's irony and what's coincidence . . .'

He handed Tom the weapon.

'Why would Rostov's daughter shoot me?' Tom asked.

Dennisov looked at him. 'Rostov doesn't have a daughter,' he said.

100

Thursday 3rd December – Kola Peninsula, Soviet Russia

'What happened?' Amelia demanded, her question almost carried away on the rising wind.

'It was an ambush.'

Tom was impressed she didn't say told you so. Instead, she snapped an order to her Soviet helpers to fetch her the medicine box, then pack their stuff and get ready to move out.

Dennisov she ignored completely.

'When we get to the bottom,' she told Tom, 'we'll be going in one direction, you and your friend will be heading the other. If we're lucky . . .'

'We'll never see each other again?'

'. . . drifting snow will cover our tracks.'

'Amelia . . .'

'I don't know what's going on,' she said. 'I don't want to know. But my two have more chance of living if they leave now. So do I. Your one-legged friend's armed. Let him keep you safe. Well, as safe as anyone can be in this bloody country.'

Telling Tom to hold her torch, she jagged a one-use morphine syringe through his jeans into the muscles below; then knelt to remove his makeshift tourniquet. She grunted at the neatness of the entry wound.

'.22.'

Tom was surprised.

'I'm a pacifist,' she said crossly, 'not blind.'

Having dusted entry and exit point with antibiotic powder, she took sterile pads from her small first-aid box and fixed them into place with long strips of plaster. She bound the dressings with a crepe bandage fixed with a safety pin.

'You'll need these.'

Tom took the spare syringes.

'Don't overdose yourself,' she said. 'Use them only when you think you can't bear the pain any longer. And don't let anyone do anything stupid like decide to stitch the wounds shut. They'll need to heal in their own . . . Christ, why am I even telling you this. You probably know it better than me.'

He'd ask her where she'd got battlefield morphine, but she'd only say something snotty about not being the kind of person to wander round the wilderness without adequate supplies.

Tom and Amelia led the way downhill, away from the ruined base and its broken trees and burned-out huts that vanished into the drifting snows behind them.

'Plane,' Tom said.

Something small and civilian materialised overhead. The noise of its thudding engine muffled by the eldritch howl of the night wind. It disappeared into darkness as quickly as it appeared.

'We should get off the track.'

'It didn't see us,' Tom told Dennisov.

'All the same . . .' Dennisov indicated a dark stand of trees in front of them. 'I suggest we hurry.'

A barely visible track led between firs and their small group took it, stopping breathless several minutes later in a looming clearing where the path divided, heading in three different directions.

'At least the wind's dropping,' Amelia said.

Tom was about to answer, when Dennisov worked the

bolt on his carbine. Amelia's two helpers were already unslinging their hunting rifles. Voices came from ahead.

'We fall back,' Tom said.

'Too late,' Dennisov told him.

Searchlights lit the snow around them. Three searchlights. Pinning their party like moths to a board. And Tom heard the whine of snowmobiles catching up with an advance party on skis.

A voice ordered Dennisov to throw down his carbine. When he hesitated, everyone heard the sound of multiple SKS bolts being worked and the order was repeated.

Dennisov let it drop.

'And you,' the voice demanded.

Tom reluctantly let go of the six-shot Röhm he'd lifted from the girl in the clearing. Instinct and training had kicked in. He wasn't even aware he'd drawn it.

As Tom watched, a KGB general entered the clearing. Her eyes were shielded by her cap. But Tom could see that she was smiling grimly.

'*You*,' Dennisov said.

101

Thursday 3rd December – Kola Peninsula, Soviet Russia

Stepping into the clearing, the woman shot both Amelia's assistants without giving them more than a glance. They fell where they'd been standing, mobile searchlights making blood gleam where it splattered snow around them.

'Kneel,' she ordered Amelia and Tom.

Amelia opened her mouth to object and looked shocked when Tom yanked her down beside him in the snow.

'Saving your skin?' she hissed.

'Saving yours.'

'Seriously,' the general said. 'What the fuck are you wearing?' She was talking to Dennisov, who looked down at his coat.

'It suits me,' he protested.

'Major Ivan Petrovich Dennisov, I am arresting you for treason,' she told him. 'You will be returned to Moscow to await trial. They are expecting you.'

'It's Colonel,' he told her. 'I was promoted.'

'Major, Colonel. It makes no difference. You will be tried, found guilty and shot.'

'For what?' Dennisov demanded.

She backhanded him, and half a dozen SKS 7.62s came up when he clenched his fist and stepped towards her.

'You know what.'

'Believe me, I don't.'

'You have been running an operation to undercut the

355

Red Army's direct commands. Starting with the attack on our allies at Heringsdorf. You will die for it.'

'Berlin acted without authorisation.'

'They did what we have become too effete to do. Act decisively. Save your lies for the court. Not that they'll believe you. We're going to televise it, you know. It's about time we reminded Soviet citizens what happens to traitors.'

'Marshal Milov won't allow it.'

'He's going to be replaced.'

'Gorbachev would never . . .'

The woman snorted. 'Things change,' she said fiercely. 'Weak links in the Politburo will be replaced. The worst shot, the rest jailed. There will be no compromises with Washington, London or Bonn. It's time this country learned to stand on its feet again. As for you . . .'

Dennisov met her glare.

'After you have been tried and found guilty, you will be shot by a firing squad. If I get my way, we will televise that too. I intend to be there.' Her lip curled. 'Hell, I intend to give the order myself.'

'What are the charges?'

'Treason. Gangsterism. Corruption. Murder.'

'Whose murder?'

Her gaze sharpened. 'Your father's.'

Tom looked up.

'As for you,' the woman said to him, 'you will also be shipped to Moscow, and I will question you myself in the cellars of the Lubyanka.'

'Leave him out of this,' Dennisov said.

'Why would I? Do you think the rest of us are fools? That no one knows that he, like you, is *Voryvzakone*? That you stepped into Erekle Gabashville's shoes? We have proof that you have used your official position to facilitate criminality. That your sordid little bar is a front for money laundering . . .'

Tom felt a shiver run down his spine.

Two years before, he'd been across the table when a Georgian gangster had shot himself, having lost his own son as the price for helping Tom hunt down the kidnappers of the British ambassador's daughter. Erekle Gabashville, known to his friends as Beziki, had passed his crime interests to Tom, who'd handed them to Dennisov. It hadn't occurred to Tom to ask Dennisov how that was going. Rather better than the authorities liked, from the sound of it.

The woman's eyes were hard when she turned back to Tom and took off her high-peaked cap.

'You don't recognise me, do you?'

He did. At least, he did now.

She smiled as fear entered Tom's face.

102

Thursday 3rd December – Hampshire

'Charlie . . .'

'It's all right.'

It was more than all right. Becca was back.

'No, it's not,' Becca said. 'He's going to shoot you.'

She sounded really worried, which was odd because she'd barely seemed to notice he was alive until after she was dead. And when she did, it was only to tell him to get out of her room, leave her things alone and stop being weird.

She called him the Accident.

He'd said, no, she was the accident.

And she'd pushed him out of her room and onto the landing, and shouted fiercely enough to be heard downstairs that, No, he was the *accident*. She was the *mistake*.

Mummy had been furious with both of them.

Charlie still wasn't sure why.

Becca had her face half turned away. She always had her head turned away these days, except for the times she had her back to him. He used to worry it was because she'd been so badly injured in the car crash, until he remembered she used to do that in life too. Now he knew it was because . . .

'You're crying,' Charlie said.

'Well, doh.' She dragged her hand angrily across her eyes. 'One of us has to live.'

'Why?' Charlie asked. That thought was interesting.

'Daddy,' Becca said. 'Mummy, me, you. He'll be sad if we were all dead.'

'He's sad already.'

'Sadder then.'

'Who are you talking to?' Dancer demanded.

'My sister,' Charlie said. 'She's sitting beside you. Just there.'

Despite himself, Dancer glanced to his right. The tank room at the top of the water tower looked empty to him.

That didn't surprise Charlie. Becca was good at staying hidden.

'She's imaginary?' Dancer asked.

'She's dead,' Charlie said.

Dancer scowled.

'She had a car crash,' Charlie explained hastily. 'Her Mini hit a tree. It was dry, the road was clear, her brakes were working, there were no skid marks.'

He recited the list from memory. A list he wasn't meant to have read and hadn't. But a boy could learn a lot by listening. 'She was pregnant, you see. Daddy used to think she'd killed herself. Until Mummy told him he wasn't allowed to think that. Mummy used to think it was an accident . . .'

'What does she think now?'

'She's dead,' Charlie said. 'I'm not sure she thinks anything.'

'You don't see her too?'

'She was ready to go,' Charlie explained. 'She'd made up with Daddy and we had a holiday. That was the holiday when she got ill. Then we had a year of hospitals and Daddy trying not to be upset and Mummy being brave, and by the end of that she'd said all her goodbyes.'

He sounded matter-of-fact, even to himself. Mostly because that was how he felt about it now. He'd had a whole year to accept that Mummy was dying. That was more than enough time when you knew something was inevitable. He hadn't even had ten minutes with Becca.

One day Becca was there, and then she wasn't.

She hadn't said any goodbyes. That was what convinced Charlie it was an accident. If she'd meant to kill herself she'd have said proper goodbyes. I mean, he knew she was Becca and could be difficult . . .

'Even Becca . . .' Charlie said.

'Even Becca what?'

So Charlie told him. 'She might be unprocessed emotion,' he added. 'That's what a psychologist told Mummy. Pretending she's still here but invisible might be my way of dealing with not being ready to accept she's dead.'

'What does Becca say?'

Charlie looked at Dancer with new respect.

'She says it's an interesting idea.'

Dancer laughed.

'Also,' Charlie said, 'if you're going to shoot me, you should probably do so.'

'Becca said that?' Dancer asked.

'No.' Charlie shook his head. 'That's me.'

'Sins of the fathers,' Becca added.

Dancer's eyes widened and Charlie realised he'd repeated that too.

'That's Becca,' Charlie said hastily. He didn't want to make things worse.

He watched Dancer drop out the magazine, shoot the bolt to eject the round in the breech and toss Charlie the rifle.

'You're not going to shoot me?'

'Not this time,' Dancer said.

103

Thursday 3rd December – Kola Peninsula, Soviet Russia

Snow had fallen in flurries, but the paths in the Moscow cemetery had been cleared overnight. Tom could remember it well. Surprisingly well, given how drunk he'd been at the time. Dead birds had been collected from beneath their trees and tossed into a bin near the entrance. It was always the small birds that died. Their faster metabolism meant they burned more energy, and they had shorter lives anyway. Comrade Vedenin, there to bury his dead son. Commissar Milov, possibly there as a mark of respect, but more likely to keep his eye on everyone. Erekle Gabashville, looking out of place. Even General Dennisov, Dennisov's father, squat and hobbling like a poisonous gnome. These were the canny ones.

Brave, wily or timid enough to survive the Stalin years.

It was the girl beside General Vedenin who attracted glances. Blonde, stiff-faced and beautifully dressed in Western clothes. Sophia Dennisova, the general's other daughter. The dutiful one. The legitimate one. The one who'd been engaged to the late Vladimir Vedenin . . .

The coffin arrived on the shoulders of six fellow officers from the Vnutrenniye Voiska. Dressing up wild dogs didn't make them any less wild, Wax Angel had said. But they stood straight and looked smart enough carrying a box containing a dead idiot.

The state paid for funerals, and by tradition funerals were open to the public; although the earliness of the hour and the suited young men with hard eyes by the cemetery entrance had been effective in putting off the curious.

'Monsters are what I do.'

Tom had told Caro that one night in Moscow, when she flew out from London with the divorce papers they'd never signed. They'd ended up in bed for the first time in years. He'd told her everything. Another first. He'd have said he'd been more honest with her then than he'd ever been with himself.

Now he knew that was a half-truth.

Here, knelt in the snow in front of Sophia Dennisova, his friend's sister, his dead enemy's daughter, the fiancée of a boy he'd killed, Tom knew he'd lied. Monsters *were* what he did, but monsters were also what those who killed monsters became.

Tom recognised Sophia now. How could he not?

The self-styled dutiful daughter. The only one of his three children that General Dennisov, that psychotic old bastard, had been proud of.

'You ruined my father's life, corrupted my crippled idiot of a brother, murdered the man I intended to marry, and you didn't even recognise me . . . ?' Sophia Dennisova's Tokarev came up and Tom forced himself to stare back as he waited for a bullet that didn't come. 'You wish,' she told him.

He'd really believed she would pull the trigger.

'Vedenin was a spoilt thug,' her brother said crossly. 'A drunk. A sadist. The marriage wasn't even your idea. Don't tell me you weren't relieved when he died.'

'I wanted what his father could bring,' Sophia hissed. 'Contacts. Opportunities. Alliances. That's what my father wanted. Our father. Your father.'

'Sophia . . .'

'You're going to be shot,' she said. 'As for him—' She gestured at Tom '—I meant what I said. He will be taken to the Lubyanka and I will question him myself. Believe it when I say I will do my very best to keep him alive until I've wrung out every whimper.'

'And me?' Amelia asked.

'You?' Sophia Dennisova considered Amelia, then her pistol. She smiled thinly. 'I'd have said you were entirely surplus to requirements, wouldn't you?'

'I have the money,' Tom said hastily.

He tossed his rucksack at Sophia's feet and bundles of $5,000 notes spilled out onto the snow. The black-market rate for dollars was fifteen times higher than the official one. The Vnutrenniye Voiska troops around her were staring in utter disbelief at sums of money larger than their wildest dreams.

Sophia barely glanced at Tom's offering.

'You killed—'

'It was an accident,' Dennisov said. 'The KGB records . . .'

Sophia glared. 'Since when do people like us believe the records?'

'That's a huge sum of money,' her brother reminded her.

'Fuck,' she said. 'You're both fools. This isn't about money. This has *never* been about money.'

'What is it about then?' Dennisov demanded.

At her nod, the nearest VV trooper clubbed him and Dennisov toppled sideways, groaning. 'It's about the State,' Sophia said, sounding offended. 'The State. The People. The Party. The things *nomenklatura* like us should care about.' Stepping closer, she kicked her brother. 'The things everyone *should* care about, even you. And I knew *you'd* come,' she said, turning to Tom. 'If we used the right bait. Did you like the photograph?'

'I don't know what you're talking about.'

'Oh, believe me. You do. Rostov's moon-faced pretend daughter . . .' Sophia jerked her head at Amelia. 'The photograph of her in the forest gazing upwards. It took some doing to get that into the right hands.' Dennisov's sister sounded pleased with herself. 'After that, all we needed was you.'

She smiled. '"*I have a teenage daughter. The love of my life. I will do anything to save her. Here . . .*"' She mimed handing over a photograph. '"*Her name is Rivka . . .*" Rivka's Russian for Rebecca, but I imagine you knew that.'

Tom felt sick at his own stupidity.

'Rostov's dead. I'm sure that won't surprise you. I didn't even need to have him killed. The radiation did it for me.' She snorted. 'He was too sick to eat and too frightened not to dangle the bait in front of you as I'd ordered.'

'You couldn't be certain I'd bite.'

'Of course I could. You're entirely predictable. Your kind always are. Rebels on a leash. We keep them too. You understand, don't you? That you will die here?'

Tom looked around him.

'No, fool. Here in the Soviet Union. In the cellars of the Lubyanka. After I've wrung every last scream from you.'

'Oh, for fuck's sake,' Dennisov said, struggling to his feet. 'We've done this bit already. And Tom didn't kill Daddy either. I did.'

'You confess to murder?'

'He was a monster.'

'He was a hero.' There was a catch in Sophia Dennisova's voice. 'A hero of the Soviet Union. A hero of Stalingrad. His photograph was in my school book.'

'He was a psychotic little bully.'

Sophia kicked his good leg from under him, and Dennisov

toppled sideways and rolled out of range. This time he decided to stay down.

'And the glass ball?' Tom said.

'*What is this idiocy?*' Sophia Dennisova asked savagely. 'Where did it come from? Who first mentioned it? I know nothing about a glass ball . . .'

'You must do.'

Tom could see in her eyes that she didn't.

Amelia still knelt beside him, her face stony. Dennisov was feeling the torn skin of his temple where he'd been clubbed. Too cold for easy bleeding, Tom thought distractedly, his mind on other matters as he took in the scene.

They were pinned in the glare of the Vnutrenniye Voiska's searchlights. But the searchlights were small, portable. Lead–acid batteries don't like the cold, and it was *very* cold. Their bulbs were already dimming in the way battery-powered lights did if left on too long. Tom knew that was something he could use. He just needed to work out how.

'Rostov mentioned an orb,' Dennisov said, looking up at his sister. 'That day at lunch with Tom in Tallinn. I was listening in from the floor above. His price was ten million dollars and safe passage to the West for his daughter . . .'

'Poor, poor Rivka.'

Dennisov ignored Sophia's comment.

'He's telling the truth,' Tom said. 'In return for the dollars and his daughter's safe passage, I was to get a Geiger counter, its readouts and a glass sphere that was apparently priceless.'

Sophia shook her head crossly. 'He was to offer the truth of what happened, the Geiger counter and the plans. I know. I wrote his lines for him. All he had to do was deliver them.'

'He called it a Fabergé egg among bombs,' Tom said.

Sophia struggled to control her rage.

'You,' she said, glaring at her brother. 'What do you know about this?'

'I'm the family drunk,' Dennisov said. 'A fool. I don't know anything about anything.'

He caught Tom's gaze and Tom could swear he smiled.

104

Whisky splashed the back of Grandpa's wrist, he jumped so suddenly. He didn't drop the decanter though. Charlie was glad. It was one of the good ones. His grandfather gazed at the rabbit rifle in Dancer's hands. It was held lightly and angled to the floor.

'At least you waited until my wife was gone.'

'My idea,' said Charlie, slipping from behind Dancer. 'Granny would only make a fuss.'

He held a reluctant Cat in his arms, and grinned when Cat struggled free, turned to sneer at the clumsy way he'd been carried, and headed for the warmth of the fire, curling up in front of it on a Persian carpet.

Grandpa's eyes widened as Charlie took the rifle from Dancer, dropped out its magazine and ejected the round in the breech.

'Wipe it down,' Dancer told him.

Taking a handkerchief from his pocket, Charlie ran it over the lock, stock and barrel to remove Dancer's fingerprints. Then he propped it in the corner, beside the Georgian side table with the Regency carriage clock. Mummy had loved that clock. Charlie wasn't sure why. It was very noisy, very big and never told the right time.

'Magazine,' Dancer reminded him.

Removing five rounds of .22 from the magazine, Charlie

wiped them down and lined them up neatly on the Georgian card table.

'And the ones in your pocket.'

Slightly guiltily, Charlie removed the remaining .22, wiped them down in turn and made himself another line behind the first. 'Looks like a chess set,' he said. 'But with only pawns.'

When Charlie looked up, Dancer was watching Charlie with a slightly strange smile, and Grandpa was watching Dancer.

'Major Fox's son,' Dancer said.

It wasn't quite a question. Or if it was, Grandpa didn't answer. He just waited.

'Your grandson says his mother's dead. His sister too. And you've sent his father away, and he might be dead by now as well.'

'I hope to God not,' Grandpa said.

Charlie wondered if he was allowed to ask why they were talking about him as if he wasn't there. At his new school, which must be about to break up soon, he'd been told there were no stupid questions, which was ridiculous because Charlie could think of dozens of stupid questions. He wondered if that would be one of them.

'I didn't take your rifle,' Charlie said.

Grandpa stared at him.

'That's what this is about?'

Charlie stared back. Of course it was. What else could it be about? Granny and Aunt Agatha said he'd taken the rifle. He hadn't. Grandpa should know that. It was his job to know that when Daddy was away. He was meant to take Charlie's side.

'I don't lie,' Charlie said.

Lying made him feel sick. He could taste the lie for days.

He always told the truth, Daddy could have told them that. Charlie never lied.

Not even when the truth got him in trouble.

'How did you get in?'

That question was for Dancer. Grandpa meant how did you get past the two men standing guard at the front. Charlie answered it for him.

'We used the side door.'

'It's locked.'

'I used the key under the big pot.'

'You hid a key under a pot?'

'Mummy did,' Charlie said. 'When she was Becca's age. It's rusty now.'

Grandpa sighed.

Outside the window, one of Grandpa's two bodyguards began his walk round the garden. It would take him ten minutes and then he'd go back to watching the road. Both guards would watch the road for half an hour and then the other one would take his own walk. They took turns to make it fair.

Grandpa didn't seem pleased when Charlie explained this.

'I couldn't let them see me,' Charlie explained.

'When?'

'When I came to get Cat's food.'

'Good God.' Grandpa glanced at the tail-less feline who opened one eye to see what the fuss was about, and then went back to dozing in front of the warm fire. 'You've been breaking in?'

'I waited until the cars were gone.'

'The alarm . . .'

'Almost got me,' Charlie admitted.

It had gone off once – Charlie was trying to get in, and so was Mrs Ross. He was lucky they hadn't met. That would have complicated things. She'd tutted at whatever mistake she'd apparently made, cancelled the alarm and reset the box in the hall. Charlie didn't tell Grandpa that. He didn't want to get her into trouble.

Instead he said, 'It's not set for the side door.' Grandpa opened his mouth to disagree so Charlie amended his words. 'Well, it was,' he said. 'But I cut the wires to the plates, joined them together and wrapped them in tape . . .'

Dancer laughed.

'You're the tramp . . .'

Dancer touched his hand to his forelock. 'Aye, sir,' he said. 'Very good, sir.'

'Dancer didn't kidnap me,' Charlie said. 'I ran away and we sort of found each other. He helped me avoid the police.'

'He's good at that,' Grandpa said.

There was something in the way Grandpa said that which made Charlie feel uneasy. Dancer didn't seem to like it either. His face sharpened.

'I left a cutting,' he said.

'I got it,' Grandpa said. 'What I don't understand—' He glanced at Charlie and then looked at Dancer '—is why . . .'

'That night,' Dancer said, 'there was a wee boy . . .'

'You?' Grandpa looked shocked. 'Of course, you. If you're here it has to be.'

'Fox never told you. Did he?'

'That he let a witness . . . ?' Grandpa shook his head. Charlie wasn't sure what was going on. He knew it was serious though.

'There's a list,' Dancer said.

Grandpa waited.

'You know which one.'

'Let's suppose I do.'

'I want my name removed from it. There can't be that many targets left anyway.'

'And in return?'

'I brought him back,' Dancer said.

'He brought himself back.'

'I told him it was time he went home. That I'd be there to witness the deal.'

'What deal?'

'He comes home, he doesn't run away again, and you let him live with his father.'

'A man you swore to—'

'People change.'

Charlie held up his hand as if in a lesson at school. Both men turned to look at him. 'Do you think I'll change?' he asked, sounding worried.

Dancer at least gave Charlie's question the consideration it deserved, watched by Lord Eddington, while two SO1 officers circled the gardens, oblivious to what was going on inside. 'No,' Dancer said finally. 'You're you. That's fine. I think you'll probably stay the same.'

105

Thursday 3rd December – Kola Peninsula, Soviet Russia

'Get up,' Sophia told Dennisov.

Her brother shook his head, and Sophia's scowl said she'd happily forego the show-trial in Moscow and shoot him here and now if he gave her much more trouble. Tom hoped Dennisov realised how close his sister was to the edge. Tom doubted it, though. He seemed drunker than ever.

'But I'm not done here,' Dennisov said petulantly. He gestured jerkily at the desolate space around them. He was indicating soldiers, Tom realised suddenly. Pushing his hand into his side pocket, Dennisov fumbled at his hip flask.

'You're a disgrace,' Sophia told him.

A moment later, she kicked the flask out of his hands.

As Dennisov went scrabbling after it across trampled snow, Tom saw him slip a hand inside his ridiculous coat, retrieve something and palm it, while grabbing for the flask with his other. Wrenching the flask's top open with his teeth, he tipped it up, groaned and threw it down.

'Empty,' he said in disgust.

Sophia was scowling. Amelia looked resigned.

Tom refocused on the Vnutrenniye Voiska around him. Six shots or seven in the tiny pistol clipped to the back of his belt. Seven, he thought. Was he confident enough to put his life on it? He wished he'd paid more attention when Dennisov talked him through the Seecamp .32 on the train. No safety catch. So nothing to thumb-off first. He was certain of that. No sights either.

It was a last-ditch definition of point, shoot and pray.

'Drag my brother up,' Sophia said.

Two soldiers stepped forward.

'Tom . . .' Dennisov said.

Reaching for the Seecamp with frozen fingers, Tom edged it free.

Too clumsily. A Vnutrenniye Voiska yelled a warning and Tom shot out his searchlight, shooting the soldier a split second later. The man jack-knifed, hands to his gut, and Tom slammed his third round into the crown of his head.

Three shots down.

One searchlight, one soldier.

At the same time, Dennisov rolled onto his back to put a bullet through the jaw of the soldier standing over him. It exited the man's brain-pan. Dennisov's next round put out another searchlight. The one after, the soldier manning it.

Three shots in unison.

Two searchlights, three soldiers.

It had taken a couple of seconds, if that.

Sophia had managed to draw her own pistol when Amelia grabbed the hunting rifle her dead helper had dropped, working its bolt with a loud clang.

'Don't!' she ordered.

'Shoot her,' Dennisov said.

Amelia gave the faintest shake of her head.

'Do it!' Dennisov shouted.

Amelia stood her ground and Dennisov rolled his eyes.

'*She's a pacifist,*' Tom yelled.

The two remaining soldiers unfroze, their rifles swinging towards Amelia, and died when Tom drilled both through the heart in rapid succession. His shots sounding high and sharp. The tiny pistol barely jumping in his hands. 'Drop it,' Tom ordered. He watched Sophia weigh her chances. She let her Tokarev drop.

'*Tom*,' Dennisov warned.

They could all hear it through a drop in the wind. The faint whine of 2-stroke motors out on the plateau. More snowcats were on their way. Flickering lights in the distance, off to the east. Dennisov looked uncharacteristically troubled.

'We need to move.'

'What about your sister?'

Dennisov raised his pistol, then hesitated.

Sophia snorted. 'You don't have the balls,' she told him. 'You never have had. If the situation were reversed, I wouldn't hesitate.'

'We're different.'

'Very,' Sophia said. 'I should have been the boy.'

Dennisov shot her through the leg. 'You talk too much,' he said.

'Give me a second,' Amelia ordered. She rolled a dead NCO over and began emptying his pockets.

'What are you looking for?'

'Anything to tell me why they're here.'

Tom opened his mouth to say they already knew.

Amelia beat him to it. 'You really think this is all about you?' she demanded. 'That this entire plan was put into place to entice you, Tom Fox, across the border, capture you and take you to the Lubyanka to be horribly tortured?'

He had.

'Men,' Amelia said.

'You're going to die,' Sophia said. 'All of you.'

106

Thursday 3rd December – Kola Peninsula, Soviet Russia

'This way.'

The headlights through the trees were getting closer, the noise of the 2-stroke engines louder. On a night this cold, in a snowscape this bleak and uninhabited, Tom and Dennisov's shots would have been heard for miles.

'Ever ridden snowcats before?' Dennisov asked.

Amelia's snort was withering.

'I'll take that as a yes,' he said. 'We ride with headlights off.' He jerked his head towards the vehicles grinding their way up the slope. 'It's bad enough they'll be able to follow our tracks.'

'Your tracks,' Amelia said. 'I'm staying here.'

'You can't,' Tom said, slinging the cash across his back and adding a dropped SVT-40 rifle to his load.

'I'll just say I have no idea who you are, why you came here or what the fuck's actually going on. Wouldn't be that far from the truth,' she added bitterly.

'They'll still kill you,' Dennisov said.

Tom grunted agreement. 'You know they will.'

'Oh, fuck the lot of you.' Flicking open a pocket-knife, Amelia slashed the starter wires on the snowcat they were abandoning, removed its spare petrol can, and hooked her leg over the saddle of another.

'Come on then,' she said.

*

There were lights following.

There had been lights for the last hour.

A thought was nagging at the edge of Tom's mind. It moved away every time he tried to nail it down.

You really think this is about you?

The horizon flickered with a wall of washed-out neon where solar winds battered the earth's magnetic field. The snow they fled across was powder fresh, and what passed for day still hours distant. The wind in their faces so cold Tom steered from instinct and hunched behind the snowcat's screen as his thoughts nagged at that.

If this wasn't about Sophia Dennisova's desire for revenge, what was it about?

Wind-shaped birches gave way to a slope, where gales had scoured the snow from ice and granite that grated under their skis. Nearing a ribbon lake, they stopped briefly to judge the steepness of the approach. Ice would hide their tracks, and they needed to be as hard as possible to follow. All this in near darkness with only a sliver of moon and the aurora to light them.

Hitting the far end of the lake, they ground up a slope, their vehicles cutting deep into the snow's crust, found another lake beyond and clattered onto its surface. Tom could smell the heat from his engine, feel its warmth rising towards him. The new lake was not as wide, but it was longer, its edge rising sharply on one side.

This time they left halfway along, Dennisov suddenly veering towards an icy slope between hills and Tom and Amelia following. The ridge at the top was so sharp Tom almost took off before gathering speed between the trees as he headed for an open expanse of snow. Abruptly, Dennisov cut his power and Amelia instinctively did the same. Swerving to avoid them, Tom clipped a half-submerged stump and catapulted from his saddle as his machine plummeted out of sight. Tom rolled to the edge of a drop.

Between the slope's edge and a new lake's surface was a fall of fifteen feet. Tom was on his knees, staring at his ruined snowcat and swearing when Amelia reached him. 'Reindeer fence,' she said, indicating the post and its snapped and rusting wire.

'Thought you couldn't fence them in?'

'Hasn't stopped Murmansk trying.'

'Broken,' Dennisov said, peering at the fallen snowcat.

'I noticed,' Tom replied.

Dennisov kickstarted his machine back to life. 'Better see what we're facing.' He headed up the slope they'd ridden down and stood for a moment silhouetted against the sky. Someone else had seen him too.

The shot was high and sharp.

A dull thud matched by Dennisov's furious shout as he toppled sideways. Then he was back on his feet, back on his snowcat and heading downhill. 'Fuckers,' he said. A neat hole in his prosthetic leg showed where the bullet hit.

'How many?' Amelia demanded.

'Eight or nine. At the start of the lake. Heading onto the ice . . .' He caught Tom's glance. 'Aye,' he said. 'Sniper. Night-sights. Dragunov SVD-63 probably.' Not standard Vnutrenniye Voiska then. Sniper training and infrared sights were altogether too sophisticated for conscripted border troops.

'Why a sniper?' Tom asked.

Dennisov shrugged.

'Make him tell you,' Amelia demanded.

'Should have left her behind,' Dennisov said. 'Let her take her chances.'

'That's not—' Tom began.

'Fuck it!' Dennisov rounded on him. 'I'm freezing to death,

I'm out of vodka, I'm in the middle of fucking nowhere, you're treating me like I'm the enemy, and my own side just tried to put a fucking round through me. I'm not interested in fair. All right? I'm interested in getting out of this alive. I'm interested in winning.'

Dragging open his mink coat, he said, 'It's about this. Okay? Everything. All of it. Every fucking moment. It's about this.'

An orb wrapped in what looked like silver foil hung in a string bag round his neck.

'Fuck,' Amelia said.

'You're taking it back to Moscow?' Tom demanded.

'Of course I'm not taking it back to Moscow. You fuckwit. We already have the plans. You're taking it to London. My job is to make that happen.'

It was the old Sami taxi-driver's memories of the Winter War in Finland that gave Tom his idea. 'Wait on the ice,' he said. 'I'll either join you in a few minutes or I won't. Don't come back for me. You stand a better chance of getting Amelia to the border. Amelia, you need to take the orb to Eddington.'

'I'm a pacifist,' Amelia said. 'That's a bomb.'

'Call it evening up the odds.'

'Call it what you like,' Amelia said. 'I'm not doing it.'

'I'll do it,' Dennisov promised. 'If necessary I'll fucking defect and take it with me. Sveta can defect too. Charlie's going to need us to fight his corner. What are you going to be doing?'

Tom told him.

Stringing wire at head height between firs as he went, Tom climbed to the ridge above to track the vehicles following them. They came in a V-formation, three riding point, the rest holding back, fanned out behind. The advance party were moving fast, headlights on full. Faster than he expected. Abandoning his ridge, with its view of the approach, Tom hurried to his firs. As the three advance vehicles crested the ridge, one after another, they accelerated, gathering speed as they raced for the new lake below.

The old Finn's idea of an ambush was as effective as it was brutal.

The wire caught the first soldier across his throat and slammed him into his pillion passenger. If the rider's neck hadn't broken on impact, enough of his throat had been sliced open to kill him anyway. His passenger was down in the snow, holding his skull, when the vehicle behind hit him, expelling rider and pillion. The third one went over the edge, crushing its riders as it landed. Tom was out of hiding and closing the gap before the second snowcat's pillion even realised someone was behind him. Tom saw the man's eyes go wide, and then it was done, his neck broken.

His companion was already dead.

One of the snowcats had a 4-gallon can of petrol strapped to its side, and the dead men carried Tokarev 7.62s. Tom slid the can over the edge and saw whiteness head for it. Dennisov's damn coat. Pocketing a Tokarev, he tossed another to Dennisov, kept the clips from the other two men and tossed their pistols into the snow. The last thing he took was a hip flask from the first man to die.

Time to move.

107

Thursday 3rd December – Kola Peninsula, Soviet Russia

Throwing himself over the edge, Tom bounced off a boulder and rolled down scree, slamming into lake ice at the bottom. He gasped, the northern lights turning black for a moment as Amelia's morphine lost its battle with the pain.

Amelia was beside him in a moment.

'Another,' he begged.

'It's not time,' she said.

'Just do it.'

'You do it . . .' She tossed Tom a tube of battlefield morphine and scowled when Tom ripped off the top, stabbing its stubby needle through his trousers. The pain lifted and for a moment he felt almost happy.

'Here,' he said.

Dennisov caught the hip flask.

'What is it?'

'I don't imagine it's water.' Tom watched his friend drain half its contents, and shook his head when Dennisov tried to pass it across. 'I fight better sober.'

'And I don't.' Dennisov had an AK-47 slung across his hip to go with the rifle ported across his back. He was looking pleased with himself.

'Where did you get that?'

'From our friend here.' Dennisov indicated a body beside the army-issue snowcat that had gone over the edge. The

Perspex windshield was shattered and its handlebars bent out of true, but unlike Tom's machine its ski wasn't broken.

'Its rider took the brunt,' he said.

'Luckily for you.' Amelia kicked her snowcat to life.

They raced away from their pursuers, their Burans newly fuelled and no longer stinking of over-hot engines and burning oil. They rode the length of the ribbon lake. Heading parallel to the aurora. Not looking back.

No shots followed.

A sudden flare of the aurora revealed a group of figures on the lake in front of them. 'Who are they?' Tom shouted.

Dennisov peered. 'Ice-fishers.'

A family were dragging long nets from a hole they'd chain-sawed into the lake's surface. Blocks of ice piled into a crude wall said it was a regular fishing hole. Tom could see a fire in some kind of bucket.

'I'm going to warn them,' Amelia shouted.

'No time,' Dennisov told her. 'We head east . . .'

'North,' Tom said. 'For Norway.'

'East,' Dennisov insisted. 'There's an SSV base. I will call Moscow. The Commissar will order the SSV to protect us.'

'*Amelia* . . .'

'Leave her,' Dennisov insisted.

She was heading for the ice-fishers.

'Go home!' Amelia shouted at the family, who stood as she approached. One of the men grabbed the chain-saw and tried to crank it into life. 'Soldiers,' Amelia yelled. 'Soldiers, police, guns!'

They scattered. By then, Dennisov was way ahead. Although Tom had slowed, then slowed again to let Amelia catch up. 'Your conscience will kill you.'

'At least I have one.'

Yanking open her throttle, Amelia caned the 2-stroke to close the gap on Dennisov, who was powering towards the far end of the lake. By the time the ice narrowed to fit between dimly lit slopes, their snowmobiles were almost side by side.

Dennisov pointed to the left.

'Fuck,' Tom said.

A turn so sharp it had to be artificial led up a ramp to an open-mouthed hangar dug into the snowy hillside. The ramp was painted a dizzying dazzle of monochrome camouflage that stopped Tom's eyes from focusing.

He had no trouble seeing the hangar. Its doors were wide, its interior lit as brightly as the Bolshoi on a gala night. A flat-bottomed speedboat, with a raised propeller behind its open cabin, blocked the way to an altogether weirder craft. This was three times the boat's length, had stub wings and an exaggerated tail. Its top half looked like a cut-price Concorde, the bottom borrowed from an outrigger canoe.

It had wing guns either side.

'Tupolev Aerosledge,' Dennisov said, nodding at the boat. 'And that's an Ekranoplan Wingship. Delivered here by helicopters, I imagine.'

He considered them carefully.

'Ugly bastards.'

The Aerosledge was white with a vermillion stripe down its side and Red Stars on the fins either side of its propeller. Its windscreen was bulletproof, finished in chrome trim and swept round to form the sides of its cabin.

A chrome searchlight graced its prow.

'Pity it's not a machine gun,' Dennisov said.

'Where's everyone?' Amelia demanded. Tom was asking himself the same question. The base looked empty, and strangers like them should never have been allowed to get this close. As for the wide-open doors and lights . . . A trap?

'Let me do the talking,' Dennisov said.

There was no talking to be done.

No one guarded the freezing interior of the hangar. The machine room backing onto it was empty. Its lathes, drilling machines, hydraulic lifts and heating turned off, for all its lights had been left on. A door beyond that was locked until Dennisov shot its lock. A sign in a corridor indicated crew quarters in one direction. The CO's office, canteen and officers' mess in the other.

The CO's door was open and his office empty.

Having read a fax not even ripped from the fax machine, Dennisov read another on the absent CO's desk and smiled sourly. It was from C-in-C North Western Command, and ordered the CO to find and hold the traitor Colonel Dennisov, a woman calling herself Dr Amelia Blackburn, and Major Tom Fox, a well-known British spy.

The fax still in the machine told him to assist Colonel Dennisov in every way possible, and provide full protection for Dr Amelia Blackburn and Major Tom Fox, both friends of the Soviet Union. This one was signed 'Milov' and copied to the Politburo. Neither order had been entered in the duty book.

Neither had been acknowledged.

Instead a hastily written, back-dated record in the daily book confirmed the CO's plan to take his entire command on an urgent seventy-six-hour night exercise. Its entry time was twelve hours before the faxes, which would have been more convincing if the CO hadn't been in so much of a hurry he left the book open on his desk, and the lid off his Union fountain pen.

'Sensible man,' Dennisov said.

'We should find the armoury,' Tom said.

Dennisov hefted his AK-47. '"There is yet powder in the powder flakes . . ." Just as well. That *will* be locked.'

'You're quoting Turgenev?'

'Taras Bulba. Gogol. We should move.'

'Which is faster,' Tom asked, 'Aerosledge or Ekranoplan?'

'Ekranoplan. But an Aerosledge is easier to handle, and a fuck of a lot nimbler.'

Dennisov was already dragging the sledge towards the ice when Tom spotted what looked like a dustsheet-covered motorbike. He yanked its cover free to reveal a bastard cross between a snowcat and a trials bike. It had studs in its fat back wheel. At the front was a single ski.

'You're grinning,' Dennisov said.

108

Friday 4th December – Kola Peninsula, Soviet Russia

Sophia's troop were nearing the ramp when the Aerosledge and Tom's snowbike broke through, the Aerosledge's search-light on full beam. Without releasing its wheel, Dennisov burned out a full clip of AK-47, taking down a snowcat and forcing the rest to swerve.

Heads down, Tom, Dennisov and Amelia raced away.

Wind had stripped the lake's surface. Repeated thaws and refreezes had produced edges and seams and changes of level in the ice. Swerving to avoid a frozen-over fishing hole, Tom's bike hit the ruts of an old ski track and he almost went down.

By the time his heart slowed, bike and Aerosledge were closing on the northern end of the lake, headlights now off and shots coming from behind them. None hit. The lake gave way to scree, and Tom fought for control as his rear wheel slid on ice-glazed gravel and his front ski ground over granite.

If he came off at this speed, he'd be dead.

Then rock and scree were done, and he was safely back on ice with a new ribbon lake unfolding into darkness ahead. Roaring past the Aerosledge, Tom swerved suddenly as a new party of ice-fishers scattered, their shocked faces frozen on his memory.

With luck, they'd have the sense to leave.

More shots came from behind. Tom only knew because one hissed past close enough to drown out the roar of his bike. He didn't even want to think about how close that was. *Weave.* A basic rule when someone is trying to put a bullet in you. *Weave, find some fucking cover, and get the hell out of there.* The weaving he could do, instinctively counter-steering as he jinked his way across the ice.

Except, weaving only worked if you were heading for cover and finding cover wasn't an option unless you counted the Aerosledge, and Tom doubted how heavily armoured that was. Which meant part three kicked in.

Get the hell out of there.

The lake split and they ran north-west, heading towards a low line of hills back-lit by the greens, purples and blues of the northern lights. There was a point, Dennisov promised them, where three time zones and three states met. You could step between Soviet Russia, Norway and Finland. Tom didn't care which of the last two he stepped into, as long as he stepped out of the first.

Twisting the grip of his bike with frozen fingers, Tom red-lined its engine, feeling the front ski lift and then shudder and jump as his bike raced over uneven ice. The lake was longer than he'd realised, and his teeth were chattering and his feet so cold he was finding it harder and harder to work the brake pedal.

He was vaguely aware of firs, wind-blasted black rocks and snow-covered slopes on either side. The ribbon lake was narrowing as he approached its end. Above him, the sky was on fire. The world rushing by. Hanging curtains of neon lit his ride. He wanted to look up and didn't dare. He wanted more morphine; and knew the shimmering edges to everything meant he'd already had too much.

How much fuel did this bike carry? How much further could it run? It couldn't be more than fifty miles from base to border. They had to be close now.

Up ahead, Amelia flicked the searchlight on, Dennisov swerved the Aerosledge into Tom's path, and Tom tried to accelerate out of their way. Leaning so far into a turn that his rear wheel lost grip and skittered sideways.

The numbness Amelia's morphine had given him was gone in a spike of adrenaline as Tom steered into the skid and managed to stop his bike going down.

What the fuck?

What the hell were they . . . ?

And then he understood. Red Army snowcats blocked their approach to the Finnish shore. Completing his turn, as the Aerosledge did the same, Tom found himself facing the oncoming Ekranoplan. Sophia Dennisova stood in its cockpit, half a dozen soldiers flanking her.

As the Wingship neared, it opened fire.

109

Friday 4th December – Kola Peninsula, Soviet Russia

Flinging his bike sideways, Tom saw bullets rake ice in a line that exploded through where he'd just been. His studs bit into the lake, his front ski ran on its edge, and he turned a circle far tighter than Sophia's Wingship could manage.

He almost made it, too.

Then his back wheel went out and the lake's edges spun as he careened across its surface towards black rocks. Kicking off from the bike, he saw it slam into a troll-backed boulder and explode, while he thudded across a frozen fishing hole and crashed into the snow piled against an old ice wall.

Clambering unsteadily to his feet, Tom saw the Aero-sledge spin round and race towards the Wingship, obviously planning to ram it. Amelia had to be steering, because its headlights were full on and Dennisov was behind the screen, an AK-47 in hand, emptying its clip into Sophia's craft.

Their gunner had his head down.

The Wingship swung away a second before Dennisov's AK-47 burned out, and Tom heard Sophia's scream of fury.

'*Ram them.*'

Turning faster than was safe, her craft ground one of its wings on the ice and ended up facing in the wrong direction.

'*Turn it! Turn it!*'

Her Wingship was faster than the Aerosledge and carried twice its crew but was designed for skimming over water and ice and not for manoeuvrability. They had to be able to use that.

'Here!' Dennisov shouted.

The sledge's propeller sent up clouds of snow as Amelia slowed, and Tom felt his arm almost yanked from its socket as Dennisov grabbed him. Ice slid under his feet and he was dragged aboard.

'Stay low,' Dennisov hissed.

Tom hadn't been planning to stand.

Taking the wheel from Amelia, Dennisov began weaving back the way they'd come, heading for where the lake had divided.

He weaved too wildly.

'Brace!' Amelia shouted.

Her shout came too late. Tom's teeth slammed shut. His wounded hip caught fire. Only grabbing the cabin's chrome rim stopped him being catapulted overboard as the Aerosledge ground its way over a spit of land where the lake divided. A handful of brutal jolts later and they were back on ice.

The lake raced beneath them. The northern lights flared above. They were riding the scar of a glacier from when the world was ice. 'They're back,' Amelia said.

The Wingship was behind them.

'Brace!' Dennisov yelled.

He took the Aerosledge up and over a moraine rather than round.

When Tom looked back, he saw they were holding their own. The gunner up front in the Wingship had stopped firing. So either he was low on ammo or playing a longer game. But Sophia was closing the gap.

On the lake ahead, another group of ice-fishers scattered. Amelia screamed at them to head for shore. Tom doubted they heard. Not that they needed to – the sight of the Wing-ship bearing down on them was enough to send them fleeing.

'One clip left,' Dennisov shouted.

Tom had lost his rifle when his bike went out of control. The .32 weekend special Dennisov had given him on the train was empty. The Tokarev 7.62, ditto.

'And again,' Amelia said.

A long row of Red Army snowcats was lined up to block their route to this shore too. Ahead lay the start of Norway. The difference this time was the bright beam of a helicopter lighting the lake's end. From the care it took not to stray from its position, it had to be NATO, with orders not to enter Soviet airspace.

'Ram them,' Tom said.

Dennisov shook his head.

Swinging the wheel, he brought the Aerosledge about, and Sophia's Wingship swerved as her brother raced straight at it and broke through, back the way they'd come.

'We're going to run out of fuel,' Amelia warned.

Dennisov tapped the dial. 'We're on fumes already.'

'You'll ram a Wingship, but you won't ram a snowmobile?'

'I don't want to bring them into this. Not if they're waiting to see how this plays out. Besides—' He flipped open his mink coat to reveal the glass orb still round his neck like an albatross '—can't risk this falling into the army's hands.'

'Give it to us,' Amelia muttered, 'and we'll destroy you.'

'No need,' Dennisov said. 'We're destroying ourselves.'

'Take me back to that fishing hole,' Tom demanded.

Dennisov stared at him.

'"Once a man gets a fixed idea, there's nothing to be done."'

'That's Chekhov,' Dennisov said.

'Well done. Now take me back to the fishing hole.' Sometimes the best thing to do with a thought was act on it, without giving yourself enough time to think through why it was a really, really bad idea.

'Do it,' Tom ordered.

'I'll take the wheel,' Amelia told Dennisov. 'You do what you do. We let Tom do his thing.'

'All yours,' Dennisov said with a bow.

Swinging the wheel abruptly, Amelia let Sophia's Wingship shoot past, watched it overcompensate for their change of direction and spin once before sliding to a stop. Dennisov fired off a handful of rounds and a man on the Wingship screamed. Then Dennisov swept the frozen surface of the lake with the searchlight until he found the nearest ice hole.

Tom held out his hand and Dennisov hesitated.

'Give it to me,' Tom said.

Flicking up a tiny panel on the orb, Dennisov turned a switch and depressed a button. 'Forty-five seconds,' he said.

Forty-five seconds?

'Behind us!' Amelia shouted. Sophia's Wingship had been joined by two snowcats from the lake's edge. It looked as if Dennisov was wrong – the watchers had chosen their side. Although both riders still had their rifles slung across their backs, so maybe he was half right.

'Ready?' Amelia asked.

'As I'll ever be.'

Yanking back on the throttle, she slowed the Aerosledge and gasped as Tom launched himself from the cabin, rolling as if landing with a parachute. Both snowmobiles peeled off, and Dennisov raked the first with what remained of his clip. The second was heading for Tom when Amelia slammed the Aerosledge into it, and soldier and vehicle went spinning across the ice.

Tom was already counting down in his head.

Forty seconds. Thirty-nine seconds.

Shit. Shit. Shit.

Ramming his fist into the ice hole, he punched through the skin of ice beginning to form. *Thirty-one seconds.*

He thrust the orb under the surface, scrambled to his feet and ran.

How far could he run in twenty-eight seconds? How deep could something that small sink in the time remaining? Blood pounded in his head and freezing air rasped in his throat. He heard metal grind against metal, and saw the Aerosledge cut in front of the Wingship, stopping it reaching him.

He could taste fear as he waited for the explosion to rip through the lake.

Seven seconds. Five seconds.

Three seconds.

Tom waited, waited some more. Nothing happened.

I I O

| *Friday 4th December – Kola Peninsula, Soviet Russia*

Ice cracked, sharp as a pistol shot.

Its echo rolled off slopes both sides of the lake. Behind Tom, a hundred yards of ice cracked as if punched from below. The slab on which he stood broke free and began to tip. Tom felt his boots begin to slip and launched himself at solid ice beyond, sliding to a halt on his knees. The rifle fire was done.

Instead, people were shouting.

'Slow down. Slow down!' a man howled.

Sophia's Wingship couldn't. It was too big, too ungainly and travelling too fast. As Tom watched, it hit a sheet of rising ice that crumpled its nose cone, shattered one wing and dropped it into an expanse of open water; where the huge craft tipped sideways and began to sink.

A snowmobile following didn't stop in time and vanished.

Its rider's desperate cry the last sound he uttered before water closed over his head. Tom looked for the Aerosledge and saw it was safe. A snowmobile heading for it turned and sped away.

From one side of the ribbon lake to the other, the ice was riddled with cracks. Only in the middle had one huge sheet of ice ridden over another, leaving wide, clear water where the ice-fisher's hole had been.

As her soldiers drowned, Sophia clung to the ice sheet's

edge, half in, half out of the freezing lake. Those behind her not already dead in the water found their lungs locked, their chests so tight they couldn't draw breath. Tom watched a corporal give up and slip under, dragged down by paralysed muscles, sodden clothes and despair.

This is shock, Tom thought. This has to be shock.

A thud as low as thunder told him the cracks were spreading. No one was firing now. Scanning the battlefield, Tom realised there were few left to fire. The riders of the last few snowcats perhaps, but they'd withdrawn, almost to the Norwegian shore, finding themselves trapped between NATO's hovering helicopter and the Aerosledge that Amelia had brought to a halt.

She stepped down beside Tom. 'Swallow this,' she ordered.

Tom looked at her hand blankly.

'Iodine tablet,' she said. 'Better safe . . .'

When he said nothing, she pinched both sides of his jaw to open his mouth and put the pill on his tongue. 'Swallow,' she told him.

'How long? Before the sickness starts?'

Dennisov dragged his gaze from his sister clinging to the edge of the ice shelf. The open water behind her already beginning to skin with fresh ice. He wanted to know the answer to that too.

'You're clean,' Amelia said.

Tom didn't understand.

'You dropped a small, heavy sphere into a lake. Two and a half metres of water reduces a reactor's fuel rods to the level of background radiation. This lake is a hell of a lot deeper than that. Between immersion and exploding, that thing sank a hundred metres, possibly more.'

'But the ice . . .'

'The explosion had to go somewhere. Water might stop radiation. It doesn't stop shock waves. It amplifies them.'

'How can you be sure?' Dennisov asked.

'This is what I do,' Amelia said.

I I I

Friday 4th December – Kola Peninsula, Soviet Russia

'Vanya . . .'

Dennisov's sister was calling to him.

Amelia readied to climb down from the Aerosledge and help Sophia onto the ice. Dennisov shook his head.

'She'll kill you the moment she's safe.'

'*Vanya!*' Sophia protested.

The one-legged Russian glanced to where three army snowmobiles waited off the frozen shingle marking Norwegian soil. All three riders had rifles. All three had their rifles still slung across their backs. None showed any sign of coming to Sophia's aid. Dennisov showed no signs of it either.

'Doctor!' Sophia called.

Amelia Blackburn turned back.

'My brother's lying.' Sophia's voice was a whisper, barely audible even in the sudden and shocking silence of the battle's aftermath. One of her shoulders looked dislocated. Her leg had its bullet wound. Blood was oozing from her scalp. It was hypothermia that would kill her though. Only her movements, as she tried and failed to climb out, stopped ice crystals seeding around her.

'I can help you,' Sophia promised. 'I'll tell Moscow you had no part of this. You're a pacifist. You can't just let me die here.'

'You had Per murdered.'

'I don't know who Per is.'

'*Yes, you do.*'

The shake of Dennisov's head was so slight that Amelia missed it. Tom didn't.

'Your man crushed him to death with a snowplough,' Amelia said furiously. 'You had his cousin crucified between trees.'

'Not me,' Sophia promised.

When Tom looked up, Dennisov was watching.

There was no point asking if the Commissar was behind one or both atrocities. The man had done or ordered far worse. The only question would be, why? Tom was still considering that when Sophia's fingers gave way and she slipped under the water. When she resurfaced, her voice was raw. Her chest so tight it hurt to speak.

'You killed Daddy,' she said. 'Now you're killing me. You're a traitor to your country. What won't you betray?'

'The family I've made,' Dennisov said, without even thinking about it. 'Sveta, who I'm going to marry. The baby Yelena. The Commissar. Wax Angel. Tom.'

'He's not family.'

Dennisov undid Tom's coat, then his shirt beneath.

'Yes I am,' Tom said.

Amelia's eyes widened at the mafia stars.

As for Sophia . . . The ice had entered her body as well as her soul. As the three of them watched, she sank for a second time. This time she didn't resurface.

112

Friday 4th December – Kola Peninsula, Soviet Russia

The helicopter over the shore drifted lower and its side door slid back. Tom saw a glint of glass, grabbed Amelia and pulled her down against an incoming shot.

'They're filming,' Amelia said.

Tom was too deep in shock to work out if that was good or bad. Maybe they'd already got the explosion, the snow-mobiles plunging through ice, the Wingship tipping sideways and sinking. Maybe they'd only got him, Dennisov, Amelia, the broken ice, the remaining snowcats, which still showed no signs of moving.

He wasn't sure it mattered.

Battles are fought on adrenaline, training, instinct and fear. In their aftermath comes a flatness that leaves heart and soul empty. Tom had no idea how much of what he felt was the morphine, how much that the battle was done and he'd had enough. He'd had enough of Eddington's games, of trying to balance the ties of flesh and blood with being used like a chess piece. He was done with a life where his main aim was simply staying alive. Caro had always said there was more.

'Are you all right?' Amelia asked.

'I'm fine.' The answer was out of Tom's mouth before he'd even thought about it. Utterly instinctive. He didn't mean it though, and he didn't believe it.

Neither did Amelia.

'Bastard,' Tom said.

398

Dennisov stared at him.

'This.' Tom pulled back his shirt and shivered. The stars had healed in the previous week, but their edges were still raw.

'Someday,' Dennisov said, 'those will save your life. The KGB card you found was fake. Those are real. In Moscow they will open doors.'

'What if I never go back to Moscow?'

'In London too.'

Tom's mouth twisted.

'We'll be there,' Dennisov promised. 'Never doubt it. We'll be everywhere. One year, three years, five? The Soviet Union is dying . . .'

He held up a hand to still Tom.

'If the Commissar says it's done, it's done. He was there at its birth. He will be there to bury it. When the fracture comes, half of us will become whatever replaces the KGB, the rest of us this. Nothing will change, and everything will change.'

'*Dennisov . . .*'

'You will welcome us with open arms for not being what we were. In the beginning anyway. Until your politicians finally realise.'

'That what you are is what you've always been?'

'Besides, we have a deal. Gabashville made you his heir. You passed control to me. I promised you half of everything. Of course, payment will be in roubles – but then life isn't perfect.'

'And what happens next?' Amelia said, looking at Dennisov, who glanced towards the three snowmobiles still offshore. Their riders watching and waiting.

'What happens now is Tom gives me ten million dollars and I give him a tatty piece of paper. It may not seem like it, but it's a fair swap. Better than fair.'

Dennisov held out his hand.

'What paper?' Tom asked.

'You don't trust me?'

'Should I?'

The Russian looked hurt. 'Always.'

By the light of the moon, with the aurora borealis tingeing the creased and crumpled page half a dozen shades of washed-out neon, Tom looked at the blueprint for what he thought was the egg, until he looked at the scale along the bottom and realised this was several times larger.

'Ignore the date,' Dennisov told him.

'1979?'

'It's a lie. So is the line saying it originated at the Joint Institute for Nuclear Research, Dubna. The design isn't even Soviet. Give this to your Lord Eddington, and only him. Those are the Commissar's orders. Eddington will be expecting it.'

Of course he would. Tom tossed the rucksack to Dennisov, who weighed it in his hand thoughtfully, shrugged and dropped it to the ice.

Stepping forward, he hugged Tom. 'I'm sorry about Caro.'

He stepped back.

'Now go.'

The helicopter came down to meet them the moment it realised Tom and Amelia intended to abandon Soviet soil. If that was an adequate description for Amelia helping Tom clamber up the slippery shingle.

Behind them, Dennisov had gone to talk to the riders of the three remaining snowmobiles, who had to be aware that they were still being filmed. Under his fur coat, he sported the shoulder flashes of a KGB colonel. The soldiers were simply Vnutrenniye Voiska conscripts. They would do as ordered.

'I'm sorry,' Tom told Amelia. 'I'm not sure you'll be able to return to Kola for a while.'

'The Commissar might protect you. If you were stupid enough to come back. But he's unlikely to protect me?'

'Something like that.'

'How's the leg?' Amelia asked.

'It has a hole in it.'

She tossed across another syringe of morphine and raised her eyebrows when Tom slipped it into his pocket.

'Maybe later,' he said.

When Tom slipped on the scree, Amelia grabbed his hand and kept hold of it, helping him to the top, while the helicopter's blades turned lazily and snowflakes rose from the ground rather than fell from the sky. When they reached a snowbank, she didn't let go. In that moment, he was glad.

113

Friday 4th December – Hampshire

Charlie looked at the telephone. This was the third time it had rung in ten minutes. That probably meant it was urgent. 'Bishops Brattan 272,' he said carefully, standing a little straighter. 'My grandfather isn't here at the moment. Aunt Agatha went home. Granny has gone to live in London. Mrs Ross has the fans on in her kitchen and can't hear anyway. Can I take a message?'

'Charlie . . . ?'

'Daddy!'

'Daddy,' Tom Fox agreed.

He gripped the hotel telephone tighter.

Coming out of the bathroom, Amelia's glance threw a question and Tom mouthed Charlie's name. There would be time to work out what the previous night meant to both of them later. In the meantime . . .

'I'll be in the lobby,' she whispered.

'Daddy?' Charlie said.

'Still here,' Tom promised.

'You're in Russia?'

'Norway,' Tom said.

'You're meant to be in Russia with the Wolf Lady.'

'I was in Russia. Now I'm in Norway.'

'With the Wolf Lady?'

'She's here.'

Charlie considered this. 'That's good,' he said finally. 'Isn't it?'

'Is it?' Tom asked him.

'I think so,' Charlie said, after a pause. 'Everyone gets lonely.'

'What about you?' Tom asked. 'Do you get lonely?'

'I have you,' Charlie said. 'And Becca.'

It seemed best to leave things there.

'Did you see any wolves?'

'A few,' Tom said. 'And some reindeer. No bears though. They're all asleep.'

'Did the wolves eat anyone?'

'Not this time,' Tom said, half apologetically.

Charlie sounded disappointed.

'Granny's not there?'

Tom tried to keep the tension out of his voice. He didn't quite manage it, and felt his son hesitate. There were emotions Charlie had trouble understanding. Others, he was so finely attuned to he could have been a fish sensing ripples from a shark that had passed that way hours before.

'She's in London. Grandpa's not sure when she'll be back.' Charlie hesitated. 'He says when, but he means if . . .'

'What happened?'

'They quarrelled.'

'What about?'

'Me, of course.'

'Ah. How's Grandpa taken it?'

'He's playing jazz very loudly and eating lots of fish. Also, he's wearing his gardening clothes indoors and doesn't change for supper.'

That sounded about right. Lady Elspeth Eddington hated fish, loathed jazz and was very particular about dress.

'How are you?' Tom asked.

'Missing Mummy.'

'Everything's all right apart from that?'

'Oh yes,' Charlie said. 'I met a man called Dancer.'

Tom felt his guts lurch.

'He's gone home now,' Charlie said. 'He had some problems with his paperwork. Grandpa made them go away.'

'Grandpa met him?'

'Afterwards,' Charlie said. 'When I came home.'

'From where?' Tom demanded, wondering how sick he should feel.

'From the woods,' Charlie said, as if that was obvious. 'I've learned lots of interesting things. I can shoot a rabbit rifle. I can wire an alarm, skin a rabbit and light a camp fire. I'm also really good at climbing ladders and high trees. And I can build a hide, and track someone. It was much better than going back to school. Grandpa can tell you all about it later.'

114

Saturday 5th December — Norwegian Airspace

There were four passengers on 32 Squadron's flight from Tromso, 200 miles north of Norway's Arctic circle, to RAF Northolt, eleven miles outside London.

Two men, a woman and a boy.

A fifth was to join them at the Oslo stopover.

A naval captain, with intelligence connections, who if he was wise would sit right at the back, keep himself to himself, and bury his head in a fat file of AFNORTH paperwork.

'Thank you for giving me a lift,' Amelia said as the BAe 146 levelled up after initial take-off, with the lights of Tromso airport behind and 500 miles of sharp mountain, deep glen and darkened fjord to go before descent into Oslo for refuelling.

Lord Eddington grimaced. 'I wasn't aware I had a choice.'

Tom smiled at Charlie. 'I wonder if the pilot would let you see the cockpit?'

'I'll take him,' Amelia said.

'Just don't mention Greenham Common,' Eddington growled.

'What's Greenham Common?' Charlie asked.

'It's a military base,' Amelia told him. 'Full of bad people who like bombs.'

'Our bombs?'

'American bombs.'

Tom nodded towards the cabin door and Amelia smiled.

'We're going,' she said.

'Of course you can,' Tom heard the pilot say.

He saw Charlie take the middle seat, while Amelia stood behind him, her hand lightly on his shoulder. A second later, the steel door closed on them and Tom was alone with his father-in-law.

'Do you trust her?' Eddington asked.

'Yes,' Tom replied.

Lord Eddington sighed.

'And Charlie likes her,' Tom added.

'It shows. He did little but talk about the Wolf Lady the moment he knew you were in Russia. He says she saved your life in Berlin by ordering a wolf to eat the man attacking you.'

'That's one way of putting it.'

'Don't feel you have to find someone to replace Caro because you think Charlie needs a mother . . .'

'No one will ever replace Caro,' Tom said tightly. After a moment, he made himself let go of the armrest to his seat. He didn't doubt that Eddington had noticed his tension. But there were so many things wrong with Eddington's statement that Tom barely knew where to start.

'Thank you all the same.'

'For what?' Eddington asked.

'You know what.'

Eddington did. He was one of those who spoke in the silences between their words. What he didn't say was as important as what he did. He'd just told Tom he'd make sure Tom got Charlie.

Tom reached into his pocket. 'This is yours.'

His father-in-law opened it, glanced at it once and put it carefully in a government-issue briefcase by his feet. 'So,' he said, 'you'd better tell me what happened.'

'People died,' Tom said. 'Mostly the right people. Some not. One or two who really didn't deserve to.'

'Take your time.'

'I'm done,' Tom said. 'You understand that, don't you? I'm out.'

Eddington considered that. 'One reason this world works,' he said, 'is that everyone has their own secrets already. We just ask them to keep ours.'

'And end up with Philby, Burgess, Blackburn and Maclean.'

'That's always a risk. Caro asked me once if I knew how damaged you were. I said, better than she did. I've seen the photographs from that children's home, Tom. Although, God knows, I never told her that. You're dangerous because you know you can survive.'

'I'm done with surviving.'

'This is about Charlie, isn't it?'

'*Of course it is.*' Tom hadn't meant to raise his voice. He hoped his frustration couldn't be heard in the cockpit.

'Immediate promotion,' Eddington said. 'Full pension. Medical discharge. We'll use that leg as the reason. You'll be out by spring. We'll weed your record of anything that might count against you.'

'Not too thoroughly. Nothing more suspicious than a man like me with a docket that comes up squeaky clean.'

Eddington chuckled.

'And in return?'

'You come back if we need you.'

'Define need.'

'If we have nobody with your skill set.'

'There's always someone with my skill set.'

'If that was true, Tom, your marriage and my relationship with my daughter would have looked very different. Now, the fifty-thousand-dollar question. Do you think the Soviets made two of those bloody things?'

'They didn't even make one.'

Lord Eddington blinked.

'Look at that blueprint again. Overlook its date and reference to Atomgrad or whatever they're calling it these days. They're lies. Don't overlook the scale.'

Eddington had. 'Christ,' he said.

'Does Heringsdorf mean anything to you?'

'If you're asking, then yes it does. An asset of ours fed us some fairy tale about Russians attacking East Germans.'

'You checked with Bonn?'

'They said the idea was absurd.'

Tom remembered the news clipping from Amelia's abandoned hotel room in Tromso. Five Greenpeace activists winning an appeal against sentences for breaking into an airbase. The West German government's refusal to admit the activists' innocence, while insisting nothing was actually stolen.

'Yes,' Tom said, 'I imagine they did. Did we ask assets in East Germany?'

'They said the same.'

There were lights below, villages giving way to the towns that ringed Norway's capital, by the time Tom finished going through his reasoning. Eddington was scowling. Not, Tom suspected, because he disagreed but because he feared Tom was right.

'You're saying the bomb was American?'

'Well . . . could the West German's have made something that sophisticated without London knowing?'

'Christ,' Eddington said. 'I hope not.'

'Do we have no-residual-radiation bombs of our own?'

'Certainly not. They're illegal.'

Tom looked at him.

'We don't,' Eddington said firmly. 'They promised,' he added, sounding cross. 'Washington promised Bonn there'd be no neutron devices on West German soil. Gods, I wonder if this means they've lied to the PM . . . ?'

'Does she lie to them?'

'Only when necessary.'

Eddington sat back in his seat and Tom could almost see him think it through. 'The East Germans couldn't admit they stole it,' Eddington said finally. 'The West Germans couldn't admit they knew it existed. The Soviets couldn't admit taking it from their East German allies. The Americans couldn't admit it was there in the first place.' He smiled. 'It's almost impressive. Any idea who attacked you on that train?'

'East German or American, Dennisov thought.'

'Best make it East German.'

They heard the cabin door open, and Charlie came out beaming. 'I'm going to be a pilot,' he announced. 'The flight lieutenant let me sit in the seat and work the levers.'

Eddington looked alarmed.

'The other set of levers,' Amelia said. She still had her hand on Charlie's shoulder, and he was leaning into her. Amelia was also smiling, just not as widely.

'You were there at the end,' Eddington said to her.

'And at the start,' she told him.

'What are my chances of persuading you to sign the Official Secrets Act?'

Amelia's smile didn't falter, although she glanced at Tom. He knew her answer before she spoke.

'Absolutely zero.'

'What's the Official Secrets Act?' Charlie asked.

Acknowledgements

First up, I'd like to acknowledge Streetmog, who makes his first appearance wandering into the second chapter of *Arctic Sun*. Without his help, this novel would have been finished in half the time.

A tip of the hat to Jonny Geller and Viola Hayden at Curtis Brown. Jonny fixed the original contract. Viola offered invaluable advice. My thanks to Rowland White. Also, to Ruth Atkins at Penguin Michael Joseph for her impressively concise and blissfully constructive editorial notes. Eugenie Todd for a great copy-edit, and Nick Lowndes for keeping me updated. A blessing in an industry that sometimes feels lonely at the writer's end.

A whole group of friends, and soon to be friends, offered support when Sam and I finally relocated to Edinburgh, decades after we said we would. Their kindness made a huge difference. In no particular order, my thanks to Jenny Colgan, Ian Rankin, Anna Frame, Simon Spanton, Joe Gordon, Gavin Francis, Shell Bryson, Dan Richards, Tom Sillar, Jacky Collins and Alister Rennie.

As always, with spy novels, there are those who can be named and those who can't or shouldn't be. You know who you are. At least one of you will recognise one of the flash-backs. My thanks to Erika Englund and Jon for their help with the Finland trip. And to Marie and Viking Kellgren for taking me out onto the Baltic ice. From darkness to darkness, via white eagles, ice sleds, kilos of pike and chainsaws. It was an incredible day. (And I apologise for the extreme liberties

I've taken in combining that memory with memories of ice fishing on lakes in Norway in my teens.)

My father died during the pandemic, in the earliest stages of writing this book, and appears very briefly as one of the passengers on the RAF plane returning from Norway. Understandably he's the one with the fat file of AFNORTH paperwork.

To bastardise Tolstoy, 'All normal families are alike; each dysfunctional family is dysfunctional in its own way.' Same goes for countries, it seems to me. *Arctic Sun* is a novel about what happens when dysfunctional countries and dysfunctional families meet.

I dedicated this book up front to all the iterations of Charlie in my family. But I'd also like to tip my hat to Tom. I'm sorry it took me this long to get round to dealing with the shit.

Finally, Sam Baker, for kindness, tolerance, and endless walks round the Meadows.

For this and far more, I owe you.

Same as it ever was.

Edinburgh

2023